RICHARD BAKER

CORSAIR

BLADES OF THE MOONSEA

BOOK II

Blades of the Moonsea
Book II
CORSAIR

Published by Wizards of the Coast LLC

Printed in the U.S.A.

Cover art by Raymond Swanland
Map by Rob Lazzaretti
Original Hardcover Edition first printing: March 2009
First Paperback Printing: November 2009

9 8 7 6 5 4 3 2 1

ISBN: 978-0-7869-5307-3
620-25071000-001-EN

The Library of Congress has catalogued the Hardcover edition as follows:

Library of Congress Cataloging-in-Publication Data

Baker, Richard (Lynn Richard)
Corsair / Richard Baker.
p. cm. -- (Blades of the Moonsea ; bk. 2)
ISBN 978-0-7869-5115-4
I. Title.
PS3602.A587C68 2009
813'.6--dc22

2008048046

U.S., CANADA,
ASIA, PACIFIC, & LATIN AMERICA
Wizards of the Coast LLC
P.O. Box 707
Renton, WA 98057-0707
+1-800-324-6496

EUROPEAN HEADQUARTERS
Hasbro UK Ltd
Caswell Way
Newport, Gwent NP9 0YH
GREAT BRITAIN
Save this address for your records.

Visit our web site at www.wizards.com

For Alex
This one's just for you.

Acknowledgments

First, I would like to thank my editors, Phil Athans and Susan Morris. Phil offered me carte blanche to choose a corner of Faerûn to explore in Blades of the Moonsea; it's been a lot of work, but a tremendous amount of fun too. Susan's eye for character development and motivation might be the best I've run across in a dozen books now, and *Corsair* is much the better for it.

I have the great good fortune to work with a number of highly intelligent, highly creative, and highly motivated people each day. Being a game designer is a pretty good way to make a living. Being a game designer who gets to work with the people I work with is a *fantastic* way to make a living. You all rock.

Finally, a special thanks to Kim, my wonderful wife, who patiently puts up with many, many hours of me chaining myself to the computer and complaining about it. Two down and one to go, sweetheart!

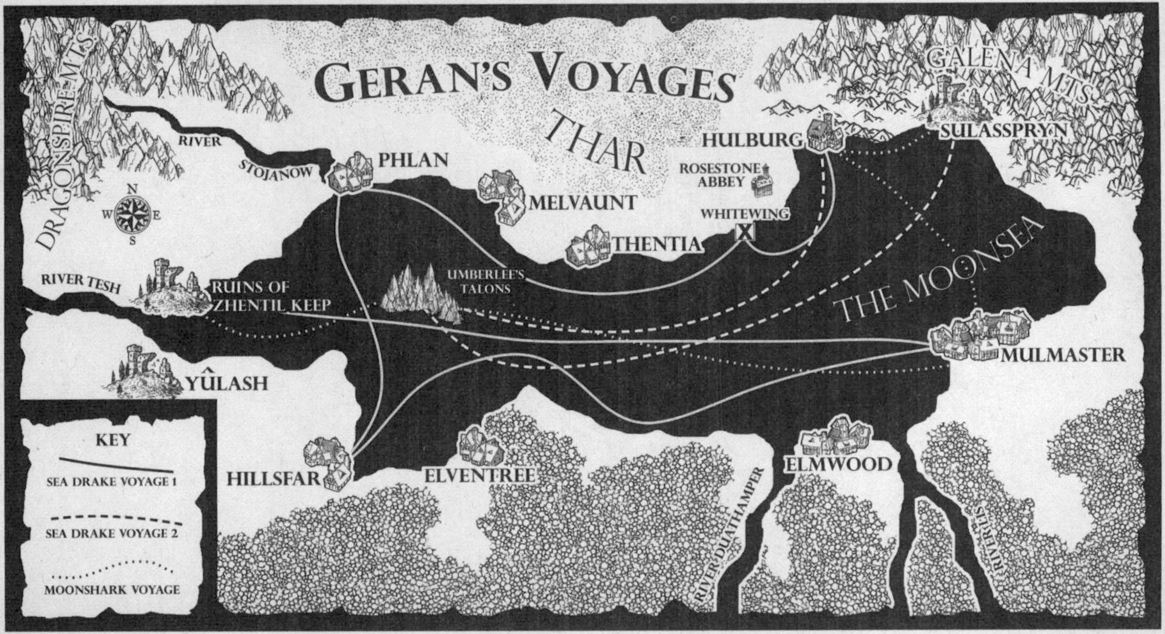

Geran's Voyages

Dragonspire Mts.
River Stojanow
Phlan
Thar
Melvaunt
Thentia
Rosestone Abbey
Whitewing
Hulburg
Galena Mts.
Sulasspryn
The Moonsea
Umberlee's Talons
River Tesh
Ruins of Zhentil Keep
Yûlash
Hillsfar
Elventree
Elmwood
River Duathamper
River Lis
Mulmaster

Key
Sea Drake Voyage 1
Sea Drake Voyage 2
Moonshark Voyage

PROLOGUE

15 Ches, the Year of the Mages in Amber (1466 DR)

The shrill ring of steel on steel woke Geran Hulmaster in the dark hour before dawn. He rolled up onto one elbow in his bed, listening with his brow creased in the darkness of his room. He could hear cries of alarm spreading through the castle of Griffonwatch, his family's ancestral home. For a long moment he wondered if he were caught in one of those strange dreams that came with a delusion of wakefulness. Then the shouts and the commotion started again, and Geran came fully awake.

He threw off his covers and jumped out of bed; the flagstones of the floor were cold under his bare feet. Fighting in Griffonwatch? he wondered. He'd lived in the castle of the Hulmasters all his seventeen years, and never had the castle come under any kind of attack. Oh, there were the occasional barracks-room brawls down in the Shieldsworn quarters, but that was down in the castle's lower bailey, where the soldiers and the servants had their lodgings. And he doubted that the fighting he heard was any kind of drunken brawl. It sounded serious and deadly.

He tucked his nightshirt into the thin breeches he usually wore to sleep and stepped into the boots standing by the foot of the bed. He was a tall, sparely built young man, with arms and legs that seemed a little too long for him and a wild mop of thick black hair that fell across his keen gray eyes. Stamping his feet to the floor to seat his boots, he stumbled over to his sword belt and buckled it around his narrow waist. Geran had been training at arms since his twelfth birthday, and his hands already had the hard-earned calluses of an accomplished swordsman. Whatever commotion was loose in Griffonwatch, it would find him ready for a fight.

Geran gave his boots one more stamp then hurried to his chamber door and threw it open. The hallway outside was empty, but he could hear the sounds of fighting echoing from the lower parts of the castle. "Who attacks us?" he muttered to himself. Orcs or goblins from Thar? Brigands from the Highfells? How could they have gotten all the way into the castle? And why would they attack the harmach's soldiers in their own fortress? He'd never heard of orc raiders or human bandits trying anything like that before.

Since the Hulmaster family quarters seemed quiet for the moment, Geran headed down the stairs leading to the tower's lower room. There he found his cousin Kara, who stood by the door leading out to the upper court. The door was ajar, and she peered out cautiously with her eerie, spellscarred eyes glowing faintly blue in the dim light, a short sword bared in her hand. She was a year younger than Geran, but she could use her blade almost as well as he could use the the sword at his hip. Like him, she wore her nightclothes, but she'd belted her gown tight around her waist so that it wouldn't hinder her. She spared him a quick look then returned to watching the courtyard.

"What's going on?" Geran asked in a low whisper.

"I don't know, but I heard fighting," she answered. "What should we do?"

He frowned and peered out into the courtyard as well. A cold, steady rain pelted down in the night, and he shivered in his thin nightshirt. The Shieldsworn guards who normally stood watch by the Hulmaster quarters weren't at their posts. All of the sudden, he found himself unwilling to answer Kara's question; his curiosity was rapidly giving way to dread. Something was terribly out of place in the house of the Hulmasters this night. Geran thought he knew what it was to be in a fight. After all, he'd held his own in a skirmish or two up in the Highfells, riding against orcs and other such savages alongside the Shieldsworn.

But it was a different matter to wake up to a battle in his own home wondering which of the soldiers or servants he knew were already lying dead in the halls.

Several armored figures emerged from the doors leading down from the courtyard to the great hall. Geran tensed, dropping his hand to his sword hilt, but Kara shook her head. She could see as well as a cat in darkness—a gift of her spellscar. "It's your da," she said.

Bernov Hulmaster strode across the courtyard with several Shieldsworn at his back. Geran and Kara stepped back from the door as he and his guards entered. Geran's father was only an inch taller than Geran, but he was a thick-bodied bear of a man with a stout beard of gray-streaked brown; Geran got his black hair and his lean build from his mother's side of the family. Bernov wore his battle armor and a heavy cape against the weather, and he filled the doorway with his broad shoulders and pauldrons. His face was set in a grim scowl.

"Ah, you're awake," Bernov said. "Are you two all right?"

"Yes, Da," Geran answered. "We're fine. But we heard fighting."

"I know." Bernov glanced around the family's hall, as if he expected enemies to burst out of the shadows at any moment. "I want you and Kara to stay here. Bar the door when I leave, and admit no one to the Hulmaster quarters except the harmach or myself. And no one's to leave, either. Keep your mother, your aunt, and Sergen here until I tell you it's safe. Do you understand me?"

Geran did not understand at all, but he managed a weak nod. "What's happening? Are we under attack?"

Bernov's scowl deepened again. "It's your uncle Kamoth. He tried to murder the harmach and seize Griffonwatch. The harmach survived, but the castle is still in doubt. I fear some of the Shieldsworn are his, so you're not to trust anyone."

Kamoth tried to kill the harmach? Geran stared at his father. Kamoth Kastelmar was husband to Geran's aunt, Terena, Bernov's sister. Their older brother, Grigor, was harmach of Hulburg, lord over the town and the surrounding lands. Geran knew that his father didn't think much of Kamoth and hadn't ever really trusted the man, but he couldn't believe that Kamoth was capable of the sort of treachery that was apparently afoot. He *liked* Kamoth. The Hillsfarian nobleman had married into the family only two years past, bringing with him his son, Sergen, but even though Geran and Sergen didn't get along, Kamoth had never had a hard word for Geran. Kamoth had a wicked sense of humor and the charm of a born rogue, but the capacity for treason and murder?

"There must be some mistake," Geran said.

"There's no mistake. Kamoth and his men killed the guards by Grigor's door, but another Shieldsworn happened by and caught them at it. They killed her too, but not before her shouts raised the alarm." Bernov reached out to set a hand on Geran's shoulder, and his expression softened. "I know you think highly of Kamoth, Geran. But he's turned against us, and he means to kill every last Hulmaster and take Hulburg for his own. He's an enemy now."

Another sharp exchange of swordplay came from lower in the castle, and Bernov glanced over his shoulder. "I have to go. Stay here, and keep the door barred."

"Wait! I'll come with you," Geran said. "I can help." He wasn't a match for his father yet, or Kamoth either, but he could best many of the Shieldsworn in the practice yard.

Bernov smiled and squeezed Geran's shoulder with rough affection. "I know it, Son. But I'm worried for your mother and the rest of the family, and I'd feel a lot better if I knew that you and Kara were here to keep this door closed and make sure they all stay safe."

Geran knew his father was simply putting a good face on ordering him to stay out of the fighting, but he acquiesced anyway. "I understand," he replied. Bernov nodded and strode back out into the rainy courtyard. Kara shot the heavy iron bolt into place.

They waited in silence for a quarter-hour or more, straining their ears for a clue as to what was taking place in the castle outside the Harmach's Tower. From time to time new shouts echoed through the halls below, punctuated by sharp cries or the clatter of steel against steel. But the sounds of fighting steadily diminished; Geran thought that one side or the other must be getting the upper hand. He wished that he hadn't agreed to remain in the tower. If he'd gone with his father, he might have been able to tip the scales in some close skirmish. He was old enough and skilled enough to fight for the harmach.

The door to the tower rattled against its bolt. Geran and Kara both jumped at the sound and turned to look. The door—a sturdy construction of thick oak planks riveted together with bands of iron—shook again in its frame. "In the tower, there! Open up!" a man called from outside.

"It's Kamoth!" Kara gasped.

Geran nodded. Together they drew their blades and stood facing the door. Its bar was sturdy enough to stop anything short of a small battering ram. There was a small scratching sound . . . and the small spyhole in the door swung open, pushed by the blade of a dagger. The panel was only about the size of a hand, but it was enough for Geran to recognize his uncle's features peering through from outside. Kamoth's bright blue eyes fell on him, then crinkled at the corners in a warm smile. "Ah, there you are. Geran, my boy! And Kara, my dear! Open the door, will you?"

Geran glanced at Kara, but she did not move. Kamoth was her stepfather, but she'd known her uncle Bernov all her life. Kamoth's brows knitted together. "Hmm, perhaps I wasn't sufficiently clear. Draw back the bolt, if you please, because I'd like to come inside the tower."

"We can't do that," Geran answered.

"Oh? Why in the world not?"

"My father told us to keep this door barred until he or the harmach tells us otherwise."

Kamoth glanced away and muttered something under his breath. But he returned to the spyhole a moment later, his eyes bright and kind. "Be that as it may, I'm sure they wouldn't mind if you just let me in for a moment. I'm in need of a few things from my quarters, and then I'll be right out again."

Geran straightened his shoulders and looked his uncle in the eye. "My father told us you tried to kill the harmach tonight. Is it true?"

"A terrible misunderstanding, my boy. I've some important letters in my room that I need to show your father to clear this all up. Now, mark my words, you two—open that door before this whole affair takes a tragic turn. It's dangerous for me to stand out here on this doorstep talking to you."

Geran felt himself starting to waver. He wanted to give Kamoth the chance to explain himself, even though he knew exactly what his father had told him to do. But he felt Kara standing at his shoulder. "Don't do it, Geran," she whispered. "There are more men just behind him."

He closed his eyes and shook his head. "We won't let you in, not against my father's orders. If you're innocent, you should give yourself up."

Anger flashed in Kamoth's eyes, but swiftly passed. "Well, I never took you for a fool, my boy. That's it, then—I'd best be on my way. Kara, give my regards to your mother. I'll certainly miss her, I will." There was a small sound of movement outside, then Kamoth's face vanished from the spyhole.

Geran waited a moment then cautiously crept up to peer from the small spyhole. The rain-slicked courtyard outside was empty.

"What's going on here?" At the foot of the stairs leading up to the family quarters, Geran's cousin Sergen stood in his nightshirt. He looked at Geran and Kara and his eyes narrowed suspiciously. "Was that my father at the door?"

Geran and Kara exchanged looks. "You'd better tell him," Geran said to her. "I doubt he'll believe it from my mouth."

"Believe what?" Sergen demanded. He was a dark-haired youth of fifteen years, wiry like his father, but he was paler than Kamoth and stood a good four inches shorter than Geran. He'd come to Griffonwatch two years past when Kamoth married Terena Hulmaster. Geran didn't like him very much; in his experience Sergen was quick to find fault with others and quicker still to take offense when someone found fault with him.

Kara grimaced and looked over to their stepcousin. "Your father tried to kill the harmach. He's got men in the castle."

"What? That makes no sense!"

"Can't you hear the fighting?" Geran snapped. "Those are Kamoth's men fighting the Shieldsworn. Your father's a traitor."

"That's a lie!" Sergen snarled. "You're a damned liar!"

"No, I'm not," Geran said coldly. "In fact, I wonder if you're in on this too." He took two steps toward Sergen and narrowed his eyes. He didn't particularly like Sergen calling him a liar for no other reason than saying something Sergen didn't want to hear. He'd earned more than a little trouble for teaching Sergen manners with his fists before, but that wouldn't stop him from doing so again if his stepcousin didn't mind his words.

"My father is no traitor!" Sergen shouted. He balled his fists and refused to give ground. Geran frowned; he'd never known Sergen to challenge him so directly. "And I'm not, either! Say it again, and I'll knock your teeth out, you lying bastard!"

Geran started forward with the intention of extracting an apology from his stepcousin, but Kara reached out to set a hand on his arm. "Wait, Geran," she said. "He really does think you're lying. He doesn't know anything about this. Kamoth didn't tell him."

"Stop saying that!" Tears of anger gathered in Sergen's eyes. "My father is no traitor!"

Kara did not reply. Geran glared at his stepcousin, but to his surprise, a small measure of compassion for Sergen stopped him from another sharp retort. By sunrise Sergen would know the truth of events. If Geran had been in his place, he knew he'd find the shame of his father's actions absolutely unbearable; he might as well allow Sergen to enjoy his ignorance for a few hours more. "Very well," he said. "I'll say nothing more on it."

Sergen looked suspiciously from Geran to Kara. "Where is my father, then?"

Kara sighed and her voice softened. "He's gone. I think he's leaving Hulburg."

"Leaving?" Sergen stared at Kara for a moment. Then, without another word, he brushed his hand across his eyes, turned, and bolted up the stairs leading back to his room.

Geran guessed that his stepcousin did not want to let him see how he'd been wounded. He watched Sergen retreat and ran a hand through his hair. He couldn't even begin to imagine what all of this meant for Sergen, for his aunt Terena . . . for all of the Hulmasters. Sergen would likely never believe it. Any pleasure Geran might have felt at his stepcousin's humiliation was rapidly souring in his stomach. Not even Sergen deserved what his father had done.

Kara cocked her head to the side, listening. "I think the fighting's over," she said. "I don't hear any more swordplay."

"Kamoth's gone, then." Geran thought about his father's instructions and decided he'd better follow them to the letter. "Go check on your mother. And you'd better keep an eye on Sergen, just in case. Watch his door and make sure he doesn't leave. I'll stand guard here."

"All right," Kara agreed. She started up the stairs but turned to look back at Geran at the bottom of the steps. "Where do you think Kamoth will go now?"

Geran shook his head. "Back to Hillsfar? Or maybe Mulmaster?" Whatever Kamoth had done, Geran almost hoped that he did get away. He didn't like the idea of watching Kamoth try to answer for what had happened in Griffonwatch this night. "I don't imagine we'll see him again. He can't very well come back after tonight."

"No, I suppose he can't," Kara agreed. She went up the steps, and Geran took up his vigil by the door. He glanced out the window. The rain was passing, and a clear, bright moon was setting over the waters of the Moonsea. Sunrise was not far off, and he'd learn more about Kamoth's treachery soon enough.

ONE

11 Eleint, the Year of the Ageless One (1479 DR)

Nearly fourteen years later and twenty miles from Hulburg, Geran Hulmaster rode over a steep rise on the coastal trail and found pirates plundering a House Sokol merchant ship.

He halted and stared down at the two ships drawn up on the beach of the nameless cove below him before he recovered from his surprise. Then he spurred his mount down from the ridgeline to take cover behind an outcropping of rock. He was fortunate; the sun was setting behind him. Anyone looking up the hillside from the beach below would see nothing but an eyeful of bright sunshine.

Geran patted his horse's neck and whispered soothingly to it. He was a tall, lean man a little over thirty, dressed in a long, weather-beaten cloak over a leather jacket, breeches of dark green wool, and high leather boots. At his hip rode a long elven backsword with a hilt fashioned in the shape of a rose. His trail clung to the hillside above the cove and didn't come all that close to the beach itself, but there was no way he could continue on without being spotted.

"Backtrack and go around?" he wondered aloud. "Or wait until it gets dark and then ride by on the trail?" He decided he preferred to ride past if he could. It should be safe enough if the pirates didn't send out any foraging parties, but any way he looked at it, he'd be riding long after sundown and making a late camp with no fire. He scowled at the thought. The presence of a corsair ship only twenty miles from his home was not a good sign. Piracy had been bad this year, growing worse with each passing month. Hulburg's ships were harried all over the Moonsea. Now here was another cargo that wouldn't reach Hulburg's storehouses. It would be a heavy blow to the Sokols and to the harmach's coffers too.

He dismounted, looping his horse's reins around a bleached pine stump amid the boulders. As long as he was waiting for nightfall, he might as well see if he could learn anything useful about the corsairs plundering ships on Hulburg's doorstep. Picking his way down the slope to find a better vantage point, he eventually settled under the branches of a wind-sculpted thicket of gorse about fifty yards up the hillside from the strand and studied the scene more carefully.

The pirates were mostly humans, with a mix of other folk—a dwarf or two, some goblins, even one ogre that he could see. They had the Sokol ship's cargo scattered all over the beach, sorting out what was worth taking and what they'd leave behind. Geran couldn't see any of the merchant's crew, but that didn't surprise him. Most likely the pirates had killed them after capturing the ship and dumped the corpses over the side.

He chewed his lower lip, thinking. He'd do something about it if he could, but for the moment it was no real business of his. It was only an accident of fate that he was in the vicinity at all. He'd spent the last few days visiting his mother, who resided in a Selûnite convent in Thentia, and was on his way back to Hulburg. It was usually an uneventful journey, since no one lived along the coastland between Thentia and Hulburg, and most traffic between the two cities went by sea. There wasn't even much reason for highwaymen or marauders from the wilds of Thar to come this way.

"They probably chose this cove just for that reason," he said to himself. They needed a quiet place where they could sort through their plunder, and they weren't likely to be troubled here. He couldn't do much about the Sokol ship now, but at least he could carry news of the attack to Hulburg and let the Sokols know what had happened to their ship. He settled in to study the pirates and their vessel closely while he waited for the sun to set. The pirate vessel was a three-masted war galley, a ship that would be equally handy under sail or oar. Geran couldn't make out any name from where he was hiding, but the figurehead was clear—a mermaidlike creature whose fishy tail was instead a mass of kraken arms. He'd never seen anything like it. There couldn't be too many ships on the Moonsea with that device.

As the sun set, the pirates built a bonfire on the beach and broke out casks of wine taken from their prize. Geran judged that it was dark enough to make his way back up to where he'd left his horse. But just as he was about to crawl out from under the gorse, he heard a scream. From behind the hull of the pirate ship, two crewmen dragged a young woman in a fine, blue dress with a bodice of dove gray into sight and roughly tied her to the pirate vessel's kedging anchor up on the beach. She'd been hidden on the far side of the ship from Geran's vantage point. One of the ruffians knotted his hand in the woman's long, golden hair, pressed his bearded face against hers, and forced a kiss. Then he reached up with his other hand and stripped her to the waist, tearing away her bodice. She snarled at him and struggled to get free, but her hands were bound behind her back. The pirate laughed and sauntered away. Geran started to draw his blade and surge from his hiding place, but he forced himself to stop and consider his actions. If he acted rashly, he could get both himself and the woman killed.

"Ah, damn it all," Geran muttered. "Now what do I do?" A moment ago there would have been no shame in slipping away and making sure the tale of the Sokol ship's fate reached Hulburg. He wouldn't have lost a moment's sleep over leaving a scene where the murders had already taken place. But it was all too clear what a beautiful woman unfortunate enough to have been a passenger on the wrong ship could expect in the pirates' camp. If he rode off and abandoned her to her fate, he'd hear her screams in his conscience for a long time. He had to do *something.* The only question was, what? He might have considered attacking a handful of enemies who weren't expecting trouble, but there must have been sixty or seventy men on the beach and likely more he just hadn't seen yet. Pirate vessels carried large crews so that they could overwhelm their victims through weight of numbers.

It'll have to be stealth, he realized. Or a diversion of some kind. I need something to take their attention away from her long enough to cut her free and spirit her away. And the longer I wait, the better—they'll get themselves falling-down drunk if I give them the chance. But how long will they wait before they turn their attention on the woman? And are there other captives I haven't seen yet?

Geran waited impatiently, watching from his hiding place. The pirates tapped another cask and drank eagerly, roaring with laughter and admiring their spoils. Several times he tensed and prepared to burst out of his place of concealment when one or another of the crewmen approached the woman, but each time the pirate retreated. Finally Geran decided that the master of the pirate ship must have been saving her for himself. She was certainly pretty enough. She slumped with her chin down, held upright by the lashings that bound her to the anchor. He wondered who she was and how she'd come to be on the ship.

Finally, he judged that the moment was as right as it would ever be. It was possible that more of the pirates would drink themselves into a stupor if he waited longer, but the leader might appear and rape or kill the woman at any time. Besides, Geran could see a silver glimmer to the southeast that hinted at a big, bright moon. Scowling at the foolishness of his own conscience, he slipped out of the brush and darted down to the water's edge. There was no surf to speak of, just small wavelets less than a foot tall. Wading out into the cold darkness until he was thigh-deep in water, he crouched down and began to creep toward the stern of the Sokol ship, which still jutted out a fair distance from the shore. The pirate vessel might be better for what he had in mind, but it was farther away, and he didn't want too many enemies between him and his horse if things went poorly.

The Moonsea was never warm even in the middle of summer; on a clear, dark, autumn evening, it was bitterly cold. Geran's teeth chattered, and he shivered from toe to crown. But the water provided the best avenue toward his goal without crossing the open, firelit beach. The pirates' shouts and coarse jests rang out over the water, filling the cove with their callousness. After wading a short distance, he reached the stern of the Sokol ship, and paused to listen closely. He could hear muffled thumps, gruff voices, and planks creaking; at least a few of the pirates still searched the holds of the merchant ship, but he didn't think he heard anyone up on the deck. As stealthily as he could, Geran clambered up the ship's side toward the quarterdeck and risked a quick look. No one was in sight.

He swung himself over the rail and moved back to the ship's sternlamp. It was a big lantern of wrought iron, suspended from a short pole fixed to the rail. He pulled it down and glanced inside; oil sloshed in the reservoir. He poured it out on the deck then splashed some on the rigging lines and the furled sail of the mizzenmast close by. From the caravel's quarterdeck he could see the pirates' bonfire on the beach. Several men were gathered around their captive, leering and pawing at her. She's almost out of time, he realized.

Kneeling by the oil he'd poured out on the deck, Geran focused his mind into the clear, still calm necessary for spell-casting. He whispered words in Elvish he'd learned years ago in Myth Drannor: *"Ammar gerele."* In the palm of his upturned hand a bright yellow flame the size of an apple appeared. He flicked it down to the oil-soaked deck. As the pool ignited and flames began to climb into the rigging, Geran quickly scrambled back over the side and dropped back into the water. Ruddy light blossomed on the quarterdeck behind him.

"The prize!" someone shouted. "She's burning!"

Geran glided away from the burning ship as quickly as he could, hoping that none of the pirates would think to look for an enemy creeping away in the water. He heard more shouts behind him and risked a quick look; men on the beach leaped to their feet and dashed for the grounded Sokol ship. Others stood staring in dumb amazement until their officers cuffed them into action. "Put it out! Put it out, you dogs!" they shouted.

Fire was the one thing that sailors feared more than anything else, for there were a thousand things on a ship that burned well given the chance. If there had been a strong wind blowing, Geran might have hoped for the flames to spread to the other vessel, but even without that, it seemed that the fire was doing its part in diverting the pirates.

He floundered back to the wet sand and gravel fifty yards from the caravel, with no cover to speak of—but he was in the darkness, and the pirates' attention was fixed on the bright fire. Men were swarming over the rail to battle the blaze now, beating at the flames with wet blankets and old cloaks or throwing buckets of water and sand as quickly as they could draw them. Several pirates still lingered near the place where the woman was tied up, but they were looking at the fire as well.

"Tymora, favor a fool," he said aloud. Then he drew his elven blade, locked his eyes on the place he wanted to be, and spoke another spell. *"Sieroch!"* he said. In a single, dark, dizzying instant he vanished from where he was standing and appeared beside the golden-haired woman. She looked up, startled, and he saw that she had elf blood in her; her violet eyes showed just the slightest tilt, subtle points graced her ears, and her features had a fine, sharp cast to them. She was slender of build and tall, but her pale bosom had a human fullness, and her hips were well curved. He pressed his hand over her mouth before she could give him away with a startled cry and quickly set the edge of his blade to her bonds.

A dozen pirates were sprawled on the ground nearby, too drunk to be roused by the fire. Three more stood within ten or fifteen feet, but they were watching their fellows fight the fire; their backs were to Geran.

"Don't speak," Geran whispered into the half-elf's ear. "I'm going to try to rescue you." The panic in her eyes faded, and she gave him a single quick nod. He took his hand from her mouth and turned his attention to slicing through the ropes binding her as quickly and quietly as he could. It was harder than he'd thought; the firelight cast dark, dancing shadows, and he didn't want to cut her by mistake. He finally found the right angle for his sword and sawed through the cords binding her wrists together.

"Behind you!" the half-elf hissed urgently.

Geran looked up and found that one of the pirates who'd had his back turned a moment ago was looking right at him. He was a burly fellow with a mop of straw-colored hair and a scarred jaw. "Who the devil're you, and what d'you think you're doing with our pris'ner?" the man demanded. The other crewmen standing nearby turned to look at Geran.

Geran seized the half-elf by her wrist and dashed off into the darkness. They struggled through the loose sand, but so did the men who pursued them. In twenty steps they were out of the firelight, and Geran began to hope that they might be able to simply outrun the corsairs' pursuit. Then he saw a brawny half-orc moving to intercept them, a heavy hand axe grasped in one thick fist. They must have posted some sentries after all, Geran realized.

The half-orc didn't waste time on challenges. Baring his fangs in a fierce growl, he flung himself at Geran with a roar of rage, his axe raised high. Geran quickly stepped in front of the captive and met the half-orc's rush with an arcane word and a lunge. His sword burst into emerald flame and took the half-orc in the notch of his collarbone, grating on bone as it struck deep. The pirate stumbled heavily and fell into the swordmage; Geran shouldered him to the side, then whirled to face the big straw-haired man and the other two pursuing from the fireside.

"Ho, so you've some fight in you after all!" the big man said. "I thought you were going to just run off there!" He had a cutlass in his hand, and he started forward with a more cautious advance than his crewmate had tried. The second man came up close behind him with a short boarding pike; the third fellow struggled to catch up.

"More are coming," the half-elf woman said. And she was right; by the bonfire Geran could see more of the pirates turning aside from the fire aboard the Sokol ship and moving in their direction. He didn't have time for a defensive fight.

He launched an attack on the big man. The fellow parried his first thrust, and blocked the slash that Geran followed with, but then Geran looped his point over the man's guard and stabbed him deeply in the meat of his sword arm. The pirate dropped his cutlass with a startled oath; before the man could recover, Geran flung out an arm and snarled another spell, flinging up a shield of ghostly white. The glowing disk caught the man with the boarding pike as he worked around to Geran's flank and knocked him down in the sand. The fellow started to scramble to his feet, but a fist-sized rock sailed over Geran's shoulder and caught him in the mouth. He fell back again, spitting broken teeth.

The third pirate looked up at Geran, realizing that neither of his two comrades was still in the fight. He was armed only with a long dagger, but he must have been daunted by Geran's longer blade or magic, because he hesitated and then backed away. "Over here!" he shouted. "The girl's getting away! Here!"

Geran snarled in frustration. He'd been within a few feet of escaping without notice! The man with the dagger realized his danger at the last moment and tried to retreat, but he lost his footing in the sand and fell. Geran silenced him with a savage kick to the jaw. Geran wheeled to face the big, yellow-haired man, just in time to duck under a wild, left-handed slash of the man's cutlass. This man was the one who'd stripped the captive and toyed with her while she was helpless. Eyes blazing with wrath, Geran slapped his cutlass out of the way and rammed the point of his backsword into the man's belly. The man howled in agony; Geran jerked back his point and finished the pirate with a cut that took off half of his face. He looked around for another foe to sate his anger, but no more were near.

The half-elf winced when he met her eyes and retreated a step. Geran took a breath, mastered his fury, and lowered his sword. Before any more foes could catch up, he seized the woman's hand again and hurried her up the beach. "You're handy with a rock, but it's time to leave," he told her. "We've worn out our welcome."

Together they scrambled through the brush at the edge of the beach and ran up the hillside. When Geran risked another look over his shoulder, he could see dozens of men seizing burning brands from their bonfire and starting up the hill after them. The slope was treacherous in the dark; loose soil and rock slipped under their feet, and he had to keep an eye ahead to make sure they didn't flee into a bluff they couldn't scale, as well as watching the pirates who followed.

He found their way blocked by a thick patch of brush at the foot of the cliff and realized they were climbing up by a different way than he'd come down. He paused, trying to find his bearings, but the half-elf took one glance and pulled him toward the left. "There's a better path over here," she said. Geran decided to trust her judgment and followed after her. With her elf blood, she could probably see in the dark much better than he could. When they got around the thicket, he took the lead again and steered her toward the spot where he'd left his horse.

They reached the boulders where Geran's horse was tethered. The animal, a big, gray gelding, scented danger and pranced nervously. Geran sheathed his sword—he hated to do that with blood on the blade, but he'd just have to clean it up as best he could later—and unlooped the reins as the half-elf climbed into the saddle. Then he hauled himself up into the saddle behind her and set his heels to the horse's flanks. They pelted out of cover along the trail as the first of the pirates reached the top behind them. The swordmage risked a glance backward and saw angry corsairs running after them brandishing torches and cutlasses. Then he leaned forward in the saddle, arms around the woman in front of him, and urged the gelding to its best speed.

His horse's hoofbeats thundering in the night, Geran galloped out of the cove with the pirates' captive on his saddle and leaping red firelight behind him.

TWO

11 Eleint, the Year of the Ageless One (1479 DR)

After a hard run of a mile or so to gain distance on the pirates, Geran slowed his horse to a canter and rode for a time. When he judged that they'd put any immediate pursuit well behind them, he let the horse settle into a trot, its breath steaming in the cool night air. The night was clear and cold, but the moon was up now; its silver light glittered on the Moonsea to their right. The woman shivered in his arms, and he realized that she was clutching only a shred of her torn dress over her torso. For that matter, he was still soaked from his moonlit swim. "I think we've outrun them for now," he said. "We can stop for a moment. I have a spare shirt and cloak in my gear."

She turned her head to look back at him. "Thank you," she said. "I didn't want to say anything, but I'm freezing."

He reined in and dropped down out of the saddle. Then he offered a hand to help her down as well, trying—but not entirely succeeding—to keep his eyes fixed on her face. She crossed her arms over her chest with an awkward grimace, and he made himself turn his attention to the satchel behind the saddle. He rummaged through it quickly and found his spare clothing. "Here. You're welcome to it."

He turned away and watched the trail behind them, giving her the privacy to dress as well as she could. There was no sign of the pirates behind them. He guessed they'd covered three or four miles pretty quickly; the marauders must be at least a quarter hour behind them, if indeed they were still giving chase. He heard rustling and the sound of tearing cloth. Then the half-elf spoke again. "I'm decently covered now," she said. Geran looked back to her; she had ripped off the ruined top of her dress and tucked his oversized shirt into what was now a very uneven-looking skirt. His cloak hung down to her ankles, and she hugged it close around her shoulders. They regarded each other for a moment.

"I'm Geran," he told her. "I mean you no harm. If you like, I'll see you to Hulburg and help you on your way once we get there."

"My name is Nimessa Sokol." She held the cloak tightly around her collar, as if she meant to hide inside it. "We were bound for Hulburg. We were supposed to land there this afternoon."

"You're a Sokol?"

"Yes. My father is Arandar Sokol." She glanced over Geran's shoulder at the trail leading back along the hills toward the cove. There was a smudge of orange light flickering against the hill-side. "Is it safe to linger here?"

"No, we should keep moving," he said. Geran didn't know any of the Sokol family personally, but he knew *of* them. They were from the city of Phlan, a few days' sail west of Hulburg. Like many of the wellborn folk around the Moonsea, they were merchant-nobles; they had interests in several cities, including Hulburg. "It's a little less than twenty miles to Hulburg, by my guess. Too far to ride tonight, but I think we can put the pirates well behind us."

"Then yes, I'll be happy to let you see me to Hulburg. But you won't have to go to any more trouble on my account. My family's coster has a trading concession there. I'll be fine."

"In that case, I suggest we ride another few miles and then get off the trail. We'll be home by noon tomorrow."

"Home?" Nimessa looked more closely at Geran. "Of course. You're Geran *Hulmaster,* the harmach's nephew. You're the one who fought the King in Copper and killed Mhurren of the Bloodskulls. We heard the story. But what in the world were you doing by that beach? You must be mad to challenge so many enemies at once."

Geran allowed himself a small smile. "I'll answer, but let's ride while we talk." He helped Nimessa up into the saddle again, not that she really needed the assistance, then settled himself behind her. They rode eastward along the crest of the coastal hills, following the winding trail. The moon draped the dark landscape in silver and shadow; it was clear enough that the promontories and inlets for several miles ahead were visible, and the Moonsea was a great, gray plain stretching out of sight on their right. With Nimessa's slim body in front of him and her golden curls just under his nose, it did not seem like such a bad night for a ride after all.

"How did you come to find me when you did?" Nimessa asked.

"An accident. I left Thentia early this morning and was looking for a place to make camp for the evening when I stumbled across the pirates and your ship. I was about to ride off when they brought you out and tied you up." He shrugged awkwardly, even though she couldn't see him. "I couldn't leave you in their hands without at least trying to help, but I had to wait until it was dark before I could move. You saw the rest."

"The fire on *Whitewing?*"

"Yes, I'm afraid that was my doing. I figured that she was a loss already, so I might as well deny the pirates their prize while making a distraction." They rode on for a short time, and then Geran sighed. He hated to ask what he asked next, but he thought he'd better. "I watched for a while, Nimessa. I didn't see any other captives. Were you the only one they spared?"

"Yes." She looked down. "There was no one else left to save."

"Were you—" he began, and then he stopped himself. He was going to ask if she'd been traveling alone, but he knew better. A young noblewoman of a good family would have been accompanied, most likely by a maid-in-waiting or a kinsman. There was a chance that the pirates would spare wellborn captives in the hopes of winning a rich ransom, but somehow he doubted that they'd intended to ransom Nimessa back to her family. And if they hadn't intended to ransom her, no one else in her party would have been worth keeping alive. He let the question die on his lips. He could only imagine what she'd seen and been through. Even if she was made of stern stuff, it would not be easy on her.

After a while he realized that she was shaking inside his oversized cloak, and she failed to stifle a sob. He frowned behind her, trying to decide if it was kinder to leave her to her thoughts for a time, distract her with meaningless conversation, or draw her out and let her tell her story. *Half an hour ago you were thinking of her as a princess in a Waterdeep romance story, and you the brave knight,* Geran fumed at himself. *She's seen more murder and cruelty in a few short hours than most people do in a lifetime.* And he'd certainly contributed his own share with his furious skirmish on the beach. All she knew of him was that he'd stolen her out of a pirate camp, savagely cutting down anyone in his path. Regardless of the reasons he gave for his actions, she had to wonder whether his motives were honorable or not.

Not knowing what else to do, he squeezed her hand and said, "It's over now, Nimessa." She nodded but did not answer.

Geran found a spot that he remembered along the track and paused to look around. They still had the trail to themselves, as far as he could tell. He spurred his horse up and over the crest of the hill. An old footpath led into the low thickets and hedgerows of a small valley where a stream descended to the sea below. They headed inland into the empty hills. If the pirates were still in pursuit, Geran figured that they'd likely follow the coastal trail. They couldn't know where Geran and Nimessa had left the trail unless they had a very good tracker with them.

A long-abandoned homestead stood at the head of the valley. It might have been wiser to keep on going, but he was exhausted, and the moon would be setting soon. There were dangers other than pirates abroad in the Highfells at night, and Geran didn't care to meet them in the dark. He dismounted and led his horse inside the old house. There was a back door leading out to overgrown fields behind the house; if they had to, they could flee deeper into the hills.

He helped Nimessa down then busied himself with setting up a small camp. "I think it's safe to rest a couple of hours," he said. "We can't ride all night, and I'm too tired to go much farther. My apologies for the accommodations."

"For some reason a lonely old ruin in the middle of nowhere doesn't seem so bad to me tonight," Nimessa answered. She found a small, rueful smile. "Do you know where we are?"

"More or less. I used to hunt up here when I was younger."

Geran found some dry brush and built a small fire inside the old hearth. He stepped around the corner to change into the last of his dry clothing and spread his wet clothes out in front of the fire. Then he shared his provisions with Nimessa, and they made a supper out of a loaf of bread, a wedge of cheese, dried sausage, and apples. She ate ravenously.

When Nimessa finished, she looked up at him and brushed a hand across her eyes. "I haven't eaten since yesterday evening," she explained.

"I understand."

"And I don't think I've thanked you yet for saving my life." Nimessa dropped her gaze. "I don't know what moved you to risk your own life to save a stranger, but I'm very glad that you came along when you did. The things they said they would do to me—I can't even think of it."

"Do you know who they were?" Geran asked gently.

"The ship's name was *Kraken Queen.* I saw it painted on her stern. The captain was a fierce man, maybe fifty or so, and almost as tall as you. He wore braids in his hair and beard. I never heard any of the crewmen call him anything other than 'Captain.'"

Geran remembered the figurehead of the tentacled mermaid. The name fit the ship. "How did they catch you?"

"They stole up on us before sunrise this morning. When the sun came up and we spotted them, they were only a couple of miles off. Master Parman tried to outrun the pirate ship, but the wind died down around noon, and after that *Whitewing* didn't stand a chance." Nimessa hesitated, and she huddled deeper in Geran's cloak. "They killed everyone else, but the pirate captain ordered his men to spare me for—later."

"You don't have to say more."

Nimessa fell silent, and Geran frowned, digesting the story. *Whitewing* made five ships he knew of that hadn't reached Hulburg in the last few months. Piracy was choking the trade of the city little by little. Something would have to be done, and soon. "Well, it's over now," he told her. "You're out of their reach. Try to sleep for a few hours."

He let her have his bedroll and went to tend to his horse. He gave the animal an extra pat on the neck by way of apologizing for a hard run at the end of a long day. By the time he returned to the fireside, Nimessa was curled up on her side under his blankets and breathing deeply and slowly. He studied her face; she had wide eyes, a delicate point to her chin, and smooth skin that seemed a pale gold in the firelight, hinting at sun elf ancestry. In sleep she looked young and innocent. It was hard to say with someone of elf descent, but he would have guessed her to be twenty-five or so. Younger than Alliere, he decided. And she was fair-haired, while Alliere's hair was dark as moonshadows. Of course he'd never watched Alliere sleep during the brief months that he'd loved her. Elves didn't sleep as humans—or half-elves—did. Strange how two peoples could be so much alike and yet so different.

"She's not Alliere," Geran told himself softly. With a sigh, he turned away and looked to settle himself for a long night. Nimessa had his bedroll, so all he could do was wrap himself in his cloak. He resigned himself to a night with little rest and found a spot where he could sit with his back to a wall and have a good view of the overgrown fields outside. The night was still and quiet.

He dozed off a couple of times during the night, but no one came along to interrupt their rest. Finally, as the eastern sky began to gray, he roused himself. He didn't think *Kraken Queen*'s men were anywhere nearby, but his trail would be easier to follow in daylight. He packed up the camp quietly, allowing Nimessa to sleep a little longer, then he woke her. "Morning is near. We should move on."

Nimessa opened her eyes, looked at him, then sat up sharply with a gasp. She frowned in puzzlement, then she remembered where she was. “Sweet Selûne,” she murmured. “For a moment I thought it was all a terrible dream.”

“I’m afraid not,” he told her. He gave her a crooked smile. “I’d offer you some breakfast, but we ate everything I had with me before we went to sleep. Lunch is in Hulburg.”

In a few minutes he packed up the last of his gear, and they set off again. A high overcast was stealing in from the west. Rather than heading back to the coastal trail, Geran decided to put the sunrise on his right and cut northeast through the hills. It would shave a couple of miles off their journey, even if it was more rugged country, and it was also much less likely to lead them into any pirates who might still be looking for them. These hills marked the rolling fall of the land from the high moors of Thar to the Moonsea. The folk of Hulburg called them the Highfells, and Geran knew them well. As a youth he’d explored every vale and hill for a day’s ride around his home. They rode at an easy pace for several miles, slowly climbing higher into the hills and leaving the coast behind them. The higher slopes were treeless and marked by wide slashes of bare, mossy rock.

“It’s so empty,” Nimessa said as they crested a ridge. “Nobody lives here?”

“Shepherds and goatherds sometimes bring their flocks into these hills in the summertime, but we’re past that now,” Geran answered. “A few people settled the coastal hills in the time of old Thentur, but that was two or three centuries ago. Now?” He shook his head. “No, no one lives up here.”

“Where are the mines? And the forests your people cut?”

Geran pointed past her at a faint, gray-green range that marched across their path many miles away. “The Galena Mountains. They lie about fifteen or twenty miles east of Hulburg. That’s where you’ll find the mining and timber camps. West of Hulburg there’s nothing but the Highfells and Thar.” He reined in and swung himself down from the saddle. “You keep riding. I’ll walk a bit.”

“I’m perfectly capable of walking a few miles,” Nimessa answered.

"I don't doubt it, but I'd feel better if you rode."

She looked at him with a skeptical expression. "You don't have to impress me with your gallantry, you know."

"Would it make you feel better if I said I was mindful of the horse, not you?"

Nimessa laughed briefly and shook her head. She had a pleasant laugh, light and soft, much like many of the elves Geran had known in Myth Drannor. He smiled and set off again, walking at her stirrup as they picked their way down a hillside. If he had his bearings right, they'd hit the inland trail from Thentia soon. "So what business do you have in Hulburg? It seems a fair distance from your home."

"I'm taking over the management of our House's tradeyard. My father isn't satisfied with the return on our investments in Hulburg. He feels that it's time a Sokol stepped in to put things in order."

Geran looked up at her. He wondered if she had much experience in overseeing Sokol business. Was her father seeing to her education in the affairs of House Sokol, or was she expected to take a direct hand in the business? He was more than a little responsible for the decline in Sokol profits over the last few months, since he'd played a large part in exposing the corruption of the Merchant Council in Hulburg—although it was Geran's own cousin Sergen who'd been behind much of that. In the aftermath of Sergen's failed attempt to seize power, Harmach Grigor had closely examined the leases and rents paid by each of the foreign merchant concessions in Hulburg. Most of the big merchant costers were now paying much more for the right to cut the harmach's timber and mine the harmach's hills than they had when Sergen was running things. Of course, that meant Nimessa would be on the other side of the table from him when it came time to negotiate those rights.

"There are still plenty of Veruna leases available," he observed. House Veruna of Mulmaster had been Sergen's chief accomplice in the recent troubles. "House Sokol could do worse than to bid on a few of those, since the Verunas won't be getting them back."

"The Verunas have made it clear to us that they'd take a very dim view of other families or costers buying up their Hulburg leases," Nimessa answered. "They feel they're still the rightful holders, and they'll retaliate against any other House that takes advantage of your uncle's draconian measures."

"Draconian?"

Nimessa tilted her head. "So the Verunas say. I wasn't here, so I really can't make a judgment about whether the harmach was within his rights to expel House Veruna and confiscate their holdings."

Geran snorted to himself. He didn't have any doubt of it, but of course he was a Hulmaster. He decided that Nimessa wasn't in Hulburg to learn anything. She was here because her father trusted her to look after Sokol interests. Nimessa hadn't forgotten that he was a Hulmaster, and despite the fact that she was riding through the middle of nowhere with a borrowed shirt and oversized cloak, she was careful to keep her thoughts to herself about her family's business.

The rest of the morning passed by quietly enough. From time to time they talked of small things; Geran told Nimessa some of the stories he knew about the Highfells and their brooding barrows, while Nimessa told him about events and doings in Phlan. They saw no signs of *Kraken Queen*'s crew or any other travelers for that matter. Eventually they struck the Thentian trail Geran was looking for, and two hours more brought them to the edge of the Winterspear Vale a couple of miles north of Hulburg itself. As Geran had promised, they came to the Burned Bridge over the Winterspear in the early afternoon.

Hulburg itself lay south of the old bridge, a ramshackle town bustling with commerce and trade. Here, where the Winterspear emptied into the Moonsea, an older city had stood hundreds of years ago. The town of Hulburg was built atop its ruins. On the east bank of the river, the castle of Griffonwatch—home of the Hulmasters—overlooked the town's landward edge, guarding against attack from the wild lands of Thar. The tradeyards and concessions of the foreign merchant companies stood mostly on the west bank, hard by the town's wharves. A steady stream of wagons and carts pushed out along the road leading inland, ferrying provisions and tools to the camps outside of town. The ruins of an old city wall meandered around the edge of the town, but stonemasons were at work in various spots—Harmach Grigor was pouring most of the Tower's newfound wealth into repairing the old defenses.

Geran stole a glance at Nimessa's face, trying to read her reaction to her first sight of the town. She frowned, perhaps taking in the unpaved roads or the smoking smelters. "It's not quite as cheerless as it looks," he told her. "The streets down by the bayside are a little more, well, civilized."

She summoned a small smile. "It's busy," she observed. "That's a good sign. Besides, I've been told that the lodgings in the Sokol concession are fairly comfortable. I'll be fine." Then she nodded off to Geran's left. "It looks like there was a fire."

Geran followed her gaze. Near the spot where the Vale Road passed through the ancient walls stood a large wooden building on a footing of old stone. One corner was scorched, and a patch of the wooden shakes over that part of the building was missing. A thin plume of smoke rose from a hole in the roof. "The Troll and Tankard," he said with a frown.

"A tavern?"

"The best ale in Hulburg." They rode by slowly. A number of workmen were busy with the work of tearing down the ruined siding with hatchets and saws. Several more stood watch over the scene, each with a blue cloth tied around the arm. Geran spotted Brun Osting, the tavernkeeper, studying the scene with his thick arms folded across his chest and a fierce scowl on his bearded face. Brun had run the Troll and Tankard ever since his father died fighting to stop the Bloody Skull orcs from pillaging the town five months past. Geran detoured closer and hailed him. "What happened here, Brun?"

The tavernkeeper looked around. He was a young man of strapping build, easily two or three inches taller than Geran and fifty pounds heavier. "M'lord Geran—and m'lady," he said, touching his knuckle to his brow. If he was surprised to see Geran riding with a pretty young yoman in the front of his saddle, he didn't say anything. "It was the Cinderfists. A gang of 'em tried to fire the Troll during the night, but they made enough noise to rouse my brothers. We drove 'em off and saved most of the building."

Geran studied the damage and frowned. "Anyone hurt?"

"The Cinderfists carried off two or three o' theirs, but I don't think no one got killed. My brother Stunder took a bad cut, but he's patched up now." Brun Osting shook his head. "There's trouble in the making, m'lord. Mark my words. The Cinderfists try burning out good Hulburgans again, and there'll be killing over it."

"I hear you," Geran said. "Is there anything I can do to help? The Hulmasters are in your family's debt."

The young brewer waved his hand. "It's just a few hours' work to cut some new shakes and planks, m'lord. The Troll wasn't that handsome to look at anyway, but I'll bet the smell of smoke's going to be in the rafters for years."

Geran shook his head and rode off, allowing the brewer to get back to his morning's work. When they were out of earshot, Nimessa glanced up at him. "Who are the Cinderfists?" she asked.

"You might call them a guild or militia, or you might call them a gang. They're mostly newcomers to Hulburg, men from places like Melvaunt and Mulmaster. Many work in the smelters and foundries." During the troubles of the past spring, Geran had spurred the common folk of Hulburg to band together against the mercenaries of the foreign merchants. It hadn't taken long for the poorer foreigners to copy their example and begin organizing their own guilds and militias to protect themselves too. The Moonshields—the native Hulburgan militia—were loyal to the harmach. The Cinderfists, on the other hand were largely dependent on foreign merchants for their livelihood. "I can't prove anything, but I suspect House Jannarsk and their Crimson Chain allies are behind them. Hulburg is full of poor men from other cities who just want a chance to do better for themselves, but there are a few that came here for different sorts of opportunities."

"Have they caused a lot of trouble?"

"Some," Geran admitted. "But Brun Osting's right—there's more on the way if things keep going on as they are." They rode into the small square at the foot of the causeway leading up to Griffonwatch. Geran reined in again and looked down at Nimessa. "Can I offer you the hospitality of Griffonwatch? I'm sure that we can find you something better to wear. Or would you rather go to your family's holding now?"

"The Sokol concession, please," Nimessa answered. "I have to tell our people there about *Whitewing* and send word to my father right away. But I thank you for the offer."

"As you wish. Consider it a standing invitation." Geran hid his disappointment behind a small nod. He found that he was reluctant to part company so soon. Once he escorted her to the Sokol compound, she would be back among the people and surroundings she was familiar with. He'd check on her in a few days, and if she recovered as well as he thought she might then he'd leave her be. It would likely be for the best.

Then again . . . he'd been haunted for almost two years now by the memories of Alliere. Maybe some part of him was hoping that Nimessa was not interested, simply so that he could go on dreaming about the elf princess he would never see again. Or was he afraid of what Mirya Erstenwold might think, if he were to start courting again? He frowned behind Nimessa, unhappy with his musings. He'd never been one to puzzle out the workings of his own heart. All he knew was that he'd spent two years living like a cloistered monk because Alliere had broken his heart, and Nimessa Sokol reminded him that he wanted to be free of her ghost.

He tapped his heels to the horse's flanks. "The Sokol tradeyard's not far off now. Allow me to see you home."

THREE

14 Eleint, the Year of the Ageless One (1479 DR)

Rhovann Disarnnyl detested his human guise. He was mortified by the unkindnesses of age, the heaviness of his sagging features, the rough whiskers on his face, and the wiry, gray hair on his chest and arms. Elves suffered none of those indignities, and in his natural shape Rhovann was a fine example of his graceful race. He consoled himself with the thought that his disguise was only a magical glamour he could end any time he chose with a few arcane words. But the difficulty was that crafting a persona as carefully thought out as Lastannor—middle-aged, balding, with a meticulously squared beard of iron gray and a coarse, dusky, complexion—required hours of painstaking work. The trouble of re-creating his disguise was a strong incentive to endure his altered appearance as long as he could. And there was always the risk that he'd overlook some small detail like the exact shape of the nose or whether the rounded ears lay flat by the skull or stuck out like cup handles, a detail that some observant enemy might notice. Fortunately he'd had the foresight to make Lastannor as close to his own natural height and build as possible, so that he would have one less opportunity to err. No human could really match the slender athleticism of a moon elf, but Rhovann avoided trouble there simply by shaping Lastannor's build as gaunt and by making a point of moving with a sort of exaggerated lethargy to conceal the lightness of his step.

He was nothing if not attentive to details.

"You have a sour look to you today, Lastannor," said Lord Maroth Marstel. The Hulburgan and his House mage rode in the human noble's carriage, rolling through the streets of Hulburg toward the castle of the Hulmasters. Marstel peered suspiciously at Rhovann with weak eyes in a red, heavy-featured face. He was a thick-bodied, white-jowled man of sixty-five years or so, with a thick mane of hair and a broad white mustache that was yellowed at the edges by his ridiculous habit of pipe-smoking. The old lord wore a scarlet tunic embroidered with his family coat of arms, which featured a leaping stag amid a whole field of gold embellishments. "What troubles you?"

"Nothing of consequence," Rhovann lied, feigning a friendly grimace. "Something disagrees with me, my lord." Of course, it was Marstel himself Rhovann found disagreeable. The man possessed a truly spectacular combination of loud bluster, oxlike wit, and ill-informed opinion. He seemed to crash through his days like a wagon rolling down a steep hill, completely insensitive to the damage he caused. If Rhovann hadn't given himself the task of elevating the man's fortunes, he might have looked on the whole affair with some small amusement. As matters stood, Rhovann had spent several months now soothing feathers Marstel ruffled every time he opened his mouth, and safeguarding the buffoon who sat in the carriage next to him from even greater disasters.

"You're a scrawny fellow, and you hardly eat at all," Marstel observed. "I can't imagine why your stomach should trouble you. I think it's a lack of exercise and fresh air. And not enough wine. Two good goblets a day would serve you well." The white-haired lord nodded to himself, satisfied that he had diagnosed the problem. "Yes, that must be it. You should come hunting with me tomorrow. It's always a good, vigorous day."

Rhovann sighed. "I am afraid I have business to look after, my lord. But you should go ahead without me. As you say, the outings are good for you." Marstel's idea of a vigorous day of hunting was to be driven up to some wild field and seated in a comfortable chair while his servants did their best to drive game in his general direction. The old lord would spend the day getting drunk and loosing quarrels at anything that moved. While one might naturally assume that Marstel rarely hit anything, the man was a far better shot than he had a right to be, and he often collected a fair assortment of game. He also occasionally feathered one of his own dogs or beaters, especially late in the day after he was well in his cups. Fortunately Hulburg had no shortage of poor foreigners anxious to earn a few coins any way they could.

"Suit yourself, then," Marstel said with a sniff.

Rhovann sighed. Now the old fool was going to be sore at him. Only a month or two more, he told himself. Endure this ox-brained fool just a little longer, and through him the fall of the Hulmasters will be encompassed. He flexed the cold metal of his silver hand—veiled under the illusion of human flesh and bone—and thought of Geran Hulmaster's destruction. To slay Geran for the injuries he'd inflicted would be simple justice. What Rhovann craved was *vengeance.* No, before Geran Hulmaster died, Rhovann meant for his enemy to see all that he loved torn away from him. Only then would the scales lie in balance between the two of them. For that worthy end, a few months of tedious and unpleasant work were a trifle.

The carriage came to the causeway leading up to the castle of the Hulmasters and climbed up the roadway. In a few moments they rolled into the cobblestone courtyard inside Griffonwatch's front gate and halted. Liveried footmen hopped down from the carriage's running boards to open the door and set wooden steps for the passengers. Rhovann climbed out and settled into the shuffling gait that was almost second nature to him now; Marstel followed him. Several other coaches were already gathered in the courtyard, and another rolled in just behind Marstel's carriage.

He leaned close to Marstel and gripped the old lord's arm in his hand. Silently he brought the enchantments that bound the two of them together to the forefront of his mind and bent the power of his will on their invisible connection. "Speak only as I have instructed you," he whispered into Marstel's ear. "If you do not know how to answer a question, stay silent and give an appearance of careful thought. I will tell you what to say."

The old man murmured in protest and tried to resist the enchantment's power, but his will was no match for Rhovann's. The wizard crushed his brief resistance without even breaking stride. Marstel stared ahead and nodded. "I understand."

They entered the castle's great hall, which was already arranged for the meeting of the Harmach's Council. A horseshoe-shaped table with nine chairs had been set up in the center of the drafty old hall, facing a low dais with a large, high-backed chair for the ruler of Hulburg. Rhovann steered Marstel toward the old lord's seat then sat beside him. In his guise as Lastannor, Rhovann himself held the post of Master Mage of Hulburg; the former Master Mage, Ebain Ravenscar, had resigned his post shortly after House Veruna's expulsion from Hulburg and returned to his home in Mulmaster. Marstel, on Rhovann's right, was head of the town's Merchant Council, as well as one of Hulburg's few native "lords"—although Rhovann found Lord Maroth Marstel's claim to nobility dubious at best.

Most of the other councilors were already present; Rhovann studied each surreptitiously. He did not believe that his magical domination of Marstel or his own human guise were detectable by anything less than a thorough study by one skilled in the arcane arts, as long as he made sure that Marstel continued to act in character. But the consequences of being caught in his game might be severe. He paid the closest attention to Kara Hulmaster, who sat directly across the horseshoe from him. She held the seat reserved for the Captain of the Shieldsworn, commander of Hulburg's tiny army. Kara worried Rhovann greatly. Despite her youth she was quite perceptive. Kara carried a spellscar in the form of a serpentlike sigil on her left forearm and possessed eyes of an eerie, luminous, azure hue. In many lands the spellscarred were looked on with distrust and resentment, but no one in Hulburg doubted Kara's loyalty or skill. She was a Hulmaster and by all accounts a very formidable warrior, the hero of the Battle of Lendon's Dike. Rhovann could never entirely convince himself that she did not see more than she let on with her spellscarred eyes, and he did not care for that feeling at all.

"The harmach!" called one of the Shieldsworn guards in the room. All of the councilors dutifully rose to their feet and waited while Harmach Grigor Hulmaster, leaning on his cane, made his way down the grand staircase of the hall and took his seat in the large chair on the dais.

Geran Hulmaster walked beside his uncle, dressed in a quilted doublet of gray and white. It did not escape Rhovann's attention that the sword with the mithral rose on its pommel rode at Geran's hip. His right wrist ached with a hot white pain; flesh and bone remembered the sharp bite of that sword.

Rhovann clenched his fists beneath the table. To have been maimed by the human swordmage was one thing. After all, if he'd had it in his power, Rhovann would have done the same thing to Geran during that fateful duel in Myth Drannor. But the offense that truly galled Rhovann was the fact that Geran's exile from the City of Song had led to his own. The exquisite Alliere had not turned her heart to him, as she should have once the upstart human adventurer had been dealt with. And the Coronal's Guard had found reason to pry into his arcane studies after his duel with Geran. They'd discovered books and ritual materials they considered unseemly for a mage of Myth Drannor. Spurned by the woman he desired, chastised for studying dark arts, Rhovann had lost more than his hand to Geran Hulmaster's blade. And he meant to settle that account before the year was out.

Rhovann realized that he was glaring at Geran and quickly looked away. Geran had no reason to fear Lastannor, the Master Mage of Hulburg and wizard to House Marstel, but if he noticed that Lastannor glared hatefully at him, he would be a fool not to wonder why. Instead Rhovann shifted his gaze to the harmach. Grigor was a balding man of seventy-five, with weak eyes and frail health. With some care he seated himself and leaned his cane against the side of his chair. As he sat, the councilors followed suit.

"Welcome, my friends," Grigor said. "You may proceed." Geran Hulmaster walked over to one of the benches along the side of the hall and sat down alongside the scribes and clerks who were in attendance.

Deren Ilkur nodded and struck a small gavel to the table. "The Harmach's Council is met," he said. He was the Keeper of Duties, the nominal head of the council since he directly represented the harmach. Ilkur was a newcomer to the Harmach's Council and had held his seat for only two months, since that post had formerly belonged to Sergen Hulmaster. A common-born Hulburgan who ran his countinghouse with unflinching honesty, Ilkur was a short, black-bearded man who wore a gold chain of office over his heart. "First on the agenda, the construction of the city wall," he began.

Rhovann leaned back in his seat and waited while Ilkur efficiently ran through the various affairs of interest to the council. Most of the business was routine, and he paid little attention. In half an hour they covered brief reports about the state of the Tower's treasury, the replacement of Shieldsworn killed or crippled during the Bloodskull war, the continuing disposition of House Veruna assets, and the growing disorder between gangs of common-born Hulburgans and the poor foreigners who seemed to collect in the town's neglected districts. He sat up and listened more carefully to that last report; Kara Hulmaster described how several brawls had turned lethal in the last few tendays. "I frankly don't know if I have enough Shieldsworn to keep the peace," she added. "By my count the Cinderfists might number as many as a hundred men, and I'd wager they could turn out two or three times that number if they put a call out to all the foreigners in the Tailings or out on the Eastpoint."

"Something must be done, Lady Kara," said Burkel Tresterfin. A farmer of old Hulburgan stock and a captain of the Spearmeet, he was also new to the council. "Cinderfists tried to burn down the Troll and Tankard the other day! The common folk of Hulburg are at the end of their patience. If you don't act soon, the Moonshields will take matters into their own hands. It'll be a bloody riot."

"Enough," Harmach Grigor said. "We certainly can't allow matters to go that far. Kara, find me someone who can speak for these Cinderfists, and I'll promise to hear him out. If they will forswear rioting and violence, perhaps we can find some way to answer their grievances." He pressed a hand to his forehead and leaned back in his seat. "We have other matters that we must discuss today. Master Ilkur, my nephew has news for the council."

The Keeper of Duties bowed slightly. "As you wish, my lord harmach. Lord Geran, the floor is yours."

Geran stood and walked around the table to stand in the open end of the horseshoe, clasping his hands behind his back. He looked around the table, brow creased as if he were trying to decide where to start. Then he said, "I'm afraid that other troubles are on our doorstep, good sirs. Three days ago, while riding home from Thentia, I came across a pirate vessel that had captured a Sokol ship. They were drawn up in a cove a few miles east of the ruins at Gazzeth. The pirates were plundering the Sokol cargo. They'd already dealt with all the crew and passengers, save one." He went on to tell a tale of spying on the pirates, giving details of the pirate ship and her crew and then matter-of-factly describing his rescue of a daughter of the Sokols out from under the noses of her captors. "I can only guess that they're lying in wait along our trade routes," he finished. "Any ship sailing to or from Hulburg is in danger."

"A grim tale indeed," said Theron Nimstar. He was the city's High Magistrate, an old servant of the harmach with a stout body, heavy jowls, and a keen mind. "You are to be commended for saving Lady Sokol. That was a bold stroke."

Most likely the pirates were all dead drunk by that point, Rhovann thought. He knew he shouldn't underestimate Geran Hulmaster's talents, but he wouldn't have been surprised if a dolt like Maroth Marstel couldn't have saved the girl in those circumstances. Well, it was no matter. Rhovann had heard the rumors within hours of Geran's return, so he'd expected this report for two days now, and he was ready to reply. Keeping his gaze directed toward the swordmage, Rhovann concentrated on Maroth Marstel, sitting next to him. *Now, Marstel,* he said silently. *Speak.*

"I've something to say," Maroth Marstel rumbled.

Ilkur nodded to Marstel. "The floor is yours, my lord."

The old lord rose slowly to his feet. "Piracy in our waters is intolerable! The Merchant Council demands action to protect our trade against the depredations of pirates. The Sokol ship makes five lost in the last three months. We are being ruined by these murderous attacks! The lost cargoes are bad enough, but need I remind the council that dozens—no, scores—of our sailors have been slaughtered mercilessly?" Marstel banged his meaty fist on the table, warming up to his customary volume. In truth, he needed little coaching from Rhovann in bombast; all the elf mage had had to do was throw the old fool an issue to fire his imagination. "We're pouring a fortune into city walls to deter an enemy that we have already defeated, while we are being pillaged on the high seas! I know of three merchant companies that cannot afford to lose one more cargo. They'll be ruined in the next attack—and if our merchant companies fail, then they'll no longer pay the harmach to cut his timber, they'll no longer pay the good folk of Hulburg for their work, and they'll no longer sell their wares in our streets! Disaster sails toward us, my lords and ladies, with cutlasses dripping blood and corpses in its wake, and yet we have done nothing! So when does the harmach intend to take action?"

Ilkur did not answer immediately, nor did anyone else. Perhaps they weren't sure if Marstel had meant the last question to be rhetorical or not. Rhovann hid a smile. The last bit about cutlasses and corpses was pure Marstel bombast; the old man had been caught up in his own topic, as Rhovann had expected he might be.

Harmach Grigor sighed and looked at the old noble. "Lord Marstel, what would you have us do?"

"Sweep these corsairs from the Moonsea, and secure our livelihood!"

"In case it escaped my lord's attention, I do not command a navy," Grigor answered.

"Then you must begin outfitting warships immediately. The Merchant Council insists on nothing less."

"Navies are expensive," Wulreth Keltor objected. He was the Keeper of Keys, the official who looked after the harmach's treasury. Rhovann found him a sour and querulous old man. "We cannot simply wish one into existence, Lord Marstel!"

"Nevertheless, if the harmach will not see to the safety of our commerce, then the Merchant Council will take steps to do so under its own authority," said Marstel. "It is a matter of self-defense!"

Grigor's eyes narrowed. Clearly he recognized the danger to his authority implicit in Marstel's threat. Only a few months ago he'd almost been unseated by the Merchant Council under the leadership of his treacherous nephew Sergen. "You are welcome to arm your ships as you like and crew them with whatever guards you can afford," he said. "But you have no authority to act in my place, Marstel. I am charged with the defense of this realm, not you."

"I hesitate to suggest it," Deren Ilkur said, "but is there some arrangement that can be made? Bribing the pirates to let our ships pass unmolested might be less costly than outfitting warships to deter them."

"That leaves a bad taste in my mouth," Geran Hulmaster said. The swordmage shook his head. "Forgive me for speaking out of turn, but those arrangements have a way of growing more expensive over time. And you'd still lose ships every so often, because you can't bribe every pirate on the Moonsea."

"If bribery isn't an option, then how can we best defend our sea trade?" Burkel Tresterfin asked. "Can we guard the merchant coster ships with detachments of Shieldsworn? Or do we do as Lord Marstel suggests and build warships?"

"We don't have Shieldsworn enough to man every ship sailing from Hulburg," Kara Hulmaster said. She leaned back in her chair, thinking. "For that matter, even if we could afford to build warships, I don't know how we could crew them. It would take at least two or three well-armed vessels to secure the waters near Hulburg. We would need several hundred sailors and soldiers."

"Impossible," Wulreth Keltor said. "We haven't the treasury."

"So we can't afford a navy, and we don't believe bribery is the answer. What is left to us, then?" the magistrate Nimstar asked.

No one spoke for a long moment. Rhovann nodded to himself. Even if the Hulburgans had settled on building a navy, it would take too long and cost too much to interfere with his designs. "There are other cities on the Moonsea that maintain fleets," he said into the silence. "Perhaps we could ask Mulmaster or Hillsfar for protection?"

"That may prove more costly than building our own fleet," Harmach Grigor said. "If we surrender our sovereignty for the protection of a larger city, we will never recover it. I consider that the last alternative."

Rhovann willed Marstel to silence. He'd intended to catch the harmach in exactly this predicament, forcing him to choose between embarking on an expensive and most likely impractical scheme of fleet-building or weakening his authority by begging for another city's help. Either way the harmach opened himself to sharp criticism. The disguised elf leaned forward to speak. "In that case, my lord harmach, I must add my concerns to Lord Marstel's. What do you intend to do?"

Grigor Hulmaster gazed at the squares of blue sky outside the great hall's tall windows. He might have been old and frail, but he was not stupid; he could see the dilemma confronting him. "It must be a fleet, then," he finally said. "We'll purchase a couple of suitable hulls in Hillsfar or Melvaunt and bring them back to Hulburg for fitting out. For the crew, I suppose we'll have to hire mercenaries."

"Two ships may not be enough to protect our sea trade," Kara said. "Even if you assume that each can remain at sea half the time, it's only one ship on patrol on any given day."

"No, I expect it is *not* enough, Kara. But I hope that two warships are sufficient to serve as a deterrent," Grigor said. He looked around at the assembled council members. "I hope you all understand that the Tower must find funds for this somewhere. To begin with, I expect that rents must be raised on mining and logging concessions."

"Proceed with care, my lord harmach," Marstel warned. "It doesn't matter to the Houses of the Merchant Council if they're ruined by piracy or taxation. Ruin is ruin."

"You demand the harmach's protection for your shipping, but you balk at paying for the forces necessary to safeguard you?" Kara snapped. "You can't have it both ways, Lord Marstel. Where else should the harmach obtain the funds to pay for a fleet, if not from the merchant costers that will profit by the protection a fleet offers?"

Rhovann opened his mouth to counter the Shieldsworn captain's point, but Geran Hulmaster shook his head and turned to address his uncle. "Perhaps there is an alternative to a standing navy," the swordmage said. "Instead of building enough warships to defend our sea trade from every possible pirate attack, we should search out the pirates' lair and destroy them there. A single expedition of one or two ships might do as much to protect our trade in a month as a fleet of four or five ships could in years of patrols."

"Yes, Lord Geran, but where would you start?" Deren Ilkur asked.

The swordmage shrugged. "*Kraken Queen.* The Moonsea isn't that large. She can't hide for long against a determined search. As for other pirates, we should invest in information. Spread some gold around in ports like Mulmaster or Melvaunt, hire some harbor-watchers, and we'll know soon enough where our enemies are hiding."

"We'll need a ship and crew," Kara said.

"The Merchant Council's cargoes are at stake; they can spare some armsmen. And you can spare a few Shieldsworn, Kara. For the rest, I'd wager that we can find plenty of volunteers from the Moonshields." Geran smiled. "As for the ship, well, House Veruna left *Seadrake* behind when they chose to relocate their operations to Mulmaster. She's in need of repairs, but she could be ready to sail within a tenday."

"You're willing to command her, Geran?" Harmach Grigor asked.

Geran thought for a moment. "Yes, provided I get the funds I need to repair and crew the ship. I can't promise that I'll stop all the attacks, but if we catch a pirate or two, the rest might turn to easier prey."

The harmach glanced over to Marstel. "Lord Marstel, does the Merchant Council find Geran's proposal acceptable?"

Rhovann directed the old lord to strike an attitude of thoughtful deliberation while he quickly considered the question. Geran had stumbled upon a course of action that seemed reasonable and certainly did not require the harmach to beg help from another city or levy ruinous taxes against his merchants or his people. That was irksome . . . but, if Geran's search proved fruitless, he would be disgraced, and the harmach could be attacked for failing to take effective action. It might be highly useful to allow Geran to chase his own tail around the Moonsea for the next few tendays. In fact, Rhovann could see to it that rumors were deliberately planted in out-of-the-way places just for the purpose of wasting Geran's time. And he knew something about the pirates threatening Hulburg that Geran did not know. Once he considered the suggestion, it seemed that Geran had unwittingly proposed a scheme that Rhovann would have been hard-pressed to improve upon.

Realizing that Maroth Marstel had been thinking things over just a little too long, Rhovann directed the old lord to reply. "One ship is hardly a fleet, my lord harmach. But we will withhold judgment on the merits of the plan until Geran puts an end to *Kraken Queen* or we lose another ship to the depredations of those murderous sea wolves."

Geran frowned, weighing the deadline Marstel had imposed on him. After all, he had no way of knowing how long he had before pirates took another Hulburgan ship. "I'll do my best, Lord Marstel," he said.

Deren Ilkur looked around at the assembled councilors. "Is there any other business before the council?" he asked. No one spoke up; the Keeper of Duties took his gavel and rapped it sharply on the table. "Then the Council is adjourned."

Once again, everyone stood as Harmach Grigor rose and made his way up the stairs leading from the hall. Then half-a-dozen low conversations started as the councilors and their various advisors and assistants began filing from the hall. Rhovann watched Geran stride purposefully to the door, already speaking with Kara Hulmaster. Would it be better to help him along his way or delay him? the elf wondered. Through the Merchant Council and Maroth Marstel, he could speed his enemy's efforts to outfit his expedition and get him out of Hulburg quickly . . . or he could throw obstacles in Geran's path, keeping him mired in the effort to gather armsmen and supplies for a month or more.

If Geran sailed off with a strong detachment of Shieldsworn and Hulburgan loyalists, the harmach's hand would be sorely weakened. That suggested several possibilities. "The sooner the better, then," Rhovann murmured to himself.

"Eh? What did you say?" Marstel asked.

"Nothing of import, my lord," he replied. "I think House Marstel should generously support Geran Hulmaster's efforts to fit out his expedition. There is not a moment to lose, after all."

Marstel nodded. "Of course! The pirates must be dealt with firmly and immediately. Delay is intolerable."

"Just so, my lord." Rhovann gave Geran one more long look, wondering what the fool would do if he suspected that his old rival from Myth Drannor was standing only twenty feet away, planning the success or failure of his ill-conceived venture. Then he took Marstel by the elbow and guided the Hulburgan noble to his carriage.

FOUR

16 Eleint, the Year of the Ageless One (1479 DR)

Two days after the meeting of the Harmach's Council, Geran spent the morning on the quarterdeck of *Seadrake,* watching as a crew of carpenters worked to replace the ship's mainmast. The old mast had been badly cracked in a spring gale months ago, which was one reason why House Veruna's sellswords had left *Seadrake* behind when they sailed away from Hulburg. She'd been stripped of stores, canvas, rigging, and other such things, of course, but that could be remedied easily enough. Replacing a mainmast, on the other hand, was a tedious piece of work. Over the last two days the Hulburgan woodworkers had cut away the cracked mast and built a temporary hoist to raise the new mast—a tall, straight spruce cut in the Galena foothills and seasoned for several years in a pond owned by House Marstel. Several dozen workers sweated and swore at each other as they manhandled the long, creaking lines, carefully lowering the new mast into the socket of the old one.

The clatter of wheels on the cobblestones of the street drew Geran's attention. He glanced down as an open carriage halted by the gangway leading to *Seadrake.* A pair of armsmen in the black and sky blue of House Sokol hopped down from the running boards as Nimessa Sokol descended from her seat. She looked splendid in a dress of burgundy velvet embroidered with golden flowers. To Geran's surprise, an undistinguished dwarf with a bald pate and a forked beard of iron gray climbed down from the carriage after her, dressed in common workman's garb. Nimessa glanced up and caught him watching her. She gave him a warm smile and started up the gangway with her strange companion at her side. Geran dropped down the steps leading to the main deck and went to meet her at the rail.

"I thought I might find you here," she said. "May we come aboard?"

"Of course, but mind the work on the mast." Geran drew her past the working party and led her to a safe corner of the deck. "This is an unexpected pleasure. What brings you down to *Seadrake?*"

"I heard that you're looking for a sailing master," said Nimessa. "I think I may have found you one. May I present Master Andurth Galehand? Master Galehand, this is Lord Geran Hulmaster."

Geran offered his hand forearm-to-forearm in the dwarf manner and studied the fellow. Tattoos of dwarven runes spelled out indecipherable words on the dwarf's thick forearms, and like most dwarves, he didn't spare Geran the strength of his grip. "M'lord," the dwarf said.

"Master Galehand came to House Sokol this morning looking to sign on with us," Nimessa said. "I thought you might need a sailing master for *Seadrake.*"

"I do. Are you certain you can spare him?"

The half-elf nodded. "We've already struck terms. But his first assignment for House Sokol is to take a post as your sailing master, if you'll have him. And I'll send along seasoned deckhands and armsmen, as many as you need to fill out the ship's company."

Geran raised an eyebrow. "That's very generous of House Sokol."

"No, it's good common sense. The pirates are a problem, and Sokol ships aren't safe until they're defeated." Nimessa's eyes flashed. "Besides, I have a personal interest in seeing *Kraken Queen* dealt with. Anything House Sokol can provide is yours for the asking."

"I've got Erstenwold's looking after our fittings and provisions, but I can certainly use your sailors and armsmen." He turned back to the dwarf. "Are you willing to sail under the harmach's flag, Master Galehand?"

"Aye, I've no quarrel with it." The dwarf looked over to the crew working on the mast and nodded in grudging approval. "Yer carpenters seem t'know what they're about. Her mast never was quite true afore. She ought t'sail a sight better now."

"You've sailed on *Seadrake* before?"

The dwarf gave him a fierce grin. "I know this ship like me own beard. I was her sailing master for five years. I've been wanting t'see a new mainmast for a long time now."

"*Seadrake* was a House Veruna ship. Were you a Veruna man, then?"

"Aye, but we parted ways four years ago. The Double Moon Coster made me a better offer, so I jumped ship. I've been with them since, but now I'm needing a new billet."

"Why'd you leave the Double Moon?" Geran asked.

The dwarf made a sour face. " 'Twasn't me notion. The Double Moon sacked me."

Geran glanced at Nimessa. She shrugged. He looked back to Galehand and said, "That's not the sort of thing to inspire confidence."

"Oh, I'm good enough at me job, Lord Hulmaster. I've sailed these waters for nigh on thirty years, half of that as a sailing master. No, the Double Moon decided t'do without me services last month after I called one of the High Guilders a dung-brained dunderhead and knocked him down."

Geran frowned. The *Seadrake* was in need of a sailing master, but he wasn't anxious to saddle himself with a surly officer inclined to argue orders. "I can see you're a plainspoken dwarf," he said carefully. "What led you to do that?"

"Ye might recall a wicked set of thunderstorms that blew through early in Flamerule. We were southbound out of Melvaunt, thirty miles from Hillsfar. I came up on deck for me watch and found that instead of turning our stern t' the squall line and reefing the topsails, the High Guilder had countermanded the captain and told the crew t' crowd on all canvas and run across the wind. He'd some idea of trying to make Hillsfar before the storm caught up, I guess. The squall line was hard on us by then, and it nearly set us on our beam ends." Galehand shook his head. "After we set out a sea anchor and reefed in, I told the High Guilder what I thought of 'im. He objected, and that's when I knocked him down. They paid me off the next day in Hillsfar."

"You're lucky the ship's captain didn't throw you in irons for striking one of the owners."

Galehand snorted. "Well, I think the captain would've liked t' hit the High Guilder too, truth be told."

Geran laughed. He didn't know a thing about Andurth Galehand, but the fellow had no fear of speaking his mind, and if he was telling the truth, then it wasn't any lack of competence that had brought him to grief. "All right, Master Galehand. You're my sailing master; I'll have the papers drawn up. Your first job will be to see to the rigging and the sail locker. I mean to sail by the end of the tenday, and I'll judge you by how quickly and how well you make *Seadrake* ready for sea."

"Fair enough, Lord Hulmaster. If you can spare me for an hour, I'll fetch me kit and come back straightaway."

"Very good, Master Galehand."

The tattooed dwarf made his way back down the gangplank.

Geran watched him depart then glanced up at the sky; it was a little before noon, a fine, clear fall day with a light wind out of the west. "You didn't have to bring him down here yourself, you know," he said to Nimessa. "A word of introduction from you would've been fine."

"I suppose I'm still looking for a way to thank you for my life." Nimessa gave him a shy smile then turned to run a hand over the gleaming wood of the ship's rail. "You seem to be a man of many parts. Swordsman, wizard, and now sea captain too."

"I've studied a few sword spells, I suppose, but that's all the wizardry I know. As far as sailing, well . . . before I came home this summer, I spent a year and a half with the Red Sail Coster of Tantras, voyaging all over the Sea of Fallen Stars." He laid his hand on *Seadrake*'s rail next to hers and imagined that he felt the ship growing restless under his palm, like a good horse that was eager to run. Nimessa waited for him to continue, a small smile playing across her face. He found himself speaking again before he knew what he was saying. "I've always longed to see new shores. I'm not made to stand still for long, I think."

"What drives you on?"

"It's certainly not any concern for Red Sail business." Hamil Alderheart emerged from the passage leading under the quarterdeck to the officers' cabins. The halfling wore a fine green doublet over a buff-colored shirt, with a matching cap to cover his long russet braids; for as long as Geran had known him, Hamil had prided himself on his elegant clothing. "Geran's not much of a merchant. I did all the work, keeping the books and managing the buying and selling. He was really nothing more than a glorifed wagon driver. What brings you aboard *Seadrake,* my lady?"

"Nimessa, this is my old comrade Hamil Alderheart. We adventured together in the Company of the Dragon Shield years ago and bought owners' shares in the Red Sail Coster afterward," said Geran. He'd only stayed a short time before his wanderlust led him to Myth Drannor, but Hamil had allowed him to buy back into the coster without a word of complaint when Geran returned to Tantras after his years in the coronal's service. "Hamil, this is Nimessa Sokol, of House Sokol. She's come to Hulburg to take over the Sokol concession here."

Hamil swept off his cap and bowed low before lifting Nimessa's fingers to his lips. "I am charmed, my lady," he said. "I see now why Geran took on a fleet of pirates for your honor. I would leap into a dragon's gullet for one as beautiful as you!"

Geran looked down to hide a smile. Hamil had never met a beautiful woman he could resist flattering, whether she stood a foot and a half taller than he or not. For her part, Nimessa laughed and blushed. "I thank you for the thought, Master Alderheart, but let's hope that never becomes necessary!"

I'm pleased to see you've rediscovered your eye for beauty, Hamil told Geran silently. He was a halfling of the ghostwise folk, and his people had the ability to speak without sound when they wanted to. *If you won't court this one, I will myself!*

Geran ignored his friend's silent comments. "Nimessa found a sailing master for us," he told Hamil. "A dwarf by the name of Andurth Galehand. He was sailing master of *Seadrake* for years."

"Good," said Hamil. "But I'm surprised you'd take on a Veruna man. Or dwarf."

"It was five years ago, and he seems to know *Seadrake.* Besides, he's a dwarf, not a Mulmasterite. The Verunas don't keep other folk in their confidences." Andurth was likely paid well, but he would have been given little authority or scope for action in pursuing the company's interests. That was one of House Veruna's weaknesses; they treated their hired hands like not-quite-trusted servants and kept the best coin and real authority for Mulmasterites with blood ties to the family.

"We still need a half-dozen sailors and a few more armsmen," the halfling said. "And we could use a pilot."

"House Sokol will see to your deckhands," Nimessa told Hamil. "I'm certain I can find a few skilled armsmen for you too."

"Don't worry about a pilot," Geran said. "It's been a few years, but I know the Moonsea well enough, and it seems our sailing master does too. I'll handle the navigation."

"If you get lost or run us up on a reef, I'll remind you that you said that," Hamil replied. "Oh, and one more thing: Initiate Mother Mara sent word that she's directed a young friar named Larken to sign on as the ship's curate. He's supposed to be here tomorrow."

"That's almost everyone, then," Geran said. "I'm impressed, Hamil. I never would have imagined that you could gather a crew that quickly."

The halfling shrugged. "It wasn't my doing, Geran. When word got out that you'd be fitting out, people started lining up to sign on with you."

"How many will you sail with?" Nimessa asked.

"Well, *Seadrake* needs about twenty seamen to handle her comfortably," Geran answered. "But we also need a large number of armsmen to deal with the pirates we hope to catch, so we'll have well over a hundred, counting the Shieldsworn and merchant House mercenaries."

"Is that enough to deal with *Kraken Queen?*"

Geran allowed himself a predatory grin. "Oh, yes. If I can find her, I can finish her. It's just a matter of tracking her down."

"Good hunting, then." Nimessa stepped close and brushed her lips to Geran's cheek. "I must be going. I still have much to put in order in our tradeyard." Then she drew back, nodded to Hamil, and made her way back down the gangway to her waiting armsmen and carriage. The driver tapped his reins, and the carriage rolled away.

Geran gazed after the coach. Absently he lifted his hand to his cheek.

"I think that young woman is fond of you," Hamil remarked. "I suppose it's understandable. You have an unfair advantage, since you gallantly saved her from a fate worse than death. Damn the luck!"

The swordmage shook his head. "I don't know. Even if you're right, well, how many times can I rescue her from pirates?"

Hamil rolled his eyes. "Trust me, Geran. It's a good start."

Geran tried to put Nimessa Sokol out of his mind. He looked over at the carpenters engaged with the work on the mainmast. The stepping of the mast was almost finished, but it would take hours to rig the stays, the braces, and the heavy tackle for the sails. "There isn't much more we can do here. I need to check on the provisioning order at Erstenwold's."

"A fine suggestion," Hamil said. They paused to speak with Worthel, the ship's first mate—a wiry Red Sail shipmaster of middle years from Tantras, one of a dozen Red Sails who'd volunteered to sail under the harmach's banner. After advising him to keep an eye open for Galehand, Geran and Hamil left him to oversee the rest of the mast repairs and headed down the gangplank to the crowded wharves of Hulburg.

Compared to some of the other cities on the Moonsea, Hulburg was small and rustic. Laborers from a variety of foreign lands almost outnumbered the native Hulburgans. As they walked north up Plank Street, Geran and Hamil passed dwarves in their heavy boots and iron hauberks, Melvauntians and Thentians in the doublets and squared caps that were the fashion in those cities, and all sorts of clerks and scribes and armsmen in the colors of the various merchant companies who had concessions in Hulburg. In the ten years Geran had been away in the southern lands, Hulburg had filled up and overflowed. Even after five months he was still getting used to the sights and sounds of this bustling, broad-shouldered trade-town that had mysteriously replaced the sleepy little town of his youth.

They passed several groups of foreign laborers standing around on corners or waiting by storefronts—waiting for work, or so Geran guessed. People came to Hulburg from all over the Moonsea to seek their fortunes, since the timber camps and mines of the foothills offered a chance to earn a wage. They were poor, desperate men, gaunt and hollow-eyed, with tattered cloaks and threadbare clothing. Some had spent their whole lives drifting from one city to another, wandering Faerûn in search of some place to call home.

When they crossed Cart Street, Geran noticed a commotion to his right. A band of a dozen dirty men in ragged cloaks marched down the center of the street, pushing other passersby aside. Most carried cudgels or short staves, with knives or short swords thrust through their belts. Their left hands were wrapped in gray strips of cloth with a broad, sooty smear across the back of the hand. Townsfolk muttered and glared at them as they shoved through the crowds, but the ruffians paid them no mind.

Geran tapped Hamil's shoulder to get his attention. "Cinderfists," he said in low voice. "I don't think I've seen them in the mercantile district before. What are they doing here?"

"Looking for trouble, as far as I can tell," Hamil answered. He looked around. "Just as well there aren't any Moonshields nearby. I think we'd have front-row seats for a riot."

The two paused and watched the gang members pass. Most of the other people in the street hurried on by, avoiding the eyes of the Cinderfists and steering well clear of their path. Geran stood his ground, which earned him a few hostile glares from the ruffians. But he and Hamil were both well armed, and their clothes marked them as men of high station; the Cinderfists either knew who Geran was, or weren't quite so bold as to accost gentlemen in the middle of Hulburg's trade district. Geran met the eyes of one Cinderfist, a tall, lank-haired fellow with bad teeth and a sallow cast. The man snorted as if amused by Geran's attention and muttered something to his comrades as he sauntered past. Several snickered.

I don't like the look of the tall one, Hamil said silently. *I've got half a mind to teach him some manners.*

"Leave him be for now," Geran answered. "They're not breaking any law of the harmach's—not yet, at least."

A technicality, Hamil answered. But he smiled pleasantly at the ruffians and allowed them to continue on their way. The gray-cloaked men wandered on down Cart Street, leaving the two companions behind.

"You'd think a dozen fellows like that ought to have some trade to practice in the middle of the day," Geran said.

Hamil nodded. "The Verunas employed hundreds. When the House pulled out of Hulburg, they just left their woodcutters and miners and drivers and the rest to fend for themselves. No wonder some of them have fallen in with the Cinderfist gang."

"What choice did the harmach have? He couldn't let House Veruna stay after they helped Sergen in the attempt to unseat him."

"No, he couldn't," Hamil admitted. "Your uncle did what Darsi Veruna forced him to do. But until some more trade costers or merchant Houses take over Veruna camps, those Cinderfists won't have anything to do other than stand around on street corners and trouble passersby."

"That isn't so easy as it seems. Nimessa told me that House Veruna threatened retaliation against any other Moonsea companies that buy up their former rights." Geran fell silent, thinking over the Cinderfist situation. His friend was right about the unintended consequences of House Veruna's exile, but there was more to it than that. He'd also heard stories of Cinderfists threatening or beating other foreigners in search of work, pushing them to either join their movement or leave Hulburg and search for prospects elsewhere. A thought struck him, and he looked down at Hamil. "Have the Verunas threatened the Red Sails anywhere?"

"Us?" Hamil shook his head. "No, I would've told you if I'd heard anything like that. You're a stakeholder, after all. But if you want my guess, I'd say that the Verunas have already assumed we're no friends of theirs."

"True enough." Geran clapped Hamil on the shoulder. They walked on another half block and came to the sign for Erstenwold's Provisioners, which hung above a large, somewhat ramshackle old wooden building. Several clerks and customers counted, haggled, or carried goods in and out of the store. Business had been good for the Erstenwold store in the months since House Veruna's banishment from Hulmaster. No one was extorting native Hulburgan establishments anymore; the wary truce between the large foreign merchant companies and native Hulburgan establishments was holding. Only now there was the Cinderfist situation to complicate matters, Geran reminded himself.

Geran and Hamil took the steps up to the old wooden porch and pushed their way into the store proper. A long wooden counter ran the length of the room on the right side, with a familiar clutter of stocked shelves and various pieces of tack and harness hanging on the walls. The uneven floorboards were worn to a glossy polish by decades of foot traffic, and dust motes drifted in the sunlight slanting through the windows. Geran had always liked the place; the old wood, the fresh leather, and the pipeleaf all blended into a rich, comfortable aroma. "Mirya?" he called.

A tall, dark-haired woman with her hair tied back in a long braid looked up from her ledger-keeping at a small standing desk behind the counter. She wore a plain dress of blue wool and a stern expression on her face, but she smiled when she caught sight of them. She closed her ledger and came over to the countertop. "Here to see to your order? It's not even been two days, you know."

“The carpenters were about ready to throw Geran overboard,” Hamil answered. “We thought it might be best to let them oversee themselves for an hour or two.”

“So you decided to trouble me instead?” Mirya snorted. “Well, you’ll be glad to hear that I’ve almost all of your ship’s goods laid aside in the storehouse. Provisions, canvas, plenty of line, bedding, lumber, casks of ale, spars, hand tools, oakum, pitch—here, come around the counter, and I’ll show you.”

Geran and Hamil stepped around the long counter and followed Mirya into the storehouse that adjoined her shop. Large doors stood open to the street outside, allowing the afternoon light to stream in. Barrels and wooden crates lay stacked up in orderly rows on the dusty old floorboards. “I fear the harmach’s to pay dearly for all of this,” Mirya said. “To fill *Seadrake’s* hold in the time you gave me I had to pay half again what I should have. It was no help that all of Hulburg knew that I had to have your provisions as soon as they could be found.”

“My uncle knows you wouldn’t cheat him,” Geran said. He paced down one of the aisles, glancing over the assembled material. It filled a substantial part of the Erstenwold storehouse, and Mirya’s clerks were wheeling in more tubs and barrels as he watched. It seemed hard to believe that it would all fit below the decks of the ship down by the old Veruna docks, but he knew from experience that ships could carry a lot more than one might expect. “I’m amazed you found this much in Hulburg in just the last two days. Is there anything important you couldn’t find?”

“I’ve only half the canvas here that you should carry,” Mirya said. “I’ve sent word to provisioners in Thentia and Mulmaster—quietly, of course—to see if I can get my hands on more, but I doubt I’ll have it before you mean to set out. You’ll want to be careful of your sails.”

“I hope your new sailing master knows his business,” Hamil said.

Geran nodded. “The winter storms are still two months off. With good fortune, we won’t see any bad gales until after we’ve had a chance to fill the sail locker.” He looked over to Mirya. “I’ll have my crew send up a working party first thing in the morning. We'll have most of this cleared out of your storehouse by suppertime tomorrow."

"We'll be ready." Mirya looked over the provisions and shook her head a little. "Strange to do business with you, Geran. All the years I've known you, and I have never thought of you as the sort of man who'd take an interest in it. You always seemed to be cut from a different sort of cloth."

"The indolent nobility? The brooding romantic?" Hamil asked. "I certainly don't trust him with anything important for the Red Sails."

Geran laughed. It was true enough. "My thanks, Hamil."

"I didn't mean I thought him too lazy for it," Mirya said. "Too impatient, perhaps. Too anxious to be off to the next thing, whatever that happened to be. He used to be a hard one to keep anchored for long."

"Four years in Myth Drannor taught me a few things," Geran said. He glanced down at the rose-shaped pommel and mithral wire of the sword hilt at his belt. He'd won it in the service of the coronal. Somehow he doubted that many of Ilsevele Miritar's armathors had spent much time in storehouses such as Erstenwold's. "I suppose I'm not the man I used to be."

"No, you're not. You're a better man." Mirya gave him a lopsided smile. "Selsha and I mean to see you off when you set sail. Take care of yourself while you're chasing after pirates, Geran Hulmaster. I'm becoming used to having you around again."

"I will," he promised her.

FIVE

19 Eleint, the Year of the Ageless One (1479 DR)

Seadrake sailed on the morning tide three days after Geran's visit to the Erstenwold storehouse. As promised, Mirya and her daughter, Selsha, came down to the wharves to see them off, along with a couple hundred prominent Hulburgans and curious onlookers, including Nimessa Sokol and Harmach Grigor, who was driven down from Griffonwatch in an open carriage. Geran enjoyed the fanfare until Hamil punctured his mood by pointing out that all of the Moonsea would know of *Seadrake*'s sailing within five days. They wouldn't be surprising any enemies for the foreseeable future.

The breeze was light and fitful; the caravel nosed her way slowly past the spectacular Arches guarding Hulburg's harbor. In the morning light the soaring columns of stone seemed to glow with an emerald luminescence. As Hulburg receded behind them, the breeze freshened and *Seadrake* began to throw back a small wave from her bow.

"Master Galehand, make your course south by southwest," Geran told the dwarf. "Hold that for an hour or so, and then bring her around to a northwesterly course. We're going to keep in sight of land and work westward until we pass Thentia. I doubt *Kraken Queen* is still on this shore, but we might as well make sure she isn't."

"Aye, Lord Geran," the dwarf replied. He shouted orders at the sailors on deck, followed by colorful oaths in Dwarvish as the untried crew set about their work.

Geran retreated to the lee side of the quarterdeck and left Galehand to supervise the watch, leaning against the rail to observe the crew at work while he considered his course. Sarth Khul Riizar climbed up onto the quarterdeck and glanced at the town falling into the distance behind them. The tiefling was an intimidating sight, with ruddy red skin and black horns sweeping back from his forehead. At his belt hung a long scepter of iron marked with golden glyphs. Geran knew they held powerful spells of battle and ruin; Sarth was a talented sorcerer. "Hardly any breeze to speak of," Sarth observed. "We might as well have waited for better winds."

"I was anxious to begin." Geran straightened up and clasped Sarth's arm. "I'm glad you decided to join us, Sarth."

"It's nothing." Sarth shrugged. "I am happy to be of service, but I fear that I have no spells to summon a more favorable wind." Five months ago Sarth had emerged as one of the heroes of the Battle of Lendon's Dike. The people of Hulburg knew he'd battled furiously on their behalf, and few held his devilish appearance against him. From what little Geran had gathered of Sarth's travels and adventures before his arrival in Hulburg, that was an unusual circumstance for the tiefling to find himself in.

"The wind suits me well enough for now. No one else is sailing any faster than we are today," Geran replied. With the wind out of the west, they'd need to tack back and forth across it to beat their way westward. "But since you mention spells . . . do you have any means for divining the location of *Kraken Queen?*"

"Not without some tangible connection to the ship. Find me something or someone that was actually part of the ship, and I might be able to discern the direction and distance to her."

"What about Nimessa Sokol? Should we go back to Hulburg for her?"

"I spoke with her already. She was held on *Whitewing,* and didn't set foot on the pirate vessel. And even if she had, it might not have left a strong enough psychic impression. It takes time for such a link to form and grow strong, and Nimessa was only in the pirates' keeping for a few hours."

"I suppose that would have been too easy," Geran said. "Well, we might find something you can use at the cove where *Whitewing* was sacked."

It took *Seadrake* most of the day to work her way along the deserted coastlands between Hulburg and Thentia. Geran remained on deck, learning the feel and sounds of the ship, watching the crew handle the sails, and watching the sailing master and the other officers handle the crew. Two hours before sunset, *Seadrake* rounded the last cape and came within sight of *Whitewing*'s burned skeleton.

There was no sign of the pirate ship. "Damn," Geran muttered to himself. He hadn't really expected to find *Kraken Queen* here after eight days, but it certainly would have been convenient. He looked over to Worthel, who'd replaced Galehand on watch. "Drop anchor here and lower a boat, Master Worthel. I'm going to have a look ashore."

"Aye, Lord Geran," Worthel said. He frowned under his broad mustache of red-streaked gray. "But I don't think there's much to see there. She's burned down to her keel."

A quarter hour later, Geran, Sarth, Hamil, and Kara waded ashore from the ship's boat. They inspected the burned wreck of *Whitewing,* and the scattered remains of the Sokol ship's cargo, still strewn across the pebbled shore. Kara carefully studied the tracks and refuse left behind by the pirate crew, pacing back and forth across the cove as she followed the story she read there. Geran knew of no better tracker on the north side of the Moonsea, and he waited for her to finish. If there was anything to be found in the cove, she would find it. After a time, Kara brushed her hands off against the mail aprons of her armor and rejoined him. Her eyes gleamed with the uncanny azure of her spellscar in the fading light of the day.

"What do you make of it?" Hamil asked her.

"They left five or six days ago," Kara answered. "I make their numbers at eighty or ninety, mostly humans with a few orcs and ogres. Most of the crew slept on the beach for the two or three days they stayed here." That was not unusual; most captains, pirate or merchant, preferred to make camp ashore if conditions permitted. As long as the crew posted a few sentries, it was undoubtedly safer than continuing to sail through the hours of darkness, and most vessels plying the waters of the Moonsea or the Sea of Fallen Stars offered very little in the way of accommodations for their crews.

"Did you find anything that might have belonged to *Kraken Queen?"* Sarth asked. "A scrap of canvas, some discarded rope, an empty water cask?"

"Not very much, I'm afraid," Kara answered. She held up a battered old wooden baton about two feet in length—a belaying pin. "I did find this near where they had their ship drawn up. It's the best I could do for something that was part of the pirate ship . . . but there are several fresh graves over there in the brush above the high-water mark."

Geran nodded. "I killed at least two men when I fought my way out of the camp." He didn't think he'd mortally wounded anyone else, but perhaps the pirate captain had decided to settle some question of discipline during *Kraken Queen*'s stay in the cove. The bodies might serve Sarth's requirement, but he kept that thought to himself. They were too near the Highfells and the domain of the lich Aesperus to unearth corpses, regardless of what they intended to do with the remains. Better to leave the pirates' dead in peace.

"Let me have a look." Sarth held out his hand for the pin and examined it closely. The tiefling murmured the words of a spell and then closed his eyes in concentration. After a moment he snorted and shook his head. "It belonged to *Kraken Queen,* but the aura is weak or the ship is far away," he said. "I cannot discern her direction."

"It was worth a try," Geran said. He sighed and looked out over the purple-hued waters lapping against the pebbled shore. "Very well, then. We'll have to search out *Kraken Queen* the hard way. We'll stay here for the night and begin in the morning."

Over the next five days Geran steered *Seadrake* westward along the Moonsea's northern coast past Thentia and Melvaunt as far as the River Stojanow and the small city of Phlan, with no luck. The weather worsened, as cool gray skies settled in with sheets of cold rain every night. By day *Seadrake* crashed through heavy swells, throwing white spray over the bow and running across the wind with a strong heel to her decks. They crossed the Moonsea to the southern shore near Hillsfar and spent another five days working eastward as they searched the numberless islets and forested coves that crowded the shore between that city and the River Lis. Still they had no sign of the ship they sought, and Geran decided that his quarry was not in the southern Moonsea either. That left only the two far corners of the Moonsea unvisited: the west end by the River Tesh and the Galennar, the wild eastern reaches of the Moonsea, where the mountains ringing Vaasa met the coast in mile after mile of spectacular cliffs. But Geran hesitated before ordering Galehand to set his course for either end. Both were desolate and unsettled, with no merchant shipping to speak of. Pirates would find no prey, no safe harbors, and no markets for their stolen goods at either end of the Moonsea. Geran worried at the puzzle for most of a rain-soaked afternoon then decided to call at the port of Mulmaster before he settled on his next move. If he heard nothing of *Kraken Queen* in the crowded city, he'd venture into the desolate Galennar.

It was only a few hours' sail from the Lis to Mulmaster. *Seadrake* sculled slowly into Mulmaster's narrow, fortified harbor at the end of the cool, rain-misted autumn day. Beetling ramparts and dark towers loomed over the harbor; Mulmaster climbed steeply toward the barren mountains at its back, a sprawling, grim-faced city. Under the city's ruling nobles—or Blades, as they styled themselves—Mulmaster was a city where those with gold did anything they wanted, and those who didn't have gold did anything they could to get it. The harbor was crowded with roundships and galleys from many different cities and trading houses, but *Kraken Queen* was not among them.

"I never much cared for Mulmaster," Hamil remarked as Galehand steered the ship toward an open anchorage. "The first time I came here, I had to bribe someone just to find out the proper way to bribe someone! Hardly a friendly or forthcoming people, these Mulmasterites."

“That’s been my experience of Mulmaster,” Geran agreed.

Kara nodded toward the stone quays as they came abreast of them. Several merchant ships rocked gently alongside, their decks illuminated with lanterns. Even at the end of the day, porters still worked to unload one of the ships, carrying casks and bundles up out of her hold in a steady stream. “The Veruna yards,” Kara said. She looked at Geran. “*Seadrake* may be recognized here, you know.”

Geran nodded. He was a little nervous about bringing the ship into House Veruna’s home waters too. “I doubt the Verunas would try to seize *Seadrake* by force,” he said. “We have enough fighting power on board to resist a merchant company’s armsmen.”

“True, but the Verunas might convince a magistrate or the High Blade to order the ship impounded. We can’t outfight Mulmaster’s navy or escape the port if they raise the harbor chain behind us.”

“We’ll choose an inconspicuous mooring,” Geran decided. “Master Galehand, steer for that one there; it’s not very close to shore.” With darkness falling, any Veruna retainers ashore who might recognize *Seadrake* wouldn’t see much more than one more dark hull riding at anchor out in the harbor.

“Aye, Lord Geran.” The dwarf took the helm himself and steered for the spot Geran had pointed out. *Seadrake* was no galley; she was slow and ungainly under oars. Geran couldn’t shake the impression that the whole city was silently watching their tedious progress to the empty mooring spot he’d selected. Finally Galehand brought the ship to a stop and ordered the crew to drop anchor.

“Master Galehand, put the longboat in the water,” Geran said. “Keep the crew at the sweeps and be ready to slip the cable and make for the open sea if anything goes amiss. Hamil and I are going ashore to see what we can learn. Kara, take command here.”

Kara nodded.

“What of me?” Sarth asked.

“I’d like you to come with Hamil and me,” Geran told the tiefling. “Your talents may prove useful ashore.”

Half an hour later, six of *Seadrake*'s sailors rowed the ship's boat up to the quay along the south side of the harbor and tied up. Geran, Hamil, and Sarth clambered out of the boat and climbed the short flight of stone steps leading up to the street by the harborside. Choosing a direction more or less at random, Geran set off into the dank, foggy streets. It was still early enough that they passed many people, most of them laborers and workmen still engaged in the business of the day, but they also encountered men and women dressed for the evening's revels and the occasional patrol of watchful soldiers.

They visited several different tradeyards and countinghouses near the waterfront, asking about *Kraken Queen* and spreading coin discreetly to help loosen tongues. Few of the Mulmasterites seemed inclined to be helpful, but in a wineshop across from the city's chief customshouse, Hamil discovered a handful of touts and clerks from the Moonsea's larger trading houses drinking after a long day in the merchant yards. The halfling brought a dour, gray-haired man in a House Jannarsk tunic to the table where Geran and Sarth sat, and set a flagon of good Sembian wine in front of him.

"This is Master Narm, a senior clerk who works for House Jannarsk," Hamil said. "He's on the Jannarsk wharves pretty much every day and deals with the Mulmasterite harbormasters. He's not averse to supplementing his salary by answering a few harmless questions."

Narm shrugged. "The Jannarsks care not, so long as I keep their business to myself. I'll not speak of Jannarsk cargoes."

Most likely that meant that Narm wouldn't speak of Jannarsk cargoes without a more substantial bribe, but that didn't bother Geran. He didn't really care what House Jannarsk was sending into or out of Mulmaster. "I understand," he said. "Have you ever seen a good-sized war galley—a ship with a black hull and the figurehead of a mermaid with a kraken's tentacles on her bow—in the harbor here?"

The Jannarsk man shook his head. "No, no such ship's called in Mulmaster so long as I've been posted here, and that's two years now. But I've heard a tale about a ship like that. She's a pirate."

Geran allowed himself a small sigh of relief. He'd been a little afraid that *Kraken Queen* might be anchoring openly in Mulmaster and sailing under a letter of marque from the High Blade. If the pirates harrying Hulburg's shipping were under Mulmaster's protection, that would have been a daunting challenge to say the least; Hulburg had no hope of forcing the rulers of the larger city to give up the practice. "Go on," he said.

"A merchant I did business with was ruined by a ship with a kraken figurehead. He owns a couple of cogs that ply the route between Hillsfar and Mulmaster, importing Dalelands grain, cheese, fruit, and such—a decent trade for a small shipowner. But his biggest cog was taken by two pirate ships a few miles off the Lis back before Midsummer. Both pirates flew the same banner—a black field with a crescent moon and a cutlass." Narm lowered his voice. "The banner of the Black Moon Brotherhood."

"The Black Moon Brotherhood?" Sarth asked.

"I'm afraid that it's little more than a story to frighten children into good behavior," Geran answered. "There have always been rumors of a pirate league in the Moonsea, and any time pirates appear in these waters, people begin to tell those stories again."

Narm scowled. "It might've been little more than a fable a year or two ago, but it's true enough now. I spoke with a man who survived the attack—an armsman paid to defend the cog—and he told me what he saw."

"Pirates don't often leave witnesses behind," Hamil observed.

"The armsman went over the side during the fight, but was lucky enough to find a bit of flotsam to cling to until another ship picked him up." Narm shrugged. "Believe me or not, as you will. The shipowner's cog was certainly taken, of that I have no doubt."

"I don't doubt you about the pirate attack on the cog. It's the pirate league I wonder about." Geran rubbed his jaw, thinking. "You're certain you haven't seen the black galley with the kraken-maid under her bowsprit here? You haven't heard anyone speaking of a ship named *Kraken Queen?*"

"No, she's never called in Mulmaster." The clerk shook his head. He hesitated a moment then offered, "However, I might know of someone who would know more about such matters."

Geran nodded to Hamil, who paid off the man with a half-dozen gold crowns. Narm quickly scooped the coins into his pouch. "Sometimes we find it useful to avoid the formalities of customs," he said in a low voice. "There's a man named Harask who helps us arrange matters. You can find him in the storehouse across from the Bitter End, a taphouse on the southwest wharves. Be warned that he's not above robbing a couple of strangers and dumping their bodies in the harbor." The clerk gave the three companions a shallow bow and withdrew.

Geran waited until the man was out of earshot and leaned in close to speak to Sarth and Hamil. "What do you make of it?" he asked them.

"We could seek out the armsman who survived the attack," Sarth said.

"I doubt that it's worth the effort," Hamil said. "After all, Geran's seen *Kraken Queen*. What else would we learn from the armsman?"

"I don't recall a standard on *Kraken Queen* when I saw her," said Geran. "But my attention was fixed on Nimessa Sokol and the danger she was in. I might have missed it."

Hamil smirked at him. "You mean you were distracted by the beautiful, half-naked woman tied up on the beach? Honestly, Geran, a hero of your quality should be able to keep his mind on business."

Geran remembered Nimessa's bare shoulders and the feel of her slim body before him in the saddle. He quickly pushed the idle thought aside. "I'll ask Nimessa if she recalls a moon-and-cutlass standard the next time we call at Hulburg," he said. If Narm's secondhand story was accurate, then *Seadrake* might be hunting a flotilla instead of a single ship. And the fact that Narm had told them about an attack on a Mulman ship suggested corsairs who were preying on any Moonsea traffic they happened across, instead of waylaying Hulburg's trade alone. "I say we pay a visit to this Harask and see what he can tell us about Black Moon pirates."

They left the wineshop and headed back down toward the wharves, where the taphouses and taverns were filled with a rougher crowd. "It's possible that we've just missed *Kraken Queen* so far," Hamil pointed out as the three companions strolled down the center of the street, avoiding the filthy gutters. "If she was on the north shore while we were on the south shore, we could easily have passed her by. For that matter, she might be lurking near Hulburg again by now."

Sarth snorted. "Best not to dwell on that possibility. We could chase the pirate ship around the Moonsea for tendays, if that's the case."

They made their way toward the poorer side of the city, passing a series of progressively more disreputable and dangerous establishments. The night grew clammy and cool, and a foul-smelling fog settled over the city's waterside districts. It took them the better part of an hour to find the Bitter End. From the darkened street outside, they heard the muffled sound of voices, the clinking of tin cups, and the occasional shout or harsh bark of laughter. Across the street a dilapidated storehouse loomed in the fog.

Sarth frowned. "After hours of searching, I believe we have found the foulest establishment in this dismal city. Our prospects can only improve after this."

Geran raised an eyebrow. Was that a jest from the straitlaced tiefling? He wouldn't have expected it from Sarth. "If we learn nothing new here, we'll give up for the night," he said. "Come on, we might as well get it over with."

He went to the storehouse door and knocked sharply. There was no answer at first, but then voices muttered and floorboards creaked inside. Someone drew back a bolt with a rasp of metal, and Geran found himself looking at a pair of sullen Mulmasterites in dirty workman's garb, standing in a small clear space at the front of cluttered stacks of crates and casks. Both men wore long knives at their belts. "What d'you want?" one growled.

"We're here to speak with Harask. Is he here?"

The two men looked at each other then stepped back from the door. "He's here. Come in."

The three companions entered. Their sullen guides led them through the leaning stacks of cargo to a clear space near the back of the storehouse, where a small crowd of dirty humans and half-orcs lounged on rough-hewn benches or sat on old barrels. The ruffians glared at the three of them suspiciously. In the middle of the room stood a ham-fisted, round-bodied, black-bearded man who wore an ill-fitting jerkin of leather studded with steel rivets.

"Well, well," the fat man rumbled. His voice carried the thick, throaty accent of Damara or Vaasa. "A human, a halfling, and a devilkin walk into a room. I'm waiting for the rest of the joke."

"Are you Harask?" Hamil asked. "We may have a business proposition for you."

Harask spread his hands. "I am listening."

Geran spoke next. "We're looking for a ship that sails under a black banner—a banner with a crossed crescent moon-and-cutlass design. Have you ever seen such a ship or such a banner?"

"I might have," Harask answered. "What's it to you?"

"We'll pay well for news of her whereabouts," Geran answered.

"Ah, so you are a man of means," Harask observed. His eyes darted to the ruffians lounging behind Geran. Geran whirled and reached for his sword, just in time. Without a word the smugglers waiting in the storehouse threw themselves at the three companions, producing knives and cudgels hidden under their cloaks and tunics. For a furious instant, Geran feared that they might be overwhelmed. He dodged back from a knife slash, parried the fall of a club with his blade then slashed the truncheon out of his enemy's hand with a cut that also removed two fingers. Behind him, Hamil put a man on the floor with a cut to the hamstring then threw himself at the shins of another ruffian to send him crashing to the floor. Geran knocked that one unconscious with a kick to the face while he was on the ground. Then a brilliant, blue flare seared the room, and lightning crackled across the space. Several of the ruffians shrieked and fell convulsing. As quickly as it had started, the brief assault fell to pieces.

Sarth held up his rod that was glowing with a dangerous blue light. "I do not care to be accosted by the likes of you!" he snarled. The ruffians still on their feet stared at him then bolted for the door.

Geran turned back to Harask and found the fellow halfway out a small, concealed door. He lunged after him and dragged him back into the room, throwing him into his seat. Then he tapped his sword point on the man's chest. "Now where were you going?" he asked.

The fat man glared at him. "You'll be sorry for this," he said. "I have powerful friends in this city! They'll see to you soon enough."

"I don't much care about your friends," Geran replied. He reached down and seized Harask by the collar, giving him a good shake. "Now tell me, what do you know about the Black Moon?"

"To the Nine Hells with you!"

Geran was out of patience. Some of the ruffians might already be on their way to summon more help or even find the local Watch, and he had no particular desire to explain himself to the lawkeepers in Mulmaster. He cracked the flat of his blade across Harask's left ear, a stinging blow that elicited a howl of pain and raised a bright welt on the side of Harask's face. "Mind your manners," he said. "Now, tell me: Have you seen a ship with that banner? Where did you see her?"

"Zhentil Keep," the man replied. "Damn it all, she was in Zhentil Keep! Now leave me be!"

"You're lying. No one goes to Zhentil Keep. It's a monster-haunted ruin."

"Cyric take my tongue if I am lying!" the man snarled. "Outlaws and smugglers from the cities nearby hide in the ruins along the Tesh. No one troubles them, and there's always a ship or two there looking for a few hands."

The swordmage narrowed his eyes, studying Harask, who sat glaring at him with a hand clapped up against his ear. If he'd been in the ruffian's place, Zhentil Keep was exactly the place he might have told his interrogator to go to. The ruins happened to lie all the way at the other end of the Moonsea, and they were infested with monsters. But Zhentil Keep was about the only place in the western Moonsea that he *hadn't* looked already. Merchant ships had no reason to go any farther west than Hillsfar and Phlan, so he'd turned *Seadrake* back to the east without working his way another hundred miles into the prevailing wind to search deserted coasts and ruined cities. The prospects for a pirate lair in the ruins seemed almost as dim as those for a base in the Galennar . . . but Geran had heard stories that brigands and such outlaws occasionally laired in Zhentil Keep. It was at least plausible that pirate ships might lurk there too.

I believe he's telling the truth, Hamil said to him.

Geran knew that the talent of the ghostwise for speaking mind-to-mind didn't allow Hamil to read the thoughts of others, but it did mean that the halfling had a better sense for truthfulness than most. *I think so too,* he answered Hamil. To Harask he said, "If I find that you've lied to me, I will come back for you." He jerked his head toward Sarth. "My friend the sorcerer here will invert you with his magic. You'll walk on your tongue and carry your eyes on your arse, so you'd better hope that we find what we're looking for in Zhentil Keep."

Sarth gave Geran a startled look, but Harask didn't see it; he was cringing. "I've told you what I know!" he said.

The swordmage looked at his companions and nodded toward the door. They filed into the fogbound street outside. None of the men who'd fled the storehouse were in the vicinity; Sarth's magic had well and truly put them to flight.

"So it's off to Zhentil Keep, then?" Hamil asked in a low voice.

"So it seems," Geran answered. A shrill whistle rang through the night, piercing the fog. Apparently some of the ruffians had run straight for the Watch to report dangerous sorcery on the loose. Geran winced then exchanged looks with Sarth and Hamil. "Let's be on our way. I think we've worn out our welcome in Mulmaster."

SIX

29 Eleint, the Year of the Ageless One (1479 DR)

"A foul night," Sergen Hulmaster muttered. From the gate of the Five Crown Coster's tradeyard, he frowned at the murk gathering around the streetlamps outside. He detested the evening fog of Melvaunt. On days when the brisk western wind failed, the stink of the city's smelters and cookfires and sewers covered the town like a great foul blanket. He'd been careful to purchase a villa that overlooked the city from the heights of the headland west of the harbor—a neighborhood that was distinctly upwind of the town itself, at least most of the time—but his storehouses were located in the heart of the commercial districts, and it seemed that if the air started to grow still and foul, it always started here.

"Is everything well, m'lord?" asked his chief armsman Kerth. The sellsword hovered close by Sergen. Magical tattoos covered the man's brow, part of the elaborate enchantments that made him absolutely incapable of turning against his master. The precaution had cost Sergen a fortune, but he had too many enemies to worry about the loyalty of his bodyguards. They were well compensated for agreeing to undergo the necessary rituals.

"Well enough, so long as one doesn't mind smelling like the harbor for the rest of the evening," Sergen answered. He was a fastidious man, and he took great care in maintaining his wardrobe. Tonight he wore a lavender tabard over a shirt of black silk, with a broad belt and high boots of expensive Sembian leather.

A wide-brimmed hat with a rakish tilt matched his tabard. He was just about to retreat inside the dubious comforts of his storehouse when he heard the muffled clip-clop of hooves on slick cobblestones and the creaking of wooden wheels.

"Wagons coming, m'lord," Kerth said.

Sergen smiled in a distinctly predatory fashion, pleased that his late vigil would be rewarded after all. "About time. Kerth, turn out your men to lend a hand. Quick and quiet now!"

"As you wish, m'lord," the armsman Kerth answered. He raised a knuckle to his scarred forehead and turned to rasp orders to the other guards waiting nearby. Sergen stood aside from the doorway as his armsmen unbarred the gate leading into the narrow alleyway between his storehouses and hurried out to guide several large wagons inside. This was not the sort of work he liked to give his highly paid guards, but he was certain of their loyalty. Unfortunately the small army of clerks, scribes, and porters who worked in the Five Crowns tradeyard during the customary hours of business was not under any sort of magical compulsion to serve with unquestioned loyalty. Oh, some of them were trustworthy enough, but Sergen knew that clerks and porters tended to gossip with their colleagues in other trading houses when the day was done. When he caught Five Crowns men making that mistake, he punished them severely, but it was impossible to stop all such talk. Better to keep the night's work to those he could trust to keep it to themselves.

Sergen unlocked a door leading to a rarely used storeroom. "In here," he told his men. The drivers of the wagons weren't in his employ, but they knew better than to ask questions or look too closely at the cargo they were hired to carry. They set their brakes and climbed down to undo the ties that held each wagon's canvas cover in place. Beneath the canvas, the wagons were laden with heavy crates, casks, barrels, and chests. Each had been seared with the black mark of the Five Crowns brand, conveniently covering the former owners' marks. Over the next tenday or so, Sergen would arrange to dispose of the stolen cargo a few parcels at a time, which would turn a tidy little profit for his merchant company.

It irked him that he had to attend to such details, but that was the nature of his circumstances. As much as he affected the habits of the nobility, he was simply one more merchant in Melvaunt, and his fortune was not so substantial or secure that he could leave it in the hands of underlings. A few months ago he'd entertained dreams of making himself lord over Hulburg, but his so-called family had somehow survived his carefully planned acquisition of power, largely through the interference of his thrice-damned stepcousin, Geran Hulmaster. Instead of ruling from the throne of Griffonwatch, he was reduced to skulking about in dark storehouses in the middle of the night, with spellbound sellswords the only minions he could trust.

Kerth interrupted his brooding. "That's all of it, m'lord," the tattooed swordsman said. "The wagonmaster's asking after his coin."

"He is, is he?" Sergen answered. He looked into the storeroom, studying the merchandise with a practiced eye. He'd been expecting at least another wagonful or two, but apparently it wasn't coming tonight. With a shrug, he closed and locked the storeroom. "Very well, then. Bring him in to my office."

While Kerth went to fetch the wagonmaster, Sergen unlocked his office and counted out the gold coins of Melvaunt—anvils, they were called—from his strongbox. By the time he finished his swordsman was back, standing at the side of a portly halfling dressed in a thick, quilted tunic. The halfling doffed his cap and bobbed his head. "Good evenin', m'lord," he said. "Is everything to your satisfaction?"

"I suppose. Were you seen?"

"Not by the shore, m'lord. No one was about; I think the fog drove most folk indoors tonight. We made the usual arrangements at the city gate, and had no trouble."

"I was expecting more merchandise."

The driver nodded. "The man who met us said you would be, m'lord. He gave me this to give to you." He handed Sergen a small envelope sealed with a blank daub of wax.

Sergen took the letter, broke the seal, and read it. It was short and to the point: "We must meet. Expect me at two bells. Take the usual precautions. —K." Sergen tugged at his goatee, wondering what new development this signaled. Well, he would find out soon enough. It was already an hour past midnight—one bell, as they said in Melvaunt—so he needed to conclude his business and return home. "Your payment," he said, handing the halfling a small pouch. "I've counted out ten anvils since your load was lighter than I'd been led to believe."

The wagon driver winced, but he did not complain. It was hard but fair, and he knew that he'd get no more from Sergen this evening. "Thank you, m'lord," he said. He bowed and withdrew.

"Kerth, have my carriage brought up immediately," Sergen told his bodyguard. "We've got company coming. Have your men lock up here."

In a matter of minutes Sergen and Kerth clattered away from the Five Crowns storehouses in a swift black carriage, driving back up to the hillside where Sergen's villa overlooked the harbor. The guttering streetlamps painted the murk hanging over the city a dull red-orange color, but as the carriage climbed, the thick stink lessened perceptibly. Soon enough the carriage clattered past the comfortable houses of the wealthy, each surrounded by its own wall, and some guarded by watchmen with pikes. Near the top of the hill they reached Sergen's estate and turned into the long, gated driveway. "Order the servants to their quarters, and douse the streetlamps," Sergen told Kerth. "I'll be waiting in the study."

"I understand, m'lord," the mercenary said.

The carriage stopped by the manor's door. Sergen allowed his footman to open the carriage door for him. As he climbed the steps to the manor's foyer, a valet took his cloak and the doorman held the door for him. He might not have a noble title, but he certainly could afford the trappings of nobility. While Kerth spoke with the servants and saw to the arrangements outside, Sergen headed back to his study, a large room with broad windows overlooking the harbor. He drew the curtains closed and then poured himself a glass of good dwarven brandy from a service he kept near his desk. Taking a seat by the room's fireplace, he listened to the faint sounds of the household staff receding and watched as one by one the lights were turned down low outside. His visitor valued discretion, after all.

Sergen waited no more than a quarter hour in the dark study before he heard footsteps in the hallway outside. He set down his brandy and stood as Kerth opened the door to admit a tall, cloaked figure. The armsman looked at Sergen; Sergen nodded to him, and Kerth stepped outside and closed the door, leaving him alone with his visitor. The man undid the fastenings of his heavy cloak and tossed it carelessly onto the nearest sofa. "This is a fine house, my boy," he said. "But living here is making you soft, mark my words."

"It's all for show," Sergen answered. "Hello, Father." He stepped forward for a quick embrace and a hearty thump on the back. Kamoth Kastelmar was a lean, well-weathered man of fifty-five years, a little taller than his son. A gray-streaked beard of black framed his square face, and his eyes smoldered beneath craggy brows. He wore a knee-length black coat with gold embroidery at the cuff and collar, and a fine saber rode at his hip in a scabbard of Turmishan leather. Once upon a time he'd been the scion of a minor noble family of Hillsfar, but he'd put his home behind him at an early age, seeking better opportunities. Fifteen years ago Kamoth married Terena Hulmaster, the sister of the harmach, and brought Sergen—his son by his first wife, a woman Sergen hardly remembered—to Griffonwatch to live with Terena's family. But Kamoth was a restless man, an ambitious man, and he soon began to plot against his brother-in-law, Harmach Grigor. When those plots were uncovered, Kamoth had been forced to flee Hulburg and seek his fortune elsewhere. He'd left Sergen to be raised by the family of his stepmother. Sergen had hated him for that for a long time, but Kamoth was his father for better or worse. Beyond the shadow of a doubt he'd taught Sergen everything he'd needed to know about how to look out for himself.

Kamoth thumped his back one more time and stepped back. "I don't suppose you have something worth drinking in here?" he asked.

Sergen nodded at the brandy service. "Good dwarven brandy."

The older lord snorted. "Well, perhaps living soft has its advantages." He poured himself a tall glass and actually took a moment to inhale the aroma. "Did that fat little halfling get my cargo to your storehouse?"

"He did, although it was only three-and-a-half wagons' worth," Sergen replied. "Was that all of it?"

"I lost almost a third of the cargo after I beached the Sokol ship," Kamoth said. He scowled fiercely. "Some madman spied out my landing and crept down after dark to set fire to my prize. What's more, he cut the Sokol lass free of her bonds and fought his way out of my camp while my lads were busy fighting the fire. Killed two men and crippled another."

Sergen grimaced. "Your madman was named Geran Hulmaster."

"Geran? He was the one that fired my prize?" Kamoth turned away with a muttered oath. He glared into the fireplace for a long moment before he composed himself and turned back to Sergen. "All right, then. How did you find out about Geran's little visit to my encampment?"

"Geran told his uncle about it the hour he returned to Hulburg. Grigor called the Harmach's Council together to discuss the matter, and my ally on the council heard Geran's story for himself. He keeps me informed of the council's business; I heard the tale several days ago."

Kamoth looked past Sergen, his eyes fixed on old memories. "Bernov's son," he murmured. "I saw him from a distance before he fled the beach, fighting his way past my lads. I thought he seemed familiar, and now I know why." He shook his head and seated himself in one of the chairs by the fireplace. "Nine years now that Bernov Hulmaster's been dead, and his wanderfooted son shows up to ruin the best part of a prize I took with my own two hands. Damn that man! Even from the grave he's finding ways to hinder me."

"The fire ruined that much of the Sokol cargo?"

"No, not that—the lass. She was a splendid sight, my boy. I had designs upon her, I did."

Sergen grimaced. Kamoth was a man of violent appetites. When he said he had designs on a woman, those designs often ended in the most heinous sort of murder. It was one of the reasons his father had never bothered to establish himself in civilized society again after fleeing Hulburg years ago; his proclivities would have soon enough earned him a death sentence in all but the most lawless of settings. Sergen considered himself a pragmatic, unsentimental man, and he did not shy from the idea of taking what he wanted, but he'd never been able to understand the demonic urges that moved Kamoth. At its best Kamoth's cruelty was simply wasteful. At its worst it was the very soul of wickedness, something so spiteful and nihilistic that even Sergen shrank from it. "I'm sure she was," he temporized.

"How in the world did Geran know to lie in wait for me on that deserted shore?" Kamoth mused aloud. "I didn't know myself where I'd put in until I saw the cove and decided it would serve."

"Sheer accident. According to what my man on the council heard, Geran was off visiting his mother in Thentia. He was on his way home to Hulburg when he stumbled across your camp. A day or two to either side, and he never would have seen you."

"By all the misfortunes of Beshaba. What did I do to deserve that?"

If ill fortune followed the guilty, Sergen thought, then his father had certainly earned his share and more. He decided not to voice that sentiment. He hesitated for a moment, then he said, "I'm afraid there is something more to Geran's involvement. The Harmach's Council ordered Geran to fit out a warship to deal with *Kraken Queen*. Geran is likely at sea by now, searching for you."

"By all nine of the screaming Hells!" Kamoth leaned forward, his eyes fierce. "Warship? What warship?"

"Apparently the Verunas left a serviceable caravel named *Seadrake* behind when they abandoned the city. They've got a large detachment of Shieldsworn and mercenaries aboard." Sergen smiled. "They believe it will be easier to track you to your lair than to patrol the sea lanes near Hulburg, awaiting the next attack."

The pirate lord stifled a snort of derision. "Grigor Hulmaster thinks one impressed ship is a match for the Black Moon Brotherhood? I should go burn Hulburg to teach the harmach some respect."

Sergen shrugged. So far events were proceeding more or less as he'd expected. His father's pirate flotilla had virtually strangled trade going to Hulburg by sea over the summer, creating no small amount of difficulties for the Hulmasters. He'd originally planned for Kamoth's corsairs to slowly tighten their grip over the next few months, bringing the harmach to his knees. "We expected that the Hulmasters would take steps to protect their shipping," he said. "They have no choice. If Grigor does nothing, the Merchant Council has to act in his place."

"I expected that they'd arm their merchantmen, perhaps send a few soldiers to sea, or maybe strike a deal with Hillsfar or Mulmaster for protection," Kamoth said. "I didn't think they'd fit out a warship so quickly. Why in the world did House Veruna leave anything that useful behind?"

"She couldn't sail, and they didn't have enough hands for the oars." Sergen frowned; he'd spent his last few days in Hulburg hiding in the Veruna compound, and he remembered the Mulmasterites' retreat all too well. "I told them to burn anything they couldn't carry off, but Darsi chose not to listen to me. She thought she'd be able to convince the High Blade of Mulmaster to demand the return of the storehouses and *Seadrake* from the harmach."

Kamoth waved his hand. "Bah. If you can't protect your own, you deserve to lose it. I don't blame the High Blade for ignoring her complaints."

"So what do we do about Geran and his ship?"

"Let him chase his own tail all around the Moonsea, as far as I care. Or set a trap for him." Kamoth grinned fiercely and set a hand to the pommel of his dagger. "Yes, I like the thought of that. The day I see the son of Bernov Hulmaster dead on the point of my blade would be a fine day indeed."

Other than the fact that Sergen hoped to be the one holding the blade, he approved of his father's sentiment. "If my source is correct, there are close to a hundred of Hulburg's soldiers and militia aboard *Seadrake* . . . along with Geran and Kara Hulmaster. Geran is little more than a reckless adventurer, but he is a formidable swordsman, and Kara is far and away the best commander in the harmach's service. Can you defeat him?"

"So many, eh? Then I'd need two ships or a ruse of some kind." Kamoth frowned, his eyes fixed on some distant vision of mayhem as he considered the problem. "Damn, but it might be better with three ships at that. I know Geran can fight, and those Shieldsworn'll be tough bastards. It makes you wonder who's left in Hulburg."

Sergen looked sharply at his father and laughed. A bold idea had just occurred to him. "In fact, that is exactly what I'm wondering. With both Geran and Kara away from Hulburg and a shipful of Shieldsworn absent from the town's defenders, I think a bold stroke might be called for."

The pirate lord raised his eyebrows and sat back in his chair. "Raid the town? Now that *is* a bold idea, my boy. If I summon the Black Moon together, we could land better than six hundred men. Would that be enough to take Hulburg?"

"Take it? No, you'd never be able to fight your way into all the merchant compounds or storm Griffonwatch. But with even a little bit of surprise, you could pillage the harbor district and fire as much of the town as you liked." That would in fact serve Sergen's plans even better than slowly choking off the town's trade; the harmach's weakness in the wake of such an attack would demand action. And it would wound Geran to the heart if Hulburg suffered while he was wandering aimlessly hundreds of miles away. Sergen had much to repay Geran after the swordmage's interference in his plans.

"A bold stroke nonetheless," Kamoth mused. "Ah, the stories they'd tell about the Black Moon Brotherhood after a feat like that! I like the thought of it, my boy. You might be worth something after all."

Sergen allowed himself a small smile. It wasn't often that he found a way to earn his father's approbation. Kamoth was quick to praise one of his cutthroats or laugh at the coarse humor his crewmen enjoyed, but Sergen had always had to come up with something exceptional to earn that fierce grin. He took a deep sip of the brandy and said, "In that case, when does the Black Moon sail against Hulburg?"

SEVEN

29 Eleint, the Year of the Ageless One (1479 DR)

A cold, steady rain fell as Geran and Sarth rowed *Seadrake*'s skiff toward the broken towers of the ruined city. Hamil sat in the stern of the small boat, his hand on the rudder. It was a dark and dreary night, the sort of weather that would persist over the Moonsea lands until the bitter winds of winter arrived sometime in early Nightal. The steady hiss of rain falling into the sea masked the creaking of the oars in their locks and the soft slap of water under the small boat's hull. They'd only been rowing for half an hour, but they were already soaked. Geran didn't mind; the foul weather meant that fewer unfriendly eyes would be watching them.

Seadrake was a mile behind them, invisible in the darkness. She showed no lights, since Geran hoped that their landing in Zhentil Keep would go unnoticed. As an additional precaution, they wore the same sort of common garb that any deckhands might wear on a sodden Moonsea evening. Instead of a fine jacket and jaunty cap, Hamil glowered under a drenched hood. Geran had left his fine elven backsword in his cabin on *Seadrake* and carried a plain cutlass instead, while Sarth had used his magic to disguise himself as a sellsword of Teshan descent, with a thick black mustache and dark, fierce eyes under a heavy brow.

Hamil surveyed the crumbling buildings of the ruined city with a dubious expression. "That looks like the sort of place you venture into when you've a mind to feed yourself to some horrible monster," he said. "Are you sure of this plan, Geran?"

"Sure of it? No, but I think it's worth a try." Geran paused to glance over his shoulder as the city's ramshackle docks drew closer. Zhentil Keep sprawled on either side of the mouth of the River Tesh. In better times it had been the busiest harbor on the Moonsea, and both banks of the river—as well as some of the lakefront too—had been lined with broad stone quays that could accommodate scores of ships at a time. He would have liked to bring *Seadrake* into the Tesh and drop anchor in the river mouth, but he guessed that the sort of brigands and outlaws he was looking for would have vanished into the rain and rubble at the first sight of a hostile warship. "We'll find the sort of cutthroats we're looking for soon enough. Or they'll find us."

Sarth frowned as he pulled at his oar. "Are you not concerned that the sort of villains we seek might rob and murder three strangers the moment they catch sight of us?"

"A fate easily avoided. We have to appear too poor to rob and too dangerous to pick a fight with." Geran smiled humorlessly. "Trust me, we should fit right in."

Hamil looked past his larger companions and shifted in his seat. "We're getting close. Steer for the docks on the north bank here, or do you want to tie up on the other side of the river?"

"The first spot you see. If the fellow in Mulmaster was right, there may be a ship or two moored up the Tesh, and I don't want to run into them." Geran paused in his rowing and turned around to get a better look at the looming shadows around him.

A hundred years ago, Zhentil Keep had been the most powerful city in the Moonsea lands. Its soldiers held the Tesh vale, the mighty Citadel of the Raven in the Dragonspine Mountains, and the ruins of Yûlash; Hillsfar they subdued in Myth Drannor's War of Restoration. Gold flowed into Zhentil Keep's coffers from a dozen far lands intimidated by Zhentarim sellswords or inveigled by Zhentarim spies. But the Zhents, for all their ruthlessness and might, had inevitably aroused the wrath of an enemy beyond their strength.

The unliving archwizards of the newly reborn Empire of Netheril did not look kindly on such an aggressive neighbor, and they'd turned their fearsome sorcery against Zhentil Keep. In the years before the Spellplague, the Netherese razed the city and scattered its lords, its priests, and its wizards to the four winds. Zhentarim expatriates dotted the lands of the Inner Sea, but their native city was now a shadow-haunted ruin that all decent folk gave a wide berth.

Except, of course, for Geran and his companions.

Geran's eye fell on a dark quay that seemed like a safe spot to leave their boat. "There, that will do," he said. He and Sarth resumed pulling, and in a few minutes the skiff bumped up alongside the old landing. Hamil scrambled out and looped the skiff's bowline around a rusted bollard, then the swordmage and the tiefling followed. Geran paused on the cobblestone street to gain his bearings, hand on his sword hilt. The old buildings loomed over him, most standing five or six stories in height and crowded shoulder-to-shoulder like tired soldiers standing in ranks. Dark doorways and empty windows looked down over the street. It was said that the curse of the Netherese archwizards still lingered over the city, some nameless doom waiting to swallow anyone so foolish as to venture into the darkest shadows. Geran had no idea if that was true or not, but he sensed brooding menace just beyond his sight.

"This is an accursed place," Sarth said. "Terrible spells were spoken here."

"We'll keep to the riverbank. The stories I've heard about this place claim that whatever lingers here doesn't like the water, or that the Tesh has washed away some of the curse," Geran said. "Either way, I don't think it would be a good idea to explore any of these buildings."

Hamil stopped and looked up at him. "It's also a bad idea to leave a fire untended, speak a demon's name, or run while you've got a knife in your hand. Is there anything else we should go over?"

Sarth snorted through his mustache. Geran sighed. "I've known you to ignore common sense once or twice," he said to

Hamil. "I remember some times with the Dragon Shields when you leaped before you looked."

They left the skiff tied up by the quay. Since there were no ships visible at the river mouth, and Geran didn't see or hear anything to suggest that other folk might be around, he decided to follow the riverside street westward, deeper into the city. They gave the old buildings on their right a wide berth, staying out in the open street.

After a half mile or so, they passed the remains of one of the city's great bridges, now little more than a series of six stone piers in the river. Beyond the bridge piers, several ships were moored to the old quays—a couple of small coasters that were likely smugglers of some sort, a round-hulled cog, and a half galley with a long, slender hull. A few dim lanterns illuminated the streets by the riverside, and the distant strains of voices and faint music carried over the water. Geran and his friends exchanged looks, then they continued.

Along the riverbanks above the first of the bridges, a dismal little town of sorts had grown up in the city ruins. Although the looming stone buildings here were still mostly abandoned, the lower floors of a dozen or so in the immediate area had evidently been reoccupied. Lanterns hanging from posts outside marked the locations of taverns, festhalls, boardinghouses, provisioners, fences, armorers, sailmakers, and others who did business with the sort of brigands and pirates who lurked in the ruins. Despite the late hour, dozens of men—and a few women—loitered out in the street, staggered drunkenly from one place to the next, or simply lay sprawled on the cobblestones wherever they'd fallen asleep or passed out. More than a few seemed to be half-orcs, goblins, hobgoblins, and other such creatures, but the humans seemed to pay them no special attention.

"We'll try the taverns first and keep our ears open," Geran said. "Let's get the mood of the place before we start asking dangerous questions."

They headed for the first taphouse they saw. A crude signboard hung above the door, showing the image of two busty mermaids. Directly under the sign a gray-bearded sailor slumbered in the street. Geran stepped over him and pushed open the door. Inside, raucous sailors crowded a small room that looked like it might once have been a well-off merchant's parlor. Simple tables and benches replaced all of the old furnishings, and an overturned skiff served as the unlikely bar. In one corner, a man in a patched cape strummed at a lute, but no one was paying him much attention. They were watching a contest of knife throwing, with the target hanging close by the door. As Geran ducked through the door, a small dagger *thunked* into the wood not far from his face. Drunken sailors and their rented lovers roared with laughter as he flinched aside.

"I think you've found what you're looking for," Hamil said. "What a charming place."

Geran gave the knife thrower a hard look and made his way over to the bar. Hamil and Sarth followed, while the game resumed behind them. The barkeep was a balding dwarf with a striking scar across his mouth that notched his beard. He looked up at Geran with a yellow-toothed grin. "Dun't think I've seen ye before," he said. "Are ye lads from the Impilturian merchant lying on t'other side o' the river?"

Geran was momentarily tempted to say yes just to satisfy the fellow's curiosity, but of course he had no idea whether any of the other crewmen were in the room. He decided that it would be best to say as little as possible. "No, we're new in town. What do you have to drink?"

"I've got a keg of Hillsfar's own Moonsea Stout tapped, and I'll draw ye a mug for half a silver talent. Or I could find ye a bottle of southern wine, though that'll cost ye dear. It's hard to come by."

"The stout, then," Geran told him. He fished two silver coins out of the purse at his belt and handed mugs to Sarth and Hamil. His companions found stools fashioned from old barrels sawn in half around a battered old capstan salvaged from some wreck or another, and settled in to nurse their ale and observe the crowd. Geran lingered to speak with the barkeep, and motioned for him to stay a moment.

"What more are ye wantin'?" the dwarf asked.

"The warship out in the river. Who is she?"

"That would be *Moonshark.*"

"Is she a Black Moon ship?"

"Why, are ye lookin' for a billet?"

"We might be." Geran shrugged and glanced at the patrons of the taphouse. "Are any of these fellows *Moonshark* crewmen?"

"Dun't think so," the dwarf answered. He took up a rag and started wiping down the bar; Geran decided to leave him to his work instead of pressing the question. He joined Hamil and Sarth at their table.

They drank a round, listening to the people around them. Geran and Hamil made a point of keeping up an animated discussion about various taverns in the cities of the Vast, providing Sarth with the opportunity to study their neighbors surreptitiously. The tavern-goers included seamen from the ships hidden in Zhentil Keep's ruined harbor, sellswords on hard times, and brigands and outlaws who preferred the company of others of their kind.

After half an hour, Geran leaned in to speak to Sarth and Hamil. "I think we've heard everything we're going to," he said. "Let's see if we can find some of *Moonshark*'s crewmen on the street. We might find one that's talkative when drunk."

"A good idea," Sarth agreed. The three of them drained their mugs then filed out into the dark street outside. The hour was growing late, but there was little sign of it in the pirate den. The faint strains of music still echoed across the water, broken by the occasional sound of breaking glass or a shouted oath. They headed upriver, toward the next island of lanternlight they could make out.

A door on their right burst open, and a party of boisterous men flooded out into the street. Geran halted to let them pass, but one of the men—actually a bandy-legged half-orc with one tusk at the corner of his mouth—turned and met his eyes. A dark scowl came over the half-orc's features. "Now what d'you think you're lookin' at, you goat-buggering bastard?" he demanded.

Geran bit back a retort and nodded down the street with more friendliness than he felt. "Just on my way to the next taproom. Don't mind me."

"I'll mind whatever I decide to mind," the half-orc growled. The fellow's companions—five of them—moved to surround Geran and his comrades. They were a dirty, ill-favored lot, dressed in ill-fitting leather and armed with cutlasses or cudgels at their belts. At least a couple of them seemed unsteady on their feet, more than a little in their cups, but the sallow half-orc was unfortunately not one of them. "I don't think I've seen you lot 'round here before. You ain't in any crew I know. That means you're mine."

It seems we've seen this more than once, Hamil remarked. The halfling shifted a half step behind Geran, hiding his hands from view.

Geran glanced over his shoulder at Sarth and gave the tiefling a subtle shake of the head. "No magic," he mumbled under his breath. Sarth scowled, but he nodded. It would be hard to masquerade as common sellswords if thunderclaps and blasts of fire erupted in the street. Then he looked back at the half-orc glaring at him. He doubted it would work, but he had to try. "We've got no cause to quarrel," he said. "We'll go our way, and you can go yours."

The half-orc spat something in Orcish and swept out his cutlass. Geran had no idea what he'd said, but as far as he could tell negotiations were at an end, and he drew his own cutlass an instant later—nearly sticking the blade in the scabbard because the shape and weight were different from the fine elven steel he was accustomed to. The other brigands followed suit; the sound of steel rasping on leather filled the air, followed an instant later by the ring of steel on steel. Geran blocked the half-orc's first vicious cut by passing it over his head then stepped close to smash the heavy handguard into the side of the half-orc's head. The half-orc staggered back, and Geran immediately turned and leaped at the man to his right. They hacked at each other for three quick passes of steel, then Geran slashed the cutlass out of his hand with a nasty cut to the forearm. The cutlass dropped to the cobblestones with a shrill ring, and when the brigand doubled over holding his arm, Geran surged forward and planted a boot in the center of the man's belt. With a strong shove of his leg, he sent the wounded brigand stumbling over the side of the quay and into the water.

Sarth blocked the cudgel of the man attacking him with a two-foot iron baton—actually his magical rod, disguised by his illusion magic. Then the tiefling bludgeoned his foe to the ground with a rain of blows to the head and shoulders. Meanwhile Hamil efficiently hamstrung the swordsman moving in to attack Sarth from the side, and kicked the man unconscious when he fell to the cobblestones. "Behind you!" he called to Geran.

Geran turned and found the half-orc rushing in again despite the vicious clout he'd taken. But the fellow was unsteady on his legs, and the swordmage easily twisted aside from a clumsy thrust. This time Geran hammered the pommel of the cutlass to the nape of the half-orc's neck as he stumbled past, and stretched him out senseless or dead on the street. He leaped over the half-orc to smash the flat of the cutlass against the skull of a brigand stabbing furiously at Sarth. The man crumpled to the ground; Sarth dealt him a heavy clout as he fell for good measure. The tiefling looked up at Geran and scowled. "My way is easier," he muttered.

"And louder," Geran reminded him. He straightened up and looked around, just in time to see Hamil test the balance of the dagger in his hand and let fly at the last brigand, who had turned to flee. The blade turned over three times before the pommel cracked the fellow on the back of the head and knocked him to the cobblestones. Silence fell over the scene, and Geran realized all of the brigands were on the ground or in the river. Several bystanders stood nearby, including one tall, strongly built woman with a shaven head, who had her fingers wrapped around the hilt of her own sword.

Hamil looked at the bald woman. "You want a part of this too?" he demanded.

The woman let go of her sword and held up her hand. She was no beauty; her shoulders were almost as broad as Geran's own, and her face was square with blunt features. Geran could easily have mistaken her for a man, if not for the heroic expanse of her bosom and the fine point to her chin. "Not I, friend. I'm just an interested spectator," she said. She looked down at the thugs on the ground and twisted her mouth into a hard smile. "Consider me impressed. You handled those wretches easily enough, although I can't imagine why you saw fit to leave them alive."

"We're new in town," Geran answered warily. "I have no idea who these fellows belong to. It didn't seem wise to kill them without knowing who might take offense."

"You're a man of uncommon wisdom, then." The woman nodded toward a ramshackle establishment on the other side of the river. "Those fellows work for Robidar. He's the half-orc that runs the bar, festhall, and gaming hall over yonder. They're in the habit of rolling drunks and stragglers. You'll want to watch your backs if you stay here long. Sooner or later Robidar's boys'll want to even up the score."

"Thanks for the warning," Hamil answered. "I'm in the habit of watching my back anyway."

"Indeed." The woman hesitated, studying the three companions for a moment, then she spoke again. "By any chance, are you three looking for billets? I could use a few more sharp fellows who can fight like you can and have a good share of common sense too."

"What sort of billets?" Geran asked.

"Deckhands on *Moonshark.* She's the half galley tied up by the bridge, a good ship and swift. My name is Sorsil. I'm her first mate."

Geran glanced toward the shadowed outline of Sorsil's ship to hide his quick grin. It seemed that fortune had smiled on him. To conceal his interest, he rubbed at his jaw as if in thought. "As I said, we're new in town. We intended to weigh a few opportunities before making any decisions."

Sorsil gave a short laugh. "You won't find many better opportunities, no matter how long you stay moored here. We sail under the Black Moon's flag, my friends. Things are going well for us these days. A deckhand's share'll make a wealthy man of you after three prizes—maybe just one or two if they're rich. And for men of ability, there's even more to be had."

Geran made a show of thinking over Sorsil's offer, while he considered his next step. He'd hoped to catch a rumor of the Black Moon by visiting Zhentil Keep, but it seemed he'd caught a pirate ship. Now that he'd confirmed that the Black Moon Brotherhood had more than one ship at their command, he found himself wondering how many more vessels belonged to the pirate flotilla and where they might be found. He had the woman he wanted to talk to right here in front of him. The question was how to engage her without making Sorsil suspicious.

Tell her we're interested in signing on, Hamil said silently. *It can't hurt to see what more she'll tell us.*

"That's an interesting offer," Geran said slowly. "But, truth be told, we'd sort of hoped to sign on with *Kraken Queen.*"

The bald mate looked at him oddly. "Really? Why?"

Hamil glanced up at him. *You put your foot in it now. Why indeed, Geran?*

Geran affected a small shrug, thinking furiously. "I haven't heard of *Moonshark* before. But I know *Kraken Queen* took a Sokol cog just a couple of tendays ago, and it wasn't her first."

Sorsil shrugged. "Well, you'll have a long wait if you hope to catch *Kraken Queen* in port. But she's a Black Moon ship also, and we see her from time to time. If you can convince the captain to let you cross-deck, you might get your wish. *Moonshark*'s your best bet for now."

"All right, then. I guess we're in," Geran said. "When do we sail, and where are we bound?"

"Good!" the mate said. "We're sailing tomorrow morning. As far as where we're going, that's the captain's business for now and none of yours until we're at sea. Come on with me, and I'll introduce you to him."

Sorsil indicated the shadowed quay with a wave of her well-muscled arm, and they set off toward the slender warship lying by the ruined bridge. Geran studied the ship as they approached. *Moonshark* was a half galley, built for sailing instead of rowing. She was smaller than *Kraken Queen,* a two-master instead of a three-master, but she looked like she'd be swift and handy under oars or sail. Geran decided that *Seadrake* would have a hard time catching her on the open sea unless she gained the weather gauge on the pirate. Sorsil led them up the narrow gangplank and gruffly acknowledged the greeting of the deckwatch—a pair of dispirited-looking men who evidently wished they were free to spend the night in the ruined port's taverns. The mate went aft to a companionway beneath the quarterdeck and knocked. "Captain?" she called in a low voice. "New hands."

"What have you got there, Sorsil?" The voice was not quite human, wetter and more throaty, with a hint of a growl deep in the chest. A tall but curiously hunched figure appeared in the small companionway, ducking beneath the doorway as it stepped onto the main deck. The creature stood almost seven feet tall despite its posture, and as it moved into the lanternlight by the head of the gangplank, Geran saw that it was a gnoll—a savage beast-man with a hyena-like muzzle and a short coat of mangy yellow-gray fur. It wore a shirt of black mail and carried a curving scimitar at its belt.

"Three hands as say they want to sign on, Captain Narsk," the bald woman answered. "They handled a gang of Robidar's lads well enough, and I thought you might want to meet them."

"Rrrobidar's men aren't worth a cup of warm piss. Still, we need the crew, don't we, Sorsil?" the gnoll—Narsk, Geran reminded himself—said. The mate remained silent, and Narsk paced closer, looking over the three companions. The swordmage did his best to look surly, violent, and desperate without challenging the gnoll by holding his gaze too long. Narsk twisted his lips away from his fangs and then looked down at Hamil. "The other two might do, but I don't need a little rrrat like this one on my ship. I need fighters."

Hamil planted his feet and looked up at the gnoll. "I'll try any man on this ship—you included, Captain."

The gnoll scowled at that, but Sorsil spoke up. "He can fight, Captain. I watched him hamstring one man and kick him unconscious just as neat as you please and then knock out a second man with the pommel of a thrown dagger. He's worth a share."

"Rrreally?" Narsk looked down at Hamil and smiled unpleasantly. "Well, we'll find out soon enough. If he's not as good as you think, the rrrest of the crew'll kill him within three days, or my name's not Narsk. Are you still willing to sign on with *Moonshark,* little one?"

"I can look after myself."

"It's your neck." Narsk pointed one clawed finger at Hamil. "I won't spare a word to save your worthless life if you are wrrrong."

"What are your terms, Captain?" Geran asked.

"The crew divides half the value of any prize we take, one share each. The three of you make fifty-five hands. You can sleep wherever you find space, and you'll be fed twice a day. There's no other pay. I'll keep your shares in the ship's chest until you decide to leave, and then I'll count you out if you want." The gnoll grinned. "Better that way, less thieving and killing among the crew."

Hard terms, Hamil said to Geran. *He doesn't care whether his crew likes him much.*

They seemed more or less in line with what Geran would have expected of a pirate captain. "What are the rules of the Brotherhood?" he asked.

"There aren't many," Narsk answered. "Sorsil can explain them. All you need to know is that you'd better do what I say—or what Sorsil says in my place—or you'll be damned sorry you didn't."

"I wouldn't expect otherwise. All right, Captain, I'm willing. When do we sail?"

"Tomorrow at sunrise," Narsk said. "You'll be pulling oars with the rrrest of the crew."

"Then if we're sailing tomorrow morning, I've a mind to say my farewells to the ladies of the port before we cast off," Hamil said. He winked at Geran and gave the gnoll a sly grin. "When do we have to be back on board?"

For a moment Geran was afraid that Narsk was going to tell them that they were finished with their port call and had to remain aboard; after all, why give them a chance to change their minds? But a sly look stole over the gnoll's face, and he bared his fangs in what Geran supposed was meant to be a friendly grin.

"Go say your farewells, then."

Geran relaxed. He'd judged the gnoll well. Sailors with full purses were all too likely to jump ship at the first opportunity, but penniless sailors were more or less at the captain's mercy. Narsk was all too happy to let his three new hands spend their last remaining coin ashore, since that would put them well and truly in his power when they straggled back aboard *Moonshark*. Chances were he had no intention of paying them at all, or at least not until it suited him to do so.

"Back by sunup, or I'll leave you," the gnoll warned. Then he ducked back through the small door leading to the aft cabin, shutting it behind him.

Sorsil looked over the three companions and shrugged. "Well, you heard the captain," she said. "You can go back ashore, or I can show you where to sling your hammocks now. But I'll warn you that the best spots are taken."

"The night's still young," Geran answered. "We'll be back before dawn." Then he trotted back down the gangplank, with Sarth and Hamil a few steps behind. He turned back toward the yellow lanterns marking the location of the taverns along the ruined quay and walked away from *Moonshark* without a backward glance.

"Well, what now?" Sarth asked quietly.

"I think that a bold opportunity is before us," Hamil replied. "The question is: should we take it?"

"Do you mean to attack *Moonshark* before she sails?" Sarth asked.

Geran thought he knew what Hamil had in mind. "Not exactly. What do you think about becoming pirates for a while?"

Sarth stopped in midstride and fixed his dark eyes on Geran. "It strikes me as pure madness," he said. "Do you have any idea how hard it will be to keep our identities a secret in the close confines of a ship filled with enemies? You may be able to pass yourselves off as deckhands, but I know nothing about ships."

"I prefer to think of it as audacity, not madness," Hamil said.

"In any event, I have a hard time imagining a better way to spy out the plots of the pirate captains or to find out where the Black Moon ships are lairing."

Geran chewed on his tongue for a moment, thinking it over. He'd gone along with Sorsil's offer simply because that seemed a plausible cover for approaching the pirates—nothing more than a ruse to ferret out some rumors of Hulburg's enemies. A couple of miles away under the clouded Moonsea night, *Seadrake* waited. He and his companions could slip out of Zhentil Keep and bring the ship into position to catch *Moonshark* in the morning. But *Moonshark* wasn't the prize he was after; he wanted *Kraken Queen,* and his intuition warned him that she might prove an elusive quarry. All he had to do was board *Moonshark* before dawn, and Narsk's ship would take him exactly where he wanted to go. Once he spied out *Kraken Queen*'s lair, he could slip away to summon *Seadrake* and bag the Black Moon Brotherhood with a single efficient stroke. With his arcane magic—and Sarth's—at their disposal, abandoning Narsk's ship should be simple enough.

"I don't ask either of you to come with me," he told Hamil and Sarth, "but I intend to sail with *Moonshark* in the morning. *Seadrake*'s in Kara's command. I want her to take the ship back toward Hulburg and protect shipping as best she can until I return or send word."

"I'm with you," Hamil said. The halfling looked up at him with a fierce grin. "You'll need someone to watch your back."

Sarth sighed and looked up at the dark skies overhead. "I, too," he said. "There is an excellent chance that you will have to fight your way off that ship. If so, my magic may be of some small use. But I am going to be a very inept deckhand."

"Hamil and I can help you with that," Geran told him. "Besides, there'll be plenty of men on that ship who know just as little as you do. Narsk needs fighters even more than he needs sailors."

"Very well," Sarth said. He frowned unhappily. "I will trust your judgment."

"Good. That brings up two more things. First . . . Sarth, you have a spell of flying. Can you return to *Seadrake,* explain to Kara what we're doing, and come back swiftly?"

Sarth nodded. "Of course, but we should get out of sight before I take to the air."

"The place where we left the skiff should do. I don't think many of the people here are in the habit of roaming the ruins at night."

"What else?" Hamil asked.

Geran smiled. He knew it was a foolish thing, but it amused him nonetheless. "We'll need to come up with good pirate names."

EIGHT

30 Eleint, the Year of the Ageless One (1479 DR)

Moonshark sailed at dawn, as Narsk had promised. Before the lower limb of the sun had cleared the horizon, the half galley hauled in her lines and sculled slowly eastward with the current of the Tesh. By daylight the taverns and dens huddled in the ruins of Zhentil Keep struck Geran as squalid and small. None of the people living there showed themselves as the pirate ship set sail.

As he bent his back to one of the oars and pulled, Geran began to second-guess his strategy. The moment the ship got underway, Narsk and Sorsil dropped any pretense of civility. The burly first mate armed herself with a small cudgel and roamed the main deck freely employing the weapon against anyone who seemed to be shirking. Narsk prowled the quarterdeck, snarling savagely as he issued his orders. Worse yet, Geran's new shipmates seemed a vicious lot. Most of the crewmen were humans from a wide variety of lands, but some were dwarves, some were half-orcs, some were goblins or kin to goblins, and there was even one ogre—a strapping, dimwitted creature called Kronn, who manned one of the ship's oars by himself. They wore threadbare tunics, scraps of armor, tattered cloaks, and sodden hoods or misshapen hats. Geran caught more than a few studying him and his friends with calculating looks. Some grinned threateningly at him when he met their gaze. If there weren't a dozen ready to slit his throat for a silver talent, he would have been astonished.

"Pull, you sorry bastards!" Sorsil roared. "The captain doesn't want to bob around in the river all damned day! The sooner we cross the bar, the sooner we'll raise sail! Now pull like you mean it!"

The man sitting beside Geran at the oar bench chuckled to himself. He was a weatherbeaten old Shou, with a face like seamed leather and a topknot of gray-streaked black hair. "Every time we leave port, it is the same," he said between strokes. "Pull harder! Pull faster! But do not worry, stranger. Narsk knows that the crew does not like to row, and he'll take the oars in soon enough."

"You've sailed with Narsk a long time?" Geran asked.

"I joined *Moonshark* three years ago. Zaroun was the captain then, and *Moonshark* hunted the Sea of Fallen Stars." The Shou gave Geran a bitter smile. "Zaroun was a good captain, but he was not a good judge of men. Or gnolls. He signed on Narsk in Impiltur as we sailed west toward the Dragon Reach and within the month he was dead and Narsk was captain. That was a year ago now."

Geran looked up at the quarterdeck, where the gnoll paced. "Did Narsk challenge Zaroun or just murder him?"

"Challenge, of course. That is the Black Moon way. But you should know, stranger, that a captain is within his rights to order a challenger killed. If the crew thinks the challenger is not fit to seize the ship, they'll deal with him. No, one should be sure that the crew will stand aside before one challenges the captain."

"I see." Geran wasn't surprised to learn that the Black Moon pirates chose their leaders in such a manner, or that the challenge process didn't offer any guarantees to the challenger. Many outlaw gangs and brigand companies worked in much the same way. The captain could count on the protection of the crew against many challenges, but only so long as he held their confidence. "Has Narsk faced many challenges?"

"Some." The Shou gave Geran a sly look. "You speak like a man who has an interest in becoming captain."

Geran snorted. "I don't think so. Narsk doesn't scare me, but the rest of you do."

The Shou laughed aloud, attracting the attention of Sorsil. The mate growled and struck him across the shoulders then gave Geran a clout as well. "Enjoying the morning, lads?" she snarled. "Now pull!"

Geran saw stars. He started to surge up from his bench, but he stopped himself short. It was far too early to think about fighting anyone, and he knew that the mate had meant the blow as a sharp warning and nothing more. Instead the swordmage clenched his jaw and chose to endure the blow with a hard look at the mate.

Hamil and Sarth, sitting at the bench in front of him, hesitated half a moment in their sweep, and Hamil glanced back to meet his eyes. *Are you certain you want to continue?* he asked silently. *We can dispatch a few of these villains and make our escape any time you like.*

Geran shook his head slightly and went back to his rowing as Sorsil moved on to shout at a different crewman. He was here to learn more about the Black Moon corsairs, and if he drew blade the first time he met with something he didn't like, he would never get far. Hamil shrugged and returned his attention to his own oar.

"You were wise to hold your anger," the Shou said in a low voice. "If you had struck back at Sorsil, Narsk would have ordered her to beat you or kill you." He paused and then added, "I am Tao Zhe. I am the ship's cook."

"Call me Aram. Those two ahead of us are Vorr and Dagger." Geran nodded at Sarth and Hamil. "What else should I know about sailing under the Black Moon?"

"It would be wise to find a fist soon."

"A fist?"

"A band, a gang—they call them 'fists' here," the Shou answered. "One man alone is in for a difficult time aboard a Black Moon ship. Your shipmates will rob you, bully you, give you the worst jobs to do. The best protection you have is a strong fist. If your fist is strong enough, even the first mate and the captain must think twice before dealing harshly with you. After all, you might challenge the captain, and if your fist is very strong, the crew will stand aside. I see that you have a small fist already, you and your two comrades here, but that is not enough. No one has reason to be wary of such a small fist."

"How many fists are there on *Moonshark?"* Geran asked.

"Four that matter: Skamang and his Impilturians, the dwarves and Teshans, the Mulmasterites—they follow Khefen, the second mate—and the goblins and their kin. Remember, if you pick a fight, you're taking on the whole of your foe's fist."

"Up oars!" Sorsil shouted. Geran and Tao Zhe pushed down on their end of the heavy oar, raising its blade up out of the water, as the other pairs of oarsmen along the ship's side did the same. The mate waited a moment to make sure that all of the rowers had obeyed then called, "Take in and secure your oars!" They pulled the oars inboard and set them in chocks bolted to the deck, making them fast with iron pins that held the oars in place. The rest of the crew stood up and pushed their way clear of the oar sweeps; Sorsil ordered crew to set *Moonshark*'s sails.

"I must go and see to our stores before I prepare the midday meal," Tao Zhe said. He studied Geran for a moment. "You may not need any advice from me, but I offer it anyway: Sorsil is no one's friend, and watch your back around Skamang there." The cook nodded at a tall, stoop-shouldered Northman with blue whorls tattooed on his face. "He's got a fist that not even Sorsil wants to cross, and he's the one man on this ship other than Narsk that you do not want for an enemy."

"I'll remember what you've told me," Geran answered. The cook nodded and went forward to the ship's galley. Geran went to lend a hand with the job of raising sail. Some galleys carried masts that could be unstepped and laid down flat inside the hull, but *Moonshark* was made for sailing first; her two masts were fixed in place and carried a typical fore-and-aft rig. The pirate crew managed the task with a fair bit of fumbling and plenty of cudgel-blows from the first mate; many of the deckhands were no more familiar with the work of sailing a ship than Sarth was. *Moonshark* might be able to outsail a round-bellied cog or outrow a coaster in a light wind, but her crew needed more practice to handle her well under sail. Geran decided that Narsk had manned her with whatever fighters and outlaws he could scrape together in the most wretched taprooms of the Moonsea, whether they knew a thing about sailing or not.

They passed the rest of the day working through the dozens of tasks that kept a deckhand busy. Geran quietly related to Sarth and Hamil everything Tao Zhe had told him, and the three made a point of watching out for each other. The weather was fair and cool, with a steady light wind out of the west that drove *Moonshark* at a slow-footed, rolling pace. The pirate ship carried many more deckhands than she needed; the sailing watch could have been handled by four or five men, but a big crew was needed for rowing and fighting. Consequently, most of the crew worked little while the ship was under sail and undertook routine tasks only when unable to pass them off to some more luckless hand—for example, the three new hands signed in Zhentil Keep.

The sullen Northman Skamang held court by the foremast for most of the day, surrounded by his fist of seven or eight deckhands who did nothing at all the whole day, as far as Geran could tell. At one point, Skamang called Geran over when Geran was carrying fresh water from the ship's casks up to the galley for Tao Zhe. "Ho there, new man," he said in a rasping voice. "What do you call yourself?"

Geran set down his yoked buckets with care before answering. "Aram."

"I heard that you and your friends cut up a couple of Robidar's lads back at the Keep. Is that right?"

"That's what happened."

Skamang smiled without humor. "Six of them, they say. You, the seasick sellsword with the mustache, and the little fellow. I find that hard to believe. The three of you must be some fighters."

Geran shrugged. "Ask Sorsil if you don't believe me. She watched the whole thing." He picked up his yoke and continued on his way. He could hope that Skamang would decide that he and his friends were likely more trouble than they were worth, but somehow he doubted they'd be that lucky. He didn't need Tao Zhe's warning to sense that the tattooed Northman intended trouble for them sooner or later.

The rest of the day passed peacefully enough, and the night as well. Late in the afternoon of their second day out, *Moonshark* came in sight of a group of black, jagged rocks jutting up out of the Moonsea. Geran recognized them; they were spearlike towers of changeland known as Umberlee's Talons, and they served as a useful landmark to ships navigating in the western reaches of the Moonsea. Most ships gave them a wide berth. Not only did the jagged rocks offer plenty of chances to rip out a ship's bottom, but the place had an evil reputation—they were haunted, or cursed, or concealed the lair of a mighty sea monster, or some combination of the three, depending on which tavern tale one favored. Narsk steered a course straight toward the menacing islets, and none of the other deckhands seemed very concerned when he did so.

Sarth stood by the rail next to Geran, gazing at the sinister rocks; Hamil was below, sleeping after staying up most of the night on watch. Some of the rocks rose well over two hundred feet out of the water, but no seabirds hovered around them or roosted on their steep sides. "Is this the secret Black Moon refuge?" the tiefling asked in a low voice.

"I doubt it," Geran answered. "The Talons are well known in these waters. If there was anything here but empty rocks, I think the story would have got out."

"Could there be some hidden anchorage here? Something hiding in plain sight?"

"Your guess is as good as mine." The swordmage shrugged. He peered more closely at the Talons as *Moonshark* drew near. If there was some sort of stronghold or secret harbor hidden in their midst, he couldn't see it. Soon enough Sorsil ordered the sails to be taken in and called the crew to the ship's oars. She prowled the narrow walkway between the oar benches, truncheon in hand, while Narsk carefully piloted the ship between the looming rocks to a reach of clear water he liked. They dropped anchor and settled in to wait.

At sunset the wind shifted to the east and strengthened.

Moonshark rocked at her anchor, and the breeze moaned eerily as it blew though the sharp edges of the rocks looming overhead. Sarth and Geran exchanged looks; there was some subtle sorcery in the air, a breath of the supernatural, and both the sorcerer and the swordmage could taste it on the wind. "Something is approaching," Sarth said.

"The High Captain's on his way," said a dwarf sitting on the capstan nearby. His name was Murkelmor, and he smoked a simple clay pipe. He'd struck Geran as the sort to keep to himself in the few brief hours he'd been around the fellow. "This is where we meet him. The wind always seems t' turn when he's near."

Sarth looked at the dwarf. "Why here? Is there some harbor nearby?"

Murkelmor shook his head. "None t' speak of. No, as I've heard it told, there's a black isle that only the High Captain knows how to find. This easterly wind is the wind he needs t' put to sea."

"A black island?" Geran asked. Clearly, the Black Moon ships had some way of staying out of sight when they wanted to; he was fairly sure he would have found something other than a single half galley lurking in the ruins of Zhentil Keep if the Black Moon kept to the known harbors of the Moonsea. But he'd never heard of anything like a black island in the Moonsea.

The dwarf shrugged. "I've no' seen it myself, mind ye. But that's the tale that's told."

"Ship abeam to starboard!" called the lookout by the bow.

Geran turned to look over the starboard rail, expecting to see a distant glimmer of sail on the horizon. Instead he blinked as the long black hull of a half galley slid through the Talons, not more than four hundred yards distant. "Now where in the world did she come from?" he muttered to himself. He'd been looking in that direction only a few moments ago, and he would have sworn that no ship could have slipped so close to *Moonshark* without his noticing. Its approach might have been screened by one of the larger Talons, but somehow he didn't think so.

"It's *Kraken Queen!"* the lookout called again. "I can make out her figurehead!"

Murkelmor smiled and tapped the ashes out of his pipe. "See? The High Captain, as I told ye."

Geran leaned over the rail, staring into the gloaming. Sure enough, the mermaidlike device with the twining tentacles in place of its fishy tail glimmered in the light of the rising moon. "This is an interesting development," he murmured to Sarth. "Now we know what Narsk was waiting for."

The gnoll climbed up from his cabin to the quarterdeck. "Put the longboat in water, Sorsil," he snarled. He turned to pace the quarterdeck, eyes narrowed as he stared at *Kraken Queen* lying amid the Talons.

"Aye, Captain," Sorsil answered. She turned and snarled at every hand who happened to be on deck at the moment. "You heard the captain, you miserable dogs! Quickly now, or I'll peel the hide off the lot of you!"

Geran moved over to the ship's boat stowed across her midsection on a raised deck. He wasn't particularly worried about Sorsil's threats, but if Narsk wanted to go over to *Kraken Queen,* he wanted to go too. There was a chance that someone from the other pirate ship might recognize him from the skirmish on the beach, but the last time they'd seen him it was by firelight, and he hadn't been dressed like a common seaman with a thickly stubbled chin. And he sincerely doubted that any of the deckhands on the other ship would be expecting to see him again in the crew of another Black Moon ship. Several other crewmen joined him by the boat, and together they lifted it from its frame, turned it right-side up, and maneuvered it to the rail to fix hoisting lines at its bow and stern. They lowered the boat to the water under Sorsil's watchful eye.

"All right, I need oarsmen," the mate said. Geran made sure he was standing in plain sight, and a moment later Sorsil singled him out. "You there!"

The swordmage feigned a grimace of annoyance, but swung his leg over the rail and dropped down the shallow rungs bolted to the ship's side to take up one of the oars. More of his shipmates followed. He glanced up at the rail, now rocking over his head, and caught Hamil looking at him. *Good thinking, Geran,* the halfling told him. *But pull down your hood, you look like you're up to something.*

Geran reluctantly pulled his hood back down to his shoulders and waited by his oar. A moment later Narsk clambered down the ladder and took the steersman's seat himself. He was wearing a heavy black coat and a large, wide-brimmed hat that seemed oddly out of place atop his bestial features. "Push off and let's go," the gnoll ordered. The boat crew cast off the lines, pushed away from *Moonshark,* then fell into a strong rowing rhythm as Narsk steered them toward the other ship. The Talons seemed to catch the light chop of the surrounding waters and reflect them in confused eddies; Geran decided that he wouldn't want to bring a ship too close to the towering rocks.

They reached *Kraken Queen* and caught a line tossed down from the rail; the crew of the other ship crowded around the rail, calling down offers to trade or good-natured jibes at *Moonshark*'s expense. As they bumped alongside the larger ship's hull, Narsk growled, "Wait for me," and scrambled up the side.

"Ho there, Narsk! You're the first to arrive!"

I know that voice! Geran realized. He twisted around on his bench and peered up at the quarterdeck of *Kraken Queen.* There stood the captain of the other ship, a lean man of middle years with a gray-streaked beard of black around his craggy face and a big scarlet cloak bedecked with gold braid.

"Kamoth," he whispered. "I don't believe it." Kamoth Kastelmar was supposed to be dead. The last Geran had heard, he'd gone down with a pirate galley cornered and sunk by Mulman warships years ago. But there was no doubt of it; the captain of *Kraken Queen* was the same man who'd married Geran's aunt, Terena, fifteen years ago and brought his son Sergen to live in Griffonwatch with the Hulmasters. A "gentleman of fortune," as he'd called himself then, Kamoth was the scion of minor nobility in the city of Hillsfar, a reasonable match for the sister of the harmach. But only two years later Geran's father discovered Kamoth engaged in all manner of foul plotting against

Harmach Grigor and drove the traitor into exile. Kamoth had left his teenage son Sergen behind—by chance or design, Geran had never determined—but Harmach Grigor had decided that the boy was not to be held responsible for the crimes of his father and raised Sergen as a member of his own family.

"What's the matter with ye?" Murkelmor growled at Geran. The dwarf had the seat next to Geran's. "That one's as mad as Manshoon. He'd just as soon kill ye as look at ye. Meet his eye, and he's like t' think ye mean to challenge him."

Geran shook his head and turned his face away. He doubted that Kamoth would recognize him; he'd been a lad of seventeen years the last time Kamoth had seen him. The strangest part of it was that he'd always *liked* Kamoth. During the brief time he'd spent in Hulburg, Geran hadn't seen anything other than the man's bluff good cheer and roguish charm. It was only much later that he'd discovered how thoroughly he and the rest of his family had been taken in. "Who is he?" he asked the dwarf.

"That's the High Captain o' the Black Moon," Murkelmor answered. "All the other captains—including our own Narsk—sail at his word. Kamoth, his name is. *Kraken Queen* is his."

Geran risked another look. Narsk and Kamoth were deep in conversation, the gnoll towering over the pirate lord but bobbing and nodding his head in response to Kamoth's words. Kamoth turned aside, calling for someone near him . . . and Sergen Hulmâster stepped into view, a leather lettercase in his hands, and handed the packet to Kamoth to give to the gnoll. Sergen glanced out toward *Moonshark* and down to the longboat bobbing at the side of the pirate lord's ship. At the last moment Geran averted his eyes and turned his back to the quarterdeck. Kamoth was unlikely to recognize him, but Sergen knew him very well indeed. A momentary hint of recognition, a single suspicion, could set a hundred blades at Geran's throat. Not knowing what else to do, Geran kept his face turned toward *Moonshark,* looking away from the quarterdeck, and imagined Sergen's eyes boring into his back, a black smile of satisfaction twisting Sergen's haughty expression, the first snort of derisive laughter.

Well, now I know why the Black Moon pirates have been seeking out Hulburg's shipping, he thought furiously. Sergen enlisted his father's pirate fleet to continue his effort to unseat the Hulmasters. Or was it the other way around? Had Kamoth directed Sergen's plots and betrayals all along?

A sudden clatter on the ladder steps climbing the ship's side caught Geran's attention. He glanced up, expecting to see pirates scrambling down to seize him where he sat—but instead it was simply Narsk returning to the longboat. The gnoll tucked the mysterious lettercase into his coat pocket and seated himself by the rudder. Sergen was nowhere in sight, but Kamoth still leaned over the rail. "Seven nights, Narsk!" he called. "Don't get caught up in any other sport between now and then."

"*Moonshark* will not be late, High Captain," the gnoll answered. He waved at the oarsmen, and Geran started pulling with the rest, keeping his eyes in the longboat's bottom.

Geran didn't look up again until *Kraken Queen* was a good hundred yards astern. He could still make out Kamoth's scarlet cloak on the quarterdeck and thought he saw Sergen's black coat close by. He heaved a breath of relief and put his back into the sweeps. For the moment it seemed that he was safe, and neither of the two traitors suspected that a Hulmaster had been bobbing up and down in a small boat not twenty-five feet from their quarterdeck. He'd hoped to find a way to eavesdrop on Narsk and Kamoth, but for the moment he was glad to have avoided discovery.

"Pull, you dogs," Narsk snapped. "I mean to be underway in half an hour, and I'll flog the first ten men I see if we aren't!"

Geran joined the other oarsmen as they threw themselves into their work. His hands throbbed and his shoulders ached, but he smiled to himself when his eye fell on the leather lettercase sitting in Narsk's coat pocket. He might not have missed his opportunity to eavesdrop after all, if he could only examine Narsk's letter. All he had to do was find a chance to break into the gnoll's cabin and steal it without getting caught.

NINE

30 Eleint, the Year of the Ageless One (1479 DR)

Evening was descending over Hulburg as Mirya locked up Erstenwold's Provisioners and prepared to go home for the evening. It had been a slow day, but right before closing time a farmer from the Winterspear Vale had shown up with a whole wagonload of cheese, bacon, smoked hams, and other foodstuffs to sell. By the time she'd finished with their business and had overseen the unloading of the wagon, it was an hour past the time that she normally locked up. Most of Hulburg's shopkeepers lived above or behind their places of business, but the Erstenwolds were a family that had been in Hulburg for a long time, and Mirya's house was a comfortable cottage surrounded by a small apple orchard on the river's west bank, a little less than a mile distant. Anxious to start for home, she went to the store's back door, the one that let out into the alleyway behind Plank Street, and looked up and down the narrow way for any sign of Selsha.

"Selsha!" she called into the gloaming. Her daughter was nowhere in sight, but Mirya knew that she was rarely out of earshot. She could remember her own mother calling for her at the end of the day when she was a child and supposed that she probably sounded a lot like that to Selsha's ears. A mother's voice carried a long way, as she recalled. "Selsha! It's time to go home!"

She heard nothing at first and peered up and down the alleyway behind the storehouse. She rarely stayed at the shop this late into the evening, and the shadows were long and dark in Hulburg's streets. The buildings surrounding Erstenwold's did not seem so friendly or familiar as night descended over the town. During the day these streets were busy with scores of neighbors that Mirya knew well—the cooper across the alley, the tinsmith next to him, old Mother Gresha and her laundry tub two doors down, and Auntie Tilsie who sold scores of simple meals to the town's porters and drivers every day from her kitchen around the corner from that. All of them doted on Selsha and were happy to let her pester them during the day, but they were all closing up or indoors now. After sunset Hulburg's taphouses and taverns filled up, and instead of watchful neighbors the streets would be left to strangers searching for a place to drink themselves into a stupor. Mirya frowned at that thought and raised her voice. "Selsha! Where are you?"

"I'm coming, Mama!" Selsha appeared at the end of the alleyway and ran to the door. She was a slip of a girl, just nine years old, with wide blue eyes that had a way of disarming Mirya's most furious moments and with silky black hair just like her own.

"Where were you? Did you not hear me calling?" Mirya scolded her. She bustled Selsha into the store and pulled the door closed behind her. "I was worried about you, Selsha!"

"I'm sorry, Mama," Selsha replied. Then she held out her hand. "But look, I found something."

Mirya looked down into her daughter's hand. It was an amulet of some kind on a silver chain. She could see at once that it was valuable, and she reached down to gently lift it from Selsha's grasp. "What is this?" she murmured, and she looked closer. The amulet was formed in the shape of a sunburst, but the rays were jet, and in the center gleamed a jawless skull of silver. She stared at it in growing horror, realizing that what she held in her hand was a holy symbol of Cyric, the Black Sun, the god of lies and murder. With a small cry she let it drop to the floor.

"What? What is it?" Selsha asked.

"Something that we are not to handle lightly," Mirya answered. She rubbed her hand briskly against her skirt, unable to stop herself. "Selsha, where did you find this?"

Selsha looked down, and her lip started to quiver. Mirya realized that her own sudden alarm had frightened the girl. "I'm sorry, Mama. I'm sorry. I didn't mean—I didn't know—"

Mirya took a deep breath and kneeled down by Selsha, wrapping her arms around her daughter and stroking her hair. "No, no, Selsha, all is well," she said softly. "I am not angry with you. I was only surprised. Now, tell me, how did you find the amulet?"

"Kynda and I were playing in the empty storehouse on Fish Street. I know we're not supposed to, but no one was around. Anyway, I found it on the floor. See, the chain's broken—I think someone dropped it and didn't even know. Kynda and I were looking at it when we heard some men come in. They sounded angry, and we were afraid we would get into trouble, so we hid until they left."

"Did the men see you?"

The girl shook her head.

Mirya picked up the amulet from the floor, suppressing a shudder of distaste. "Do you think they were looking for this?"

This time Selsha nodded slowly. "I heard one man say he thought it might have fallen through the floorboards, and the other man told him to go get a crowbar so they could pry up the floor and look for it."

"You shouldn't have been in someone else's storehouse, abandoned or not, and well you know it." She gave Selsha a stern look and stood up, slipping the amulet into a pocket of her dress as she turned away, thinking about what to do with the thing. A token of Cyric was not prohibited by any law she knew of, nor was it an evil thing in and of itself. The Black Sun was not a god that she cared to honor, but then again few people truly revered such things as murder or strife. Most people either gave Cyric his due in order to avert his attention or looked past the darker aspects of his doctrines and instead saw him as a deity of ambition and determination—the sort of god who encouraged his followers in their desire to fight their way up out of their circumstances no matter what it took. The poor foreigners who huddled in miserable neighborhoods such as the Tailings sometimes turned to grim gods like Cyric out of simple desperation. Mirya couldn't blame them for being attracted by promises of prosperity and success. Of course, she didn't doubt that there were truly malicious followers of the Black Sun in those same neighborhoods. Slavers, thieves, and robbers of all sorts looked to Cyric for favor too, and there were plenty of those in the Tailings.

But what Selsha had found wasn't simply a charm or token. It was a holy symbol of the sort a high-ranking priest might carry. She could sense the enchantment of the thing; it was precious to somebody. "Now what should we do with it?" she muttered to herself. She certainly didn't want to keep it. She could have Selsha put it back where she found it—but if Selsha was right, the men she'd overheard were already looking for it, and Mirya was not about to send her daughter into the hands of someone who might be a zealous follower of Cyric. Either she'd have to take it back herself, or she'd have to throw it away somewhere.

Someone knocked sharply on the alley door. Mirya started and looked at the door. Only a neighbor would come by that door, and her neighbors were all at their supper tables by now. The knock came again.

"Who is it, Mama?" Selsha asked in a small voice.

"I've no idea." Mirya frowned at the door and smoothed the front of her dress. This is ridiculous, she told herself. It's probably Tilsie come to borrow some flour. Still, her intuition told her that wasn't so. She set a hand on Selsha's shoulder. "Stay here, dear. I'll see who it is."

She went to the door, calmed herself for a moment, then lifted the bar and pulled the door open a foot or so. "Yes?" she said.

Outside in the alley stood a pale, fair-haired man in a laborer's garb. Streaks of gray marked his temples and the neatly trimmed square of beard under his chin. He stood with a strange, distracted smile on his face, but his eyes were dark and intense. "Ah, you must be Mistress Erstenwold," he said.

"I'm afraid we're closed for the evening. If you come back tomorrow—"

"I'm not here on business," the man said. He held up a hand to forestall her protest. She noticed a fine gold ring on his little finger and the smoothness of his palm and found herself doubting very much whether he was as poor as his clothing suggested. "I understand that you have a young daughter who might have been playing out in the neighborhood today. A dark-haired girl, perhaps ten years of age. Is that so?"

A cold stab of fear sank into Mirya's heart. "Aye, it is," she said slowly.

"Then perhaps she might have found something I lost, something rather valuable to me. By any chance have you seen a silver amulet? It would be marked with the emblem of a silver skull." The man affected a shrug. "A keepsake, but one I would very much like to find."

Mirya kept her face neutral. She was sorely tempted to deny it outright, but a small voice warned her that the stranger wouldn't be at her door unless he had a very strong suspicion about the amulet's location already. Priests sometimes knew finding spells of different sorts, and he might have already divined where his holy symbol was. She wished a couple of her clerks were still on the premises; she did not like being alone with this man at her door.

The stranger took her hesitation for confusion. "Perhaps you could call your daughter to the door? I'd like to ask her about it—just in case, you understand."

As little as she liked the half-smile on his face or the strange intensity of his eyes, she liked the idea of this man speaking to Selsha much less. She reached into her pocket before she even realized what she was doing and held the amulet out to him. "There'll be no need for that," she said. "She found this in the alley a little ways from here. Is it yours?"

The pale man gently took it out of her hand and glanced at it. He smiled broadly and inclined his head, but his eyes remained cold, almost serpentine. "Why, it is indeed!" he said. "Now I wonder how it came to be lying out in the alleyway? Doesn't that seem strange?"

"It looks like the chain has a broken link."

"It does." The man carefully gathered up the silver skull and slipped it into his pocket. She noticed a gray smudge across the back of his hand as he did so, and her eyes narrowed. It seemed to her very much like the sort of smudge that someone who marked his fist with soot might have on the back of his hand. Either her visitor was one of the Cinderfists, which seemed unlikely since he did not strike her as a man who'd seen the inside of a foundry or had shoveled coal into a furnace, or he at least wanted people to believe that he was. Then the man leaned to one side, looking past Mirya into the hallway behind her. "And look! That must be your daughter."

Mirya glanced behind her and realized that Selsha was standing just a few feet behind her, staring at the pale man. Her daughter must have come out from the store's front room while Mirya was speaking with the stranger. She looked back quickly to the man, but he just smiled again—a smile that still did not reach his eyes—and said, "What a lovely child. You are quite fortunate, Mistress Erstenwold. Quite fortunate indeed."

"Thank you," said Mirya, her voice thick. She did not know what else to say. The idea of this man making small talk with her about her daughter chilled her to the marrow.

"You should speak to her about picking up things she finds in *alleys,* though. Good evening, Mistress Erstenwold." The man nodded to her and strode off into the gathering shadows.

Mirya shut the door firmly and shot the bolt. Then she hurried Selsha home, starting at every shadow along the way.

The next day passed without event, but at noon of the day after that Mirya thought she saw the hooded man watching Selsha when she came back to Erstenwold's after playing with her friends in the morning. She stepped out into the alleyway and looked again, but the man was nowhere in sight. The encounter was unsettling enough that she dwelled on it all day long. She moved through the rest of her day in a distracted, pensive mood, her mind turning over the implications. She'd seen the man's face, and she knew him for a servant of Cyric; if he wanted to be sure of keeping his identity a secret, he would have to make sure she did not speak of it again. Perhaps he was simply allowing her to see him to intimidate her . . . or it was possible he contemplated more stringent measures to keep his secret. By the middle of the afternoon, she called Selsha back inside and told her that she had to remain inside in the Erstenwold store and storehouse until she told her otherwise.

The next morning she slipped away from Erstenwold's for an hour, hurrying up to Griffonwatch to speak to the Shieldsworn. Geran and Kara were both away at sea, but her brother Jarad had served as the captain of the harmach's soldiers for years before his death, and they'd thought the world of him. She met with Sergeant Kolton and told her story, but the veteran had little he could offer her. "We've not found out much at all about who runs the Cinderfists," he told her. "They're a closemouthed lot, they are. Mostly men from Impiltur, and they know their own—there's not a single native-born Hulburgan who works in the foundries. I might've guessed that an outlander priest of Cyric is mixed up in it."

"So you've no idea who he is or what he might be up to?" she asked.

Kolton shook his head. "You know as much as we do, Mistress Erstenwold. I can make sure the Shieldsworn check on Erstenwold's regularly, at least for a few days. If you see the fellow you spoke with lurking nearby, I'd appreciate it if you pointed him out to the harmach's men. You're the only native-born Hulburgan who knows his face, as far as I can tell."

Mirya frowned at that thought. It might be very important to the stranger to remain unknown, and she could think of only one way that a man in his position might make sure of his anonymity. She found herself wishing that Geran was in town. It wasn't in her nature to play the damsel in distress, but in the months since Geran had returned to Hulburg they'd slowly fumbled their way to something like friendship again, and perhaps a troubling flicker of something more than that—when it came to Geran Hulmaster she was not necessarily the master of her own heart. She knew herself well enough to keep any such nonsense at a very safe distance indeed, but she also knew that Geran would turn the Tailings upside down to ferret out the hooded man if he found out that someone had threatened her or Selsha. In any event, Geran was away on *Seadrake* chasing after pirates, and that left matters squarely in her own lap.

Kolton took her silence for a reproach. The blunt-faced sergeant sighed. "We're stretched thin, Mistress Erstenwold—you know that. There's nothing the Shieldsworn wouldn't do for you or your daughter, for Captain Jarad's sake if nothing else. But if you're worried, you might also speak to the Moonshields. They don't like the Cinderfists much at all. I'm sure that Brun Osting can make sure a couple of his lads are close at hand whenever the Shieldsworn aren't."

"Thank you, Sergeant Kolton. I might, at that." Mirya took her leave and drove back down to Erstenwold's, wrapped in her thoughts as her wagon rattled through the rough cobblestone streets. She'd hoped that the Shieldsworn would know who the hooded man was, but clearly that wasn't the case. That didn't mean there weren't people in Hulburg who might know more. There was one other place she could turn to . . . but that was a bridge she'd burned a long time ago. Mirya reined in the two-horse team just a few dozen yards short of the Lower Bridge at the end of East Street and sat there thinking things through. Then she tapped her switch to the horses and turned left, climbing up Hill Street instead of crossing the Winterspear and heading back toward Erstenwold's.

Hulburg's East Hill was a strange mix of old and new. Much of its seaward face had been ruined during the Spellplague of a century ago, replaced by the jumble of soaring green stone known as the Arches. On its western side a poor, working-class neighborhood clustered hard by East Street and the Winterspear; around the point to the east, the homes became little more than shanties housing the hundreds of men who toiled in the smelters and foundries a mile downwind of Hulburg proper. But the higher elevations of the East Hill above the crowded neighborhood overlooking the Winterspear were the places where Hulburg's wealthy lived in grand old houses and gated manors. Mirya drove her team to a fine old house hidden behind a screen of low, wind-twisted cedars. She set the brake, slid down from the wagon's seat, then climbed a short flight of stone steps to the house's front door and knocked firmly before she could change her mind.

Nothing happened for a long moment, and Mirya began to wonder if anyone was home. But then the door opened, and a young woman with long black hair and a plain dress of gray wool looked out. "Yes?" she said.

"I'm here to call on Mistress Sennifyr," Mirya said. "My name is Mirya Erstenwold. I'm not expected."

The servant studied her for a moment before answering. "Wait here. I will see if the mistress is available." She disappeared back into the shadows of the house—the front room was dark, with heavy drapes drawn over the windows—while Mirya waited on the porch. Then the servant returned and offered a slight bow. "She will see you. Follow me, if you please."

The servant showed Mirya to a sitting room as dark as the foyer, and Mirya took a seat on a plush couch. She did not have long to wait. Just a moment later, a woman in an elegant purple gown glided into the room, her hands folded at her waist. She was perhaps forty-five years of age, but her hair was still a soft brown untouched by gray, and her face was smooth. Only the shadow of frown lines at the corners of her mouth and a cool, commanding sternness to her dark gaze hinted at her age. She looked at Mirya with a small smile then said, "Well, well. Mirya Erstenwold! You haven't stopped by my home in years and years. I confess I am surprised to see you here."

Mirya rose and bowed her head. "Mistress Sennifyr. Thank you for seeing me."

"Not at all. We have missed you, my dear. Tell me, how is young Selsha?"

"Very well. She just passed her ninth birthday."

"Indeed." Sennifyr raised an eyebrow. "What have you told her about her father?"

Mirya kept a neutral expression on her face, but flinched inwardly. There were few things in her life that she truly regretted, but what she had done to the man who'd fathered Selsha was one of them. Sennifyr knew that, of course. She was the one who had arranged the whole thing, drawing Mirya deeper and deeper into her snares at a time when Mirya had been younger, more foolish, anxious to find approval in her eyes.

It was a mistake to come here, she told herself. Sennifyr had not forgotten any of her old cruelty. But to flee now would gain Mirya nothing. Instead, she made herself answer the question with iron truthfulness. "I told her that I knew him only for a short time and that he died soon after she was born. I'll tell her no more than that for now."

"Poor Mirya. You were always so strong, so clever, and so much was asked of you." Sennifyr offered her a small smile. "The Lady chose a difficult path for you. I know it. But you must understand that you will find no easing of your pain as long as you refuse to go as you have been called. Surcease lies in surrender to the Lady's will. It is never too late to return to the path awaiting you."

"I've not forgotten it, Mistress Sennifyr. For now I choose to go my own way."

"The day will come when no other comfort avails you, my child. The Lady knows her own, and once you have been in her embrace, you will always be hers. We will await your return." Sennifyr folded her hands in her lap. "Now, I doubt that you came to my house to seek the Lady's comfort. You want something of the Sisterhood."

Mirya grimaced. Sennifyr had never been stupid, either. "Well, aye, though I hope that you'll see it to be in your own interest too."

"No justification is necessary, my child. I have not forgotten your devotion to the Lady, even if you have for a time. How may I be of service to you?"

Mirya smoothed her skirt. She had never been one to fence at words. The worst of it was that some long-buried part of her ached to answer Sennifyr's words of forgiveness, to return to the Sisterhood she had left and make amends for the faithlessness of the intervening years. She fixed her mind firmly on the task ahead and ignored her old guilt. "I found out a servant of Cyric a few days ago—a pale man in a hood, masquerading as a common laborer. He knows that I know his secret. I need to learn his name and what purpose he has in Hulburg."

"And you thought we might know something about him?"

Sennifyr reached over to the table next to her and poured herself a cup of tea. "My dear, we have nothing to do with the Black Sun's minions."

"I know. But there's not much that happens in Hulburg that the Sisterhood doesn't see. If the servants of Cyric are preaching to the poor folk of the Tailings or stirring up trouble with the Cinderfists, the Sisterhood would know of it."

"And if you did learn this man's name, what would you do?"

"See to it that the harmach knew it too."

"I see." Sennifyr sipped at her tea. "It is no secret that Geran Hulmaster is close to you. I imagine that a word whispered in his ear would reach the harmach soon enough. For that matter, I would be surprised if Geran did not act on such information himself. He is not one to hesitate over such matters. But how do you see this as a concern for the Sisterhood?"

"It seems to me that the Cinderfists are exactly the sort of trouble a servant of Cyric would foment among the poor outlanders of the town." Mirya paused, choosing her next words carefully. "I'd imagine that the hooded priest teaches the folk of the Tailings to rebel against their circumstances, to fight against their sorrows. Where would those folk turn if he were to leave? More than a few might seek comfort in the Lady's embrace, mightn't they?"

Sennifyr gazed thoughtfully at Mirya. "It pleases me to hear you speak so, Mirya."

"I'm weary of the troubles plaguing my home, Mistress Sennifyr. Someone is stoking the fires, and I want an end to it." Mirya didn't doubt that there would be trouble of a different sort if the Lady of Sorrows came to hold the hearts of Hulburg's poorest folk, but at least the Sisterhood wouldn't incite riots and rebellion in the streets. Besides, she was sure that she was not saying anything that hadn't occurred to Mistress Sennifyr already.

"The Sisterhood would approve," Sennifyr said. She took another sip from her cup and set it down in its saucer. "Very well. We have heard something of this. As you guess, a few of our Sisters are newcomers to Hulburg. They hear things from the other outlanders that the native-born do not. I think that one of them might know the man you encountered. I do not know who he is, but she might. Go to the Three Crowns and ask for Ingra."

"Thank you, Mistress Sennifyr."

"It is nothing, dear Mirya. But you must go in secret. Ingra will help another Sister, but only if no one sees her to do so."

"I understand." Mirya stood and inclined her head to Sennifyr, who returned a gracious nod.

"I hope you will visit again soon, Mirya. I know in my heart that the Lady's full purpose for you is still to be revealed." Sennifyr stood and watched as the servant returned to show Mirya to the door.

After the gloom of Sennifyr's house, the overcast day seemed clean and whole to Mirya. She drew a deep breath and climbed back up to the seat of her wagon. She thought now that it would have been better if she hadn't come, but she'd done it, and there was nothing to be gained by second-guessing her decision now. The only question was whether she'd find an answer at the Three Crowns worth the price of reminding Sennifyr and the Sisterhood that she remembered them.

TEN

2 Marpenoth, the Year of the Ageless One (1479 DR)

Narsk set his course eastward from the meeting at the Talons, swinging far out to sea around Hillsfar then closing on the Moonsea's southern coastline once the well-defended port was a good thirty or forty miles astern. *Moonshark* ran under a full spread of canvas by day, making good time. By night Narsk ordered Sorsil to take in sail and slow their pace, which was not unusual for ships sailing the Moonsea. For the most part the great lake was deep and uncluttered by islands or reefs, so most captains kept some sail on during all but the darkest of nights.

It proved much harder to find an opportunity to slip into Narsk's cabin than Geran would have imagined. The chief difficulty was that Narsk rarely left his cabin and did not linger for long on the deck when he did. The gnoll took all his meals in his room and issued most of his orders through Sorsil. Geran had several ideas in mind for actually slipping inside without being seen, if Narsk would simply vacate his cabin for a decent amount of time; if nothing else, he knew a spell of teleportation he could use from the usually empty storeroom under the captain's cabin. He considered trying to surprise and overpower the gnoll by teleporting into the cabin without warning, but he couldn't be certain that he could do it in absolute silence and slip away again unseen. That meant he and his friends might have to deal with the rest of *Moonshark*'s crew, and Geran didn't care for the odds if it came to that.

While waiting and watching for the chance to move, Geran and his friends settled into the ship's routine. The weather turned cold and damp on their second night from the Talons, and the ship slipped through intermittent showers as she continued eastward. As the newest hands on board, they were assigned to the midwatch under the second mate, a portly Mulmasterite named Khefen. That meant they had to stand watch in the middle of the night and catch what little sleep they could before and after. At least Khefen was more or less indifferent to the three of them, so long as they didn't bungle the few adjustments to the sails he saw fit to make during the night. The second mate drank steadily from a large leather flask he kept hidden under his cloak throughout the watch, without showing any sign of growing drunk, and ignored the deckhands otherwise.

During their second midwatch with Khefen, the rains were especially persistent. After several hours of standing lookout and scrambling aloft when the second mate ordered them to, all three companions were soaked, shivering, and generally miserable.

"I am not enjoying this," Sarth muttered to Geran as they went back below. "Truly, is this necessary?"

"We'll give it two or three more days," Geran replied under his breath. "Something may turn up, and I'd still like to know what Kamoth is planning."

The tiefling grimaced under his magical guise. "Very well, but I will think twice before I accompany you on your next ill-considered venture."

Later that morning Geran was hard at work splicing an old, well-worn line—a particularly tedious and exacting job that the tattooed Northman Skamang had foisted off on him—when the cry of "Sail ho! Fine on the port beam!" came from the lookout aloft. He stood and shaded his eyes with his hand, looking for the other ship. This time it was indeed a fair distance off, easily seven or eight miles, and all that could be seen of it was the mast. Sorsil summoned Narsk to the quarterdeck, and the two conferred quickly before the gnoll ordered the helmsman to turn and sent the watch aloft to crowd on more sail. The wind favored *Moonshark;* by good fortune the pirate galley was well positioned to run down her quarry with the morning sun at her back and a freshening crosswind that let Narsk aim the galley's bow a little ahead of the other ship.

Geran glanced at the sky. It was overcast, but no storms or squalls seemed likely to appear. And they were at least thirty or forty miles from any sort of harbor. Unless the cog was faster than she looked, he guessed they'd catch her in a couple of hours. Most of the crew was gathered along the rail, gazing greedily at the other ship. Some were already picking out weapons for the anticipated boarding.

Hamil and Sarth climbed up from the galley, where they'd been sent to help Tao Zhe with his scullery work. The halfling looked around at the pirate crew then up at Geran. "What's going on?"

"Narsk's sighted prey," Geran said in a low voice. He pointed. "We're trying to chase down that cog there."

"Well, there it is," Hamil murmured after peering over the rail. *What do we do if Narsk catches her?* he asked. *Do we go along with the rest of the crew and keep to our ruse? Or do we interfere and keep Narsk from taking that ship?*

Geran looked down at his friend, brow creased in worry. "I don't know," he said. He should have anticipated they might find themselves in this very situation. He didn't doubt the three of them could find a way to fight ineffectively or hang back from the worst of what was coming, but their shipmates might notice, and that would do very little to advance their standing in the crew. More to the point, it would hardly absolve the three of them of responsibility for not thwarting a pirate attack that they were in position to foil. But it was hard to see how that wouldn't give away their ploy and bring their effort to infiltrate the Black Moon to an end.

Sarth glanced at Hamil; the ghostwise halfling was evidently repeating his question for the tiefling. Sarth looked around to see if any of the crew were in earshot and leaned on the rail beside Geran. "A difficult decision," he said. "I am not sure how to counsel you, Geran, but I suppose you could consider the matter in this way: What would have happened if we weren't aboard? If it seems that *Moonshark* would catch the merchant and take her without our help, our participation wouldn't change what fate had already intended for that ship. For that matter, it might not be in our power to prevent an attack. There are only three of us, after all. If we *can't* prevent Narsk from taking that ship, then we might as well maintain the ruse. What we learn here may save other lives on some other day."

"I hear you," Geran answered. "But, as it turns out—we *are* aboard and nothing is fated at the moment. Besides, we'd have the advantage of surprise and your magic as well. If we deal with a few key crewmen right at the outset, the rest might lose their nerve."

"I think I'm with Sarth on this," Hamil said softly. "I'm not anxious to pick a fight with fifty enemies for the sake of total strangers. But we might be able to interfere in another way. If the ship were to lose a sail or the rudder were to fail . . ."

"It will mean a fight if we are caught at it," Sarth answered.

Geran thought of what Nimessa had told him about the fate of *Whitewing*'s crew. If they stood aside or went along because the merchant was doomed anyway, they'd still be a party to the worst sort of murder. They *might* be able to defeat *Moonshark*'s crew by killing Narsk, Sorsil, and perhaps Skamang or Khefen quickly . . . but it was probably more likely that any such mad assault would succeed only in getting all three of them killed, and he was not any more eager than Hamil to lose his life for a handful of strangers.

"If we can keep Narsk and the rest of the cutthroats on this ship from murdering the crew and passengers of some hapless ship, I think we have to try," he said. "Hamil's suggestion has merit. We'll just have to make sure no one notices."

Over the next hour, *Moonshark* steadily closed on the cog. Geran was surprised to see that the merchant ship didn't try to flee, but instead kept to her original course. Either she hadn't noticed the pirate galley on her beam—which seemed more and more unlikely—or the captain blithely assumed that he sailed in friendly waters. He supposed it was possible that the merchant captain had already determined for himself that there was no escape and therefore hoped to bluff his way out of an attack by a simple show of boldness, but that struck him as even more unlikely. As the pirate galley slowly overtook the merchant cog, Geran and his comrades began to plan their act of sabotage.

They were well along in their planning, and the cog was a little less than a mile off, when Sorsil shouted down at the main deck from her position by the helm. "Back to your stations!" the first mate called. "Go on, you dogs! There's nothing for us here!"

Geran and his companions exchanged looks then turned to the quarterdeck. Narsk gripped the rail, glaring at the cog with his fangs bared. Then he snarled something to Sorsil and stormed off the quarterdeck, disappearing into his cabin once more. Sorsil took one more look at the cog then ordered the helmsman to turn away. *Moonshark* turned smartly to starboard and cut across the wake of the ship a mile astern of her, now running downwind.

"What in the world?" Geran asked aloud. "What was that about?" He heard a few murmurs from other crew too, likely expressing the same sentiment.

"Narsk gave up the pursuit," Sarth observed. "Why would he do that?"

"Look!" Hamil said. "The merchant's raised a pennant."

Geran turned back to the cog, now falling astern. A pennant floated in the breeze from the ship's mainmast; he was sure it hadn't been there a few minutes ago, so the cog's captain must have just ordered it flown. It was a quartered flag of red and gold, and Geran knew it well. "That's a House Marstel ship," he said.

"Marstel? As in the Marstels of Hulburg?" Sarth asked.

"Yes," Geran replied. "That double-dealing bastard! He's paid off the Black Moon to leave his ships alone. And he was the one who argued for the harmach to do something about piracy."

"Badgering the harmach to do something likely kept other merchant companies from making a deal with the pirates," Hamil said. "Lord Marstel's a sly old fox if that's the case. I never would have thought he had it in him."

“Nor would I,” Geran said. He frowned, trying to figure out what to make of it. Then the pirates crowded along the rail drifted back to their duties and the ship returned to its routine.

The crew’s disappointment at being turned away from a prize in their grasp likely accounted for what happened that evening. *Moonshark* was too small to have anything like a mess deck; the galley was located in the forecastle, and Tao Zhe, the cook, ladled the evening’s stew into whatever cup or bowl each man brought to him. After receiving warm food and a hunk of coarse bread, the deckhands retreated to whatever corner of the main deck they could find that offered shelter from the weather and a good place to sit and eat. Geran, Hamil, and Sarth had just settled down to their unappetizing meals when several crewmen belonging to Skamang’s fist sauntered up to them. A round-bellied Chessentan named Pareik, who shaved his head and wore large gold earrings, led the band. “Get up, new fish!” he snarled. “That’s our place you’re in.”

It looks like Skamang’s decided to try us out, Hamil observed. With a sigh, he carefully set his dinner on the deck.

“It suits me well enough,” Geran answered Pareik. It would have been easier to defer and avoid what was coming, but he suspected that he’d be at Skamang’s beck and call for the rest of the voyage if he did. Standing up to Pareik now and showing a quick and violent temper might save him no end of trouble later, as well as furthering their ruse. Besides, he was in a foul temper, and he didn’t like the look of the fellow. “Go find a different place.”

Pareik grinned. “So you’re too good to take your supper somewhere else,” he said. He slapped Geran’s dinner tin out of his hands, spilling the stew. “You can eat it off the deck, then! What do you think about that, new fish?”

Without a moment’s thought, Geran seized his dinner tin from the deck and leaped to his feet. He didn’t have to feign his anger; before he could think better of it, he threw the tin and the remaining stew in Pareik’s face. Pareik recoiled, belatedly raising his arms to defend himself, but Geran planted his boot at the Chessentan’s belt buckle and propelled him back across the deck. The pirate stumbled to the deck and rolled, fetching up against the opposite gunwale. "I think I'll knock out your damned teeth, that's what I think!" Geran snarled at him.

He took two steps toward Pareik, intending to administer the beating of a lifetime to the Chessentan, but heavy footsteps to his right caught his attention. The ogre Kronn stood close by, glaring down at him with his piggish little eyes. Behind him, the tattooed Northman Skamang sat watching with a small smile on his face. Kronn spoke in a rumbling voice. "You hidded Pareik," he said. "Thad mean any Skamang's fisd can hid you. Kronn belong Skamang's fisd. Kronn hid you!" The ogre lashed out with one enormous fist, mashing it straight down as if he meant to drive a nail into the deck.

Geran leaped backward out of the way, not with any particular grace. His old mentor Daried would have winced; he'd always said that Geran had the slow-footedness of any big human. The elf bladesinger could have evaded Kronn's fist with half a step and a twist of his shoulders. Hamil could have too. But Geran's off-balance jump was enough to get him out from under Kronn's blow. The ogre bellowed in annoyance and sprang after him; Geran skirted around the mainmast to put it between him and his foe, buying himself a moment to think.

Sarth and Hamil surged to their feet and moved forward to join the fray, while the rest of Pareik's little gang dropped their own suppers to the deck and stood their ground. But Murkelmor the dwarf moved between them and held up his hand. "None of that now!" he shouted. "Your man laid hands on one o' Skamang's fist, and Skamang's fist chose one o' their own t' answer him. It's the way it's done. Take another step, and it's a matter for th' captain t' settle!"

"I will not stand aside and watch that ogre bludgeon my friend!" Sarth snarled.

"You will if you know what's good for him an' for you," the dwarf answered. "Two men fight, it's between them. Any more join in, and th' captain has to put a stop to it."

"Stand your ground!" Geran shouted at Sarth. "Keep it between Kronn and me!" Geran had faced ogres before. They were immensely strong, and big enough to shrug off wounds that would have incapacitated a human opponent. But they were slow and lacked skill, relying entirely on their size and strength. With a sword in his hand he wouldn't have shied from a duel against Kronn. But he had only his bare hands for this fight.

He circled the mainmast again. Kronn went low and lunged forward, and this time the ogre managed to catch hold of Geran's ankle. He yanked Geran's foot out from under him and dragged the swordmage across the deck, raising one meaty fist to crush Geran while he had hold of him. Geran tried to wrench his foot out of the ogre's grasp and failed. In desperation he used the ogre's grip to anchor his left leg while he scissored up with his right. He caught the ogre on the point of his heavy jaw with a strong kick, spoiling Kronn's aim. Kronn's fist mostly missed him as it crashed into his ribs, batting him down to the deck again. Geran's breath left him in a whooshing exhalation, and he gasped for air, but before Kronn could finish him with a solid punch, he drove his right heel into the meaty paw gripping his ankle and bent the ogre's thumb in a direction it was not supposed to go. Kronn howled, and Geran scrambled free, still trying to find his breath.

"Keep after him, Kronn!" Pareik cried. "You almost had him there!"

"Don't let the ogre grab you like that!" Hamil shouted at Geran.

"Never . . . would've . . . thought of that," Geran wheezed. Kronn lunged for him again, and this time he threw himself under the ogre's long arms and drove his head into Kronn's gut. The ogre lost his breath this time, and before he recovered Geran threw several wild uppercuts under Kronn's chin. It was like punching a bull; the ogre's head barely moved. The blows had little effect other than enraging Kronn, and Geran quickly backed away again as Kronn swung wildly and stumbled to one knee. A reckless idea struck Geran, and he paused just in front of the mainmast as the ogre wound up for another punch. This time the swordmage stayed still until the very last instant before dropping to the deck under the punch. Instead of pulping Geran's head like a melon, Kronn drove his fist into the mainmast.

The whole mast shuddered, but not even an ogre could damage it with a punch; he howled and clutched his mashed knuckles. "Kronn *kill* you for thad!" the ogre roared.

Geran rolled away across the deck and regained his feet. But Kronn seized a heavy block and chain from its place by the mainmast, wielding the wooden pulley like a crude flail. He lashed out furiously at Geran, each whistling blow smashing splinters from the deck or crashing against mast and gunwale. Corsairs gathered around to watch the brawl yelped in alarm and scrambled back out of the way, although one unfortunate fellow caught the heavy block high on his shoulder on Kronn's backswing and was knocked spinning to the deck. Geran wheeled from side to side, searching for a weapon of his own. He didn't know what the Black Moon had to say about weapons in a brawl, but he'd have to deal with that later. First he had to avoid getting killed.

Dagger coming! Hamil warned him. Geran looked back over to his friend just in time to catch the heavy poniard Hamil tossed to him. It was not much of a defense against Kronn's overwhelming strength and reach, but the feel of steel in his hand was reassuring. He realized that, oddly enough, he was now in the exact position Hamil was whenever the two of them sparred. He was facing a bigger, stronger, slower opponent with much greater reach. And that meant he had to get in close without getting killed.

What would Hamil do in this sort of fight? he wondered. The answer came to him quickly; he'd watched Hamil fight enough times to guess how his friend might handle a big, clumsy foe. A smile flickered across his face as he ducked under another swing of the block and circled to his right, moving next to the mainmast again. "Come on, Kronn! Can't you hit me?" he taunted.

The ogre howled in fury and lashed out again—but Geran ducked to the other side of the mast. The block and chain wrapped around the mainmast, momentarily entangled, and he made his move. He dashed forward up under Kronn's guard and slashed the ogre several times across the belly and chest, holding back from a mortal thrust simply because he didn't know what would happen if he actually killed his opponent. When Kronn threw up his left arm to shove Geran away, he laid open the ogre's forearm from wrist to elbow. Blood splattered the deck, and the ogre cried out in pain. Then he let go of the block and chain and fell back on his broad bottom, shielding himself with his arms.

Geran stepped closer to strike again, but Narsk suddenly appeared on the main deck, brandishing a mace with a spiked head. "Damn the lot of you! What is going on here?" the gnoll roared. Geran quickly backed away from his foe.

"The new man shoved me to the deck and cut up Kronn when he stood up for me," Pareik said quickly. "He would've killed Kronn, Captain!"

"Skamang's man started it!" Hamil retorted. "He knocked Aram's dinner to the deck, looking for a fight. He's damned lucky Aram didn't kill him for it."

"He's lying! The halfling's a liar!" several of Skamang's supporters shouted. Hamil surged forward to answer them, but Sarth restrained him.

The gnoll captain snarled in anger. He might not have had any reason to care what happened to his new crewmen, but at least he seemed to know Skamang, Kronn, and their gang well enough to guess what had happened. He stalked over to where Kronn crouched groaning on the deck, hands clamped around his midsection. "Who drew the first weapon?" the gnoll demanded.

The ogre looked up at Narsk. "Kronn dint do nuttin', Cap'n. Th' new fellah jusd wend mad. He cutted Kronn. Thad's th' troot!"

Narsk swore and wheeled back on Geran, his mace clenched in his hairy paw. He loomed over Geran, his canine fangs bared. "And I suppose you'll tell me you were willing to fight the ogre with your empty hands until he armed himself?"

Geran met his gaze without flinching. "None of this was my idea, Captain. The ogre took the block off the mainmast. I had to defend myself."

Sorsil cleared her thoat and looked over to the dwarf

Murkelmor, who sat on a cask, watching the whole scene. "Did you see what happened, dwarf?" she demanded.

Murkelmor shrugged. "Pareik picked a fight with Aram, and when Aram took him up on it, he had Kronn t' step in for him. I'm guessing that Kronn's no' so happy with the whole business now." He paused and then added, "Kronn was th' first to arm himself."

Narsk turned away, still muttering to himself. Geran watched him carefully, poniard still in his hand, steeling himself in case the gnoll turned back and swung at him. He'd kill Narsk if he had to, and damn the consequences. But the gnoll looked down at Kronn instead. "You're beaten, you fat oaf. Is this done, or do you and Aram go on until one of you is dead? It seems to me that won't be Aram."

"It's over, Captain," Skamang said. The Northman gave the ogre a stern look. "Kronn won't trouble him again."

"Is that so, Kronn?" Narsk asked.

The ogre looked at Skamang then nodded. "Kronn say it done."

"Then get up and get someone to stitch you back together," the gnoll snarled. He looked at the assembled deckhands and waved his hand angrily. "Back to work, all of you!"

Kronn slowly got up, still bleeding profusely. He gave Geran one sullen, hate-filled glare then shuffled back toward Skamang and his gang. Geran watched him just in case he had any thought of a sudden rush and only rejoined Sarth and Hamil when he felt safe in turning his back on his adversary. He handed the poniard back to the halfling. "My thanks," he said.

Hamil glanced toward the ogre on the other side of the deck. "You'd better keep it. I've got a couple of spares."

Sarth looked closely at Geran. "How badly are you hurt? Do you need help?"

Geran felt his ribs with a wince. "I'm well enough," he managed. He discovered that he ached all over, in fact—his ribs, his left ankle, his right foot from kicking the ogre's thick jaw, even his back from being thrown (or throwing himself) on the deck. "If you're so concerned, next time I'll allow you to fight the ogre. That seems to be the way it's done."

The sorcerer surprised him with a sudden laugh. "I will bear that in mind," he said. "But I doubt you'll be troubled for a while. You bested Kronn, and that should earn you no small respect from the rest of the crew."

"Narsk too," Hamil said in a low voice. He nodded at the quarterdeck, where the gnoll paced. His red eyes, narrowed with thought, were fixed on Geran. Narsk watched them a moment longer, then he descended from the quarterdeck and ducked into his cabin again.

"He suspects something," said Sarth.

Geran gazed at the cabin door. He still needed to find out what it was that Kamoth had given Narsk. And they were another day closer to whatever event the pirate lord had in mind. "We can't do much about it," he answered. He picked up his dinner tin from the deck, trying not to wince as his injured ribs protested. "Come on—I want to see if Tao Zhe has anything left in the galley, since Pareik and Kronn spoiled my supper."

ELEVEN

4 Marpenoth, the Year of the Ageless One (1479 DR)

Geran soon learned how much he'd risen in the estimation of the rest of the crew. Early the next morning, as he once again aided Tao Zhe with the scullery work, Murkelmor wandered over and took a seat on a hatch cover, watching him scrub. The dour dwarf studied him for a long time without speaking, busying himself by scraping out the caked soot from a worn old pipe.

"If you're interested in the pots, you can find yourself a brush and pitch in," Geran finally said.

Murkelmor made no move to help him, but gave him a humorless smile. "That was a fine brawl yesterday," he said. "No one's ever bested Kronn wi' nought but bare hands. Never thought I'd see it happen, neither."

"It might've gone the other way if Dagger hadn't thrown me his knife."

"Aye, but you held your own until th' ogre gave your friend a reason to help." Murkelmor leaned forward. "You're a stout fighter, no doubt of it, and maybe the other two as well, but three's not enough to watch each other's backs. You'll be needin' more allies, Aram."

Geran stopped scrubbing and straightened up. There were three more dwarves on board. Murkelmor and fellows formed a tight, close-mouthed gang, watching out for each other. And he'd seen that several of the human crewmen—mostly Teshans, men and women of the Moonsea lands—stayed close to the dwarves. Murkelmor's gang numbered eight or nine crewmen, then, and the addition of Geran and his companions would strengthen it significantly. "Allies we're happy to have," he said after a moment's thought. "But we're not looking for a master. I'm my own man."

"I hear you," the dwarf allowed. "I speak for me fist more often than not, but I'm no petty king like Skamang. I'll not try to tell you what to do. An ally's good enough for me. Keep an eye out for me lads, and we'll do the same for you."

"Done," Geran told him. He'd have to talk it over with Hamil and Sarth, but Murkelmor was exactly the sort of ally the three of them were looking for. The dwarf nodded in approval and ambled off.

On the evening of the fifth, two days after Geran's duel with Kronn, *Moonshark* rowed into the walled harbor of Mulmaster a little before sunset. The reek of scores of forges and foundries hung in the steep streets and clung to the rooftops; like most of the other Moonsea settlements, Mulmaster was a city that thrived on ironwork and the mining of precious metals from the mountains nearby. A different collection of merchant ships rocked softly in the swell, but otherwise little had changed in the harbor since Geran's previous visit aboard *Seadrake.*

"Mulmaster again," Hamil noted as they pulled their oar at a quarter-beat. "Well, now we know that at least one Black Moon ship calls here. One of those fellows we talked to a few days ago lied to us."

"Possibly," Geran said. "But it might be true that *Kraken Queen* herself hasn't been here. Maybe Kamoth sends other ships to run his errands in the larger ports."

It came as no surprise to Geran that no alarm attended the arrival of *Moonshark* in the city's harbor. A harbormaster approached in a rowboat and hailed the ship as the galley glided into the city's narrow bay. Narsk remained out of sight, but Sorsil spoke with the man and passed him a small bribe. With that business concluded, the harbormaster directed *Moonshark* to a vacant spot along the city's stone quay and departed. Sorsil took the helm herself and steered the corsair ship expertly to the quay, where the deckhands made her fast to the pier with four heavy lines.

As soon as the ship was tied up, Narsk emerged from his cabin, dressed in a heavy, hooded cloak that shadowed his bestial features. A small number of the so-called savage races could be found in any large city in Faerûn, but most of those would be goblins or orcs—a gnoll couldn't help but attract attention. He picked out several deckhands of Skamang's fist as the men were securing the ship and growled, "You three, arm yourselves and come with me. I have business ashore. Sorsil, let no one else leave the ship before I return. I will not be long."

"Aye, Captain," the mate replied. She took up a post by the gangplank as Narsk and his guards swept down the ramp and headed off into the town.

Geran watched the gnoll disappear into the narrow streets as Hamil and Sarth worked to secure the ship's oars. "I think this is my opportunity," he said to his companions. "If I'm ever going to get a look inside Narsk's cabin, now is the time."

"Agreed," Hamil said. "The plan we talked about?"

Geran nodded. "We'd better move fast. I don't think Narsk will be away from the ship for long."

Hamil climbed up to the quarterdeck and began to occupy himself by coiling lines there. His real job was to serve as the lookout and warn Geran if anyone was coming. Geran and Sarth headed below to the midships crew quarters and from there worked their way aft to the storeroom directly beneath Narsk's cabin. Sarth closed the door behind them and set his back to it. He was also a lookout. Geran needed the storeroom to stay empty, and it was Sarth's job to make sure that no other crewmember wandered in at some inopportune time. "You understand that we may have to fight our way off the ship if this goes poorly?" the tiefling asked.

"I know it," Geran answered. Still, this was the first chance he'd seen in days to find out what was in the letter pouch that Sergen had handed to Narsk. He only hoped that the gnoll hadn't taken it with him when he went ashore.

Before he could begin to second-guess the plan, he focused his mind into the still, silent readiness he'd learned under the leaves of Myth Drannor. He brought to the forefront of his thoughts the mystic words of the teleportation spell, sensing the power locked within the arcane syllables. He drew Hamil's poniard with his right hand and held it at the ready, just in case he was about to find himself in the middle of a fight. Then the swordmage hurled the force of his will into the arcane syllables fixed in his mind as he spoke a single word in Elvish: *"Seiroch!"*

There was a dizzying instant of darkness, a sense of bitter cold, and Geran found himself standing in the cabin directly above the place where he'd been standing in the storeroom. He turned quickly, dagger held before him, but there was no one else in the room. Narsk's cabin was empty for the moment. With a small sigh of relief, he sheathed the poniard and studied his surroundings more carefully.

The cabin was dark and cluttered, and a heavy animal smell lingered in the air. Geran wrinkled his nose in distaste; Narsk was none too tidy in his living arrangements. He realized that he'd need a little light to see by, so he took a copper coin out of his pocket and quietly murmured the words of a light spell. The coin began to glow with a bright, warm light; Geran quickly wrapped it in a bit of scrap cloth to mute its brightness as much as he could. He didn't want it shining from the row of windows across the stern end of the cabin. By the dim light, he studied his surroundings. Discarded clothing lay strewn where Narsk had dropped it, plates with the half-eaten remains of old suppers, and an assortment of odd baubles—gold goblets, pearl-handled cutlery, small idols, and other such things likely gleaned from the pillage of a dozen ships—lay scattered about, along with what seemed to be half an armory's worth of weapons.

"Now where did Narsk put that pouch?" Geran asked softly. He moved over to the small desk in the cabin and searched through the old charts and cargo manifests strewn there. Just like the baubles of gold and gems that were lying around the cabin, they'd probably been seized from *Moonshark*'s prizes too.

Finding nothing there, Geran rifled through the desk drawers. Then he moved to the bookshelves—hard to believe that Narsk was literate; he'd never heard of a gnoll who could read—but found nothing there. With a sinking feeling, he realized he'd have to seriously search the cabin.

It took him a quarter hour, but he finally found the leather pouch underneath Narsk's mattress. Hoping that the master of the ship was going to be tied up in his business ashore for a while longer, Geran sat down at the desk and carefully drew out the pouch's contents: two letters on parchment, one short, the other long. He looked at the short letter first. It read:

Narsk:

Proceed to Mulmaster, making port no later than the 5th of Marpenoth. Go to the concession of the Red Wizards and ask for Iomauld. Tell Iomauld that you have come for the starry compass and that the High Captain will arrange payment as is customary. Iomauld will explain the device's operation to you. Install the compass and proceed to the rendezvous. If the Red Wizards desire immediate payment, pay them whatever they ask for the compass. I will compensate you. If the starry compass is not available or you run into some other difficulty, then do not linger in Mulmaster. You must be at the rendezvous without fail.

Kamoth

"'Starry compass'? What is that?" Geran wondered. Some sort of magical device, it seemed. The Red Wizards were known as purveyors of enchanted items. Their fortresslike concessions were scattered throughout the cities of the Inner Sea, forbidding places where the mysterious expatriates of old Thay wove their sinister spells for anyone who could afford their services. In any event, that was likely what Narsk was doing this very moment ashore.

Geran set that letter aside and picked up the second letter. He'd just unfolded it when he heard Hamil's voice in his mind: *Narsk is returning, Geran! You'd better hurry up in there.*

"Damn it all," Geran muttered to himself. Quickly he skimmed the second letter:

Narsk:

No later than three hours after sunset on the 7th of Marpenoth, bring Moonshark *to a point three miles south of the ruins of* Seawave, *on the shoreline twenty-five miles west of Hulburg. There will be a large bonfire ashore to aid in navigating to the rendezvous. Do not arrive too early, since we do not want the fleet to be spotted as it assembles. Stand off well out to sea until after dark if you need to. Once the Black Moon is gathered together, we will proceed to Hulburg and attack the city in the early hours of the 8th. Your assignment is to land* Moonshark*'s crew on the wharves by the House Sokol concession. This is the westernmost of the merchant tradeyards in the city, hard by the bluffs of Keldon Head.* Wyvern *will make her landing on the Double Moon wharves immediately to your right.*

Your crew is to burn the Council Hall, where Hulburg's Merchant Council meets. After that, they are free to slay, pillage, or burn as they please. There will be Black Moon men posted in front of places that are not to be harmed; make sure that your crew knows to listen to any man wearing a black armband. The rest of the town and its folk are yours to do with as you please.

All Black Moon ships will withdraw together at sunrise, unless the High Captain personally instructs you otherwise. Make sure your crew understands that stragglers will be left behind. If you are in possession of the starry compass, you will accompany Kraken Queen *to Neshuldaar—it is the eleventh islet. Otherwise, you are to make for the River Lis and the Inner Sea.*

No pirate has ever assembled a five-ship raid in the Moonsea. Strike hard, strike fast, and the harmach's men will never know what hit them.

Kamoth

"Merciful Ilmater," Geran breathed. The Black Moon intended to attack Hulburg, and only four days from now! With five ships they could easily carry five or six hundred men. Given the advantage of surprise, they could cause unimaginable damage. Somehow he had to find a way to warn Harmach Grigor. The corsairs expected to strike a sleeping town without any idea that danger approached from the sea, but if the harmach called out the Spearmeet and mustered the merchant company armsmen to meet the pirate attack on the wharves, Hulburg might drive off the Black Moon with little harm.

Geran, Narsk is coming up the gangplank! Hamil shouted in his mind. *You have to get out of there now!*

Geran stuffed the two letters back into the pouch and then put the pouch back under the mattress where he'd found it. He could hear Narsk's snarling voice just outside the cabin door. He took one quick look around the cabin to make sure he hadn't left anything obviously out of place, then jammed the coin with the light spell back into his pocket and cleared his mind. The key rattled in the lock as he closed his eyes and whispered, *"Seiroch!"*

There was an instant of icy blackness, and then he stumbled as he appeared in the darkness of the hold beneath Narsk's cabin. Sarth reached out to catch him by the arm and steady him. "I'm here, Geran," the tiefling whispered. "Did you find Kamoth's instructions?"

"I did." Geran started to say more, but then he heard the door in the cabin above creak open and Narsk's footsteps overhead. The gnoll's harness jingled, and he heard the muffled sounds of something heavy tossed onto the bunk, followed by a cloak dropped to the floor. Then Narsk paused and snarled low in his throat like an angry wolf. Quick footsteps crisscrossed the cabin several times, then they heard the gnoll hurry back out to the deck.

"Did you leave something behind?" Sarth asked Geran.

"I don't think so. But I must have left something out of place." He grimaced. It couldn't be helped now. All they could do was rejoin the crew and try to behave innocently.

They picked up casks of salted pork from the storeroom and carried them through the midships crew quarters—where they passed several of their crewmates—forward to the galley. Tao Zhe was not there; Geran breathed a sigh of relief. He hadn't really come up with a good reason why he and Sarth would bring the Shou cook something he hadn't asked for yet, but they had to have some reason for being in the storeroom under the captain's quarters.

They climbed back up onto the main deck and found Hamil waiting for them there. "Trouble," Hamil said quietly. *I think Narsk has got your scent.*

"My scent?" Geran looked back toward the captain's cabin. Narsk was standing just outside the door, sniffing the air. Geran had no idea how keen a gnoll's sense of smell was, but given Narsk's hyena-like muzzle, he had to believe it was sharper than his own. The question was, did he have enough of Geran's scent to identify him or not?

"If you found what you needed in Narsk's cabin, this may be the right time to jump ship," Sarth murmured. "What more do we have to gain by remaining on board?"

Geran thought quickly. He needed to find a way to warn Hulburg about what was coming. That was the foremost consideration. He'd like to find out more about the starry compass and what it was for, or continue his corsair career and see what more he could learn about the Black Moon Brotherhood, but those were secondary goals. He looked over to Hamil and asked, "Did Narsk bring anything aboard when he returned? Maybe a parcel of some kind?"

"Yes, something about the size of a hatbox. I thought it strange that he carried it instead of giving it to one of the men who went with him. Why, what is it?"

"I think it's something called a starry compass. It may be important." Geran turned to Sarth next. "Do you know any sending spells?" he asked.

"I do not have my tomes with me," the tiefling answered. "They are still aboard *Seadrake.*"

"Then we have to remain aboard *Moonshark.* The Black Moon ships are gathering to attack Hulburg two days from now. We won't find any vessel that will get us to Hulburg faster than that. Somehow we will have to find a way to warn the harmach that the Black Moon is coming."

Hamil winced. "That's not much of a warning. Won't we get to Hulburg at the same time that the other Black Moon ships do?"

"We might find some way to warn Hulburg of our presence," Geran said. "If nothing else, Sarth might be able to go ahead and provide at least a few minutes' warning."

"In that event, it seems that we're continuing as corsairs for a little longer," Sarth said. "And that means we have to throw off Narsk's suspicions. We have to hide your scent somehow, Geran. How, I don't know."

"Sorsil! Assemble the crew," Narsk shouted. "I want every hand before the mainmast now!"

"Aye, Captain!" the first mate replied. She started bellowing for the deckhands to muster on the main deck.

Geran stood petrified for a moment. He was certain that he needed to stay on board, but if Narsk could tell he'd been in his cabin . . .

"Quickly, Geran!" Hamil said. "Go below to Sarth's locker. Change into his spare clothes, and dump what you're wearing over the side. It may reduce your scent."

It was worth a try. Geran retreated into the galley and from there went belowdecks to the midships crew quarters. His fellow deckhands were complaining as they clambered out of their bunks and made their way up to the main deck; no one paid much attention to him. He found Sarth's locker, grabbed a tunic and a pair of breeches, and returned to the galley. He stripped, splashed himself with water from the large cask there and scrubbed briefly with a handful of scouring sand Tao Zhe kept in a bucket, and dressed in Sarth's clothing. He crept back up to the main deck, where most of the ship's company was assembled, and threw his own clothes over the side before he went to join the rest of the deckhands.

Sorsil spied him trying to slip into the rear of the assembled crew. The fierce first mate stepped over and struck him across the arm with her truncheon. "Laggard!" she snapped. "Next time don't be the last man to muster!"

Geran saw stars. Holding his arm, he glared after Sorsil, but the first mate had already moved on. Maybe it would have been better to jump ship in Mulmaster after all, he thought.

Before he could rethink his plan, Narsk moved slowly into the middle of the deckhands. "Keep silent and hold still," the gnoll growled. He went from person to person, towering over most of them, his red eyes gleaming ferally in the lanternlight. He sniffed audibly from time to time, pausing in front of some and then moving on. Geran tried to will himself to calmness. If he allowed himself to start sweating, he would lose the temporary benefit of donning Sarth's clothing. But he kept his hand close to the hilt of the poniard Hamil had given him, just in case.

Narsk reached him and sniffed several times. Geran met his eyes without flinching. Narsk didn't expect him to act like he was afraid, so he didn't. The gnoll narrowed his eyes and asked, "Where were you, Aram?"

"In the galley. I wanted something to eat."

The gnoll studied him for a moment longer then moved on. Geran kept himself from sighing in relief. When the gnoll finished with the crew, he paced back toward the quarterdeck, muttering to himself.

Geran noticed his fellow deckhands exchanging puzzled looks. No doubt they were wondering what in the world Narsk was looking for, but they kept their thoughts to themselves. He looked over to Hamil and Sarth and found them looking back at him. That had been too close.

"Sorsil, make rrready to sail," Narsk snarled at his first mate. "We are leaving now."

A mutter ran through the crew, and Sorsil looked as if she intended to protest before thinking better of it. Few ships left harbor after dark; in the first place it was usually better to have daylight for the careful piloting necessary to navigate close to shore, but more importantly crews expected opportunities to go ashore and spend their hard-earned coin on whores and drink. *Moonshark's* crew was chafing for the chance to escape the ship for a time, and Narsk was denying them their sport. Of course, they didn't know what Geran knew—the gnoll captain had an appointment to keep in the waters near Hulburg in just two days' time.

In a quarter hour, Sorsil gave the order to cast off, and the crew manned the rowing benches again. The waning moon peeked through a high overcast as they rowed quietly out of Mulmaster's harbor; for once the first mate didn't snarl and shout at the deckhands at their oars. They rowed until they were a good two miles clear of the harbor mouth, then Sorsil ordered the crew to ship and stow oars. "Stay at your benches, and shut your mouths!" she told the deckhands. "The captain wants to speak."

Narsk stood on the short ladder leading to the quarterdeck. The gnoll bared his fangs in what passed for a smile on his canine visage. "It's time to tell you where we sail!" he said. "At sunset the day after tomorrow, we'll be three miles off the rrruins of Seawave. There we'll meet *Kraken Queen, Wyvern, Daring,* and *Seawolf.* All five Black Moon ships assembled together in a single fleet! Together we'll set our course eastward and attack the town of Hulburg in the dark watches of the night!"

The deckhands around Geran raised a hearty cheer at that. Somewhat belatedly, Geran remembered to join in, thrusting his fist into the air. Narsk continued: "We're to burn the city's Council Hall, and then we're free to do as we please. I mean to fill the hold with loot and captives! Every dog among you will be rrrich—if you're rrready to take what you want from those fat, stupid townsfolk!" That brought another cheer.

Narsk grinned again. "The Hulburgans won't want to be parted from their trrreasures," he said. "Once they rrrealize what's happening, they'll try to fight us off. So stay away from the drink, go in groups of five or more, and kill anyone you come across. We can loot and drink all we want *after* the fighting's done, but we've a battle to win first. Umberlee help the dog who comes back to my ship without blood on his sword!"

The pirate crew roared their approval again. The gnoll laughed savagely. "The night after next! Hulburg won't forget the name of *Moonshark* for many a year, that I promise you!" He waved his hairy paw in salute then dropped down the last few steps of the ladder and left Sorsil to dismiss the crew.

Hamil twisted in his bench to look back at Geran. *Well, there it is,* the halfling said silently. *How are we going to stop this, Geran?*

The swordmage looked at the pirates swarming over the deck, already boasting to each other about what they were going to do in Hulburg. He frowned and met Hamil's eyes, the only way that the halfling could hear his thoughts in return. *I don't see any way around it,* he answered. *Tomorrow night we'll have to get to Hulburg, if we have to seize the ship and sail her there ourselves.*

TWELVE

5 Marpenoth, the Year of the Ageless One (1479 DR)

The night air was cool and damp around Rhovann Disarnnyl as he flew above the roofs of Hulburg's wretched Tailings. He remained in the guise of Lastannor, the Turmishan mage who advised Lord Maroth Marstel, and as he arrowed through the dark sky a long, hooded brown cassock fluttered behind him. Ironically he'd invested enough time and effort into cultivating Lastannor's place in this miserable human town that he couldn't allow Lastannor to be seen going from the Marstel villa to the place he was going. Therefore he'd made use of a spell of flying to leave his quarters in Maroth Marstel's house unseen by any on the ground, and intended to return the same way later.

Few folk were out and about at this hour, and he was fairly certain that no one would notice a silent, dark shape overhead, not when the guttering yellow streetlamps scattered here and there through the streets below obscured sight of what moved overhead. Rhovann crisscrossed the Tailings for a moment just to be sure of his bearings then he descended toward the building he sought. Without a sound he dropped down out of the night sky into the lightless alleyway behind the ramshackle inn and taphouse he was looking for. He looked around carefully, aware that robbers and thieves sometimes lurked in this very alleyway to prey upon the drunken patrons of the taphouse.

For now, it seemed that he had the alley to himself. The reek of garbage and emptied chamberpots was thick in his nostrils, and he scowled. Humans—the poor ones, anyway—were a filthy race, at least by the standards he was accustomed to. Elves would never have permitted such a thing in one of their cities. Not for the first time, Rhovann cursed the misfortunes that had joined his fate to crude, boorish, stinking humans rather than the cultured *Tel'Quessir* among whom he belonged. It would have been better to raise a lonely tower in some remote wilderness and live as a recluse than to accept permanent exile among the towns and cities of humankind. Once he brought about Geran Hulmaster's downfall, he might choose that very course of action.

With a sigh, he picked his way out of the alleyway, turned to his left, and made his way into the inn's front door. Above the door a battered old wooden signboard showed a faded painting of three golden crowns above crossed swords. Rhovann glanced up and down the street then went inside. The taproom adjoined the foyer, and through the heavy wooden beams of the open doorway, he could see dozens of humans engaged in drinking themselves into a stupor with the worst sort of swill he could imagine. Some looked up as he entered, but he was well hidden in his voluminous cloak. Only a shadowed wedge of coarse brown skin showed beneath the cowl, along with a wiry gray beard cut in the distinctively squared-off style favored in Turmish.

Rhovann found one of the serving maids hurrying past and stopped her with a touch of his hand. "A friend expects me," he said in a low voice. "It would be a private room. Where does he wait?"

The serving-maid looked up at him, and a shadow of fear flickered over her face. She quickly brought her knuckle to her forehead and averted her eyes. "If you please, this way, m'lord," she said. She led him back through the taphouse to a small dining room behind the common room, knocked, then let Rhovann into the room. Inside, a pale human with a patch of yellow-gray beard under his mouth waited by one end of the table, dressed in the tunic of a workman. "Your guest is here, m'lord," the serving maid said.

"Excellent," the pale man replied. "Bring us a flagon of your very best wine, my dear. None of that swill you normally serve, mind you; we are gentlemen of discriminating tastes."

"As you wish, m'lord." The servant bobbed her head and withdrew.

Rhovann stepped into the room, pulling the sliding door closed behind him. "Could you have found a more squalid tavern for our meeting, Valdarsel?"

"I know it's not much, but they know me here," the pale man replied. He offered a humorless smile. "The proprietor impresses me with the zeal of his service to the Black Sun. Inspired by his example—or, perhaps, simply fearful of losing their employment—his people do Cyric's work readily enough. They understand my requirements, and they are careful to meet them. And, speaking of my requirements . . ."

Rhovann reached into his cassock and drew out a small leather pouch that jingled softly. He set it on the table and slid it over to the Cyricist priest, who weighed it in his hand then tugged the drawstring open to peer inside. The mage was all but certain that Valdarsel was in fact already in the pay of some other power with an interest in Hulburg, but he was prepared to pretend otherwise if the Cyricist thought it important. Besides, what did he care about Marstel's money?

"It is the customary sum," Rhovann told him. "Count it if you like."

"I will later," Valdarsel answered. He tied the pouch closed and slipped it under his own tunic. "My thanks, good mage. This should allow me to recruit and arm another fifty Cinderfists, although I'll likely need to bring some in from the nearby cities. Naturally, I will see to it that the Cinderfists cause no difficulties for House Marstel."

"Naturally, although the time may come when I ask you to arrange for some selective damage to befall unimportant Marstel assets. It wouldn't do for my lord's properties to remain completely untouched by your mob. Some might grow suspicious."

"A wise precaution," the Cyricist remarked. "Let me know when and where you would like the Cinderfists to strike."

There was a knock at the door behind him. The serving maid

slid it open and carried in a tray loaded with a jug of wine, two goblets, a loaf of black bread, and a wedge of cheese. She set it on the table between the two men, poured wine in both goblets, then curtsied and withdrew. Rhovann waited for the door to slide shut before continuing.

"I have news that will interest you," he said. "Sometime after midnight two nights from now, the Black Moon Brotherhood will attack Hulburg. I understand that it will be a large raid, the greatest pirate raid in the Moonsea in a hundred years—five ships full of corsairs. I expect that they will cause much damage to the neighborhoods close to the harbor."

Valdarsel stared at him for a moment before leaning back in his chair with his goblet of wine. "Indeed," he murmured. "Have your magical divinations shown you this danger descending on the city?"

Rhovann smiled. "If you would like to think so."

"And what leads you to provide me with warning of the attack?"

"In the wake of a devastating raid, there will be outrage and recriminations. The harmach's inability to adequately defend Hulburg from the depredations of the Moonsea pirates will be plain for all to see. I wish the Cinderfists to run amok in the days following the raid, Valdarsel. Riot in the streets and scream for Harmach Grigor's head." Rhovann raised his own goblet and sipped at his wine. He heard the serving maid hurry past in the hall outside, her footsteps light on the floorboards, while in the common room of the inn someone began to strum a lute with little skill. "With the rule of House Hulmaster shown to be fatally weak and incompetent, the Merchant Council will have no choice but to wrest power from the harmach. The Cinderfists will enthusiastically support this measure, of course. Should the harmach resist, the combined might of the Merchant Council and the Cinderfists will force him out."

Valdarsel nodded to himself, his eyes focused on the events Rhovann outlined. "It is easy to see what Lord Marstel gets from all this," he said, "but it seems to me that the poor, honest outlanders of the Tailings and the foundries will simply exchange one master for another. The Cinderfists may go along with the idea of overthrowing an incompetent government, but they'll turn against your council next. I have to have something more to satisfy the rabble."

Rhovann shrugged. "Doubtless there will be Hulmaster loyalists remaining among the population after the harmach has been dismissed, especially among the so-called native Hulburgans who own most of the land in these parts. As those people are found to be conspiring to overthrow the council and restore the rule of the harmach, the council can deal sternly with them and confiscate their property. Reward citizens loyal to the council with Hulburgan land and goods, and I think you'll find that the Cinderfists may become enthusiastic supporters of the new regime."

"It wouldn't take much for a wealthy Hulburgan to be found to be resisting the council's authority, would it?"

"Some semblance of procedure should probably be followed," Rhovann replied.

"Oh, of course." Valdarsel grinned like a wolf. "It is said that wizards are subtle and dangerous, Lastannor. In your case, that strikes me as an understatement. A plan such as you propose warms the Black Prince's heart, it truly does."

Rhovann inclined his head, acknowledging what the Cyricist intended as a compliment. It was possible that the Merchant Council alone might suffice to oust the harmach in the wake of the Black Moon raid, but he needed to make sure that the Cinderfists would not interfere. In truth, he could not care less what became of the city or Valdarsel's ragged mob once the Hulmasters were dealt with. He expected to shake the dust of Hulburg from his boots and never look back. Leaving the town to be torn apart among an idiot like Maroth Marstel, a viper such as Valdarsel, and the desperate gangs of foreigners who lurked in its poorer neighborhoods was one more little gift for Geran Hulmaster.

He returned his attention to the priest of Cyric. "The pirate raid depends on surprise. If you choose to move your Cinderfists out of its path or get them in place to strike during the chaos, make sure that you keep the reasons to yourself." The mage wished he did not have to confide in Valdarsel, but if he failed to warn the man about the coming attack, the Cyricist might very well wind up unleashing his rabble to some counterproductive cross-purpose. He simply had to hope that the prize was tempting enough for the priest.

Valdarsel snorted. "I am not stupid." He took another sip from his goblet then nodded to himself. "Best not to tell my people anything, I think. I'd rather make use of their unfeigned outrage in the days to come. In fact, I rather hope that the pirates do some damage to the Tailings and Easthead. A few deaths or abductions would be just the thing to stir up anger."

"I consider that the safest option. You and I are the only people in Hulburg who know what is coming the night after next. I prefer to keep it that way." Rhovann drank again from his goblet—the wine was exactly what he might have expected from a place like the Three Crowns—and stood. "We will speak again soon."

He set his hand on the door and was about to let himself out when he heard a thump from somewhere behind the wall where Valdarsel sat. Someone in the adjoining room said clearly, "Ho, what are you doing there?" There was a muffled reply, another couple of thumps, then the speaker shouted, "Come back here!"

Rhovann wheeled on Valdarsel with sudden fury. "You had someone spy on me?" he demanded.

Valdarsel ignored him. The Cyricist surged out of his own seat and looked at the wall. The Three Crowns was rather shoddily built; the interior walls were little more than a thin weave of wooden slats covered in plaster between the rough timber posts. Valdarsel angrily threw aside several spare chairs standing against the wall, revealing a coin-sized hole in the plaster just a little above the floor. "Not I," the man spat. "It seems there was a mouse in the wall."

Rhovann threw open the sliding door and hurried down the hall, only to find that the room he was seeking backed onto the dining room from a different corridor. He snarled and rushed around through the foyer linking the taphouse to the inn, turned right, and found a hallway that paralleled the one in the taphouse. A gangly, teenaged servant lad stood in front of an open storeroom, a small keg in his arms. Rhovann pushed past him to look in the storeroom. Amid the clutter of casks and barrels, he saw the gleam of light shining through from the dining room on the other side, with a small space cleared by the spyhole. There was even a blanket on the floor.

He turned on the serving lad standing there. "Who was in here? Where did he go? Speak, boy!"

The youth gaped at him before he found his voice. "It—it was a woman, m'lord, with black hair and a blue cloak. I opened the door to fetch this keg and found her on the floor there, looking through the hole. She—she leaped up and ran out."

"Which way?" Rhovann demanded.

The boy nodded down the hallway behind him. "There's a door to the alleyway back there. I heard her go through."

Rhovann ran to the end of the hall and burst out into the dark alleyway behind the inn. He looked left, then right, but he saw no sign of his quarry. A moment later Valdarsel appeared behind him. "No sign of our mouse?" he asked.

Rhovann shook his head. "No. She's gone. The boy said she was a black-haired woman in a blue cloak."

Valdarsel scowled. "That could be anybody. Damn it all to the depths of Nessus!"

"No one followed me here or knew that I was coming," Rhovann said. He looked at the Cyricist. "Our mouse was spying on you, not me. Perhaps the folk of the Three Crowns have come to know you better than you would like."

"Oh, trust me, I intend to question them rigorously." The cleric kicked at the ground and walked in a small circle, composing himself. "How much did she hear, I wonder?"

"Assume that she heard everything until we have reason to believe otherwise."

"We need to find her, then. Tonight." Valdarsel took a deep breath and looked at Rhovann. "Do you have any divinations that might help?"

"Divinations, no. But I might be able to do something else." Rhovann headed back inside with the priest trailing him and returned to the storeroom. The serving boy was gone; he'd fled back to the taphouse with his keg as quickly as possible, it seemed. He kneeled by the place where the spy had crouched, and spoke the words of a light spell to illuminate the scene. There was the blanket—an old saddle blanket, he saw—a small candle in a tin holder, and a few crumbs of bread and cheese. Whoever it was, she had waited for some time for Valdarsel to arrive. Then something glinted in the light. He reached down and retrieved a long, fine strand of black hair from the blanket.

"Have you found something?" Valdarsel asked.

Rhovann showed him the hair. "It may be enough. I must return to my chambers and make some preparations."

"Go swiftly, then. We must catch this mouse before she squeaks." The priest smiled cruelly. "While you essay your magic, I will find out what I can from the servants of the house. Someone besides that boy knew she was here."

"Very well," said Rhovann. He hurried outside to the alleyway and spoke the words of his flying spell. In the space of a moment he soared up over the rooftops, leaving the dark alleyway behind the Three Crowns behind him. This time he did not have to search out his destination with care; he could see the lights of the Marstel manor from the moment he rose above the rooftops of the Tailings. With all the speed the spell allowed him, he raced back toward Lord Marstel's home, high above the town in the richest part of the Easthead.

He easily avoided the guards at the front gate by alighting in a little-used garden behind the grand house. Rhovann had appropriated the northerly wing of the Marstel manor as his own months ago, evicting the other residents. It gave him space to set up a library, a laboratory, and a conjury for his arcane studies, and also made it easy for him to leave or return to the estate without being observed. He knew he would have been wiser to keep his quarters right next to Maroth Marstel's own chambers, but he detested the old man and wanted an excuse to keep him at some small distance when he could. Instead he made sure that Marstel's servants and guards never left the old man's side and knew to summon him the instant Marstel did anything he wasn't supposed to.

The elf made his way into his rooms and went at once to his conjury. This room he kept sealed with a spell of locking, which he undid with a word and a gesture. In the center of the room a large, magical diagram of beaten silver was inlaid into the polished stone floor; shelves and worktables along the walls held a variety of arcane reagents and materials. When he entered the room, a hulking figure in a vast black cloak stepped into the light—a pale creature almost the size of an ogre, with doughy flesh and lusterless black eyes. It reached one great hand toward him.

"It is I, Bastion," Rhovann said absently. The golem halted at once, its arm falling to its side. "Has anyone tried to enter since last I left?"

The creature shook its head in a slow, deliberate gesture.

"Good," Rhovann muttered. He looked around the room and found the item he was searching for—a large, thick glass jar filled with dark liquid. Inside floated a small, malformed creature about the size of a cat. He carried the jar over to the center of one of his worktables then used a small chisel to break apart the old, brittle wax seal that fastened the lid to the neck of the jar. Bastion stood by and watched him at his work, its eyes dead and dark. A rank, briny smell greeted Rhovann's nostrils when he pried off the lid.

Rhovann held his left hand over the jar then used a small, sharp knife to cut the tip of a finger. He squeezed a single drop of blood into the dark fluid where the creature floated. Nothing happened at first, but then the thing inside began to move slowly. Its limbs twitched weakly, and its beady eyes opened. "Come, little one," he said to the thing in the jar. "I have need of you tonight."

The creature—a homunculus, it was called—climbed awkwardly out of the jar and slid to the tabletop in a splatter of dark brine. It unfurled a pair of batlike wings and flapped them slowly, drying itself. Its motions were growing stronger, more confident, with every moment. Rhovann allowed himself a smile of satisfaction. Creating a homunculus was a tedious and unpleasant task, but now he was going to reap the reward of his own foresight from many months ago. He took the strand of hair he'd found in the spy's nest at the Three Crowns and gave it to the creature.

"Find the woman whose hair this is," he said. "Do not allow yourself to be seen. Then return, and tell me who she is, and where she may be found. If you do not find her by sunrise, return and tell me so."

"Yes-s, mas-ter," the homunculus said in a small, wheezing voice.

Rhovann went to the room's window, opened it, and threw open the heavy shutter outside. "Now go," he said to the homunculus. The creature hopped from the tabletop to the windowsill, tested its wings, and threw itself out into the night. It flew clumsily at first, but quickly grew stronger and steadier. When it flapped out of sight, it was flying as well as any big, heavy-bodied bird. The mage tended to the cut on his finger and then settled down to wait. Since there was little more he could do until the homunculus returned, he motioned for Bastion to withdraw and seated himself cross-legged on a low divan against one wall. The elf allowed himself to doze off into the half-memory, half-dreaming state that served as sleep for elfkin. His mind wandered and time passed.

A little more than an hour later, he heard a sudden fluttering and scratching at his window. He rose and went to let in the homunculus. The little creature scrabbled across the windowsill to the table nearby. "Well, let us see what you have learned," Rhovann said to the creature. It could not truly understand him, of course, but it knew what it was supposed to do. It crouched down and held still. The elf mage reached out to rest his living hand atop its head and intoned the words of the spell that would reveal to him what his spy had discovered.

He closed his eyes, the better to focus on the images of the creature's memories. He saw its wild, fluttering flight across the rooftops of Hulburg. It stopped frequently, clinging to the eaves of houses or prowling over the rough wooden shakes of roofs, snuffling and tasting the air as it sought the woman. At first it seemed to move more or less at random, a few hundred yards this way, then a few hundred yards back, but soon its movements became more urgent, more focused. It moved to the east side of the Winterspear River and headed to the north side of town, not far from the foot of the castle Griffonwatch, flapping past a handful of passersby and drunks staggering through the streets despite the late hour. The homunculus steered wide around any people it encountered. Once Rhovann saw a Shieldsworn guard by the castle's battlements look up with a startled expression on his face, but no one else seemed to notice the winged monster. It soon alighted on an old split-rail fence by a small farmhouse in the middle of an apple orchard and crawled closer on its wings and feet. In his mind's eye Rhovann saw the thing climb up beside a window and peer inside.

The woman he sought was sitting by the table in her kitchen, frowning as she fixed herself a cup of tea. The blue cloak hung on a peg by the door. Rhovann smiled coldly and lifted his hand from the homunculus's head. He knew where she was. "What is her name?" he asked the homunculus.

"Mir-ya," the creature hissed. It possessed no real intelligence of its own, but sometimes it could learn things about the people it spied on, things it didn't necessarily observe or hear aloud. That was the nature of its magic.

The name sounded familiar to Rhovann. "Mirya Erstenwold? That is Mirya Erstenwold?"

"Yes-s," the creature wheezed.

"Why would Mirya Erstenwold spy on me?" he wondered aloud. The homunculus just gazed up at him without answering; the creature simply didn't understand. He knew that she was a friend of Geran Hulmaster, but he'd thought she was a simple shopkeeper. As far as he knew Lastannor had given her no reason to pry into his business . . . but he hadn't been the only person in the Three Crowns, had he? She must have been there to spy on Valdarsel instead of him. Either way, he had to assume that she knew things she was not supposed to know. She might not have overheard much during the time she'd been spying on them—after all, she'd gone home instead of going straight to Griffonwatch—but he couldn't take the chance that she had.

It seemed that he had one more errand for the night. He found a piece of parchment, scribbled out a short note, and handed it to the homunculus. "Take this to Valdarsel. He was at the Three Crowns Inn earlier tonight and may still be there. Do not allow yourself to be seen by anyone other than Valdarsel if you can help it. Return by daybreak if you do not find him."

"Yes-s, mas-ter," the creature replied. It seized the note in its tiny paws and flapped away again.

Rhovann watched it for a moment, then he donned his hooded cassock. "Come, Bastion," he said to his golem. "We must pay a visit to Mirya Erstenwold."

THIRTEEN

6 Marpenoth, the Year of the Ageless One (1479 DR)

Hulburg's Arches stood ninety miles north-northwest of Mulmaster's fortified harbor. With favorable winds and a full spread of sail, a swift ship such as *Moonshark* could make the crossing in twelve or thirteen hours. However, Narsk had Sorsil and Khefen run at half-canvas during the night of the fifth, so that as morning broke on the sixth of Marpenoth, they were only about thirty miles out of Mulmaster. The jagged line of the Earthspur Mountains still showed above the horizon behind them, although they soon vanished into an overcast that thickened throughout the morning.

Shortly after daybreak, Narsk and Sorsil summoned Murkelmor, who served as the ship's carpenter, to the quarterdeck. Murkelmor was soon hard at work building a frame or stand of some sort in front of the helm, using some of the ship's spare timber. Most of the deckhands paused in their day's work to peer up at the quarterdeck or look over Murkelmor's shoulder, curiosity which was sharply discouraged by Sorsil when she noticed it. When the dwarf finished, Narsk brought the mysterious parcel from Mulmaster up from his cabin and carefully removed a strange, dark glass orb about the size of a man's two fists held together. Tiny pinpricks of light seemed to glimmer in its dark depths. The orb spun freely inside a collar of silver metal; Murkelmor secured the collar to the wooden stand he'd built for the device.

"The starry compass," Geran murmured to Sarth and Hamil as they watched from the maindeck. They were halfheartedly pushing mops around the deck as they did their best to spy on the installation of the device. They weren't the only ones; more than a few of the ship's crew were looking for an excuse to take a look at it, whatever it was.

"What is it?" Hamil asked. "Some device for steering by the stars? A magical lodestone? And what does Narsk need one for?"

"I don't know," Geran answered. "Kamoth's letter didn't say much more than 'Pick up the starry compass in Mulmaster.'" He looked over to Sarth. "Have you heard of anything like it?"

Sarth shook his head. "As I've told you, I know nothing about seafaring. That ignorance extends to arcane devices that might have uses at sea. I could imagine that it would be useful to have an enchanted compass, though."

"We'll have a look at it later," Geran decided. He was more than a little curious about the device, but at the moment the threat to Hulburg occupied the greater part of his attention. He returned to his mopping. On the quarterdeck, Sorsil and Murkelmor cut a piece of spare sailcloth to serve as a cover for the compass and its frame. They slipped the cover over the device and lashed the canvas securely in place. Clearly, Narsk and Sorsil didn't want it pawed by every member of the crew.

Moonshark passed the day lazily pacing northward under half-sail, as Narsk dallied in the middle of the Moonsea well out of sight of the shore. Geran willed every ounce of speed from wind and wave, but the half galley refused to hurry her steps. Under cheerless gray skies he paced the decks anxiously, chafing as the hours dragged slowly by. The rest of the crew, on the other hand, spent the hours eagerly anticipating the looting of the town. They told stories of rich prizes from the past, boasted about their sexual prowess, or speculated about where the best loot would be found. The larger fists in the crew—Skamang and his men, Murkelmor with his dwarves and their Teshan allies, the goblins and half-orcs, the Mulmasterites—clustered together, laying their plans to go their own way once the ship's business was taken care of. Some of the smaller fists struck alliances with larger ones or grouped with each other. A few men who'd been to Hulburg before did their best to sketch out maps of the town for the others, which ranged from fairly good to wildly inaccurate. The pirates laughed and jibed at each other in a rough good cheer that lasted throughout the day.

A little before midnight, Geran, Hamil, and Sarth arose and prepared themselves for their watch. But the swordmage motioned for his companions to follow him forward instead of going up to the deck. When he was satisfied that no one was in earshot, he said, "We're taking the ship tonight."

Hamil and Sarth glanced at each other, then Hamil nodded. "What do you have in mind?" the halfling asked.

"We'll take care of the rest of the watch and steer due north for the rest of the night. I can't wait for Narsk to reach the Black Moon rendezvous."

"A dangerous ploy," Sarth said. The tiefling frowned unhappily behind his human guise. "Narsk roams the ship at odd hours. If he discovers us . . ."

"We'll have to deal with him along with the rest of the watch," Geran answered. He wished he could think of some other way to get to Hulburg in advance of the Black Moon raid, instead of risking all on such a reckless plan, but they were out of time. "Let's get to it, then. The sooner we change course, the closer to Hulburg we'll get."

Hamil held out his fist and looked up to his companions with a bold grin. "Good fortune to us, then," he said. Geran fought down his fears of what might happen if they failed and set his hand on top of his friend's.Sarth shrugged and set his hand atop Geran's.

"Good fortune," they both repeated in low voices. Then the three companions turned to the work ahead.

First they visited the ship's armory. Hamil expertly picked the lock, and Geran helped himself to a good cutlass. With a little work he rigged the scabbard to lie across his back, where a hooded cloak might help to hide the fact that he was armed. Then, in the privacy of the arms locker, Geran quietly invoked the swordmage wardings and spells, which served as his armor, for the first time in days. They were not normally noticeable, but someone trained in the arcane arts might sense their presence, and anyone who struck at him—for example, the first mate with her cudgel—would likely notice their effect, which was why Geran had gone without the wardings. He hoped he wouldn't need them, but it was better to be ready. Tonight would be a night of decision, and the time for fitting in with their fellow corsairs was drawing to an end. "All right, let's head up for watch," Geran told his friends.

They quietly closed the arms locker and went up on deck, reporting for their watch under the second mate, Khefen. Although Khefen's watch consisted of a full third of the ship's company, twenty men weren't needed on deck at all times. Normally *Moonshark* sailed with the mate and a helmsman on the quarterdeck, a lookout in the bow, a lookout aloft, and a couple of roving deckhands who kept an eye on the rigging, tended the braces and stays, and looked after the lanterns belowdecks. Their primary task was to go below and rouse more of the watch if the mate had to change the set of the sails. Some minor adjustments could be handled by a couple of men easily enough, but other adjustments—for example, breaking out or taking in a mainsail—required the whole watch. Those men who weren't on deck were allowed to catch as much sleep as they could, so long as they were quick to come up on deck when summoned. Over the course of a watch it was customary for the helmsman, lookouts, and rovers to trade places with their watchmates so that most of the crewmen had a chance to sleep at least four or five hours a night. However, *Moonshark*'s stronger fists made new and unproven hands stand more of the watch than they should have. For tonight that would serve Geran and his friends well.

Geran took the helm after the watch change, while Sarth was kept on as roving hand, and Hamil was sent aloft to the crow's nest. The night was cool and dark; the moon was hidden behind thick clouds, and a light drizzle fell. *Moonshark* rode sluggishly on a west-northwesterly track as the wind was light, and she still didn't have her full spread of canvas aloft. For half an hour he held the ship on course, biding his time to make sure the second watch was settled below. Khefen said little to him, sipping from his flask as he leaned against the lee rail.

Finally he decided the moment was right. He looked over at the second mate. "Take the wheel for a moment, Master Khefen?" he asked. "I need to relieve myself."

Khefen sighed, but he shook himself under his damp cloak and nodded. "Don't be long," he said.

Geran let the man get his hands on the helm and stepped back. Then he quietly drew a leather sap from beneath his cloak and struck the second mate across the back of the head. Khefen groaned and slumped; Geran caught him and lowered him softly to the deck. Quickly he looped a keeper over the topmost spoke of the helm, then dragged Khefen to one side. He arranged the unconscious man against the rail and liberally sprinkled him with the contents of his own flask. Things would go hard for Khefen in the morning, but at least it wouldn't seem overly suspicious. Then he hurried forward.

Hamil dropped lightly to the deck from the foremast as Geran approached. The halfling winked at him, and together they moved forward to take care of the remaining two men on watch. But atop the fo'c'sle they found that Sarth had caught both the forward lookout and the other rover together. Both men lay sprawled on the deck in an enchanted slumber, overcome by the tiefling's spells. "Did you deal with Khefen?" Sarth asked.

"Not as neatly as you managed these two, but it's done," Geran answered. Together he and Hamil securely bound and gagged the unconscious men then hid them under a bit of spare canvas.

"The deck's ours for the moment," Hamil said. "So what now?"

"Now we run toward Hulburg at our best speed," Geran answered. "If we can get within a dozen miles or so of the northern shore, we'll put the longboat in the water and part ways with *Moonshark.* With luck we'll reach Hulburg by noon and warn the harmach about the pirate raid. But I think we'll need a good three or four hours on a northerly course to get close enough for the boat, and then we'll have to get the boat in the water without waking half the crew."

"What can I do?" Sarth asked.

"Go forward and act like you're on watch. If anyone comes up on deck, try not to let on that anything's out of the ordinary. Hamil, you'll do the same. I'm going to turn us slowly to our new course and see if I can't quietly put on a little more sail without anyone noticing."

"If this works, I'll be astonished," Hamil muttered. "But I guess it's worth a try." The halfling shrugged and moved to take up his position near the mainmast.

Geran returned to the quarterdeck, checked briefly on Khefen—the mate seemed to be well and truly out—and took the wheel again. Working just a few degrees at a time he brought their course a good fifty degrees over, settling on a heading just a little east of due north. Then he put the keeper back on the helm and hurried down to the main deck to help Hamil and Sarth square the yardarms back around, now that they were sailing further from the wind. Geran sorely wanted to break out more sail, but he'd need most of the watch for that. He might be able to bluff his way through by propping Khefen up at the rail and telling the watch that the second mate wanted more sail on, but there were just too many things that could go wrong if he roused a dozen more of their watchmates. He settled for having Sarth and Hamil quietly break out the staysails, which were comparatively small, close to the deck, and easily handled. They didn't add much to *Moonshark*'s speed, but every little bit helped, and the wind was beginning to pick up a little bit.

They ran for most of the night with little difficulty. Several times sleepy crewmen came up to the deck to answer calls of nature. None seemed to notice that the ship was not on the heading she was supposed to be on, but that didn't surprise Geran. Very few deckhands knew anything about navigation, and Narsk was hardly in the habit of informing the crew exactly where he was bound at any given moment. Usually no one other than the mate on watch and the man standing at the helm knew what course the ship was steering, if there weren't any landmarks in sight. One or two noticed the staysails and said something, but Hamil deflected the questions easily enough by simply saying "the captain told Khefen to break 'em out." The deckhands took Hamil at his word and made their way back down to their hammocks.

Two hours before dawn, Geran judged that they'd pushed their luck far enough. In an hour or so Tao Zhe would be rising to begin making breakfast. Geran wanted to be off the ship before then. He was just about to call Hamil and Sarth to the quarterdeck when he heard heavy footsteps on the portside ladder. A moment later, Sorsil appeared on the quarterdeck. "How goes the night?" the first mate asked. Then her eye fell on Khefen's motionless form, propped up by the rail. "What in the—Is that miserable bastard asleep on his watch?"

Geran stared at her in horror. Fortunately, Sorsil's attention was fixed on Khefen. The first mate crossed the quarterdeck and kicked Khefen savagely. The second mate fell over with a strange grunt but didn't awake. "By Cyric's black blade! He's dead drunk!" she fumed.

"Master Khefen said he wasn't feeling well," Geran stammered. "The night was quiet enough, so I just kept on as he told me."

Sorsil looked at the lodestone in front of the helm and then glanced up at the sky. The night had cleared a bit, and a few stars were shining through the overcast. "Bloody hell, we're sailing due north! And who put on the extra sail? How long have we been going like this?"

"Only half an hour or so," Geran said. "It was the last thing Khefen told us to do before he . . . fell ill."

Sorsil was livid. The first mate kicked Khefen's unresponsive body again, and Geran winced. The last thing he needed now was for the second mate to wake up. But evidently he'd sapped the man harder than he thought, for Khefen still didn't rouse. The first mate rounded on Geran again. "Half an hour, you say? You didn't think to send the rover to tell me that he was gods-damned unconscious? How much longer were you going to go on without letting anyone know that you were the only man on the quarterdeck?"

Sorry, Geran, I didn't see her come up on deck! Hamil's silent voice cut into Geran's thoughts. A moment later the halfling hurried up the ladder from the maindeck. "Is all well?" he asked aloud.

"Ask your friend here," Sorsil snapped. The first mate looked one more time at Khefen and then scowled at both Geran and Hamil. "Bring the ship back to west by northwest, damn you," she finally said. "And you there, Dagger, you go below and rouse the whole watch. We're going to take in sail like the captain wanted, and then you're going to explain what in the Nine Hells is going on here."

Distract her, Geran, Hamil told him. *We can't afford a scene.*

Geran grimaced. He knew he wouldn't like what came next, but he couldn't see any way around it, not if he still hoped to spare Hulburg the brunt of the Black Moon raid. He looked at Sorsil and said, quite deliberately, "I've had enough from you, Sorsil. I think the sails are fine as they are. Take them in yourself if you don't like the way they're set."

The first mate paled in rage. "You think—?" she snarled. She reached for the truncheon at her waist. And at that moment Hamil glided up behind her, reached up to clap a hand over her mouth, and sank his poniard into the first mate's back. Sorsil staggered forward two steps; Geran caught her and wrestled her over to the rail. They struggled for a moment, but the first mate's strength was already failing. With one final effort Geran toppled her over the side with a splash, although Hamil had to catch the swordmage by the belt buckle to keep him from going in after her.

I doubt that Daried Selsherryn would have approved of that, he thought grimly. It was murder, pure and simple, and Geran was none too proud of it. But Sorsil had killed more than a few of *Moonshark*'s victims with her own steel, or so he'd heard from Tao Zhe and others aboard. And scores, perhaps hundreds, of Hulburgan lives were at risk if he failed to warn the harmach of the pirate plan. He looked over to Hamil and nodded his thanks.

"I think we're out of time."

"Agreed," the halfling said. "How far to Hulburg, do you think?"

"It might be fifteen miles, it might be thirty." That would be a brutal distance if they had to row it, but the longboat had a small mast that could be stepped into place with just a few minutes' work. Geran hoped to sail to Hulburg, not row.

"They'll come after us once they find us gone," Hamil pointed out.

"I know." Geran thought for a moment, considering how best to sabotage the ship. Unfortunately there was nothing nearby to run her aground on, so he decided to disable the rudder. He kneeled, slashed the ship's rudder cables with his poniard, and began to haul up the loose cabling. Rigging a new rudder cable ought to occupy *Moonshark* for a couple of hours at least, and by the time they were ready to pursue Geran and his companions, they'd have long since disappeared. "Go on back and get the longboat ready to launch—quietly!"

Hamil grinned at him. "Maybe this will work after all." He dashed forward to the main deck, while Geran yanked length after length of the rudder cable up from below. Without her rudder, *Moonshark*'s bow began to fall off downwind, and she rocked a little as she passed through the swell.

Geran got the last of the rudder cabling that he could reach, picked up the tarry mess, and dropped it over the side. He brushed off his hands, hurried down the ladder to the main deck, and headed forward to help Hamil and Sarth wrestle the longboat over the side. This was by far the trickiest part of the whole business; lowering the longboat was a six-man job, not a three-man job, and it was nearly impossible to do it quietly. With sheer brute force they managed to lift it out of its cradle and stagger over to the rail, but not before the boat's gunwales thumped the deck a couple of times. Geran winced, but they were getting close to the moment when speed would count more than stealth.

At the aft end of the main deck, the door to the captain's cabin opened, and Narsk stepped out. The gnoll took in the scene at a glance, catching Geran and his friends with the longboat half in its davit. "What is this?" he snarled. Then he leaped over to the ship's bell and began to strike it vigorously. "All hands on deck, now!" he shouted. "Trrreachery! All hands on deck!"

Despair paralyzed Geran for five heartbeats. "So close," he muttered. The first pale glimmers of dawn were beginning to streak the sky to the east. In a matter of moments, the deck would be full of enemies. They wouldn't live long enough to get the longboat in the water. He could see only one slender chance—to kill Narsk quickly and hope to cow or contain the rest of the crew long enough to make their escape.

Before he could second-guess himself, he dropped his end of the longboat. *Moonshark* rolled heavily under Geran's feet, running clumsily before the wind with her helm spinning freely on the quarterdeck. "Guard my back!" he hissed to Sarth and Hamil. Then he drew the cutlass hidden under his cloak and charged across the deck at the pirate ship's captain.

FOURTEEN

7 Marpenoth, the Year of the Ageless One (1479 DR)

"You!" Narsk snarled. "It was you in my cabin in Mulmaster! I know your scent now, human!" The gnoll greeted Geran's attack with a snarl of pure rage. He yanked out the mace he carried at his belt and drew a long, curved knife to meet the swordmage. Leaping aside from Geran's first thrust, Narsk answered with a furious onslaught of whistling mace swings, using his long knife to protect himself when the mace's weight left him out of balance and exposed.

Geran didn't answer. He leaned away from the mace, parried a knife slash at his belly, and ducked low to cut Narsk's legs out from under him. But the gnoll leaped over his slash with surprising agility. Narsk threw himself closer after Geran's sword passed, and lunged for the swordmage's neck with a snap of his powerful jaws. The swordmage fell back again and survived a knife thrust at his right side only because his spellwards deflected the blade. The tip of the blade gouged a bloody gash against his ribs, but it didn't sink more than an inch or so into his flesh. The stab still knocked the breath out of him and left him with warm blood trickling down his side, the wound throbbing in pain.

I need to end this quickly, he realized. Otherwise there would be no hope of escaping *Moonshark*.

With the instant, diamond-sharp focus he'd learned in Myth Drannor, Geran invoked a sword spell even as his steel flew to meet Narsk's attack. *"Arvan sannoghan!"* he cried, and the pirate cutlass in his hand blazed with blue flames. Narsk swore and recoiled, but not before Geran slashed his knife out of his left hand, leaving the gnoll's fur smoking.

Narsk snarled in pain. "Foul sorcery!" he shouted. "Kill him! Kill him now!"

Geran risked a quick glance over his shoulder. *Moonshark*'s crew was boiling up out of their quarters under the main deck, most with knives, belaying pins, or boarding pikes in hand. They gaped at the spectacle of their captain fighting for his life then started to close in behind Geran—until Sarth raised his arms and wove a fence of lightning across the deck. "This is between Aram and Narsk!" he shouted. "No one else is to interfere!"

The corsairs halted, unsure about whether or not they should intervene, and were dissuaded in any event by the sudden revelation of Sarth's magic. Narsk roared in fury when he realized that his crew would not cut down his challenger. "You miserable rrrats!" he screamed. "You will all pay for your cowardice!" He threw himself at Geran recklessly, pounding his mace against his foe with a furious barrage of overhand blows.

Geran parried or dodged the blows, although one carried through his block with enough power to drive the back of his cutlass—fortunately not sharpened—into his left shoulder, almost buckling him to the deck. Narsk snarled and redoubled his effort, but this time Geran deflected the mace past him and stepped aside. The gnoll was left off balance and stumbled forward as his mace head brushed the deck. Geran spun in the opposite direction and took off Narsk's head with one clean cut to the back of the neck. The body crashed heavily to the deck, and the head rolled into the companionway leading down to the crew quarters, disappearing down the steps with several dull thuds.

A stunned silence fell over the crew of *Moonshark*. They stared down at Narsk's body, and then they stared at Geran.

We lost the longboat, Geran, Hamil told him. The halfling stood next to Sarth, a pair of daggers in his hands. *It slipped from the davit when the trouble started. I sincerely hope you have another plan in mind!*

The Northman Skamang pushed his way to the front of the crew and fixed his eyes on Geran. The blue tattoos on his face seemed to writhe and jump in the flickering light of Sarth's crackling, spitting barrier. "Where's Sorsil? And Khefen?"

"Khefen's passed out on the quarterdeck, dead drunk," Geran answered. "Sorsil's somewhere astern of us, floating in the water with a knife in her back."

"Someone had better explain why the captain and first mate are dead and your friends were getting ready to launch the longboat," Skamang said. He hefted a boarding axe in his hand. "And soon, at that."

Murkelmor crossed his arms in front of his chest and scowled. "I'm wi' Skamang," the dwarf said. "I'd like t' know what in th' Nine Hells you're about, Aram."

Geran stared back at the two pirates and tried to think of something to say. He was not a good liar, and he knew it. Fortunately, Hamil knew it as well, and the halfling had a knack for thinking quickly in situations such as this. *Blame it on Sorsil! That's the best chance I can see,* the halfling said to him. Geran glanced over and found Hamil kneeling by Narsk's body, quietly checking the gnoll's pockets.

The halfling offered a small shrug and nodded in the direction of the rest of the crew. *I thought I'd better have a look,* he said. *There was a letter in Narsk's pocket. I've got it now.*

The swordmage frowned and returned his attention to the pirates confronting him. He let the point of his cutlass drop. "It was Sorsil," he said. "She came up on deck and ordered us to put the longboat over the side. It seemed strange to me, but she didn't explain herself, and Khefen was dead drunk. Then she went to the quarterdeck and sabotaged the rudder. I caught her at it and tried to stop her. Narsk came out of his cabin just in time to see Sorsil knifed and knocked over the rail."

"Narsk didn't give us much of a chance to explain ourselves," Hamil added. He stood up from beside Narsk's body and moved over to stand beside Geran. "He rang the bell and called all hands on deck, and then he went after Aram. His final mistake, as it turned out." To Geran he added, *Not bad, but don't say too much more!*

"Narsk is dead, Sorsil is dead, and Khefen's naught but a fat, useless drunk," Murkelmor said. "I'd like to know who captains *Moonshark* now."

"I do," Geran said at once. If he was going to try to bluff his way out of this, it might as well be a brazen ploy. He winced a little, realizing that he had no idea what that might mean at the moment. Before he could think better of the idea, he pressed on. "By the traditions of the Black Moon, I claim command. Narsk is dead by my sword. I'm captain of *Moonshark.*"

The crew muttered uncertainly. Some men shouted "No!" or "Not so fast," while others cried "No, Skamang!" or "Khefen!" instead.

I hope you know what you're doing, Geran, Hamil said. *This'll be another fight.*

"He's got th' right t' make his claim," Murkelmor said. The old dwarf shook his head. "We all saw it. This is no' the way it should be, but Khefen's no captain, and Sorsil's as dead as Narsk if Aram's speaking true. My fist stands for Aram."

"Mine doesn't," Skamang snarled. "I won't follow some stranger who's been aboard *Moonshark* less than a tenday simply because he bested the gnoll." He pointed the spike of his boarding axe at Geran. "I say I'm the captain of this ship."

Before Geran, the sixty-odd brigands, outlaws, cutthroats, and pirates who made up the ship's crew stood watching him—and each other—as they waited to see whether he or Skamang would seize control of the ship. No one wanted to be remembered later for backing the wrong man now. Geran forced himself to put on a cold, confident sneer as he studied the ship's crew. The appearance of confidence might be the difference between life and death—not just for himself, but for hundreds of Hulburgans too. He had to make the crew think he was as hard and deadly as a well-sharpened blade, or Skamang might succeed in overthrowing him. In that case, Geran had no guarantee that the Northman would let him live, let alone sail *Moonshark* in the direction he needed to go.

"A ship can't have two captains," Murkelmor growled. "It's no' possible."

"No, it's not," Geran agreed. He fixed his eyes on Skamang, mustering every ounce of icy contempt that he could find. "Will you fight me yourself this time, or do you want to send your ogre to die in your place? My fist will stay out of this if yours does the same."

"Your fist? All two of them?" The Northman laughed. "Drop that cutlass, let every man on this deck hear you call me captain, and I'll let this whole thing pass. You and your friends can go ashore the next time we make port, with no hard feelings."

I doubt that it would be that simple, Hamil told Geran. *He'll kill you if you give in now, just to make sure no one else thinks they ought to be in command.*

"In other words, you don't want to meet me with steel in your hand," Geran retorted. If he could goad the Northman into a duel, he might be able to take the ship with a single sword stroke. He risked a quick glance over at Sarth, who stood near the foot of the ladder up to the quarterdeck. Sarth had a tight grimace on his face, but he gave Geran the slightest of nods. Whatever came, he would be ready.

Skamang's laughter faded, and a hard edge came into his voice. "I won't be in such a generous mood if you keep up with this nonsense. You might not care whether you live or die, but I'll gut any man that stands with you and toss him over the side."

"D'you mean to gut me too, Skamang?" Murkelmor said. The dwarf took two steps toward where Geran and his friends stood, and turned to face the Northman. "Aram's got me fist at his back, if that's slipped your mind. We stand wi' him."

Skamang scowled at Murkelmor. But then Tao Zhe stepped out of the crew and went to stand by Geran too. The old Shou cook's footsteps broke the remaining indecision among the crew, and in twos or threes most of the rest of the men shifted over to Geran's side. Only the half-dozen goblins and half-orcs remained by Skamang's fist, and they began to mutter and shift restlessly as they realized that their party was now outnumbered.

Seems like Skamang and his allies haven't endeared themselves to the rest of the crew, Hamil observed to Geran.

Geran straightened his shoulders and allowed himself a small smile. He'd been afraid that the crew would choose the devil they knew instead of the devil they didn't. The Northman was a longtime veteran of *Moonshark,* after all, and no one had any doubts about his prowess or his ruthlessness. On the other hand, all they knew of "Aram" was that he knew how to use a blade and that he'd been caught in the middle of some sort of mischief during the watch. Based on that alone, he would have expected the crew to turn against him . . . but then he realized that no one on *Moonshark* missed Sorsil or Narsk, and Skamang would have been just as bad as the preceding captain in his own way.

"It looks like the vote's in, Skamang," said Geran. "I say I'm the captain. This is your last chance: Yield, or it's over the side with you and yours. Alive or dead, I don't much care."

The Northman's face darkened in fury, but he could count as well as Geran. He looked around the deck, and then he gave Geran a curt nod. "So be it. You're the captain. But we'll be watching you, Aram. Make one mistake, and you'll see just how quickly those dogs on your side of the deck will turn against you."

Geran held his eyes for a long moment and then looked around at the rest of the crew assembled on the deck. "Does anybody else take issue with me? Speak now, or hold your tongues later."

The pirates looked at each other, but no one else stepped forward. Geran nodded. "I thought not," he said. "Very well, then. Dagger is the new first mate. Vorr is the ship's mage, as you've all seen by now. When they speak, they speak for me. Murkelmor, you're the second mate. The midwatch is yours."

"What about Khefen?" the dwarf asked.

"Take him below and lock him in his cabin. I'll put him ashore the next time we make port. I've got no use for him, but he hasn't done anything to me. You can take Sorsil's cabin, Murkelmor."

"Aye, Captain," Murkelmor said.

Hamil sheathed his daggers, brushed the hair away from his eyes, and stepped out in front of the crew. "What are your orders, Captain?" he asked.

Geran glanced up at the sails, luffing awkwardly as *Moonshark* drifted downwind. The wind had shifted and strengthened during the last hour, coming around to the northwest. It was promising to be a blustery autumn day on the Moonsea, with a stiff wind that would make for fine sailing—if he didn't have to sail straight into it, which it now seemed that he did. Already he suspected that the ship was too far east to make Hulburg without hours of laborious tacking. When he'd planned to abandon *Moonshark* and strike out for Hulburg in the ship's boat, it would have suited his purposes quite well for the pirate galley to find itself adrift with a damaged rudder, unable to pursue him and too far away to join the attack on the city. Now, with the longboat gone but the ship at his command, he'd have to find a way to bring *Moonshark* to the shore somewhere near Hulburg. He could order the crew to the oars, but Geran wasn't so sure of his position that he felt ready to try them with a long stint of rowing just yet.

"The first thing we need to do is repair the rudder," Geran answered Hamil. "Until we get the rudder fixed, take in all sail. The Black Moon is gathering near the ruins of Seawave at sunset today. By my reckoning that's a good ways north and west of us yet, and this wind is driving us farther east every minute."

Rather ironic to order the repair of the rudder you sabotaged not an hour ago, don't you think? Hamil told Geran with a small smirk. Then he turned to the crewmen around him. "You heard the captain!" he shouted. "First watch, get aloft and take in the sails! I don't know about you lads, but I don't want to spend all day rowing to Hulburg. Looting and pillaging's no fun when your back's sore and you're dog-tired. Master Murkelmor, I know you're a mate now, but you're the best carpenter we've got on the ship. Have a look at the rudder, if you please."

The crewmen started to move as Hamil badgered them. Some started aloft to begin reefing in the sails, while Murkelmor motioned for a couple of his fellows to join him on the quarterdeck. Two more men came up to carry Khefen below. Sarth leaned close to Geran. "You'd better have that cut tended," he said in a low voice. "If you pass out on your feet, we might have to repeat the whole round of challenges."

Geran lifted his hand from his side and saw blood on his palm. He winced and then looked around for Tao Zhe. The Shou cook was the closest the ship's company had to a healer. "Tao Zhe! Fetch some hot water and your sewing kit," he said. "Narsk left me something to remember him by."

Murkelmor and his helpers began to lay out a new rudder cable. Geran didn't bother to press him to hurry his repairs; the dwarf knew that the ship's participation in the attack on Hulburg depended on regaining the ability to maneuver as soon as possible, and he drove his small crew of woodworkers and ropelayers as hard as they could be driven. Geran remained on the quarterdeck, watching Murkelmor work as Tao Zhe in turn worked on him. Narsk's blade had left a deep gash, but he'd been lucky not to have worse. "I thought Narsk had killed you with this one," the Shou told him as he stitched the wound. "You were fortunate this morning."

"It's not so bad." Geran gritted his teeth against Tao Zhe's work. He'd had his wounds sewn more than once, and each time it seemed worse than receiving the wound in the first place.

"Truly I did not expect you to move so quickly against Narsk when we left Zhentil Keep that morning," Tao Zhe remarked. "Nor did I expect you to be adept in magic. You seem to be a man of hidden talents."

"Narsk forced this fight on me. I had no intention of challenging him, but he left me with no choice."

Tao Zhe nodded. "I am not greatly troubled, mind you—Narsk was not much of a seaman, and he was a greedy and vicious brute. Almost anybody would be a better captain than he was."

Geran snorted. "My thanks for your confidence."

The Shou smiled. He glanced around and leaned a little closer, lowering his voice. "What really puzzles me is why Sorsil was attempting to leave the ship. It seems hard to believe that she would desert *Moonshark* without anything from her cabin, or that she would subdue the other two men on watch and hide them under a canvas but leave you and your friends free to stop her from going. I am not a very clever man, but it would seem much more likely to me that three men who'd only been aboard for a tenday were instead conspiring to steal the boat. But if that were the case, then I would still be left to wonder why they wanted to leave *Moonshark*. How strange that events transpired in the manner you described!"

Geran studied the old Shou carefully. It seemed unlikely that Tao Zhe was the only crewman aboard *Moonshark* entertaining such thoughts. "Speculation is pointless, Tao Zhe," he said after a moment.

"Of course. But it is certainly not speculation to observe that you and your comrades are hardly the typical sellswords or outlaws who sail under the Black Moon."

"What does the crew make of this, then?"

"Because they fear your magic, they will follow you for now," Tao Zhe answered. "No one liked Narsk—or Sorsil. But you should watch your back. And you should not expect the crew to deal with challengers for you, not until you demonstrate that you are a captain worth following."

"I understand."

"I only say what is plainly true," Tao Zhe answered. He finished with his needlework and covered the wound with a hot compress. "There is little more I can do. It will trouble you for a tenday or so. Try not to get stabbed there again."

"I'll take it under advisement."

The old Shou grinned. He collected his medicine kit and retreated to his galley.

Murkelmor managed to rig a working rudder cable only a couple of hours after sunrise. With the rudder repaired, Geran was able to turn *Moonshark* back to the northwest and Hulburg. But the strong autumn wind was directly out of that quarter, and so he had to resign himself to a west by southwesterly tack, heading back out toward the middle of the sea as the pirate ship fought its way back to windward. A gray, stiff chop arose by afternoon, so that *Moonshark* battered her way through whitecapped waves as she ran, soaking the decks with cold spray. The rough seas ruled out any idea of taking in sail and putting out oars that Geran might have entertained; rowing was possible under such conditions, but just barely.

In midafternoon Geran decided that he couldn't afford to extend his tack any farther to the south, and came north to run across the wind. He wasn't sure if he'd strike the coastline east or west of Hulburg at this point, but he was fairly certain that he'd be nowhere near as far west as the ruins of Seawave. Due to their night of sailing off course and the morning of drifting ahead of the wind, there was no way they'd reach the Black Moon's rendezvous point. If he had been intending to join the raid on Hulburg, he'd have to steer straight for the city at this point and join the rest of the flotilla there.

Since the afternoon was growing late, he figured he'd better prepare the crew for a change of plan. He called Murkelmor, Tao Zhe, and a few of the other fist leaders together on the quarterdeck about an hour before sunset. "Between the rudder damage and the shifting of the wind, I think we're too far east of the Black Moon rendezvous to meet up with the other ships," he told them. "They're gathering a good twenty miles west of the town in just a couple of hours. But I think we can reach Hulburg by midnight without too much trouble, and that's what I intend to steer for. We know that's where the rest of the Black Moon is bound, and we can join the flotilla there."

"The High Captain will no' be pleased with us," Murkelmor said.

"It can't be helped at this point," said Geran. "If the attack on Hulburg succeeds, I'd wager that many sins will be forgiven. If not, well, I'll take the blame."

Moonshark kept on her northerly tack for the rest of the afternoon and through the sunset. Still no sight of the northern shore greeted them, and Geran began to fear that he'd somehow completely lost his reckoning in the last few hours. He couldn't bear the idea that *Moonshark* might be too far away for him to get some word of warning to Hulburg. At least the raid would be one ship short if that were the case, but then he and his companions would have to deal with an extremely—perhaps lethally—disappointed crew. Finally, as the last embers of sunset gleamed low in the sky to the west, the lookout aloft called out "Land ho!" Geran hurried to the bow, peering into the gloaming to see what he could make of their position, and his heart sank.

They were still ten miles east of Hulburg, perhaps more. He quickly calculated time and distances in his head, trying to envision the course they'd have to follow. With this wind, *Moonshark* could make perhaps seven or eight knots running close-hauled, but they'd have to cover maybe three times as much distance on the tack as they actually managed to make good against the wind. That meant another four or five hours of sailing before they reached the Arches. He returned to the quarterdeck, thinking furiously.

"Do you know this stretch of coast?" Hamil asked him. "How far from Hulburg are we?"

"I do, and we're too far east," Geran answered. "I think we're out of time."

Hamil and Sarth exchanged looks with each other. The sorcerer frowned. "So what do we do now?" he asked.

Geran didn't see any other alternatives. He pointed at the coastline, perhaps three miles distant. "Unless I'm badly mistaken, that's Sulan Head. It's about ten miles east of Hulburg by the old coastal road. I'd bring the ship in to land on the beach at its foot, but that might take another hour, and I don't dare let the crew see me do something like that. They would surely suspect treachery. Sarth, can you reach the coast from here with your flying spell?"

Sarth studied the distance and nodded. "Yes, and perhaps a little more."

"Then I need you to leave the ship, get to Hulburg, and warn Kara, the harmach, whomever you can find that the Black Moon raid is on its way. I don't know if I can beat the Black Moon ships to Hulburg from here, not with the way the weather is running, but you may be able to on foot. By my reckoning, you've got three or four hours to cover the distance. Can you do it?"

"It must be done, so it will be done." Sarth looked back at *Moonshark*'s deck. "What about you and Hamil? If the crew notices that I am missing, they may rise against you."

"I'll tell them you're below, using Narsk's cabin to study your spells. That should work well enough for a short time." Geran paused as a stray thought crossed his mind. "That reminds me—Hamil, what's in that letter you found in Narsk's pocket?"

Hamil frowned. "I'd forgotten it. Just a moment." He pulled it out and carefully opened it under the light of the swinging stern lantern. After a moment, he shook his head and passed it to Sarth. "It looks like some kind of incantation."

Sarth glanced at it and shrugged. "Arcane words are written in several different tongues, and I had thought I would at least recognize a few words in any of them. But this is nonsense to me. Keep it safe, and I will see if I can use magic to decipher it when I have the opportunity to study it carefully." He looked back to Geran. "What will you do with *Moonshark?*"

Geran smiled grimly. "I still need to get to Hulburg, and *Moonshark*'s going to take me there. Now, let's get you on your way, because I've got to turn the ship and run away from the coast again in just a few minutes."

FIFTEEN

8 Marpenoth, the Year of the Ageless One (1479 DR)

Kraken Queen raced past the Arches of Hulburg's harbor an hour after midnight, her oars sweeping her eagerly ahead through the whitecaps and the wind-driven rain. At her back came *Daring, Wyvern,* and *Seawolf*—all told, almost five hundred Black Moon corsairs thirsting for blood, rape, and treasure. Few lights showed in the town, only a handful of streetlamps and the occasional lanternlit doorway of a tavern or merchant tradeyard. Sergen Hulmaster shaded his eyes from the wind and the rain, peering anxiously at the shoreline. If some word of the Black Moon fleet had come to Hulburg, he expected that ranks of Shieldsworn, merchant coster mercenaries, and even the laughable militia companies of the Spearmeet would be waiting by the wharves to repel the attack. But the waterside streets seemed abandoned.

Sergen allowed himself a small smile. "You were right, Father," he said. "I think we've surprised them." Given the mysterious absence of *Moonshark,* he'd spent most of the three-hour sprint from the ruins of Seawave fighting down his own misgivings about the enterprise. It seemed an inauspicious beginning to the night, and he'd urged his father to wait. But Kamoth had been impatient to launch the attack, worried that the worsening weather might make it impossible to strike in a timely manner and that delay would result in the fleet's discovery.

The High Captain grinned fiercely, throwing a challenge to

fate. "Of course I was right!" he said. "You've no stomach for this sort of stroke, Sergen. Caution and forethought are fine, but sometimes you need to throw fortune to the wind and see what comes." He held out his arms, allowing the crewmen who attended him to finish strapping on his scarlet armor. It was fashioned in the shape of a long coat of piscine scales, with fin-like embellishments at the joints and an open-faced helm with a fanged sea-serpent design.

Sergen glanced down at his own armor, a light shirt of black chain mail beneath a tough leather coat. "I hope we don't miss *Moonshark's* complement. Another seventy men would greatly fortify my confidence."

Kamoth waved one gauntleted hand at the sky. "Perhaps, but the wind and weather favor us too much to wait for that sluggard Narsk, my boy. A swift run from the rendezvous, a dark night to hinder anyone trying to organize a defense of the town, and a quick escape when it's time to go. The Prince of Demons will drink his fill tonight!"

Sergen nodded but did not answer. Long ago Kamoth had sworn him to the service of the demon lord Demogorgon, but the exiled lordling had never found much use for groveling in front of bloodstained altars. He was content to allow his father to glorify Demogorgon in any way he wished, so long as Kamoth didn't expect him to do the same. "Any sign of *Seadrake?*" he called to the lookouts.

"No, Lord Sergen! She's not in port!" the man aloft called back down.

Sergen relaxed a little. Outnumbered four to one, *Seadrake* wouldn't have lasted long against the Black Moon flotilla, but he knew better than to underestimate his stepsister, Kara, or his stepcousin, Geran. He'd done so only a few short months ago, and it had cost him the lordship of Hulburg, the friendship of Mulmaster, a great amount of wealth and power, and very nearly his life. Somehow they would have found a way to cause him more trouble with their one warship than they should have been able to in any reasonable world. "But if she's not here, then where is she?" he wondered aloud and began to worry all over again.

"Likely sniffing after our trail in the waters of the west end," Kamoth answered. He finished donning his armor. The pirate lord checked the fit with several hard slaps to his shoulders and chest. Then he moved over to the rail and looked at the other vessels following *Kraken Queen* into the harbor. "Give the signal!" he told the deckhand standing there.

The fellow lifted above the ship's sternrail a bullseye lantern that held a red-tinted piece of glass. He opened and closed its shutter three times. From the quarterdecks of the other ships, red lights winked back at *Kraken Queen* in answer. The flotilla split up as each ship began to steer toward its own assigned landing point. "Damn *Moonshark,* and damn that fool Narsk," Kamoth muttered. "I hope for his sake that I don't find reason to wish I'd waited for the fifth ship."

"The weather might've delayed him, High Captain," *Kraken Queen*'s first mate said. "He might be only an hour behind us."

"He'd better be, or the next time I see him, I swear I'll strap him to the foretop with his own guts and leave him there for the gulls!" Kamoth went back to the ship's wheel and peered ahead over the rowers. "Easy right rudder now, helm! There, steady as she goes. All right . . . all right . . . avast rowing! Raise and ship oars!"

Kraken Queen glided ahead on momentum, coasting closer to the town's wharves. The abandoned Veruna pier was Kamoth's target, and the old pirate expertly guided his ship alongside. It seemed too fast to Sergen, and he surreptitiously braced himself against the rail. But then gangs of deckhands leaped to the pier with mooring lines, checking the large galley with the heavy creaking of taut lines and timber pilings. The whole wharf trembled as *Kraken Queen* came to a stop.

"Well done!" Kamoth called. "Now go! The town's yours for the taking!"

With a wild chorus of shouts, laughter, and battle cries, *Kraken Queen*'s crew swarmed over the side and ran into the town. Kamoth himself grinned once at Sergen and followed after his crew, a wicked cutlass gleaming in his hand.

Sergen summoned Kerth and the rest of his magically bound bodyguards and followed more purposefully to the streets of town. He didn't see any particular need to murder, loot, or rape anyone; he was a very wealthy man, and he could afford all the women he cared for. His task for the night was to watch for resistance and direct the Black Moon corsairs against any trouble spots. If his father wanted to lead from the front and set an example of bloodthirst for the men, that was Kamoth's concern. Sergen wanted to make sure the raid would have the effect on Hulburg that he desired—no more, and no less.

The first screams rang out in the night, followed by the clash of steel on steel. Shouts of alarm arose from the sleeping town. It was not exactly the triumphant return to Hulburg Sergen had envisioned for himself during the long months of exile in Melvaunt, but he couldn't suppress a predatory grin. He was likely the single most dangerous enemy of the Hulmasters, the man who'd come closer to unseating the harmachs than anyone in a hundred years, and for tonight at least he roamed the streets with impunity. Geran or Kara would have a fit if they knew I was standing here watching the sacking of the harbor, he thought. The smell of smoke drifted to his nostrils, and the ruddy red glare of fires began to grow in the shadowed alleyways and winding streets. "This might turn out even better than I'd intended," he said.

"Not for the Hulburgans," his armsman Kerth answered with a hungry grin.

"It's the cost I must pay to unseat the harmach, Kerth. The Hulmasters brought this on themselves when Geran and Kara thwarted me before." Sergen studied the scene for a moment longer and then walked back to the base of the wharf where *Kraken Queen* was tied up. Dozens of corsairs waited there anxiously, whooping with delight when another building caught fire and shouting encouragement at those of their fellows who remained in view. One man in five from all four ships had been ordered to assemble here, forming a strong reserve of manpower in case the Hulburgans managed to mount some unexpectedly determined defense of their town or tried to retaliate against the pirates' ships. That, of course, was Sergen's addition to Kamoth's plan of attack. None of the fellows assigned this duty were happy about it, since they wanted to be released to participate in the sack. But Sergen was pleased to see at a quick count that most of the men promised had actually reported for this duty.

"Can't we just have a look in some of those storehouses over there?" one of the corsairs waiting in the reserve asked. He pointed across the street. "We won't be far off, Lord Sergen."

"And what would the High Captain say if he called for you to help him, but you'd run off to start stuffing your pockets?" Sergen answered. "I think I'd mind my orders, if I were you. If all goes well, you'll be relieved in an hour, and it'll be your turn to enjoy the town."

The fellow looked glum, but he gave up the argument. Sergen decided to have a look around to see if there was someplace he could put the reserve to work, and led his small knot of bodyguards along Bay Street, searching for any signs of trouble. Gangs of pirates ran from building to building, some already burdened by armfuls of loot. First he checked on the Marstel merchant compound and was relieved to see that the Black Moon corsairs were avoiding it as they were supposed to. Then he headed inland a block and walked eastward along Cart Street, passing more pirates at their work. It might defeat my purpose if the Black Moon actually razes the town, he thought with a grimace. He wanted something left of the place, after all.

The clash of arms grew heavier ahead—much heavier. Sergen frowned and hurried forward to take a look. He reached the corner of Cart Street and High Street, the heart of the town's commerce district, and saw ahead of him a solid phalanx of the harmach's own Shieldsworn. The Hulburgan soldiers, a small company of perhaps thirty or forty, fought their way down the street, driving the pirate gangs ahead of them. Sergen scowled at the show of early resistance. The Shieldsworn company was interfering with his long-laid plans to humble Hulburg, and he didn't care for it in the least. They needed to be broken, and the sooner the better. "Damn them!" Sergen snarled. "Where did they come from?"

“Simple chance, I would guess,” Kerth answered. He moved in front of Sergen and eyed the approaching soldiers nervously. “It seems that not all the harmach’s soldiers were asleep tonight. That’s too many for us to deal with, Lord Sergen. We’d better move on.”

“Agreed,” said Sergen. He frowned and reminded himself that no clash of arms ever went exactly as one planned. It was only to be expected that some of the town’s defenders would organize a brief resistance; fortunately the Black Moon was ready for them. “We’ll go back toward the docks and draw from the reserve to chase off these fellows.”

They turned and retreated down Cart Street to the intersection with Plank Street, and here more fighting greeted Sergen and his guards. A large mass of Hulburgans, most wearing hastily donned coats of old mail or leather jerkins, held Plank Street against the roving gangs of pirates and likewise were advancing toward the harbor. It was more of the sort of resistance that Sergen had hoped to overwhelm with the initial surprise of the Black Moon attack, and he made a note to himself to send more pirates here too. But a dark suspicion was growing in his heart. “I don’t like the look of this,” he said to Kerth. “Come on!”

He backtracked through the alleyway south of Cart Street and jogged westward to avoid the Spearmeet company. At the small square by the Council Hall, he found a strong detachment of Double Moon Coster and House Sokol sellswords standing watch, and he swore viciously. There were too many soldiers and militiamen ready to fight in the streets of the town. A few he might have expected, but there seemed to be companies of Hulburgans and mercenaries all over the town. “By Bane’s black hand, they were ready for us! They knew we were coming!” he snarled.

“Do you think this is a trap, m’lord?” Kerth asked.

“I have no idea, but we’ve got a fight on our hands.” Sergen turned back toward the water, and this time he ran. He shouted for roving gangs of pirates to follow him as he passed by; some did, and others ignored him, but he had no time to argue. He emerged onto Bay Street and hurried back to the corsairs waiting at the pierside where *Kraken Queen* was tied up. Quickly he detailed off half their number and sent them up Plank Street to scatter the Hulburgan militia there, and dispatched runners to gather in the roving gangs of corsairs. They needed to bring together the strength of the Black Moon, or they'd get cut to pieces in fours and fives as they blundered into the town's defenders. Then he sent another man to go ring *Kraken Queen*'s bell to signal a general recall—three sharp strikes, a pause, then three more, repeated several times. Pirates began to straggle back toward the ships.

Resplendent in his scarlet-scale armor, Kamoth jogged into view from an alleyway, with a dozen cutthroats at his back. He strode angrily up to Sergen. "Did you order the ship's bell struck?" he demanded. "We haven't been here half an hour yet! What is the matter?"

"Hulburgan companies are sealing off the streets leading to the waterfront!" Sergen said to his father. "They mean to trap us here by the docks. They were ready for us!"

"Then why weren't they waiting for us on the waterfront? Why isn't *Seadrake* here?" Kamoth scowled fiercely, considering the situation. "Didn't you say that your ally in town would warn you if the harmach caught wind of our plan?"

Sergen stopped and thought about that. "Yes, I did," he said. Rhovann was well placed in the councils of the town's leaders. If the harmach had learned of the coming attack, the elf mage would have told him. In fact, they'd made arrangements for just that eventuality. "They were warned, but only a short time before we arrived," he concluded. "They didn't have time to summon the Harmach's Council or make plans for a stronger defense, and my ally here hasn't had the chance to contact me. This is an improvised defense."

Kamoth turned on Sergen with a bloodthirsty grin. "Then it doesn't matter that they were warned. The harmach's guards are spread out all over the town trying to pin us down by the harbor. We'll smash them one street at a time, and the town will be ours by sunrise. Where are they?"

"I saw detachments on High Street, Plank Street, and Fish Street. I just sent fifty corsairs up Plank Street to drive off the Spearmeet gathered there. I imagine there must be a force blocking the Lower Bridge too."

"Good. You stay here and muster all the pirates who answer your recall. I'll take what you've got here and go deal with the Shieldsworn." Kamoth stepped close and seized Sergen's shoulder in one hand. He painfully ground his steel-armored fingers into Sergen's flesh as he lowered his voice; Sergen flinched away. "Do not ring that damned bell again unless the fleet of Hillsfar is standing into harbor, boy. I'm not to be called away from my business here every time you take a fright."

Sergen winced, but he did not protest. If he had to guard Kamoth from his own recklessness he would, regardless of his father's anger. He watched as the High Captain gathered the corsairs standing nearby and led them back into the town at a run. Meanwhile more pirates slowly trickled back to the dockside. Fuming over his father's insinuation of cowardice, he paced back and forth by the waterside, struggling to master his anger.

"Lord Sergen? There's someone asking for you—an elf." A deckhand from *Kraken Queen* stood with his cap in his hands nearby.

"Rhovann?" Sergen murmured. He wondered what the mage wanted from him. They'd made no plans to meet face-to-face during the raid, but then again, Sergen hadn't been sure he would accompany the Black Moon against Hulburg. He motioned to the messenger. "Bring him here."

He waited on the pier, listening to the sounds of the fighting that raged throughout Hulburg's streets. Half a dozen sizeable fires now burned in scattered places throughout the town. If the night hadn't been so damp, Hulburg might have lost everything west of the Winterspear. As matters stood, he thought the townsfolk would likely save most of the town. Then Rhovann Disarnnyl appeared through the rain and the smoke, dressed in a long hooded cloak. An enormous figure the size of an ogre towered behind him, dressed in a long brown robe with a heavy hood of its own. The creature's hands were pallid, almost waxy, in complexion. It carried two captives with their hands bound—a young, dark-haired girl not more than nine or ten years of age, and a black-haired woman in a blue dress whom Sergen recognized as Mirya Erstenwold. The girl must be her daughter, he realized. But what is Rhovann doing with Mirya as his prisoner? She certainly had value as a hostage, but he hadn't realized that the elf mage even knew of her existence.

"Good evening, Lord Sergen," Rhovann said. He offered a tight smile. "I see you brought your friends with you."

"Lord Disarnnyl," Sergen answered. "I'm surprised to find you out and about. I would have thought that you'd be well away from Hulburg tonight. It's not safe on the streets, after all."

"Bastion—my large friend here—deters a good deal of trouble," Rhovann answered. Sergen looked up at the huge, cowled figure standing behind the elf and glimpsed a pasty face, almost doughy in its complexion, beneath the hood. Dull, lifeless eyes regarded him in return. He realized that the thing was a construct or golem of some sort, likely created through Rhovann's magic. The elf mage motioned for his huge guardian to set down the Erstenwolds, and continued. "I have a problem—two problems, really—that I hope you can attend for me."

"So I see." Both Erstenwolds seemed unconscious, although Mirya's eyelids fluttered and a frown creased her brow. Gags covered their mouths. "What exactly do you expect me to do with them?"

"Mirya had the poor judgment to spy on me during a sensitive conversation. The little one had the misfortune of being at home when Bastion and I came to collect her mother. They both have seen too much to remain in Hulburg. Since there will doubtless be some number of people carried away by your Black Moon friends in the morning, I thought these two might be added to your catch."

"There's a simpler alternative, you know."

"Of course, but I am no common murderer. These two are not my enemies and are harmless to me once you remove them from Hulburg." Rhovann glanced at the unconscious Erstenwolds, now lying side by side on the rain-slick wood of the wharf.

"Besides, they are dear to Geran Hulmaster. It may prove very useful to keep them alive as long as he is at liberty."

Sergen pursed his lips. He was not anxious to burden himself with a couple of captives and was not as squeamish about such matters as Rhovann seemed to be, but his elf ally had an excellent point about their potential usefulness. If nothing else, simply selling them into slavery in the Inner Sea lands might make for an even more vicious flavor of revenge against his nemesis than killing them out of hand. Alive, they were far more useful against Geran than they would be dead.

"That's a fair point," Sergen conceded to Rhovann. "The day may come when I need to bait a trap, and these two would serve nicely. If you please, have your large friend pick them up and follow me."

Rhovann gestured, and Bastion silently picked up Mirya and her daughter again. The creature followed Sergen and Rhovann to the pier where *Kraken Queen* was tied up, and handed them to the corsair crewmen when Rhovann directed it to do so. "Lock them in my cabin for now," Sergen told the pirates. There would be plenty of other captives for the ship's hold, and he wasn't exactly certain what he was going to do with the Erstenwolds yet.

"Is there anything else?" he asked Rhovann.

"No, I must return to my quarters and resume my disguise." Rhovann's lip curled contemptuously. "I will report the harmach's counsels to you as soon as I can. I expect I'll know something by tomorrow evening."

"Very good," Sergen answered. "I will—"

From the deck behind him there came a shout: "A ship's entering the harbor!"

Sergen and Rhovann turned at the lookout's cry. "*Seadrake* or *Moonshark?*" Sergen wondered aloud. He climbed up to *Kraken Queen*'s quarterdeck and peered seaward. Rhovann followed just a few steps behind. By the dim glow of the city's fires, they could make out the long, low, scarlet hull of a half galley standing into harbor, her oars sweeping vigorously.

"It's *Moonshark!*" the lookout shouted.

"About time," Sergen observed. Whether the raid succeeded or failed mattered little to him, but it was very important to preserve the strength of the Black Moon no matter what happened here tonight. Narsk might have been tardy, but his sailors might turn the tide in the battle raging along Hulburg's waterfront. Better late than never, as they said. "Good. An hour late, but we can certainly use Narsk and his men now!"

Moonshark raced toward the wharves at a full battle pace, straining at her oars as if eager to join the fray. "He is certainly making up for lost time," Rhovann remarked. "You seem to have matters well in hand here, and I must return to my place before I am missed. Make sure you keep your men under control; we don't want the city razed."

"I will," Sergen murmured, but his eyes were still fixed on the approaching *Moonshark.* Narsk didn't bother to veer off to his left and make for the empty dock by the Sokol merchant yard; he simply came straight in, aiming at the center wharf where *Seawolf* and *Daring* were tied up. Sergen frowned and peered closer, his hands gripping the rail. The confident grin on his face faded, and he gaped at the approaching warship. With a ragged motion she raised her oars into the air and began to fold them inboard. "It can't be," he said. "Narsk's gone mad!"

Rhovann paused at the ladder and looked back at him. "What is it?"

Sergen threw out his arm and pointed. "He's not going alongside *Daring.* He's going to ram!"

SIXTEEN

8 Marpenoth, the Year of the Ageless One (1479 DR)

Rain and wind lashed Geran's face as he steered *Moonshark* into Hulburg's harbor. Firelight painted the whole harbor a ruddy red, and threw garish shadows against the streaming pillars of smoke rising above the town's burning buildings. His heart sank at the sight, but then he realized that the whole town wasn't aflame—five or six different fires were scattered across the harbor district, and the wet weather was doing its part to keep the flames in check. In the murk and firelight he could see bands of warriors fighting furiously on the streets leading up from the harbor. Whether Sarth's warning had reached the harmach in time, he couldn't say, but the fact that someone was still fighting by the docks was a good sign. If the Black Moon had surprised the town completely, there would have been very little fighting at all.

"It seems the issue is still in doubt," Hamil murmured beside him. The two of them were the only ones on the quarterdeck. *Moonshark* was somewhat shorthanded now, and Geran had ordered every man to the rowers' benches in order to make the best time he could to Hulburg. "Now what do we do? If we land, our crew's going to join the melee ashore. If we don't land, they'll likely throw us over the side and land anyway."

"I can see it," Geran answered under his breath. Then he lifted his voice and called out to the crew, "Well done! It's been a hard run, but we're not too late!"

The crewmen raised a ragged cheer as the ship slid past Hulburg's Arches, and bent themselves to the oars with renewed vigor. At the foredeck, Tao Zhe beat the time with a baton and a small drum. Geran gave the helm an easy turn to the right, angling around the last plunging column of the Arches. After hours of furious tacking and crowding on reckless amounts of sail for the strong winds, he'd finally reached Hulburg, only to find that he was not exactly certain what to do now.

"Somehow we need to throw the attack into confusion," he said quietly to Hamil. "We've got to do what we can to limit the damage to the town and catch Kamoth in a snare. I don't want him to get away again."

"Run *Moonshark* aground. That should keep us out of the fight."

"A good idea, but not enough," Geran said. The town—parts of it, anyway—was burning in front of his eyes, and as they drew closer he could see hundreds of people battling on Bay Street. Shouts, screams, and the shrill sound of steel on steel rang across the harbor. Those were his neighbors and friends fighting to protect life and property, fighting because of the greed and murderous designs of Sergen and his black-hearted father. Geran's eyes narrowed and a dark tide of anger surged up from the soles of his feet to his hands on the ship's wheel. "That's not enough by half," he continued. "I mean to *hurt* these bastards. They'll think twice before they attack my city again."

He quickly scanned the waterfront, searching for an opportunity to strike some telling blow. Four pirate galleys lay alongside the city's wharves, along with the usual handful of merchant ships and small craft. On the east side of the harbor, he could see *Kraken Queen* by the old Veruna wharves; straight ahead of him two more galleys lay side by side at the wharf in front of the Marstel storehouses; to the west one more galley was tied up near the Jannarsk docks. Geran wanted *Kraken Queen* most of all, but the Black Moon flagship was protected by a wharf that was in *Moonshark*'s way. Instead he pointed the bow at the two corsair ships in the middle. "Increase your tempo!" he shouted at Tao Zhe. "Battle speed!"

The Shou looked startled, but he began to strike his drum more swiftly. In the rowers' benches, the rest of the crew could not easily see where *Moonshark* was headed; they sat with their backs to the bow, and the covered bench galleries were low along the sides of the ship anyway. But the crewmen looked at each other, and many tried to catch glimpses forward between oarbeats. "Are you sure of your speed, Captain?" Murkelmor called from his place between the rowing benches. "It's no' so big a harbor!"

"Maintain your beat!" Geran called back. "We're going to ram!"

"Ram?" Murkelmor asked incredulously. "Who's there to ram?" The dwarf started to climb up to the main deck to look for himself.

Ram? Hamil repeated. He looked up at Geran. *Have you lost your mind?*

"There's a Hulburgan warship dead ahead of us, and she's got one of our galleys pinned to the pier," Geran answered. "We're going to make sure she can't pursue us when we leave! Now back to your places!"

A bold ploy, Hamil said. He winced, steadying himself by the rail.

Geran watched the distance narrow. At the last instant he shouted, "Raise oars! Bring 'em in and brace for impact!"

Carried forward by momentum, *Moonshark* buried her iron-sheathed beak in the side of the outboard Black Moon galley—*Daring,* if Geran read her name right in the uncertain light—with an awful sound. Timbers groaned and snapped like thunderbolts, the horrible sound echoing across the harbor. *Daring* was driven into *Seawolf* beside her, which in turn plowed into the wharf with enough force to upend the pilings and send the planks making up the boardwalk hurling through the air like matchsticks. Men screamed in terror or shouted in dismay. Aboard *Moonshark,* the hands at the rowing benches hurtled forward at the impact, and every loose item on the deck—barrels of sand and water, coils of rope, blocks and tackle—flew forward. One of the top yardarms aloft broke free and landed in the wreck of *Daring.*

Geran rebounded off the ship's wheel and found himself lying on the deck near the ladder to the main deck, tangled up with Hamil. The halfling groaned. "That is something I never want to do again," he muttered. "Ramming, indeed! That was the best you could come up with?"

"Once the notion struck me, I didn't want to examine it too closely," Geran answered. He staggered to his feet. *Daring* was already beginning to settle, her side stove in by the impact. He couldn't make out anything of *Seawolf* on the other side, since so much of *Daring*'s rigging and the wreckage of the pier covered her decks. "Back to your benches!" he shouted at the crew. "We've got to back out now, or the wreck will take us down with her!"

The crewmen started to untangle themselves from their seatmates and the benches around them, more than a few with groans of pain or muttered oaths. Murkelmor climbed to his feet and weaved forward uncertainly, taking in the damage to *Moonshark*. From the wreckage of *Daring* rose cries for help, the screams of the wounded, and more than a few streams of profanity. Suddenly the dwarf whirled back to face the quarterdeck, outraged. "You damned fool!" he shouted at Geran. "That's no Hulburgan! That's *Daring* you've killed, one of ours!"

"I can see that!" Geran answered. "Now get the crewmen to their benches, or we're going to sink with her!"

Skamang picked himself up from the oar benches and looked for himself. "You bloody traitor!" the Northman snarled. "You did that deliberately!"

"And I'll answer for it, but we're going to sink too if we don't back out! Now get to your benches before *Daring* takes us down!"

The deckhands looked from Geran to Skamang and Murkelmor. Fury darkened the dwarf's face, but he abruptly wheeled and began to shove men into their places. "Reverse your benches!" Murkelmor shouted at the crew. The men stood, turned in place, and sat down again to seize the oars that would have been behind them in normal rowing. Skamang glared at Geran, but he joined the rest. All too often a ramming ship went down with its victim, and *Moonshark*'s crewmen understood that they were at risk of joining *Daring* on the bottom if they didn't act swiftly. But angry glares were fixed on Geran and Hamil as the crew seized their oars.

"Oars in the water!" Geran ordered. "Tao Zhe, standard beat! Pull us out!"

Moonshark lay tangled with her victim for a long moment, her oars groping for purchase in the waters of the harbor. Then, with the groaning and popping of tortured wood, she pulled herself free from the wreck and backed off. Scores of *Daring* and *Seawolf* hands clung to their battered ships or the ruined wharf or shouted angrily from the street just beyond.

"What's our damage, Murkelmor?" Hamil shouted.

Murkelmor shot Hamil a resentful look, but he hurried forward and peered over the bow. Then he ducked into the forecastle. While he was below, Geran continued to let *Moonshark* back slowly, and put the wheel over to swing her bow toward *Kraken Queen*.

Trying for the big one next? Hamil asked. *The crew won't stand for it, Geran!*

"*Kraken Queen*'s the one I really want," Geran answered under his breath. He just couldn't imagine how to convince the crew to ram another ship. "Avast rowing! Reverse your benches again!" he called to the crew. "We're going ahead now."

"Where, Aram?" Skamang demanded from his seat. "Where are we going?"

"I'm bringing us about," Geran replied. "Now sit down and row!"

With grumbling and a few suspicious looks, the crewmen switched positions again. Geran fixed his eye on the Black Moon flagship, only a few hundred yards away and still moored at the pier. He could see pirates hurrying to man the ship and spotted a flurry of activity by her quarterdeck. There was a muffled *thump* from the pirate ship, followed three heartbeats later by a shrill whistling in the air.

"Darts!" Hamil cried. "Cover!" He threw himself against the gunwale, crouching under its cover. Geran ducked down behind the helm. An instant later, a dozen short iron javelins sleeted across the deck. Most clattered on empty space or stuck quivering in gunwales or masts, but a few fell among the crew packed on their rowing benches, wounding several men. Screams of pain and howls of dismay rang across the deck. One dart hissed over Geran's shoulder and took a deep gouge out of the ship's sternrail. Then a catapult on *Kraken Queen*'s foredeck snapped against its frame, and a ball of flaming pitch streaked across the smoke-filled sky to splash into the water a little short of *Moonshark*'s bow.

"*Kraken Queen*'s firing on us!" shouted one of the crewmen.

Geran grimaced. *Moonshark* had no shipboard artillery. Very few ships in the Moonsea—warship, pirate, or otherwise—did. Their only attack was to ram or grapple their foes. "Oars in the water! Give me some steerageway, or she'll rake us again! Tao Zhe, full speed!"

Moonshark started to glide forward as Tao Zhe struck the beat and the crew found their stroke again. Now she was moving forward, her prow toward *Kraken Queen*. Another flight of darts hissed through the air, most of them overshooting this time. Then Murkelmor climbed back up to the deck. "We've sprung seams by the stem!" he called. "Some oakum ought to hold her for now, but she'll need repair soon."

"Understood," Geran replied. "Get your carpenters to work on stuffing the leaks."

Murkelmor called out several of his men from their places and sent them hurrying into the forecastle. He glowered at the iron darts littering the deck, the wounded men in the benches, then ducked as flaming pitch sailed over the midships deck to explode in the water on the far side of the ship. The dwarf swore and turned to yank Tao Zhe's baton out of his hand. "Avast rowing!" he shouted. "All of you, stop! You'll drive us right into *Kraken Queen* next!"

"Stand aside, Murkelmor!" Hamil shouted. "We're sitting ducks for the catapults if we're not moving!"

"That's as may be, but none of us'll row a single beat more until the captain makes his intentions clear!" Murkelmor retorted. "Get us alongside a pier, Aram, or by Moradin's beard we'll take the wheel and do it ourselves!"

"He doesn't mean to bring us to shore," Skamang said angrily. "He's up to some black treachery! Can't you all see it?"

Geran held his course, fuming. He wanted Kamoth's ship . . . but he couldn't take her by himself, and he couldn't trick *Moonshark*'s crew into helping him to do it. His best chance to deal with Sergen and Kamoth lay ashore now, but he couldn't bring another ship full of pirates into the city. *Kraken Queen*'s catapult threw again, and this time her volley of darts fell across the center of the ship. Even with the instant of warning the darts' passage through the air provided, several more men fell to the iron javelins.

"Why did you strike *Daring?*" Murkelmor demanded. "What's your game, Aram?"

Geran spun the wheel to starboard and turned *Moonshark*'s bow seaward. "Get them rowing, Murkelmor! We have to get out of the flagship's range before we do anything else!"

The dwarf glared up at Geran, but he handed the baton back to Tao Zhe. "Battle speed," he agreed. "Go ahead, get her underway again."

The deckhands bent their backs to the oars, and *Moonshark* began to pick up speed. *Kraken Queen*'s next catapult throw brought another ball of burning pitch. This one struck *Moonshark* low on the hull, a few feet aft of her sternmost oar. A great gout of stinking smoke billowed up from the side, but the shot was too close to the waterline and was soon extinguished by the choppy waters of the harbor. By the time *Kraken Queen* was ready to fire again, *Moonshark* had drawn back out of range. The pirate flagship was still tied up alongside the old Veruna wharf and did not appear inclined to pursue while most of her crew was engaged in a pitched battle ashore.

Geran surreptitiously eased the helm over to approach the Arches from their harbor side. Hamil's idea about running the ship aground was worth a try. There were places in the forest of stone columns where a small boat could slip through, but nothing *Moonshark* could manage. Unfortunately, Murkelmor no longer trusted Geran's judgment at the helm. The dwarf moved to the side of the ship and leaned out for a good look forward. "Slow down or come about!" he shouted at the quarterdeck. "We're running short o' sea room here!"

Geran ignored him. After a moment, the dwarf swore to himself. "Did you no' hear me the first time? Where are you steering us, Aram?"

Murkelmor and Skamang won't let us run her aground, Hamil said. *Perhaps it's time to leave?*

Geran stood his ground a moment longer, trying to think of some ploy that might mollify *Moonshark*'s crew. Murkelmor swore again and began to shake the crew around them, getting them to drop their oars and stand up from their benches. The looks the crewmen turned on the quarterdeck ranged from slack-jawed puzzlement to dark fury, but none boded well for his continued command of the ship. He and Hamil might be able to hold the quarterdeck ladders for a long time—at least, until the crew remembered the crossbows below in the ship's armory—but what was the point? *Moonshark* might turn back to the docks and join the attack, but that would mean coming within range of Kamoth's catapults again. He'd already bloodied the Black Moon. There simply wasn't anything more he could do aboard *Moonshark* short of sinking her, and the crew wasn't about to let him do that.

"Come on!" Skamang roared. He pointed at Geran and Hamil. "Kill those miserable dogs before they do any more harm! They've betrayed us all!" The Northman seized a boarding pike by his bench and led the way as the crew surged up out of the benches and swarmed toward the quarterdeck.

"I think you're right," Geran said to Hamil. He retreated to the ship's wheel, spun her bow toward the Arches, and looped the keeper over the top spoke. Then, tossing his cutlass aside, he moved to the sternrail, swung his legs over, and leaped into the dark water astern of the ship. It was bitterly cold, and when he surfaced he gasped for air. Hamil followed a moment later, dropping into the water a few feet behind him. *Moonshark* swept away from them, carried by the momentum of her sprint even though her oars were no longer pulling in unison.

"Somehow I knew it was going to come to this," Hamil spluttered. "You and I in the water, watching the ship sail away."

"I think they'll keep her off the rocks," Geran said. "If we could have kept them at the oars just a little longer . . ."

"I'll point out, for the record, that your command of *Moonshark* lasted less than a single day."

"So noted," Geran answered. The water was very cold, and he couldn't stop his teeth from chattering. "Come on, we'd better get ashore. Skamang looked mad enough to come around and try to run us down."

Treading water, Geran watched the ship recede. There was a flurry of activity as the crew swarmed the quarterdeck and regained the helm. Skamang glared over the rail at him, and several other corsairs joined him. Then cries of alarm distracted the pirates; someone had noticed that the ship was drifting into new danger. The crew rushed back down to their benches, and the oars slowly began to dip into the water again. A moment later Tao Zhe leaped over the side, hitting the water with a large splash. The Shou surfaced and began to swim in the direction of Geran and Hamil.

"The ship's back the way you came, Tao Zhe," Hamil said.

"I know it," the cook said. He glanced over his shoulder and laughed. "I like my prospects better in the water. Everyone on board knows I'm your friend."

"Suit yourself," Geran answered. "It's a long swim, though."

They struck out for the closest land, which was the point east of the Veruna docks. It was hardly near the center of the action, but it already looked to be a swim of several hundred yards, and Geran was not about to lengthen it by swimming all the way to the city's wharves. It took them a quarter hour before they staggered up the pebble-strewn shoreline near the mouth of the Winterspear, shivering and exhausted. He turned and looked back over the harbor; *Moonshark* had turned her nose toward the wharves again, but she hugged the west side of the harbor, staying away from *Kraken Queen* and her catapults.

"Did we do enough, Hamil?" he asked his friend.

Hamil flopped to the ground and started to wring water from his braids. "We sank one ship for certain, and the other ship that was between her and the pier likely isn't going anywhere soon either. We kept *Moonshark* out of the fight for most of the evening, and I'll wager that Kamoth won't have much use for Narsk's ship after tonight. I don't know what more we could have done."

Tao Zhe looked at them both, his eyes wide. "I knew it! You are no pirates. Who are you?"

"No, we're not," Hamil said. "I'm Hamil Alderheart of Tantras. This is Geran Hulmaster of Hulburg, nephew to the harmach."

"Don't worry. You don't have anything to fear from the harmach's men," Geran told Tao Zhe. "I'll see to it that you get a pardon and an honest sailor's berth, if you want it."

"You rammed *Daring* on purpose! And you meant to ram *Kraken Queen* too!"

"It would've been hard to manage it all by mistake," Hamil told him.

"I'd like to know how Sarth fared," Geran said. He shivered in the cool night air. He'd lost his boots and his cloak in the swim. For that matter, he was unarmed as well. Still, he sighed and straightened up. "Come on. We might as well go see who's in charge of the town's defense and whether we can lend a hand."

Hamil nodded wearily and climbed to his feet again. They set off along the shore toward Bay Street. This corner of Hulburg's waterfront was still covered in the ruins of the older city that had preceded the town, and they stayed by the water in order to avoid the old rubble. Suddenly Hamil reached out and caught Geran's sleeve, pointing seaward again. "Geran, look! There's *Seadrake!*"

Standing into the harbor under oar and sail, *Seadrake* gracefully swept past the city's Arches, making for the wharves in the center of town. Her white sails glowed a dull red in the reflected firelight. In the distance Geran heard the ship's bells of the Black Moon vessels begin to ring in alarm. Ashore, the fighting began to slacken as bands of pirates broke off their battle against Hulburg's defenders, beginning to retreat to their surviving ships. "By Tymora, but Kara's got good timing!" Geran said with a grin. "That'll be a hundred more swords on our side. With a little luck, we might catch all of them now!"

The two companions hurried to Bay Street, with Tao Zhe tagging along after them. After being briefly confused for pirates due to their dress, they fell in with a band of Spearmeet who were pressing westward from the Lower Bridge, sweeping the street clear. By the time they reached the foot of the wharf where *Kraken Queen* had been tied up, the pirate flagship was already rowing her way clear of Hulburg's docks. Geran grimaced. He should have guessed that Kamoth would flee once a warship appeared to threaten his ability to escape. All they could do was stand on the wharf and watch the chase develop across the harbor.

"It looks like Murkelmor's thought better of landing now," Hamil observed.

Geran followed his gaze and glimpsed *Moonshark* reversing course to slip back out to sea, evading *Seadrake*. "I'm not surprised. He's not the type to throw in with a losing cause." He found he was a little relieved that the ship would get away for now. Skamang and his lot Geran had no use for, but Murkelmor and a few of the others were decent fellows after their own fashion. He hoped he wouldn't have to cross swords with them.

Seadrake tried to close with *Kraken Queen,* but Kamoth proved an elusive foe. The pirate flagship was handier under oars than *Seadrake,* and Kamoth demonstrated it by backing one side and stroking ahead with the other, spinning the ship on a copper piece and then darting away before *Seadrake* could turn around. The two vessels exchanged a few volleys of catapult fire and plenty of arrows during their close pass, to no great effect. For a brief moment, Geran feared that *Seadrake* would miss all the pirate ships, but then she turned and bore down on the last one—*Wyvern,* he guessed—catching her before she got more than a bowshot from the wharf. The fighting was over quickly;

Geran couldn't see well from the dock, but he could hear the angry shouts and fierce battle cries of the Hulburgans aboard their warship as they threw themselves against the pirates who'd attacked their town.

As the fighting between *Seadrake* and *Wyvern* died down and the remaining two Black Moon vessels disappeared into the blackness of the Moonsea night, Geran caught sight of a tall man with skin of brick red and a prominent pair of horns sweeping back from his forehead. He stood at the waterside watching the pirate vessels attempt their escape. After a tenday of seeing Sarth every day in a human guise, it took Geran a moment to recognize his friend. "Sarth! You're here!" he said.

The tiefling turned at Geran's call and gave him an uneven smile. "You sent me, in case it slipped your mind." He looked at Geran's sodden clothes and bare feet. "Might I guess that you are no longer captain of *Moonshark?* And Hamil is no longer first mate?"

"The crew was sorely disappointed by Geran's decisions during the attack," Hamil said. "It became clear to us that our presence was no longer required. Regrettably, we parted ways with *Moonshark* in the middle of the harbor."

"Did you get here before the Black Moon?" Geran asked.

Sarth nodded. "Yes, but not by very much. I became lost in those hills east of town and missed the coastal track. By the time I found the path I feared that I would be too late and pressed on with all the speed I could muster. When I arrived at Griffonwatch, no one recognized me until I resumed my normal appearance. That finally impressed upon the Shieldsworn the earnestness of my mission. They sent runners to muster the Spearmeet companies and summon the merchant company armsmen, but the town's defenders were still massing when the Black Moon ships appeared. If I'd been delayed by even half an hour more, the attack would have been much worse."

Geran reached out to grip Sarth by the shoulder. "Thank you, Sarth," he said. "You saved scores of lives tonight, perhaps hundreds. I won't forget it."

The sorcerer inclined his head. "I only did what I could."

Hamil looked around at the waterfront and sighed. "It looks like the Red Sail's tradeyard was hit hard," he said. "We'll have plenty of cleaning up to do."

Geran gazed out to sea after the fleeing Black Moon flagship. He had unfinished business with Kamoth and Sergen, and he meant to take it up again soon.

SEVENTEEN

8 Marpenoth, the Year of the Ageless One (1479 DR)

Sunrise was still an hour away as Geran made his way from the harbor districts toward the castle of Griffonwatch. More than a little fatigued by two sleepless nights and the bonechilling cold of his swim in the harbor, he'd left Hulburg's defenders to round up the last of the Black Moon corsairs stranded ashore. The swordmage resigned himself to a long, cold walk through the chaotic streets, and started up the hilly, cobblestone-paved path of Plank Street. He meant to speak with the harmach before he allowed himself to fall into bed.

He passed by Erstenwold's and noted that the store seemed mostly undamaged, although several of the windows were broken and a black smudge along one wall showed where some pirate had tried to set it afire. Mirya was not there, which didn't surprise him; her house was on the landward side of Hulburg. Given the late hour of the pirate raid, she wouldn't have been anywhere near the harbor district. He climbed up the steps to the storefront and peered into the darkened windows to reassure himself that nothing was out of place inside.

"Hey, what're you up to?" Several Hulburgans in the motley arms of the Spearmeet watched Geran warily from the street. The militiamen approached with their spears leveled, led by a strapping young man with a brown beard. "Get away from there!" he shouted at Geran.

Geran turned and raised his hand in a placating gesture. "It's me—Geran Hulmaster. You can point your spear away from me, Brun Osting."

Brun took a step forward and studied Geran with a suspicious look before recognition dawned in his face. He quickly pointed his spear skyward. "Begging your pardon, Lord Geran. I didn't make you out in those clothes. You look just like one o' those sea reavers we've been chasing after all night."

"No fault of yours, Brun. I've spent the last tenday passing myself off as a pirate." Geran came back out into the street. "I'm glad to see that you're well. From what I could tell, the Spearmeet was in the thick of things."

The young brewer smiled grimly. "Aye, we had our share of fighting. We made sure that plenty of reavers who left their ships never made it back to 'em. But now that we've handled the pirates, the thrice-damned Cinderfists are out looking for trouble. There's all kinds of fighting over in the Tailings and down along the poorer parts of Easthead. We were just heading that way to lend a hand." He glanced over Geran's shoulder at the signboard for Erstenwold Provisioners, and suddenly he fell silent. His face fell, and he looked at the ground.

"What?" Geran asked. "What is it, Brun?"

"It's Mistress Erstenwold, Lord Geran," the brewer said. "You couldn't have heard if you've been away from Hulburg, but she's gone missing."

"Missing?" Cold dread squeezed Geran's heart. Mirya missing? If she was not in Hulburg, there was no place she would have gone of her own free will. His weariness vanished in sudden alarm. "What happened? Tell me!"

"It was two nights past. One of her neighbors heard a ruckus at her house and found the place all tore up—the front door wrenched off the hinges, furniture overturned, and all that. No one's seen her or her little girl since." Brun set his knuckle to his forehead. "Every man who calls himself loyal to Hulburg's been looking for them."

Geran took a step back, as if he'd been physically struck. Someone had attacked Mirya's house? He started to ask himself why, but halted in midthought. It didn't matter. He'd been away from Hulburg, unable to protect them. That was most likely the why of it; the only real questions were where the two of them were now, and whether they were beyond his help or not. The thought of some harm coming to Mirya or her daughter made him dizzy with dread. "Who? Who did it?" he asked.

Brun and his men exchanged looks with one another. "No one knows, Lord Geran," the brewer said. "The harmach himself's taken it up."

"Lord Geran?" one of the men with Brun added. "I might've heard something new on it. My cousin serves in Tresterfin's company. He told me he saw something peculiar in the middle of the fighting down by the wharves tonight—a big fellow, an ogre maybe, carrying a couple of people like the evening's shopping down High Street toward the harbor. There was a thin man in a brown cowl with the big one. My cousin only saw the pair of 'em at a distance, but he told me that he would've sworn that it was Mirya Erstenwold the big fellow carried, all trussed up like a prisoner." The militiaman shrugged awkwardly. "Mistress Erstenwold's been on all our minds, I guess. He might've been seeing things as weren't what he thought. But I thought you ought to know."

An ogre and a man in a cowl? Geran could make no sense of that. There was no point in running off to comb the waterfront himself; if Brun was right, the Moonshields had already turned the town upside down, and the militiaman's story might have nothing to it. But he knew who might be able to help. "My thanks, Brun," he said. Then he climbed back up the steps to the store, let himself in by unlocking the door through its broken window, and hurried inside the darkened building.

A moment later he found what he was looking for and returned to the street with a well-worn white shawl clutched in his hand. Brun looked at him as if he'd lost his mind, but Geran showed him the shawl. "It might help," he said. "If anyone asks about me, tell them I'll be up to Griffonwatch as soon as I can."

"Aye, Lord Geran," Brun answered.

Geran nodded his thanks and rushed off down the street. He feared that he knew where Mirya was, but he had to make sure of it. He wound his way through the smoldering town, past bands of militia and soldiers searching for any pirates still hiding in the town, and hurried to Sarth's home on the seaward slopes of the Easthead. The tiefling lived in a modest house attached to a small round tower rebuilt from the ruins of an older watch-post. Sarth was a man of means in Hulburg and could afford to live well.

Geran found a heavy bell by the front door and pulled it urgently. "Sarth!" he called. "I need your help!" He rang the bell again.

The door opened, revealing a stout, balding halfling of middle years with a small oil lamp in his hand—Sarth's valet. The servant looked up at Geran and blinked sleepily. "Ah, Lord Geran! I'm afraid Master Sarth has retired for the evening," he said. "Can you return in the morning?"

"I fear this can't wait," Geran answered. "Wake him, please. It'll be on my head."

The valet sighed. "Very well, then. Please wait in the foyer. Master Sarth will be down directly." He retreated into the darkened house. Geran stepped inside and closed the door. Sarth's home was plainly furnished in the simple, rough-hewn style most Hulburgans favored, although the decor included several fine Turmishan weavings. He paced anxiously across the flagstones of the foyer, trying to fight down the sick dread in his stomach.

Sarth and his servant appeared at the top of the staircase. The tiefling belted a light robe around his waist and descended. "What is it, Geran? What's wrong?"

"Mirya Erstenwold and her daughter are missing. I fear they may have been carried off in the Black Moon raid. Can you find her?"

The sorcerer grimaced. "I am sorry, my friend. Of course I will do what I can. Do you have something of hers?"

Geran produced the shawl he'd picked up in Mirya's store. "Here."

Sarth took the shawl and nodded. "This should do. Come, let's go to my workshop." He led the way to the round room formed by the old tower adjoining the house. It was surprisingly uncluttered; in Geran's experience most conjuries and laboratories were hopelessly messy, but Sarth hadn't been in Hulburg long enough to accumulate the knickknacks, mementos, and curios that most sorcerers acquired over time. Over the last few months the tiefling had simply shrugged any time Geran asked him whether he was staying or not; Geran suspected that Sarth still entertained notions of recovering the magical tome known as the *Infiernadex* from the lich-king Aesperus, and spent his spare time investigating ways to do so.

"I hope you'll forgive me for waking you up," Geran said.

Sarth sighed. "I spent the last tenday unable to sleep a wink on that accursed ship. I think I managed half an hour before you woke me, but I am glad you did. Time may be of the essence." He went to a cluttered bookshelf, considered the tomes crowded together there, then selected one to carry over to a reading stand in the center of the room. A circle of intricate runes and sigils was painted on the floor around the stand, and Sarth was careful to step over them as he entered. He opened the book, flipped through the pages, and found the spell he was looking for. "There, this should do. Stand over there, if you please, and keep still. I must concentrate."

Geran did as Sarth told him. He'd learned a little about magic rituals himself during his studies in Myth Drannor, but Sarth was his superior in such things. The sorcerer ignited several candles around his rune-circle with a wave of his hand, and kindled a small fire beneath a brass bowl on a small table beside the reading stand. Into the bowl he threw pinches of various strange powders and began to intone the words recorded in his ritual book. Geran felt the stirrings of arcane power gathering in the candlelit conjury. Sarth continued with his magic and bent over the bowl to inhale deeply from the fragrant smoke that rose from it.

The candles flickered and guttered out; the sorcerer picked up Mirya's shawl, holding it close under his nose, and closed his eyes. He stayed that way for a long moment then exhaled and opened his eyes. "She lives," he said. He pointed toward one wall of the conjury. Its narrow window faced south, toward the Moonsea. "She is about fifteen miles in that direction and drawing farther away as we speak."

"*Kraken Queen,*" Geran snarled. The only other pirate ship to escape the harbor had been *Moonshark,* and she'd never landed. He struck a fist against the wall. "Damn it all! How did she wind up a captive? Her house was nowhere near the harbor!"

"What will you do?" Sarth asked him.

"Go after her," Geran said at once. "I'll take whatever crew I can gather for *Seadrake* and sail within the hour, if possible. I have to overtake Kamoth before he disappears again."

"I understand your desire for haste. But how heavy a blow have your enemies dealt the harmach tonight? Are you—and the company of *Seadrake*—needed here more?"

Geran hesitated. He understood Sarth's unspoken question: were Mirya and her daughter already beyond help? Even if they weren't, he was all too aware of the distant sound of fighting and the reek of smoke from the town below. *Seadrake* and her armsmen represented the better part of a quarter, perhaps a third, of the harmach's strength. Hulburg might have repelled the Black Moon raid, but there was still the question of the Cinderfists to deal with. How would they react to the pirate attack? It might be wiser to delay a day or two, to take the measure of the town's disorder and make sure that Hulburg was secure before setting out again. But each hour he delayed, Kamoth and Sergen improved their chances of escaping his grasp again—this time with Mirya and Selsha as their captives. He could imagine all too well what sort of fate might await the Erstenwolds in their hands.

Delay and risk losing them forever? he thought furiously. Or leave at once, hoping that he and the rest of *Seadrake*'s company weren't needed to quell the troubles in Hulburg? Geran closed his eyes and made his decision. "If there's any chance at all that I can save Mirya and her daughter from the Black Moon, I have to try, regardless of the consequences. I'll sail at once."

"So be it." Sarth nodded. "As long as Sergen keeps Mirya aboard, I should be able to repeat my divination and sense the direction and distance to *Kraken Queen*. I know Mirya well. It will be difficult for the High Captain to hide her from me."

"Thank you, Sarth."

Sarth glanced back through the doorway to his living space, already missing the comforts of his own bed. He sighed. "I will get dressed and return to *Seadrake.*"

"Good. I'll see you aboard." Geran clasped the sorcerer's arm in gratitude and then hurried back out into the night.

As it turned out, it was more than three hours before *Seadrake* could put to sea again. Geran could not leave without at least a brief visit to Griffonwatch—he had to seek the harmach's blessing for taking the ship to sea again, and more importantly he had to relate to Harmach Grigor and Kara the story of his voyage aboard *Moonshark* and what he'd learned about Kamoth, Sergen, and the Black Moon Brotherhood. Kara dispatched Shieldsworn messengers to recall the crew and order the ship made ready for sea again while Geran reported his discoveries. The Hulburgan ship hurriedly reprovisioned, and the crew returned from brief visits home in order to get the ship underway again as soon as possible.

The morning was only an hour old as *Seadrake* cast off and sculled her way clear of the harbor. Anxious to take stock of the damage to Hulburg's defenses and deal with surviving pirate gangs, Kara chose to stay behind. But Sarth and Hamil joined Geran again, and most of the warship's company remained aboard, including the first mate Worthel, Andurth Galehand, Larken the prelate, and the rest of the officers. *Seadrake*'s warriors and sailors had only lost a handful of souls in the taking of *Wyvern,* so the crew was still at full strength, or close to it.

Geran paced anxiously across the quarterdeck, watching Galehand steer the ship past the Arches. By his count, *Kraken Queen* had a five-hour head start. Pillars of smoke still rose from the smoldering ashes of burned buildings, climbing skyward in the morning light. The rain and wind of the night had abated somewhat, leaving the morning with a steel gray overcast and a light westerly wind. "As soon as we clear Keldon Head, crowd on all the sail you can and steer south-southwest," he told the sailing master. "The pirates are probably thirty miles or more south of us. I'm going to gamble that they'll eventually turn west and make for the River Lis, so let's see if we can cut the corner on their course."

"What if they run t' Mulmaster instead?" Andurth asked.

"I don't think Kamoth will want to risk getting trapped in Mulmaster's narrow harbor. He knows *Seadrake* will be on his track soon enough. If he goes east, he risks getting trapped in the Galennar, with the wind in our favor." Geran shook his head. "Besides, I've got a feeling he has some place to hide near Umberlee's Talons." He remembered the way *Kraken Queen* had appeared with such startling swiftness when Narsk sailed *Moonshark* to meet the master of the Black Moon there.

They kept on their southwest course for most of the day without sighting the pirate flagship. At sunset Sarth made use of the privacy and space in the captain's cabin to perform his divination again, and reported that *Kraken Queen* was indeed to their west, not much more than twenty miles off.

Geran gambled again on a long run to the north and back, to make the best speed westward possible with the wind, and kept up the pursuit through the night and the morning following. A little after noon on the day after they'd set sail, the lookout in *Seadrake*'s foretop cried out, "Sail ho! Two points off the port bow, hull down!"

Geran ran to the forecastle and peered over the bow. He could just barely make out the topsails of the ship ahead of them. Hamil joined him, climbing up the ratlines of the foremast to gain a better view. The halfling's sight was quite keen, but after peering for a long moment he gave up with a shrug. "I'm not sure if it's Kamoth," Hamil said.

"It's about where I would expect Kamoth to be if he's running west toward the Talons. But we'll have to close the distance to know for sure." Geran studied the distant sails for a moment and then nodded to himself. "I'm going to assume that's *Kraken Queen* and stick to her wake. Now that I have her in sight, I don't want to lose her again."

The afternoon seemed to crawl by as they slowly narrowed the distance to the ship ahead of them. Geran tried not to pace the decks or otherwise show the crew how anxious he was, but it took all of his willpower to restrain himself. Andurth had the ship in better trim than he could have managed, and they were making the best speed they possibly could. Instead, he leaned against the leeward rail near the helm and silently murmured prayers to every deity of mercy and fortune he could think of, hoping that Mirya and her daughter were simply being held on the other ship and not tormented in some way. The very idea of Mirya hurt or killed by Kamoth and his murderers made Geran's heart grow cold. He didn't know what it was that he felt for her; in all honesty, he had no claim on her heart and couldn't imagine how he might even try to win her again, not after the years that had fallen between them and the grief he'd caused her. But he'd go to the ends of the world and lay down his life, if that would see her safely home again.

"Sergen knows her value, Geran," Hamil said softly.

Geran shook himself and looked at his friend. "What?"

"Mirya. I can see you're worried sick for her. Sergen has to recognize her value as a hostage. He'd be a fool to let her come to harm without trying to use her against you. Nothing will happen to her as long as he believes she might be useful to him." Hamil reached up to set a hand on Geran's shoulder. "Sergen is rotten to the core, but he's not a fool."

"I hear you," Geran answered. "But that doesn't mean Sergen will treat her well or protect her from Kamoth. It might not be up to him."

"Hope for the best, Geran. There's no point in dwelling on the alternatives."

Geran snorted. "Since when have you become an optimist?"

"Don't let anyone else know. I've my cynical reputation to think of." Hamil squinted at the ship ahead of them and allowed himself a small smile. "I think that's her. You can make out the black hull and the gilding on the stern now."

Geran looked more closely and decided that Hamil was right. They were chasing *Kraken Queen* more or less directly into the westering sun, running as close to the wind as they could manage, but it was clear that they were gaining. The big pirate galley was not quite as slender or quick as *Moonshark,* and *Seadrake* held a noticeable advantage in speed over her quarry. "There's an old saying in the Sea of Fallen Stars that comes to mind: a stern chase is a long chase. But we can outsail her, and I think we'll overtake her in a couple of hours."

"The afternoon is getting on," Hamil warned. "We might run out of daylight before we catch Kamoth."

"See? Now there's the doomsayer I'm accustomed to." Of course, the same thought had occurred to him, but the skies looked clear, and there'd be a half-moon early in the evening. He thought they'd be able to keep *Kraken Queen* in sight as long as they were within two or three miles. If they couldn't catch her before sundown, he thought they'd catch her early in the evening.

The distance steadily narrowed throughout the afternoon, until sunset found *Seadrake* trailing her quarry by a little more than a mile. It was clearly Kamoth's flagship they had in sight; ahead, on the horizon, the sharp pinnacles of Umberlee's Talons rose out of the water. Soon enough the pirate ship would have to attempt some maneuver to break away from *Seadrake,* or she'd have to accept a fight.

Geran took a quarter hour to duck into his cabin, eat a few bites of food, and buckle on the scabbard of his elven steel. The blade felt good in his hand after the heavy, poorly balanced cutlass he'd relied on aboard *Moonshark.* Then he hurried back to the quarterdeck. *Kraken Queen* kept straight on for the stony pillars, as if they offered some refuge that the Hulburgan ship dared not enter.

I don't like this, Geran decided. Kamoth was up to something, he was certain of it. He wished Tao Zhe was at hand; it was unlikely that the cook could have offered any real insights about Kamoth's intentions, but he would have known these waters better than Geran. However, Tao Zhe was back in Hulburg, since Hamil had offered the old Shou a billet with the Red Sail Coster before they'd sailed. "Keep after *Kraken Queen*, but watch where she's leading us," he told Galehand. "Pass the word to clear for battle."

"Aye, m'lord," Galehand answered. The dwarf bellowed his orders over the deck, and *Seadrake*'s sailors and armsmen moved to take up their battle stations. The Shieldsworn and sellswords aboard the ship donned their armor, uncovered the catapult on the foredeck, and set up the arbalests in their mounts on the rails.

Kraken Queen raced on, just out of bowshot now. But Umberlee's Talons loomed ahead. The pirate ship steered boldly between two of the outlying reefs without slacking speed and made for the narrow passage between two of the great stony claws.

"She's threading a fine channel, m'lord," Andurth warned.

"Follow her in," Geran ordered. "If there's enough water beneath the keel for *Kraken Queen,* there's enough water for us."

"Aye, m'lord," the sailing master replied. He scowled but said nothing more, moving to stand beside the helmsman. *Seadrake* plunged between the towering stone columns, only a couple of hundred yards behind *Kraken Queen* now. In the pale light of the rising moon, Geran could see dark figures on the enemy ship's quarterdeck—likely Kamoth, Sergen, and the Black Moon ship's officers. He allowed himself a grim smile. They were almost through the Talons, and on the other side there was nothing but open sea, with no place for the pirate to hide and no way for them to delay the inevitable.

He was just about to order his archers and arbalesters to test the range when *Kraken Queen* began to lift out of the water. "What in the world?" Andurth muttered beside him. Other cries of alarm and consternation echoed from the soldiers assembled on deck. As the moonlight fell on the pirate ship, a silvery radiance seemed to grow around its black hull and scarlet sails. Luminous fins or sails shimmered into existence from the hull like the gossamer wings of an enormous dragonfly. Moment by moment the pirate galley rode higher in the water, until it barely skimmed the wavetops. And then, astonishingly, it climbed skyward, soaring into the air. It banked gently to the port side, looking for all the world like it was heeling over in a strong breeze, and Geran saw the dripping rudder shift in empty air. The corsair ship came around, passing *Seadrake* a few hundred yards to the south and high enough to sail over the highest of the Talons, and steadied with her bowsprit pointed toward the moon in the southeastern sky.

"Now that I did not expect," Hamil murmured in astonishment. "I suppose we know how *Kraken Queen* appeared and disappeared."

Geran stared at the airborne ship, watching it soar faster and faster as it climbed away from the sea. Far beneath its black hull the moonlight danced in a silvery road across the dark sea. He and the rest of the crewmen on the quarterdeck were so amazed that the bow lookout had to shout three times to get their attention. "Rock dead on the bow! Turn the ship! Turn the ship!"

Andurth wrenched his eyes from the spectacle of the receding pirate ship and looked forward again. With a startled oath, the sailing master leaped for the helm and spun the wheel to the right. *Seadrake* heeled sharply, and as her bow crossed into the wind her sails flapped loudly. But the ship missed the jagged fang of stone *Kraken Queen* had almost led her onto. The hull grated for one awful instant on submerged rock, but it was just deep enough and far enough to the port side for *Seadrake* to bounce away rather than rip herself open. The impact was still enough to knock crewmen off their feet and bring a cascade of loose stays and tackle from the rigging. Then Andurth turned the helm the other way, using the last of the ship's momentum to recapture the wind as the deadly rock passed down the port side.

"The black-hearted bastard did that on purpose," the dwarf muttered. "He tried t' lead us right into the thick o' it and hid that rock with his own hull until the last moment."

The swordmage breathed a sigh of relief and clapped a hand on the dwarf's shoulder. "Well done, Master Andurth. That could have been disastrous." He stared at *Kraken Queen,* still climbing into the night sky. "Steer us clear of the Talons and then bring us around to the southeast. That seems to be the way *Kraken Queen* is headed."

"How exactly do you propose to follow her?" Hamil asked. "At the rate she's going, I don't think we'll keep her in sight for much longer."

"I don't know," Geran answered. Mirya and Selsha were aboard that ship. No matter what happened, no matter where Kamoth fled, he meant to follow them. He refused to abandon them to whatever fate Sergen and his father had in mind for them. "I'll find a way. I *have* to."

EIGHTEEN

10 Marpenoth, the Year of the Ageless One (1479 DR)

The cessation of the ship's sounds woke Mirya sometime after sunset. She'd had two days to learn the noises of the ship: the steady rushing of the hull through the water, the creaking of timbers and spars, the ruffling of the sails in the wind, the footsteps and voices of the crew. Now those sounds had changed or simply ended, rousing her from her sleep. She could still hear the crewmen as they moved about the ship, but something was very different. The pirate vessel no longer rocked with the swells, and the sound of the wind had died away. The cabin in which she and Selsha were locked canted noticeably from forward to aft, as if the ship were aground on some sandbank or shoal.

She sat up, peering at the gloomy cabin. A fresh tray of food and a new waterflask had been set on the floor near the cabin door. Moving carefully to avoid waking Selsha, Mirya swung her feet out of the cramped bunk and stood up. She could feel the ship rocking side to side and the deck under her quivered. We're still moving, she realized. But that made no sense. The deck remained inclined as if the ship were climbing over a wave, but it never seemed to reach the top and began to sink downward again. And it had grown cold too, startlingly cold. Her breath steamed in the air, and she shivered. Fortunately the drawers beneath the bunk held several spare blankets; she took one to wrap around her shoulders and another to cover Selsha.

"Where *are* we?" she murmured to herself and went to the cabin's single small porthole to look. It was a thick piece of poor glass, green and bubble-pocked, and dirty on the outside as well. Through it she could tell night from day and perhaps discern the vaguest impression of coastline outside, but now all she could make out was darkness with what seemed to be a surprisingly bright moon low on the horizon. If she hadn't lost track of the time, it was the second night since they'd left Hulburg and perhaps the third or fourth night since the wizard in the brown robes and his gigantic servant had broken into her house and carried her and Selsha away.

"Why didn't I go to the harmach right away?" she murmured, berating herself once again. As soon as she'd heard Lastannor plotting with the Cyricist and speaking of an attack on the city, she should have done exactly that. But she'd been badly shaken by the discovery that Hulburg's Master Mage, a member of the Harmach's Council itself, was dealing with vicious Moonsea pirates and violent Hulburgan gangs. She'd lingered too long, listening on as she tried to decide what to do with what she'd learned. Then, after she'd been discovered and had made her escape from the inn, she'd found the streets of the Tailings filled with Cinderfists, all too clearly searching for her. She'd decided to head home to change out of the dingy hand-me-down garb the Three Crowns servants wore, hoping that a change of clothing might throw the Cyricist's servants off her scent. But after she'd picked her way back to her house, dodging down dark alleyways and creeping through empty buildings, she hadn't dared to set out again until she was certain she could reach Griffonwatch without meeting any of her pursuers.

It had *seemed* wiser to wait for morning to venture into the streets again, when the streets would be full of honest folk going about their business . . . but Hulburg's enemies hadn't given her the few hours she'd hoped she had. "What a fool you've been, Mirya Erstenwold," she told herself angrily. She'd discovered the seriousness of her error when that . . . *creature* of Lastannor's had wrenched her door off the hinges and seized her in its huge, clammy hands. Then the wizard had fixed his eyes on hers and had whispered a sibilant spell, the last thing she remembered before waking with Selsha in this tiny cabin a day—or was it two days?—ago.

Lastannor means to silence me by sending me away from Hulburg, Mirya thought unhappily. Like as not, Selsha and I are to be sold into slavery in some distant land. She supposed she should be grateful that the mage of House Marstel hadn't settled on a more immediate and permanent method for silencing her, but then again, there hadn't been any reason to take Selsha too. That was the one thing for which she absolutely could not forgive herself in this entire fiasco; through her own foolishness she'd managed to endanger her daughter's life as well as her own.

Selsha stirred in her sleep. She sat up and whimpered when she realized Mirya was no longer in the bed. "Mama?" she cried.

"Ssshh, I'm right here, my darling," Mirya said. She sat down on the edge of the bed and put her arm around the girl's shoulders. "I'm here."

"I dreamed of the big gray man again," Selsha said. "He was chasing me. I couldn't get away from him."

"I know, Selsha. He's one I've seen in my dreams too."

"The ship stopped moving."

"I'm not so sure of that. I think we're still moving, but in a different way. How, I can't imagine."

Selsha nodded. She could feel the deck's gentle motion too. "Where do you think they're taking us?" she asked.

"I've no idea." That mystery puzzled Mirya sorely. If she was right in her reckoning of the time, they could be anyplace in the Moonsea. They might even be passing down the River Lis to the Sea of Fallen Stars. But the coldness and clarity of the air felt more like the mountains to her. Perhaps they'd sailed into some secret passage leading under the mountains to Vaasa, or had used some sort of magic to leave the familiar waters of the Moonsea.

"Do you think Geran will come find us?"

Mirya draped her blanket around Selsha's shoulders, sharing its warmth. "Oh, darling, I know he will," she said. "When

Geran Hulmaster finds that we're not in Hulburg, he'll set out to find us, wherever we end up." She meant it to comfort her daughter, but she realized that she was comforting herself as well. Geran would return to Hulburg sooner or later, and he'd discover their absence. Whatever it was that bound the two of them together—friendship, the memory of innocent love, perhaps the hope of what might come someday—she trusted in it. He'd follow to the four corners of the world if he believed she and Selsha were in danger.

Of course, that didn't mean that she intended to wait for a rescue. She remembered a thing or two about sailing from long ago. Given a chance, she might be able to steal a boat and find her own way back to Hulburg. It would be difficult and dangerous, but surely taking her chances on the open sea would be better than going along with whatever her captors had planned for her. With that in mind, she began to search the cabin for anything that might be useful in an escape attempt. For the better part of an hour, she scoured the cabin and its sparse furnishings. Eventually she did find an old, well-worn copper coin stuck between the deckplanks. Finding little else that she could use, she turned her attention to using the coin's slim edge to loosen the screws holding the door's deadbolt in place. But the confident stride of approaching bootsteps interrupted her. Hurriedly she stood back up, slipped the coin under the mattress, and brushed off her hands.

The lock turned, and into the room stepped a man dressed in a long red coat with gold embroidery at the cuffs. He was a lean, fit, middle-aged man of average height, with a gray-streaked beard of black to frame his wide jaw, and a sword hanging at his belt. Mirya glimpsed a couple of big, poorly dressed sailors behind the man in the coat. "Well, now, I see you're up and about," he said. "How do you find your accommodations, Mistress Erstenwold?"

"I've little liking for cages, no matter how they're furnished." Mirya folded her arms and studied the fellow. She'd seen him before, she was sure of it, but it seemed like it might have been a long time ago. "Are you the captain?" she asked.

"Not much for chit chat, are you? No matter. I'm a direct fellow myself. I am the captain, as you've guessed. Kamoth Kastelmar's my name, and you're aboard my ship, *Kraken Queen.*"

Mirya's eyes widened. "The Kamoth who once was wed to the harmach's sister?"

"I'm surprised you remember me! You'd have been a young girl when I lived in Griffonwatch, not too much older than your daughter there." The corsair lord grinned broadly. "I suppose I'm not entirely forgotten in Hulburg."

That was true enough, Mirya thought. There were few adults in Hulburg unfamiliar with Kamoth's story. Fifteen years ago, he'd come out of Hillsfar to woo and win the harmach's younger sister, widowed for several years. But almost as soon as he'd settled into the Hulmaster family home, he'd been caught out in some dark plot against the harmach and was driven into exile. From time to time Hulburgans gathered around a warm fire might wonder aloud what had ever become of Kamoth. It seemed Mirya had stumbled upon the answer.

"You're a pirate now?" she managed to ask.

"So I'm called, but I prefer corsair. It has a better sound to it."

"What do you mean to do with Selsha and me?"

"Sell you, of course. After all, you're a fine-looking woman." Kamoth allowed himself a hungry grin. His good humor didn't reach his eyes, which remained as cold and dark as the eyes of a serpent. "Of course, you'd fetch a better price if you were five years younger, but I suppose you'll do."

"If it's gold you're after, there's no need to sell my daughter and me into slavery," Mirya said evenly. "I'm not rich, but I've some means and property. My daughter and I ought to fetch a fair ransom, more than we'd earn you in a slave market. You'd do better by the deal, and so would we."

The captain raised an eyebrow. "Ah, so you think to bargain with me? Well, now, I must say I admire your backbone, Mistress Erstenwold. Not many women in your situation could look me in the eye and make such an offer. Were it up to me, I might take you up on it. But I'm afraid it's not entirely in my hands. You were sent aboard *Kraken Queen* to keep you out of trouble, and my allies in Hulburg expect me to take you a long, long way from home before I set you ashore again."

"Whatever they're paying you, I'll arrange to pay more."

"A reckless offer, Mistress Erstenwold, since you've no idea what they might have offered me," Kamoth said. He shook his head. "As it so happens, we're bound for a port where your means and property are useless to me. Your value as a slave, however, travels with you."

Mirya pressed her lips together to keep from snapping in frustration. She willed herself to calm and then said, "Then I don't suppose I understand what it is you want from me."

"Why, I am simply seeing to the comforts of my guests—and taking stock of the value of my property," Kamoth answered. He let his eyes travel down Mirya's body and then back up again. Then he set his hand on her shoulder. For a moment Mirya feared he meant to strip her on the spot, but he simply turned her to one side, continuing his appraisal of her. "Thirty years or so?" he said in a low voice. "Hmm, a few years younger would be better. But you're not a bad-looking woman at all, Mistress Erstenwold. Why, I must say I might have *designs* upon you myself. Yes, I might."

Something in the way the pirate captain studied her body and spoke sent a shiver of pure terror through Mirya. It was simply unendurable—cold and almost reptilian. She was property at best, perhaps some manner of plaything, and his show of courtesy was intended for his own amusement, not her comfort. He stared silently at her with a bemused smile on his face, his attention drifting in his own thoughts, and then he shook himself. "We'll have to see about that later, I think. No reason to hurry! We're almost at the Black Isle, and I've some things to do."

He leaned to one side to look at Selsha, who crouched in the narrow bunk staring back at him, the blanket clutched to her chest. He winked once at the girl—it was all Mirya could do to keep from screaming—and then turned away and let himself out again without another look at either of the Erstenwolds. Mirya heard the key turn in the lock and rapid footsteps receding down the passage outside the door.

"Dear Lady," Mirya breathed. Then she allowed herself to slump against the wall, hugging her arms to her torso to hold in her fear. Suddenly she was not at all sure that either she or Selsha would survive their captivity long enough for Geran to find them.

"What's to become of us, Mama?" Selsha asked in a thin voice.

"I don't know, my darling. But I think he means to keep us as his prisoners for a little longer." She mustered a confident smile for Selsha and sat down beside her. "As long as we're together, I'll look after you."

Selsha nodded. Then she sat up and looked around. "I think we're going down now."

Down? Mirya wondered. Sure enough, her sense of balance was telling her that the ship's motion had changed again. The cant of the deck was different, and she thought she felt the air growing warmer. "Where in the world are they taking us?" she murmured.

She went to the porthole again and tried to make out something, anything, of their surroundings, but it was dark outside now. Even if the glass had been clear and clean, she suspected she wouldn't have seen much. Frowning in puzzlement, Mirya picked up the tray by the door and went back to the bunk to sit by Selsha. They ate together. Selsha said that she was not hungry, but Mirya insisted that she eat something; there was no telling where they were bound at this point, and who knew when they might see their next meal?

After an hour or more of sharply descending, the ship finally bumped and slid against some sort of pier or wharf. Mirya could hear the taut mooring hawsers creaking as they arrested the ship's motion, and the footsteps of the crewmen as they hurried back and forth across the deck. For a long time nothing else happened, and she began to wonder if the tiny cabin was to be their prison cell as well. But then she heard several heavy footsteps approaching outside her door again, and the jangle of keys on an iron ring.

The lock turned, and several of the pirate crewmen stepped into the room. They were dirty, dangerous-looking men in frayed breeches and worn-out tunics, and they leered at her shamelessly. "Come along, you," one of the men said. "Make any trouble for us, and you'll regret it."

"Mama!" Selsha screeched.

"Be calm, Selsha!" Mirya answered as steadily as she could.

She remained docile as two of the pirates stepped forward to seize her by the arms. "Now you're a pretty thing," one of the pirates said. He leaned forward to whisper in her ear. His breath stank. "What's your name, love?"

Mirya turned her face away and refused to reply. The pirate snorted. "As you wish, then, but soon enough you'll wish you had a friend or two here." He and his companion dragged her out of the cabin and down the passageway to a ladder leading up to the deck. A third man brought Selsha, who sobbed in fear but managed to stay on her feet and keep up with Mirya despite her terror.

Bright lanterns illuminated the ship's decks. It was dark outside, but Mirya caught a glimpse of a starry sky outside the warm, yellow halo of light cocooning the pirate ship. The air was cool and damp, with a strange, sickly sweet odor like rotting flowers hanging thickly in the air. The jagged silhouettes of treetops moved softly against the background of stars overhead. *There's no land nearby Hulburg with trees such as that,* she thought. *They must have passed down the River Lis to some port on the Sea of Fallen Stars, but where? Turmish or Akanûl, perhaps? Chessenta? Or even farther?*

The pirates hustled her across a wooden wharf to an iron-barred gate at the foot of a stone tower and then swept her inside before she could make out anything more of their surroundings. They descended through wide, low hallways made of a series of intersecting vaults. Each barrel vault was divided from the main passage by a row of iron bars and could evidently serve as storage space or a prison cell as the pirates needed. Most of the vaults were full of supplies and cargo, the same sort of clutter of barrels and crates that filled the Erstenwold storehouses back in Hulburg. Others held richer loot—clay amphoras of olive oil and wine, fine carpets, large bolts of good cloth, arms and armor. Clearly the stone keep, wherever it was, held the plunder of dozens of prizes taken by the Black Moon pirates.

They came to a large hall, where several corridors like the one they'd been following met. The pirates marched Mirya and Selsha toward the passage immediately to their left, barred by another gate of iron bars, and started to unlock the door.

Behind her, Selsha screamed in pure terror. *"Mama!"*

Mirya's heart leaped in her chest. She wrenched herself around in pure, automatic reaction to her daughter's fright, expecting that the man dragging her along had done something terrible. But the corsair gripping Selsha looked just as startled as Mirya felt. He fumbled to secure the flailing girl, swearing to himself, while the pirates beside Mirya quickly stepped in to grab her again.

"Monsters! Monsters!" Selsha shrieked.

Mirya looked past her daughter and saw them. Two creatures had just emerged from one of the intersecting corridors in the hall. The first was a fat, little spiderlike creature about the size of a human child or a largish dog. Its head rode atop a long, eel-like neck, and two dark eyes glittered in the lanternlight. A short cape was clasped around its neck, and strange greenish white runes and whorls were marked on its dark, stiff-haired limbs. It glared at Selsha and hissed in annoyance. Behind the small spider-monster stood a hulking, bipedal thing that looked like some bizarre cross between a powerful ape and a gigantic beetle. Its massive forelimbs ended in mighty claws, and large, insectile eyes stared blankly ahead. It carried a large coffer marked in the same whorls and runes that decorated the smaller creature.

"Silence that noisy thing!" the small spider-monster said in a chittering voice.

Selsha screamed all over again as she realized that the little monster was talking about her, but then the pirate holding her managed to clap one of his hands over her mouth. "The girl just took a fright," he said to the spider-monster. "It's our business, not yours."

"Bah! You should cut the speech out of it if it carries on like that—or eat it. It's better to eat the noisy ones first." The spider-monster spun around and scrambled deftly up the torso of the bigger monster, perching on its broad shoulder. Then the big monster shambled off, carrying both its smaller master and the heavy chest with no apparent difficulty.

Selsha still screamed into her captor's hand and struggled. Mirya tried to get closer to her. "Selsha! Selsha, my darling! They're gone. You must be quiet, please! The monsters are gone now!"

"You heard your mum," the pirate holding Selsha said. "There's no need for all this, girl."

Selsha looked up to Mirya, her dark eyes wide with fright. Then she stopped fighting against her captor's grip and gave in with a weak nod. The pirate carefully released his hand, and Selsha took a gulp of air. "I'm sorry," she whimpered. "They frightened me!"

"They frightened me too," Mirya said. She thought of the spider-monster and its ugly threat and shuddered. "But you mustn't scream like that again if you can help it at all."

"I'll try."

"Good girl," Mirya breathed. She looked at the two pirates holding her arms. "What kind of place is this?"

"Ah, so now she's not too good to speak to us!" the pirate steering her along laughed. "You're in the Keep of the Black Moon, love. Don't worry; you'll soon grow used to the sight of neogi and their big pets!"

Neogi? Mirya wondered. The spiderlike creature, she supposed. But she had no more chance to ask about it. The pirates took Mirya and Selsha down the new passage for a long distance and then came to a vacant cell. This one was fitted with bedding of old straw and dirty blankets. They took the keys to the door down from a hook nearby and opened up the cell. Mirya decided to try one more time before their captors left them.

"Where are we?" she asked.

"You mean you don't know?" The man laughed harshly. "Above the sea, behind the moon, beneath the sun, and among the stars, that's where you are! You're on an island in the Sea of Night, and here you'll stay until the High Captain says otherwise."

"Above the sea—?" Mirya asked. But the pirate wasn't listening to her any longer. He shoved her into the cell so forcefully she stumbled to her hands and knees. The other pirate flung Selsha into the cell after her. Then they pulled the heavy door of iron bars closed and left the two Erstenwolds alone in the shadows of their cell.

NINETEEN

10 Marpenoth, the Year of the Ageless One (1479 DR)

They lost sight of *Kraken Queen* an hour after moonrise, when not even the keen-eyed Hamil could make out the tiny, dark hull any longer. Geran stared up into the starry night for a long time after that, hoping against hope for some glimpse of Kamoth's flagship, but finally he had to admit that the pirates had escaped him. Tales of flying ships, stories of brave seafarers who dared to sail the starry waters of the Sea of Night above the skies—Geran had heard such things all his life, but he'd always dismissed them as fanciful nonsense. He'd seen the battle spells of mighty wizards, the eldritch glades of elven Myth Drannor, the strange wonders of soaring earthmotes and magical changelands that dotted the world in places where the Spellplague had touched it so long ago, but he'd never imagined that a bloodthirsty band of marauders such as the Black Moon corsairs might command the arcane learning to sail the skies. Red Wizards he might have thought capable of such a thing, or perhaps the legendary High Mages of distant Evermeet. But simple *pirates?*

He sighed and returned his attention to the moonlit quarterdeck. "Andurth, you've got the ship," he said. "I'm going below."

"What course?" the sailing master asked.

"Keep on this way until you hit the coast. After that . . . east toward Mulmaster, I guess. Maybe that's where Kamoth's headed." Geran didn't really believe so, but it was the only thing he could think of. He looked over to Hamil and Sarth. "Would you join me in my cabin? We're in need of a new plan, and I'm in need of some drink."

He led the way down to *Seadrake*'s master cabin, a comfortable room beneath the quarterdeck. Unlike Narsk's quarters on *Moonshark,* Geran's cabin was neat and uncluttered. He hadn't been aboard long enough to make a mess of it, and Kara hadn't really settled in during the time she'd used it. Geran asked the steward to fetch a flagon of wine and several cups then took a seat at one end of the cabin's table. The steward returned with their wine, and Geran poured himself some and took a deep swallow. Hamil and Sarth followed his example.

"So what do we do now?" Hamil asked. "We can't follow *Kraken Queen* into the sky!"

"No, we can't, but I refuse to abandon Mirya to Kamoth and Sergen," Geran replied. "Sooner or later, Kamoth's got to bring his ship to port. Wherever that is, we'll find him again." If nothing else, he might be able to find an archmage to teleport him there. Perhaps Hamil was right, and she was relatively safe so long as she had value as a hostage. But if Kamoth and Sergen decided they no longer feared pursuit, they might not see any reason to continue to spare Mirya and her daughter.

He stared into his cup, absently rolling the dry red wine across his tongue as he considered the puzzle before them. There had to be a way to follow her! "Sarth, what do you know about flying ships?" he finally asked.

"Little, I fear," Sarth said. "I have heard it said that great ports such as Waterdeep or Westgate sometimes see ships that call from far places indeed—cities in different planes or lands beyond the Sea of Night. And I have read accounts of some such visits in old tomes. For instance, there was a wizard named Gamelon Idogyr who visited Waterdeep a few times in the years before the Spellplague. He called on the Blackstaff on occasion, and one of the Blackstaff's apprentices recorded Gamelon's accounts of his voyages in the Sea of Night. Gamelon was said to arrive and depart aboard a mysterious ship of strange design that no seafarer had ever encountered elsewhere."

"A flying ship?" Hamil asked. Sarth nodded in reply, and Hamil continued. "Then all we have to do is find one of those mysterious ships, so that we can follow Sergen and Kamoth to their lair. How hard can it be?"

"Most such vessels hide their origin. They shift planes or take to the skies a few miles away from their destination and simply sail into harbor like any seagoing ship would." Sarth smiled bitterly. "And I've heard nothing of any visits in a very long time. I suspect that the masters of sky-sailing ships—if any still visit Faerûn—keep their secrets to themselves in these darker and more dangerous times."

"Well, we know of at least one that is still around," Hamil observed. "How did a pirate like Kamoth come by a ship like that? Is he a wizard of some kind?"

"Kamoth is no wizard," Geran answered. "And I can't believe that he has any powerful mages at his command, or we would have seen their magic at work in Hulburg."

"In that case, how does one make a ship fly? Or shift planes? Or otherwise behave in a manner that ships shouldn't?"

"According to the account of Gamelon, skyfaring or plane-sailing vessels are powered by some sort of magical device, such as a helm or a keel carved with potent runes," the sorcerer answered Hamil. "Creating such a device requires a powerful and knowledgeable wizard, but controlling one that has already been installed on a ship is much easier. Kamoth might not need a mighty wizard. He would only need a little training in the arcane arts and the knowledge of how to steer."

"In which case, why did he wait so long before taking to the air?" Geran mused. "Was he simply toying with us? Did he hope to avoid us without giving away his secret? Or was there some other reason?"

"Could it be something about the Talons?" Sarth asked. "Or sunset? Perhaps to sail the Sea of Night he must wait until the skies grow dark?"

They fell silent, nursing their goblets of wine. The ship rode lightly over the swells, stretching out her legs with a full spread of sail and a following sea. Geran finished his cup and began to pour himself another. He realized that he was exhausted. Between the last desperate days on *Moonshark* and the hurried pursuit of the fleeing pirates, he'd hardly slept in three or four days.

Hamil cleared his throat. "You mentioned a magical device, Sarth," he said. "For example, a compass?"

Geran and Sarth stared at the halfling. "The starry compass," Geran breathed. "That's why Kamoth sent Narsk to Mulmaster. He wanted *Moonshark* fitted with one too. And we left it on *Moonshark*'s quarterdeck!"

"We had more pressing matters to deal with at the time," Hamil reminded him. "However, if it's something that you have to know how to use, I don't think we need to worry about Murkelmor or anyone else left on *Moonshark* taking to the skies. Whatever the Red Wizards taught Narsk about using the device died with him."

Geran stood and paced toward the stern end of the cabin. A wide row of windows provided a fine view of the darkened Moonsea and the stars low in the sky. *Kraken Queen* sailed somewhere in that sky, even as he stood gazing out at the night. Wherever she was going now, *Seadrake* could not follow without a starry compass of her own. It was possible they could obtain one from the Red Wizards in Mulmaster . . . if the arcane merchants had another one they would be willing to part with, and if their price was something he'd be able to meet. On the other hand, he *knew* there was a starry compass aboard *Moonshark*. The pirate galley was damaged and shorthanded; she'd be easy prey for *Seadrake*.

"We need *Moonshark*'s compass," he said over his shoulder. Maybe he could persuade Murkelmor to part with it peacefully and leave the Moonsea; he didn't relish the thought of crossing blades with his former shipmates. "Sarth, can you divine her location?"

"I will attempt it immediately," Sarth answered. He stood up and left the cabin.

"The last I saw, *Moonshark* was headed southeast past Hulburg's Arches," Hamil said. "Where do you think Murkelmor would have taken her?"

Geran thought about it. The gale blowing from west-northwest would have made it nearly impossible to make any progress toward the west, so *Moonshark* would have stood south—straight out to sea and ultimately to Mulmaster on the opposite coast—or turned east to hug the shore and flee into the uninhabited coastlands of the Galennar. Mulmaster probably offered the best haven available in the eastern half of the Moonsea for a pirate ship on the run, but he doubted that Murkelmor would have wanted to chance stormy, open water with a damaged bow. No, it was more likely that the dwarf had steered eastward, searching for some deserted cove or sheltered bay in the desolate Galennar where he could make repairs and reorganize the ship's crew.

"My coin's on the Galennar," he told Hamil. "It's a hard and dangerous coast, but there are places where a ship can lie hidden. And it's uninhabited, so Murkelmor won't have to worry about the rest of the crew deserting the ship—or some local lord seizing it." Of course, they'd been much closer to the Galennar two days ago when they had sailed from Hulburg. "On the other hand, I've already guessed wrong in chasing *Kraken Queen*. If Sarth's divinations can tell me something about which way to set my course, I'd feel much better about sailing to the far end of the Moonsea."

Sarth rapped on the door and then came in with a heavy leather satchel. "My cabin's too small for this," the sorcerer explained. Geran and Hamil retreated, giving him space to work. Sarth opened the satchel and took out a stub of charcoal, drawing a circle about ten feet across behind the table and marking it with runes. He arranged candles at several points around the circle, lighting them with a wave of his hand. Then he removed a plain iron nail from his satchel—a fitting from *Moonshark*, or so Geran guessed. The swordmage watched as Sarth repeated the ritual he'd performed in the conjury of his small tower, reading from an old tome and flinging pinches of mysterious powders into a small brazier he set up beside his reading stand. Sarth inhaled the fragrant smoke rising from the brazier and stared blankly into space.

Hamil glanced at Geran, but Geran motioned for him to wait. Thirty heartbeats passed, and then the sorcerer exhaled and shook his head. "*Moonshark* lies in that direction," he said, pointing toward somewhere that would have been off the port bow had they all been standing on the quarterdeck. "She is perhaps two hundred miles distant, drawn up on the beach in a cove surrounded by steep bluffs. There are ruins above. I see a bonfire on the beach, and many of our former shipmates. They are all armed. They fear the night."

"Does that seem familiar to you, Geran?" Hamil asked.

"Ruins . . . it might be Sulasspryn, but they'd be fools to put in there. In any event, the direction and distance confirm my guess. They're hiding out somewhere in the Galennar, all the way at the far end of the Moonsea." Geran sighed. The winds favored them, but it would be a day and a half to cross the Moonsea again . . . assuming *Moonshark* stayed where it was and didn't sail off somewhere new in the meantime. At least they'd have a good night's sleep. "I'll tell Andurth to change his course. I doubt that we can crowd on any more sail, but he might find a way."

Sarth and Hamil returned to their own cabins. Geran went back on deck and told the sailing master to steer for the eastern end of the Moonsea at the best speed *Seadrake* could manage. Then he came back to his cabin and fell into his bunk. He lay awake for a time, desperately hoping that Hamil was right and that Mirya was unharmed. He couldn't bear the thought of harm coming to her, not on his account. Yet that seemed to be exactly what had happened. Five months ago House Veruna's sellswords had tried to deflect him from uncovering their crypt-breaking and their extortion of Hulburg's folk by striking at Mirya. Now a new enemy had chosen the same course—likely at his treacherous cousin Sergen's urging, he reminded himself. He didn't think he loved Mirya, not in the way he once had; a foolish, wishful part of his heart still clung to the memory of Alliere and the leaves of Myth Drannor, and at other times his arms remembered the slender waist of Nimessa Sokol before him as they rode across the moonlit hills of the Highfells. But he would rather have stabbed himself with his own sword than see Mirya Erstenwold hurt on his account. After much tossing and turning, he finally fell into a discontented sleep.

The morning broke gray and dreary. Geran awoke to find that the wind remained cold and blustery, a restless autumn gale that veered wildly throughout the day but stayed more or less west and north despite its sudden changes. Whitecaps danced across the Moonsea, and *Seadrake*'s bow kicked hissing sheets of cold spray over the foredeck as she flew over the swells. Late in the afternoon they struck the Moonsea's northern shore about twenty miles west of Hulburg, not far from the ruins of Seawave, and here Geran reluctantly decided to anchor for the night. The waters at the eastern end of the Moonsea were poorly charted, and more to the point, it would be all too easy to sail past *Moonshark* in the dark. He felt reasonably confident that Murkelmor wouldn't have sought shelter so close to a city the Black Moon had just attacked, but he didn't care to run too much farther to the east without carefully checking the bays and coves of the steep coast as they passed by. If *Moonshark*'s damage was severe enough, Murkelmor might not have had much of a choice about putting in to begin repairs.

They passed the night in a small, poorly sheltered bay, straining at the anchor. The wind slackened before dawn, but heavy rain moved in after the gale. When they raised anchor and steered east out of their small bay, they did so in a cold, merciless downpour. Hamil shivered and pulled the hood of his cloak over his head. "Have I ever told you how much I loathe the weather around here?" he asked Geran.

"Many times last spring, but you seemed to like the summer well enough."

"Well, summer was far too short. Clearly a cold, wind-driven rain is the natural state of affairs in these lands, and anything else is a temporary aberration."

Geran smiled humorlessly. "My apologies for the inconvenience. If it's any consolation, I don't think much of the weather either. It's going to cut our visibility to a mile, perhaps two if we're lucky. We'll have to stay close to the coast and move slowly, or we might miss *Moonshark.*"

"Have you given thought to how you mean to get the compass from Murkelmor?"

Geran nodded. "I'll ask him for it, if he's willing to parley. It's no good to him without someone to waken its enchantments. I'll even pay a fair price. But I'll take it by force if I have to." He hoped it wouldn't come to that; even though he and Hamil had parted ways with the crew of *Moonshark* under difficult circumstances, he'd sailed with them long enough to view some—Murkelmor for instance—as relatively decent fellows despite their choice of career. As far as he knew, they hadn't done any harm to Hulburg or its shipping themselves, even if their fellows in the Black Moon had. On the other hand, if Murkelmor refused to part with the starry compass, *Seadrake* was bigger, better armed, and had a full crew including heavily armed soldiers. Geran did not intend to leave without the compass.

Hamil frowned skeptically under his sodden hood. "I doubt that Murkelmor or Skamang will be interested in parley, but I suppose it doesn't hurt to try."

They stood out to sea and ran east. By late morning they passed Keldon Head and Hulburg, slowly closing with the shore again. The coastline here consisted of one headland after the next, steep and desolate. Two or three centuries ago these lands had been inhabited, in the days when Hulburg and Sulasspryn were vital cities carving out land from the wilds of the Moonsea North. Here and there the ruins of old homesteads stood on the south-facing hillsides, with the occasional stump of a crumbling watchtower atop a hill. Geran knew that a small number of shepherds and goatherds kept their flocks in the vales behind the coastal hills, at least within a few miles of Hulburg. But here they were passing into empty lands where no one lived. There was no road or path through these parts into other lands, so no travelers had reason to continue eastward from Hulburg, and the danger of monsters from the Galena Mountains or the bleak ruins of Sulasspryn kept anyone from trying to settle here.

Half an hour after they passed Hulburg by, two swept horns appeared above the ladder leading down to the main deck, followed a moment later by the rest of Sarth. Like Hamil, he wore a heavy cloak against the rain, and like Hamil, he also was soaked already. Unfortunately, few hoods fit him well, so he simply glanced up at the sky with a flicker of annoyance and endured the rain pelting down.

"I have repeated my divinations," he told Geran. "*Moonshark* has not moved. She lies perhaps fifteen miles or so ahead of us."

"Sulasspryn, then. It must be." Geran frowned. "But why lay there for so long?"

"She must have been more damaged than we realized," Hamil suggested. "If the stem is well and truly sprung, Murkelmor might have to steam a new piece of timber into shape to fix it. That could take a while."

"Or perhaps another pirate den is hidden in the ruins there," Sarth said. "We first found *Moonshark* in Zhentil Keep, after all."

"I've never heard any such story, but I suppose it's possible. We'll approach carefully." Geran rubbed at his jaw, thinking over Sarth's tidings. "Any news of Mirya?"

"Only the faintest hints. She lives still—I feel confident of that—but she has passed beyond the range of my divinations."

"Is she in Faerûn?"

"I do not know, Geran. She must be very far away if she is, a thousand miles or more." The tiefling glanced up into the sky. "I believe she is somewhere above us. She might be held somewhere high in the mountains or perhaps on a high-drifting earthmote. I have seen fortresses, even towns, on some of the larger ones. Or she might be somewhere in the Sea of Night."

"The starry compass, then," Geran breathed. He nodded to the tiefling. "My thanks, Sarth. Without your efforts we'd have no hope at all of finding Mirya and her daughter."

"I only hope that my meager talents do not lead you astray," Sarth answered.

"Of that, I have no fear," Geran said. He returned his attention to the gray coastline sliding by through the rain and mists.

They continued on for several hours, making little speed in the light wind. Eventually Geran had Andurth call the crew to their rowing stations and continued at half speed, a pace the crew could sustain for hours by rotating rowers to and from the benches. Unlike *Moonshark, Seadrake* was not really fitted out for rowing speed; she was made for sailing and could only put about twenty oars in the water through high, awkwardly sited ports.

Early in the afternoon, they rounded a headland and spied the ruins of a large city hugging the hillsides of the bay beyond. Old walls encircled the place, marred by numerous gaps. Twisted trees grew up through flagstone courts and choked what used to be the city's boulevards. High on a hill overlooking the harbor, the keep that had once dominated the place was an empty shell cleft in two by the gray scar of an old landslide; a huge mound of rubble at the foot of the hill marked where most of the castle had fallen. Many other buildings in the vicinity looked as if they'd been knocked down by similar upheavals. Those that still stood stared blankly out to sea, their windows and doorways filled with ominous shadow. Geran could not shake the impression that the city was watching *Seadrake* approach, resentful of the intrusion.

"This is Sulasspryn?" Hamil asked. "What happened here?"

"No one knows for sure," the swordmage said. "Some disaster befell the place a hundred years or more before the Spellplague, and few people survived to tell the tale. As the story goes, the ruling family feuded against a drow city beneath the Galenas and won—or so they thought. But the dark elves had their revenge in the end. They undermined the citadel and collapsed it, wiping out the city's rulers in one swift stroke. Then the dark elves and their monsters boiled up from beneath the city, slaughtering or carrying off most of Sulasspryn's citizens." Geran shrugged. "I don't know if there's any truth to it, but in Hulburg they say that Lolth's curse lies over the ruins. You can't find a soul in Hulburg who'd dare set foot within the walls."

"Including you?"

Geran pointed at a high hilltop west of the city. "When I was about eighteen or nineteen, Jarad Erstenwold and I rode to the headland there to look on the ruins. That's as close as we cared to be. And even then my father was furious with both of us. He feared that we might wake things better left undisturbed." He paused, and found that a shadow of old dread had crept over him. He was as close to Sulasspryn as anyone from Hulburg had been in a long time, and it struck him as an unwholesome place to be. "To tell the truth, I sincerely hope *Moonshark's* moved on by now. I don't like to linger here."

"No such luck, I fear." Hamil pointed over the rail at a customshouse close by the water's edge. As *Seadrake* slowly sculled across the harbor, the slender black hull of the pirate galley—concealed by the ruined building at first—came slowly into view, drawn up on the shore behind the structure. "There she is! It looks like we've caught *Moonshark* on the beach."

The pirate galley was drawn up on the strand a short distance outside the city walls, well hidden by the headland that sheltered the city's old harbor from the westerly winds. If the rain had been a little heavier, or *Seadrake* a little farther out from the shore, they might have sailed past without spotting the other ship. Geran signaled to the helmsman, who turned the wheel and brought the ship into the harbor. All over the Hulburgan vessel, the soldiers and sailors scrambled to make themselves ready for battle, quickly donning mail shirts or leather jerkins and uncovering the ship's catapult. The swordmage peered toward the shore, looking for signs of commotion—the Black Moon pirates might try to launch their ship and make their escape before *Seadrake* landed, or at the very least make ready to defend the ship. But he saw no one moving on the shore.

"Where are they?" he muttered. "They must have seen us by now."

"I don't care for the looks o' the shore," Andurth said in a low voice. "I can beach if you insist on it, but we've a deeper hull than that galley there, and I fear we'll be stuck fast. It'll be a devil of a job to get back in the water."

Geran frowned. The dwarf was right; there was good, deep water by the quays in the city proper, but he was not about to tie up in the middle of the ruins. The shore the pirate ship was drawn up on looked wide and muddy. "Very well. We'll land by boat." He hesitated then asked, "Hamil, can you see anyone ashore?"

The halfling shook his head. "It looks like there's a camp on the beach, but there's not a soul in sight. I'd suggest that perhaps they're all belowdecks on *Moonshark* or sheltering from the rain in the ruins, but somehow I don't really think they are. I don't like the looks of this, Geran."

"Nor do I," Geran answered. "But we're here, and we need *Moonshark*'s compass." He sighed and looked over to Andurth. "Master Galehand, drop anchor and put the ship's boats in the water. I'll take twenty hands ashore."

"Aye, Lord Geran," the dwarf answered. He shouted commands to the sailors on deck. The crewmen aloft began to furl the sails one by one, while others hurried to the ship's anchor or began to unlash the ship's boats.

Geran absently listened to the bustle and commotion. His attention was fixed on the mist-wreathed ruins looming over the harbor, concealed by veils of rain. Some dire peril awaited within, he was certain of it. But he had no idea what it might be.

TWENTY

12 Marpenoth, the Year of the Ageless One (1479 DR)

Wet gravel grated under the longboat's keel as it grounded on the strand a bowshot from where the silent *Moonshark* was drawn up. Geran vaulted over the side into knee-deep water and splashed ashore in the cold, steady rain, sword in hand. Weathered gray battlements and crumbling temples towered over the landing party, clinging to the edge of the steep bluff that marked the western side of Sulasspryn's bay. The harbor proper lay several hundred yards to the east, where the remnants of a stone jetty sheltered the city's old quays from the Moonsea storms. On this side of the harbor, a causeway ran out to the old customshouse across a thirty-yard-wide strand at the foot of the bluff. It was the only place in Sulasspryn's bay flat enough for a ship the size of *Moonshark* to haul her prow out of the water—and it was well hidden from ships passing by at sea, not that many ever had reason to sail along this desolate coast.

"It seems your guess was right," Sarth said to him. The tiefling pointed to the camp set up not far from the beached galley. Several fresh logs lay stacked there, partially stripped of their bark. The ship's bow was braced atop two more logs set like rollers under the keel, and a simple framework of timbers held her in place. "Murkelmor must have decided he could not sail any farther without first mending the damage to the bow."

"He would've been wiser to find a cove a few miles back, then," Geran said. He reminded himself that few in *Moonshark*'s crew had any reason to be wary of Sulasspryn. None of them hailed from Hulburg or the lands nearby, after all. But he would have imagined that any grim old ruin of a city should have commanded some respect. Everyone knew that all sorts of curses, ghosts, and hungry monsters might lurk in any long-abandoned castle or city, even if few of the pirates were familiar with the specific perils of these ruins.

"There aren't many trees along the coast, but there seems to be some good timber here," Hamil pointed out. "Or perhaps Murkelmor was counting on the reputation of the place to ward off pursuit and chose to land here for that very reason."

"We'll ask Murkelmor when we see him," said Geran, although he was beginning to doubt that they would. He had a hard time believing that the pirates of *Moonshark* would have been willing to strand themselves beneath Sulasspryn's brooding ruins even for a few hours, let alone the days of work that would be needed to effect serious repairs. He waited for his armsmen to drag their longboats up onto the beach and then motioned for them to follow him. "Come on, fellows. Stay close, and keep your eyes and ears open. Assume it's a trap until we know for certain that it's not."

They marched toward the pirate galley, boots crunching in the pebbles underfoot. As they neared, they saw that the pirate crew had set up a worksite on the beach to cut and shape new timbers for their ship. It looked as though they'd simply walked away from their work. Saws, axes, and other tools lay scattered around the site. The Shieldsworn and sellswords with Geran kept their thoughts to themselves, but Geran noticed that they redoubled their vigilance, watching the bluffs to their right and keeping a wary eye on the shadows of doorways and windows above.

Where are *they?* Hamil said silently to Geran. *Did they flee into the ruins when* Seadrake *appeared in the bay? I can't believe Murkelmor would let us have his ship without fighting for it.*

"I don't know," Geran murmured in reply. He circled around the prow of the galley with caution, just in case his former shipmates were waiting in ambush behind the ship's hull—and then he found the first of *Moonshark*'s crewmen. The body sprawled at the water's edge, facedown in the small wavelets lapping alongside the black hull. His back was a gory mess, ripped open in great furrows; several small, pale crabs scuttled away from the corpse as Geran approached.

"I think that's Khefen," Hamil said in a low voice. He grimaced. "Poor bastard."

Geran glanced around and then crouched by the body to study it closely. "Dead a couple of days, I think. The wounds show a lot of tearing. Claws or talons, not blades. If I had to guess, I'd say that some beast drove him to the ground from behind and ripped him to shreds. Kara could tell us more, if she were here."

"Whatever it was killed him here and left him," Hamil said. "Most animals would have dragged him off or eaten their fill."

"There's another over here, m'lord!" one of the Shieldsworn guards called. He stood by one of the large logs at the side of the worksite. A moment later another guardsman peering into the tangled scrub and brush at the foot of the bluff added, "And half a dozen here in the briars, m'lord!"

"None of this is our affair any longer," Sarth said in a low voice. "We should retrieve the compass and go."

"You're right." The longer they stayed, the more likely it was that whatever had fallen upon *Moonshark*'s crew would fall on *Seadrake* as well. And while Geran would have been happy to take away any surviving pirates who appeared and asked to leave, he didn't feel obligated to search them out, not when the lives of Mirya and Selsha might be hanging by a thread on some far island in the sky. To the soldiers poking around the campsite, he called, "Gather up the bodies you can find without straying too far and bury them together in the sawpit. But keep your weapons close to hand!"

The corsairs had rigged a simple rope ladder with wooden rungs from the half galley's deck to the beach. Geran caught hold of it and climbed to the main deck, followed by Hamil and Sarth. He saw two more dead crewmen on the deck, both by the door leading to the captain's cabin, which hung open.

"They must have tried to barricade themselves inside," Hamil said. "There may be survivors belowdecks."

"We'll check in a moment," Geran said. Keeping a wary eye on the dark opening to the cabin, he climbed up the short ladder to the quarterdeck. A heavy canvas hood covered the binnacle Murkelmor had built for the compass. He used the blade of his sword to slice through the cords knotting the hood together and dragged the cover away.

The starry compass was still there.

Geran breathed a deep sigh of relief and peered closely at the dark sphere. In the dull gray daylight, it seemed little more than a smooth round ball of black glass—although the longer he looked at it, the more he saw of its hidden depths, in which tiny glittering pinpoints of light hovered like stars in the night sky.

"It's here," he said aloud.

"Good," said Hamil. "Let's get it and go. I don't like this place."

"Agreed," Geran said. He produced a small sack from his belt. Together he and Hamil detached its silver collar from the wooden stand Murkelmor had built for it, wrapped it in a woolen blanket, and placed the orb carefully into the sack. Geran had no idea how breakable the thing was, but he certainly didn't want to take the chance that it was, not when lives depended on it. With that done, they left the quarterdeck. A quick check belowdecks revealed another half-dozen crewmen dead in the midships bunkroom amid a scene of extreme violence; blood splattered the bulkheads, and furniture lay splintered or upended throughout the lower decks.

"Call me a coward, but I'm not sure I want to linger long enough to provide a decent burial for these fellows," Hamil said. "What *happened* here?"

"Come on," Grean replied. "Let's go see if we can hurry things along and get back to *Seadrake.*"

They returned to the beach. Geran sent several of the soldiers to collect the bodies from the ship, slung the compass in a satchel over his shoulder, and then lent a hand with the unpleasant task of burying *Moonshark*'s dead—or the ones that were near at hand, anyway. By his count there were at least thirty or more still unaccounted for. If they were lucky, Murkelmor and the others had fled the city outright; if not, Geran guessed that most were dead somewhere in the ruins above the harbor.

Finally, after half an hour of grim work in the steady rain, the dead pirates were laid in the campsite's trenchlike sawpit. Several of the Shieldsworn began to shovel damp sand and earth over the bodies. Geran looked around the beach, making sure they hadn't missed anything or left anything behind. He certainly didn't want to leave something else on *Moonshark* that he'd have to come back for later.

Something gave voice to a harsh, croaking cry from the heights overlooking the beach.

The Shieldsworn stopped where they were and looked up. Several archers laid arrows on their strings; other men hurriedly unslung their shields and fit their arms inside. "What was that?" Hamil muttered to himself.

Geran didn't bother to guess. He watched the heights warily for a time. For a long moment nothing else happened. He was just about to relax his guard and tell the soldiers to finish up their work when several more cries of the same sort echoed back and forth through the steady pattering of the rain. A small stone, dislodged from somewhere above, fell down to the beach, bouncing from the bluff several times. The harsh voices called back and forth, snarling and rasping unintelligibly. He realized that the creatures above, whatever they were, were talking to each other. He glanced over at Sarth to see if the sorcerer had any idea what might be above them, but Sarth just shook his head.

"Let's head for the boats," Geran said to the people around him. "Slowly, now. Stay together, and keep your weapons in hand."

They started back toward the longboats, marching across the wet gravel—and then the creatures attacked. With a sudden thunderstorm of wingbeats and earsplitting cries, scores of winged creatures leaped from their hiding places in the ruins above and swooped down at the men on the beach. They were grayish black in color, with oversized talons, lashing tails, and horned heads. Fangs jutted from their wide mouths. More of the creatures raced out over the bay, heading for *Seadrake* a half mile away.

"Gargoyles!" Hamil shouted. He raised his short bow and loosed an arrow at the nearest of the plunging monsters. His hard-driven arrow struck the creature near the center of its chest, yet it barely sank an inch into the gargoyle's stony flesh. With a shrill cry of pain, the creature wrenched the arrow from its wound. More arrows sleeted up from those Shieldsworn who were holding bows, but few did much harm. Hamil swore then shouted, "Eyes or throat! Shoot for the eyes or throat!"

Sarth intoned words of arcane power and blasted a pair of the monsters out of the air with a crackling blue bolt of lightning. Then gargoyles dropped amid the shore party in a wave of rending claws and snapping fangs. Screams of terror and inhuman croaks of anger or pain rose from the fray. The monster's talons were hard enough to rend steel mail, and sword cuts tended to bounce off their tough hides, but a hard-driven swordpoint could pierce their flesh. Even as Shieldsworn went down under bloody claws, gargoyles spitted on Hulburgan steel shrieked and flailed desperately.

"Cuillen mhariel!" Geran snarled, invoking the warding of his silversteel veil. Argent mists swirled around his body, deflecting the flurry of slashing talons reaching for him. Then he invoked another spell to set his sword aflame and hurled himself headlong into the fray. His sword blazed with arcane fury as he slashed and stabbed at the flapping monsters around him, leaving long, black-scorched gashes in gargoyle hides. "Stand your ground!" he called to the Shieldsworn. "Guard each other's backs! We can fight them off!"

Just out of his reach, a gargoyle dropped down behind a soldier, clenched its talons in his shoulders, and then leaped back into the air, carrying the screaming, writhing man aloft. An archer shot through its wing and sent it crashing back to earth, only to be plucked off the ground himself by another of the monsters. Still other gargoyles clutched and dragged soldiers away, seeking to carry their victims aloft or pull them away from the melee. The creatures croaked and hissed with dark glee as they singled out their prey.

"Narva saizhal!" Sarth roared. He wheeled and flung a lethal blast of icy darts at gargoyles rushing him from behind. Geran leaped to cut down another of the monsters as it threw itself at the tiefling's back. Despite their stonelike flesh, the gargoyles were susceptible to the sorcerer's spells and Geran's swordmagic. And, as Hamil had said, they were vulnerable to well-aimed blows; the swordmage caught a glimpse of a gargoyle plummeting to the ground like a puppet with its strings cut, one of Hamil's arrows standing a handspan deep in its eye.

For a moment, Geran believed they would repel the first assault without much loss—and then a thin ray of grayish light lanced down from overhead, striking a Shieldsworn soldier in the chest. The man groaned once, staggered back a step, and then toppled to the ground, eyes staring sightlessly at the sky. More rays stabbed into the knot of fighting soldiers, rays that burned, rays that corroded, rays that knocked men senseless and left them virtually defenseless against the gargoyle attacks. Geran looked up and saw a large, round-bodied creature floating thirty feet in the air behind the gargoyles. It had one great staring eye, fixed on the battle below, and a number of tendrils with smaller eyes flailing around it. From the lesser eyes the deadly magic rays lashed out, scouring *Seadrake*'s landing party even as they fought to fend off the swooping gargoyles.

"A beholder," he groaned. The gargoyles were trouble enough, but beholders were terrible adversaries. Given a few moments, the monster could destroy the whole landing party single-handedly. He whirled to shout a warning to his soldiers. "Archers, pincushion that thing!"

Most of the Shieldsworn were busy fighting the gargoyles, but a couple still had their bows in hand. Bravely they fired at the multi-eyed monster. Sarth turned his attention to the beholder as well, hurling a blast of scorching emerald fire that clung to the thing and sizzled like acid. The beholder roared in anger and turned the full fury of its eye-rays against the tiefling. Sarth threw up a quick spell-shield but staggered under the magical assault.

Geran searched his mind for the arcane symbol of a spell he rarely used. He brought it to the tip of his tongue as he wove the point of his sword through mystic passes and unlocked its magic with a single word: *"Haethellyn!"* His blade took on a strange blue sheen, and he leaped in front of Sarth, parrying the beholder's eye-rays with the sword. He deflected a crimson ray at a gargoyle nearby, who howled and burst into flame, and caught a pale yellow ray next. This one he sent back at the beholder; it struck the monster in its own middle eye with a shower of sparks.

The floating monster wailed and spun its eye away from the battle below. But one of its smaller eyes found Geran and blasted him with a coruscating blue beam before he could deflect it. The magical beam seized Geran like the grip of an invisible titan and flung him headlong down the beach. The swordmage tumbled through the air and crashed into the pebble-strewn beach with bone-jarring force. He felt his left wrist snap under him, and a jolt of hot, white pain ran up his arm. He rolled several times before he came to a stop, dizzy and disoriented. Slowly he pushed himself upright with his good hand and reached for his sword, lying on the ground nearby.

Suddenly something hit him across the back, hard. It drove him to the ground, stunning him again, only to drag him into the air a moment later. Wings beat like thunder around him, and talons clenched with iron strength around his shoulders. Only the potent defensive wardings of his swordmagic prevented them from sinking deep into his flesh. Through the pain, the thundering wingbeats, the dizzying swings and drops, Geran realized that a gargoyle had caught hold of him and was trying to fly off. Already the beach was a good twenty feet below him, and the monster that had him was beating upward with all its strength.

"Geran!" Hamil shouted. The halfling ran after him and paused to take careful aim with his bow. But another gargoyle spoiled the shot, knocking Hamil down as it crashed into him, wounded by one of the Shieldsworn. Sarth dueled the beholder

with a blinding barrage of deadly spells and fierce blasts, holding the monster at bay.

Geran struggled in the gargoyle's grasp. "Let go of me!" he snarled. He was a heavy burden for the monster; it sagged and dipped precipitously in midair as he tried to twist free.

The monster croaked in protest. "Mine!" it rasped. "Catch! Slay! Mine!"

He managed to tear free of one talon, which had only been caught in his leather jacket. The gargoyle almost dropped him; Geran glanced down beneath his wildly swinging feet and realized that a fall from his current height would be sure to break bones, if not kill him outright. In fact, if the gargoyle wanted to kill him, the easiest thing to do would be to let go of him. Despite the searing pain of the monster's grip on his shoulder, Geran reached up with his right hand and seized one ankle in a powerful grip, determined to cling to the creature until the drop below them was something he might survive without crippling injury.

The gargoyle hissed and turned on him in midair, clawing and kicking at him. Talons scored his chest, raked his limbs, and came within an inch of eviscerating him, but his magic wardings held, blunting the attack. But one flailing kick of the gargoyle's taloned foot snagged the satchel hanging around Geran's neck and ripped through its strap. The leather pouch—with the starry compass inside—dropped to the ground below, vanishing into thick underbrush in the middle of a roofless house. Geran roared in fear and frustration, hanging on by one hand and waving his damaged left arm ineffectually to fend off the enraged monster.

Then he lost his grip at the same time the gargoyle's talons tore loose from his jacket.

For one terrible moment he plunged backward toward the earth, flailing in midair. Then he plummeted through the thin branches of a small cedar tree growing alongside the wreckage of an old temple. Limbs pummeled him in a dozen savage blows, spinning him first one way and then another, cracking and thrashing as he fell. He hit the ground below hard enough that his sight went black and his breath *whoosh*ed from his mouth. The compass! he thought. I lost the compass!

Groaning, gasping for breath, he somehow groped his way to his feet and staggered out from under the cedar. He was standing near the front of what had once been a grand old stone building, its facade now little more than heaps of rubble spilling across a densely overgrown street. His back ached, and his knee throbbed painfully; he couldn't put much weight on that leg. But he'd been fortunate—the gargoyle's flight had brought them over the buildings at the top of the bluff, so that instead of falling a hundred feet or more to the beach, he'd only fallen twenty or thirty feet through the branches of a tree. "Fortunate, indeed," he muttered. "If I'd been a little more fortunate, I wouldn't have been dragged off in the first place."

"Catch! Slay!" The gargoyle alighted atop a broken column a short distance from Geran, red rage burning in its eyes. Two more of its fellows circled overhead, apparently drawn by the struggle. The monster flexed its talons and hissed at Geran.

His sword was somewhere on the beach below. The compass was lost somewhere in the maze of ruins around him, if it hadn't been shattered by the drop. He could barely stand. And he had at least one broken bone, perhaps more. Geran bared his teeth in a fierce snarl. His death was likely moments away, a fact that filled him with fury and frustration. If he fell here, Mirya and her daughter would likely never escape from whatever fate the masters of the Black Moon consigned them to. But he meant to die fighting and die on his feet, if that was all fate offered.

Holding the gargoyle's gaze, he shaped a single arcane word with his will and whispered, *"Cuilledyrr!"*

The gargoyle sprang at him from its perch, claws outstretched. Geran stood his ground as long as he could before dodging aside. He managed to twist out of the way of the deadly claws, but his injured knee gave out under him, and he went down in the loose rubble and wiry grass of the street. The gargoyle gave one gloating hiss and threw itself back at him to finish him off. Then the shrill ring of steel on stone echoed through the air. Geran held out his right hand—and his sword of elven steel flew hilt- first into his open hand, summoned from the beach below by his word of calling. In one fluid motion Geran buried the swordpoint in the gargoyle's black heart. The thing screeched horribly in his ears, and its body slammed him back to the ground again.

He struggled to free himself from the monster's dead weight and looked up to see the gargoyles who'd been circling above swooping down on him. He didn't have the strength to fight off another of the monsters, let alone two at once. Wildly he looked up and down the street, searching for some sort of shelter, some defensible position. All that he saw was the dark doorway of a dilapidated palace across the street. There was no way he could outrun the gargoyles to the doorway, but he had one last card to play. As the two monsters swooped down on him, Geran fixed his eyes on the darkness inside the stone archway and mustered the strength for his spell of teleportation. In the blink of an eye he was no longer on his hands and knees in the rain-soaked street outside, but instead kneeling in the clutter and debris inside the palace, looking back out at the place where he had been. The gargoyles screeched in frustration, fluttering and bounding from side to side in search of their missing prey.

Geran held still, hardly daring to breathe. If the monsters peered too closely at the doorway, they would surely see him . . . but the creatures moved down the street, passing out of his sight. He heard their wingbeats and their croaking voices moving away.

With a sigh of relief, he climbed to his feet. The interior of the palace was dark and cluttered; he could barely see anything inside. He hobbled a couple of steps away from the open doorway, just in case the gargoyles returned—and then his foot plunged through the floorboards. He hit the floor hard, and the whole thing gave way, sending him into the cellar below in a cascade of rubble and dust. For the second time in the last hundred heartbeats, Geran found himself falling. He hit the bottom, struck his head on something hard, and sank into dizzying darkness.

TWENTY-ONE

14 Marpenoth, the Year of the Ageless One (1479 DR)

The smell of smoke still clung to Hulburg despite several days of intermittent rain. Rhovann believed it was an improvement over the customary odor of the city. He'd never cared for the cities of humankind, with their crowding, their cookfires and forge smoke, their garbage, their unwashed masses. In his more honest moments he might admit that the cool, damp air of Hulburg's autumn was much more tolerable than, say, Mulmaster or Hillsfar in the middle of the summer—but he was not often inclined to give Hulburg the benefit of the doubt.

A shame the Black Moon hadn't burned more of the place, he reflected as he gazed from the carriage at the street outside. Rhovann knew it ran counter to his ally Sergen's purpose to destroy the city outright, but in his eyes it wouldn't have done that much harm for a few blocks to be burned down. After all, each injury he inflicted on Hulburg was one more bitter draught of justice for Geran Hulmaster to savor. The wrongs Rhovann had endured at Geran's instigation were many and great, and it might take a human lifetime to repay each one appropriately.

In the seat opposite Rhovann, Maroth Marstel frowned as they passed another burned-out building, one that had survived the Black Moon attack only to be destroyed by a fire set during rioting two days later. "We should muster a few hundred armsmen and clean out the Tailings," the old lord muttered. "Drive those Cinderfists, those foreign criminals, out of Hulburg forever, before they ruin everything. That's the first thing I'll do as harmach, mark my words."

"Everything in its own time, my lord," Rhovann said. "First we must convince Grigor Hulmaster to step down—or force him to if he fails to see reason. After all, he is simply the wrong man for the times."

"The wrong man for the times," Marstel said softly. It was not his own thought, but he was so deeply under Rhovann's dominion, he likely believed that it was.

"Do not speak of becoming harmach again. It is a secret between you and me."

"A secret . . ." Marstel smiled, and his eyes took on a cunning cast. "I have a secret."

Rhovann frowned. Maroth Marstel was not a young man, and between besotting himself with drink and a certain native lack of wits, he very well may have started along the long, confusing road that afflicted some humans as they grew old. Rhovann had used spells of compulsion and control on Marstel for months now with little concern for the innate soundness of the man's mind. He found with no small vexation that he did not know exactly how his magic was likely to be affected by the subject's slide into senescence—one more unpleasant characteristic of humankind seemingly designed for his personal frustration and annoyance. It might be wise for Marstel to spend more of his time out of sight of others and to adopt a pretense that the House mage Lastannor was an especially loyal, competent, and trusted subordinate who conducted most of Marstel's business so as not to trouble the great man with needless details.

In a tenday or two that will be Sergen's concern, not mine, Rhovann reminded himself. After all, he didn't care what became of Hulburg after he was finished dealing with Geran. Whether Sergen succeeded in seating a puppet on the throne—such as it was in this rude little backwater—or lost control of the city as Marstel's failing mind became apparent to all didn't matter to him in the slightest. But just in case, Rhovann murmured the words of his domination charm and erased the childishness from Marstel's expression.

The carriage rolled into the courtyard of the harmach's castle, and footmen appeared to help Marstel from the coach. Judging from the other carriages in the courtyard, Rhovann guessed that they were the last to arrive. He allowed Marstel to lead the way into the castle's great hall and trailed a step or two behind. The other members of the Harmach's Council waited by the table, conversing with each other or studying their notes. Seated in the row behind the place reserved for Marstel as the head of the Merchant Council, the heads of the other great merchant companies in Hulburg—Sokol, Jannarsk, Double Moon, and Iron Ring—waited as well.

"Lord Marstel! Master Mage Lastannor!" the Shieldsworn guard by the door announced. The murmur of conversation in the room died away, and the various officials took their seats. Rhovann and Marstel sat down just in time to be called to their feet by Harmach Grigor's arrival. They stood slowly, and the mage studied the ruler of Hulburg as he descended the stairs leading to the great hall. Grigor looked pale and tired, and he sat down with an audible sigh. The councilors and assembled advisors and seconds sat down as well.

Deren Ilkur, the Keeper of Duties, rapped his gavel on the table. "The Harmach's Council is met," he said. "With your permission, my lords and ladies, we will set aside the normal agenda and proceed directly to the urgent business of the day—the rioting and unrest in the Tailings and other poor neighborhoods."

No one objected. Then Burkel Tresterfin cleared his throat and spoke. "I suppose I'll speak first," he said. "Two more buildings were burned last night. At this rate, there will be nothing left of Hulburg but ashes. What steps can we take to restore order? Can't the Shieldsworn do something?"

"The Shieldsworn are stretched to their limit," Kara said. Her brow was creased with a stern frown that hadn't lifted for days. "We bore the brunt of the fighting against the Black Moon, and many of the harmach's soldiers were killed or seriously wounded in the struggle to defend the town. The last thing we expected in the wake of the pirate raid was a full-scale revolt by the foreign laborers who have settled here in recent years. I've brought as many men in from the post-towers as I dare to, but until *Seadrake* returns with Geran's soldiers, it's all we can do to patrol the major thoroughfares of the town and try to keep the rioting contained in the neighborhoods east of the Winterspear."

"Is there any news of *Seadrake* and Lord Geran's pursuit of the Black Moon vessels that fled?" Theron Nimstar asked.

Kara shook her head. "None that I've heard, High Magistrate. We may not hear anything for many days yet."

Rhovann chose to attack the opening Nimstar had unwittingly provided him. "So the harmach's plan for quelling the unrest is to wait for *Seadrake* to return, which might be days, tendays, or never?" he asked Kara. "You have tried for days now to outwait the unrest, and it worsens every night. I think sterner measures are called for."

"Then I need more soldiers." Kara looked across the table to Marstel and the heads of the Merchant Council Houses behind him. "Your companies employ hundreds of sellswords. So far they've done nothing but guard your own storehouses and compounds. Place those armsmen under the harmach's command for a few days, and I'll check the Cinderfists, the Crimson Chains, and the rest of the foreign gangs. It won't address their grievances in the long term, of course, but it should at least restore calm to the city."

Marstel shifted in his seat. Rhovann carefully shaped the answer he intended, and willed it through the old lord's lips. "No," Marstel said clearly. "We will not place our guards under the harmach's command. The time has come for the Merchant Council to take more direct action to bring an end to this chaos."

"Direct action, Lord Marstel?" Kara asked, with a hint of suspicion in her voice. Rhovann could not really blame her for that. Marstel's bold ideas were often stunning examples of braggadocio or folly.

"It is clear to the Merchant Council that the Tower no longer has the ability to meet this challenge," Marstel answered.

"Therefore the Merchant Council has resolved to assume responsibility for the governance, good order, and security of Hulburg. We have a list of specific demands that must be immediately enacted."

Several of the council members started to protest, but Rhovann pushed Marstel ahead. Marstel rose to his feet and raised his voice, overriding everyone else at the table. "First, the illegal militia known as the Moonshields must be immediately banned. If we say that one gang of ruffians, vigilantes, and scofflaws is illegal in Hulburg, then all such gangs must be illegal. Since the Spearmeet is simply a thin justification for the Moonshields to meet and organize, the Spearmeet must be disarmed and disbanded as well. We can no longer accept so-called militias taking the law into their own hands!

"Second, the ill-considered ban on the Merchant Council's employment of a Council Guard must be rescinded. The harmach refuses to safeguard our property and our rights in his domains. Very well; we intend to protect our substantial investments in Hulburg ourselves.

"Third, since the Merchant Council is obligated to see to our own security—at no small expense of our own—we renounce all existing concessions and leases with the Tower. Why should we pay the harmach ruinous royalties for no benefits other than the right to do business in Hulburg?" Marstel glowered fiercely at Grigor Hulmaster, seated above the head of the table. "If the harmach cannot protect our interests in Hulburg, we must do so ourselves."

The chamber was still as a tomb when Marstel finished. Rhovann hid a small smile behind the ridiculous beard he wore in his guise as a Turmishan mage. Kara Hulmaster was so angry her eyes positively glowed with the tainted magic that marked her azure irises. Shieldsworn guards standing watch over the proceedings pressed their lips together tightly and glared at Marstel, well aware of how much of an insult the old buffoon had delivered to their lord.

"This is impossible!" snapped Wulreth Keltor. The old Keeper of Keys quivered with rage. "We all remember how the so-called Council Guard managed their affairs! And the concessions cannot be renegotiated!"

"I fail to see how disarming Hulburg's law-abiding citizens and taking steps to enrich the merchant companies will help to restore order," Deren Ilkur said. He frowned deeply behind his short, black beard. It was his task as Keeper of Duties to chair the council meetings and set the agenda, but it was clear that he couldn't continue until the question of Marstel's challenge had been dealt with.

For his own part, Harmach Grigor simply stared at Marstel for twenty long heartbeats, his face sagging in exhaustion. Finally Grigor gathered his strength and spoke. "And if we do not adopt these measures, Lord Marstel?" he asked in a weary voice. "What then?"

Rhovann glanced at Marstel and fixed his will on the old merchant lord. Marstel drew himself up with a pompous sniff. "Then the Merchant Council will take steps to enforce these measures ourselves. House Hulmaster has run this domain into ruin. We will not permit the Hulmasters to prevent us from saving ourselves."

Kara Hulmaster leaped to her feet, unable to sit quietly any longer. "I have endured years of your stupidity in this chamber, Marstel, but this is intolerable! The freedom to speak your mind does not give you the authority to incite rebellion! You say that the Hulmasters have brought this town to ruin. Need I remind you that only five months ago the harmach and the Spearmeet defeated the Bloody Skull orcs not five miles from where we stand, saving your precious property—and your own worthless hide—in the process!"

"But is it not true that it was Hulburg's appearance of weakness that invited the Bloody Skulls to attack in the first place? And the Black Moon as well?" Rhovann answered for Marstel. The mage had no idea if that was substantially true or not in the case of the orc tribe, but it was important to stake out the claim. "The Bloody Skull attack should have been sufficient warning that we can no longer afford the luxury of inaction and indecisiveness."

More people started to speak, but Nimessa Sokol was first. "Master Ilkur, a moment ago you remarked that you did not see the relevance of the Merchant Council's demands," she said. "The relevance is this: If the harmach cannot restore order, the Merchant Council must. I have not been in Hulburg for very long, but my family has a substantial stake in the good governance of this realm. I wish to hear Harmach Grigor's answer to the requirements laid before him."

Anger flashed in the harmach's eyes, but he kept his voice level and calm. "I will not ask the Spearmeet to disband or disarm," he said. "Lord Marstel insists that the companies of the Merchant Council have a right to protect their lives and property. Well, so do the common citizens of Hulburg. And we saw five months ago, and again only a few nights past, the value of a large and well-armed militia." He looked at Marstel and the merchant leaders behind him sternly. "Some allowances may be possible to meet your other concerns. But I will not give the Merchant Council the ability to enforce their own laws again. We have learned that there must be only one law in Hulburg."

"In other words, your answer is no," Marstel said. "We are done here, then." The old lord hesitated, perhaps uncertain of what to do next, but Rhovann bent his will upon him again. Recovering, Marstel nodded sharply to the other merchant leaders behind him. They all stood—Nimessa Sokol with a taut frown of concern on her face—and filed out of the hall.

Rhovann waited a moment to reassure himself that the harmach's soldiers would not attempt to detain Marstel or the others. He didn't think it was very likely. A stronger lord, or one less concerned with the good opinion of those he governed, would not have permitted an avowed challenger to depart in peace, but Grigor Hulmaster seemed determined to avoid coercion.

After a moment, Rhovann stood as well and inclined his head to the harmach. "Forgive me, but I must go as well," he said. "I may be Master Mage, but I am also sworn to the service of House Marstel."

"Lastannor, you must reason with Marstel," Harmach Grigor said. "If he flouts Hulburg's laws, the Tower will have no choice but to enforce them. He is forcing my hand."

"I will do what I can," Rhovann answered. He decided that one more bit of misdirection couldn't hurt, and added, "He is given to bold words and grand gestures, as I am sure you know. By tomorrow he may be of a different mind on the question." He bowed again and withdrew.

On the steps outside the door, he found Nimessa Sokol attempting to confront Maroth Marstel. The young woman had her hands folded in front of her waist and spoke calmly, but her eyes blazed as she stood in front of Marstel, barring him from climbing into his coach. "You said nothing about disarming the Spearmeet before," she said in a low voice. "I wouldn't have agreed to support you if you'd added that to our list! The harmach can never agree to that, and you know it. Now he'll reject our position out of hand!"

"It is a difficult time," Marstel said in reply. "You are quite young and simply lack experience in how matters such as this are decided. Few women have much of a head for this sort of thing, you know."

Nimessa paled in anger. Rhovann raised an eyebrow. It seemed that Marstel's native boorishness had resurfaced at exactly the right moment to deflect the young consul of the House Sokol concession from the fact that the demands were never meant to be met by the harmach. He stepped in to mollify her before Marstel said something to anger her even more. "What Lord Marstel means is that we now have a demand we can graciously withdraw when true negotiations begin," he said smoothly. "But that would have no value if the harmach didn't believe that it was serious."

The half-elf studied him for a moment. "Of course that is what Lord Marstel meant," she said, even though her narrowed eyes and sharp tone indicated the opposite. "However, next time House Sokol must insist on being privy to any such strategy before allowing the High Master of the Merchant Council to speak for us. Your ploy may backfire on us all, with disastrous consequences."

Rhovann forced Marstel to remain silent and bowed to the young woman. She eyed the two of them then nodded back to him and went her way. Rhovann ushered Marstel into the coach and signaled for the driver to go. They rolled out of Griffonwatch's courtyard and descended the stone causeway winding around to the foot of the castle's hill.

"It'll be dark soon," Marstel said, looking out the window. The elf mage ignored him. The old lord was quickly becoming useless, but it would be highly useful to keep a firm hand at the helm of the Merchant Council—or even in the harmach's throne, if it came to it. With constant attention and oft-repeated spells, Rhovann could use Marstel more or less as he liked, but the elf mage hardly wanted to pass the next few months or years playing puppeteer to an old man whose mind was beginning to slip. Sooner or later it would become obvious that Marstel was no longer suited to leadership (not that he'd ever been suited, really), and all of Rhovann's work would be for naught. No, what he needed was a sturdier, sounder, more loyal Marstel, one who could be counted on to manage affairs to Rhovann's satisfaction without constant supervision. Unfortunately, he knew no spells that could change the sodden old boor in front of him into the man he needed.

But he did know spells that could *make* the man he needed.

"A simulacrum . . . that might do," he mused aloud. It would be several tendays of work, but when it was done, he'd no longer need to play nursemaid to the detestable old lordling in front of him.

"Eh? What's that you said, Lastannor?" Marstel asked.

"Nothing important." Rhovann glanced out the window; they had arrived at the Marstel tradeyard in the heart of the harbor district. He looked back to Marstel and fixed his eyes on the old man's. "You will return to your home, eat a modest supper, and retire for the evening. I will see to it that you are not disturbed. Sleep well."

Marstel nodded and yawned. His chin drooped toward his chest. When the carriage stopped, Rhovann climbed out and closed the door behind him. "Take Lord Marstel home and put him to bed," he told the footman. The fellow nodded. All of Marstel's personal servants and guards answered to the mage they knew as Lastannor, and did more or less as he told them to, regardless of their lord's objections. "Let no one disturb him for any reason. I will return by morning."

"Yes, Master Lastannor," the footman replied. He climbed back up to the carriage's running board, and the coach trundled off into the evening drizzle.

The guards at the compound gates bowed to Rhovann as he passed between them. He ignored them, rehearsing in his mind one last time the sequence of events he'd designed for the evening. The rain continued to fall; large puddles covered the cobblestones, and a small stream had formed in the center of the Marstel compound. The elf mage ignored the steady rain and headed for the building housing the company headquarters. The day's routine business was long over, and the place seemed deserted except for more of the Marstel armsmen. One opened the door for Rhovann and stood aside as the mage ducked through the door to get out of the damp. He made his way to Maroth Marstel's office, which he'd appropriated for his own use.

Inside, Valdarsel was waiting for him. The Cyricist wore a plain brown hood and looked for all the world like one more driver or stoker looking for a chance to earn a living in Hulburg. "Well?" he asked. "How did it go?"

"As I expected," Rhovann answered. "The harmach refused to accept the council's terms. Although he indicated that he'd be willing to negotiate on some of the points, which surprises me."

"So the Cinderfists are needed tonight?"

"They are. It shall be as we planned. Take to the streets an hour before midnight and draw out the Shieldsworn and any Spearmeet companies you can. We will take care of the rest."

Valdarsel nodded. "So be it, then. But it would've been better to strike without warning. The charade of presenting the harmach with demands may only set Lord Hulmaster on his guard."

"Whether he is on his guard or not will not matter. But it might be very important later on for the Merchant Council to be able to claim that Grigor's intractability forced tonight's moves. A fig leaf of legitimacy may go a long way toward convincing the townsfolk to go along with the council's rule." Rhovann smiled. "Well, that and immediate evidence that the council has the town's disorder in hand."

"Don't worry, Lastannor. I'll allow you to quell the mob soon enough." Valdarsel stood up and raised his hood over his head. "Well, it seems we have much to do tonight. I must give orders for a riot, and you've a king to overthrow."

"Of course." Rhovann walked Valdarsel to the door and watched as the Cyricist hurried off into the street outside the tradeyard. Several ruffians lounging outside the gate fell in behind him—his bodyguards, or so it seemed. He did not trust Valdarsel—after all, what sort of man served a deity such as the Black Sun?—but he did trust Valdarsel to act in his own self-interest. The priest was about to become the second-most powerful man in Hulburg, free to garner riches and to reward those he deemed deserving. No doubt Valdarsel was already looking past that arrangement and planning for the hour when he'd subjugate the Merchant Council to the power of the Cinderfists instead of the other way around . . . but first he'd have to help the council to remove the Hulmasters from power.

"A hungry bulette on a chain," Rhovann murmured. As long as the one holding the chain had something to feed the monster, he was safe enough.

He strode across the yard to the largest of the Marstel storehouses, this one guarded by several men in Marstel's colors. The sellswords stood straight and touched their brows as Rhovann approached. He passed between them and let himself into the building they protected. It was half-filled with common trade goods, casks and crates of all sorts stacked in untidy rows. Rhovann moved to a spot in the middle of the floor and drew his wand from its place inside his robe. He made a simple pass in the air, and the thin outline of a hidden door appeared before him.

It swung open under the touch of his magic, revealing a stairway leading down. The murmur of men's voices fell quiet as the door opened. He descended into the room below.

In the hidden cellars beneath the Marstel storehouse, a company of hundreds of armsmen dressed for battle stood or sat, waiting. For two tendays now Rhovann had arranged for Marstel ships to quietly ferry in sellswords hired from Mulmaster and other cities, bringing the fighters in by fives and sixes and concealing them under the Marstel storehouses. Rhovann spied their captain—a big, beefy man with a mouthful of gold teeth and an iron brace fitted to one knee—and motioned the man over. "Are your men ready, Captain Bann?" he asked.

The big human nodded. "We're armed and dressed for war, m'lord. What are your orders?"

"In an hour, a tremendous riot will strike in the heart of the harbor district. It should lure all but a handful of Shieldsworn down to deal with the fires and the looting. You are to lead the House Veruna and House Marstel soldiers to Griffonwatch and storm the castle while its garrison is absent. The House Jannarsk soldiers will seize Daggergard at the same time."

Bann nodded. He was not a brilliant man, but he possessed a certain low cunning and a strong streak of mercilessness that made him effective as a commander of sellswords. "What of the Double Moon Coster or the Sokols?"

"I do not consider them reliable. The Iron Ring men will keep them in their own compounds until events are decided. Afterward I imagine they'll prove pragmatic enough to come to terms with the new order of things." And if they didn't, well, it would not be very hard to evict them from Hulburg after the merchant Houses dealt with the harmach and his men.

"Griffonwatch may prove difficult, m'lord," Bann said slowly. "It only takes a few men to hold a castle, and we've no scaling ladders or battering rams ready."

"A small detail that I will attend to for you, Captain Bann." Rhovann smiled coldly. Against a castle stripped of all but a handful of guards, he had no doubt that his magic could deliver the gate into the hands of Bann and his company. "Make sure you get your men to the top of the causeway swiftly once the riot begins. Leave the gate to me."

"The harmach and his family?"

"I would prefer them taken alive. After all, there will be a new harmach in Hulburg tomorrow. It would be a shame if Grigor Hulmaster were not alive to see it." Rhovann swept the hidden barracks room with his gaze, making sure that all the sellswords within earshot understood his wishes. He trusted servitors he created with his own hands, or minions magically compelled to do as he commanded. Common hired swords might prove corruptible or might misunderstand the orders he gave them; it was for that very reason that he grew his most capable servants in alchemical vats. Still, he knew well enough what motivated men such as Captain Bann. "Above all, do not allow any of the harmach's family to escape. A hundred gold crowns to each man who captures a Hulmaster!"

Bann sketched a shallow bow. "M'lord is most generous," the captain rasped.

"To a point. Do not fail me, Captain." Rhovann held the man's eyes for a moment and then left the sellswords to their preparations.

TWENTY-TWO

15 Marpenoth, the Year of the Ageless One (1479 DR)

Geran opened his eyes to darkness and cold water. His head ached, his left wrist and right knee throbbed, and when he tried to roll over, a sharp jolt in the middle of his back made him hiss in pain. Slowly he pushed himself upright, careful not to wrench his back again. All he could make out was a pale shadow over his head—most likely the hall in the ruined palace above. Rubble shifted under him as he moved, and he slipped deeper into the cold water that apparently half flooded the cellar. It wasn't deep, no more than a foot or so, but he was lucky he hadn't wound up with his face in the water after striking his head. He might have drowned.

"I've had better days," he muttered to himself. He snorted at his own dark humor and paid the price when pain seared his back again. He winced and looked around the ruined chamber. Where in the world was he again? What was he doing here?

"Sulasspryn," he murmured aloud. "I'm in Sulasspryn." *Seadrake* was anchored out in the bay. Hamil, Sarth, and a score of armsmen were somewhere down by the pirate *Moonshark* on the beach—or at least that was where he'd last seen them. If the light in the room above was any indication, night had fallen in the streets above. That meant he'd been unconscious at least five or six hours, and possibly much more. Gingerly he reached up to feel his skull and discovered a big knot and some crusted blood high on the left side of his forehead. All things considered, this was in fact shaping up as one of the worst days he'd had in a very long time.

He sat up carefully, picking himself up out of the cold water and seating himself on the mound of rubble. He still couldn't see much of his surroundings, but he decided against showing any light just yet. If there was anything in here he needed to worry about, it would've had hours to do with him as it liked while he was unconscious. Instead he tried to piece together his situation. Surely Hamil and Sarth knew he was missing—if in fact they, or anyone else, had survived the fight on the beach. Obviously, they hadn't found him yet. Either no one had been able to come looking for him, or they had no idea where he was. Both possibilities suggested that it was up to him to find his way back to the rest of the landing party, or to *Seadrake* if the landing party was no longer ashore. "Or to Hulburg if *Seadrake* has to put to sea," he added to himself. He didn't relish the idea of a thirty-mile walk home.

He looked around for the satchel with the starry compass. It was nowhere nearby. He scowled in the darkness and kneeled to feel around in the cold, foul water of the cellar, ignoring the aches and pains of his injuries. The compass was the whole reason they'd come to this accursed ruin—he couldn't leave without it, not if he had any hope of rescuing Mirya and her daughter from Kamoth and Sergen! He splashed around for several minutes in the shadows before he remembered that he'd lost the satchel during his midair struggle with the gargoyle that had tried to carry him off. The compass was somewhere outside, lying wherever he'd dropped it unless something or someone had picked it up.

"Damn the luck!" he swore. Geran stood and kicked at the water, earning himself another jolt of pain from his knee. He *had* to find the compass before he did anything else, gargoyles or no gargoyles.

The first order of business was escaping from this cellar. Now he needed a little light. He reached down and found a small stone in the mound of rubble below the collapsed floor, and murmured the Elvish words of a light spell over the stone. A bright blue-white radiance sprang up from its surface; Geran tucked it deep into his palm and closed his hand over it, so that only a small, blue glimmer showed from between his fingers. After all, he didn't want to give away his location to everyone nearby. By the stone's occulted light, he studied the subterranean chamber into which he'd fallen. It was a large hall with a dozen or more thick columns, the ceiling a good twenty feet or more overhead. An old slide had ruined the far end of the chamber, leaving a wall of rubble. Some sort of temple? Geran guessed. Or perhaps a trophy room or banquet hall? It seemed strange that any of those things might be located in a cellar, but maybe the ancient catastrophe that had destroyed Sulasspryn had caused some sort of collapse here.

The only stairs he could see were choked with rubble, so Geran held up his light and studied the hole in the ceiling through which he'd fallen. He certainly couldn't climb back up that way, not with his bad wrist and bad knee. But he didn't necessarily have to climb. He picked out a spot in the room above, gathered his concentration, and spoke a single arcane syllable: *"Seiroch!"*

The teleport spell whisked him through an instant of icy blackness, and then he was in the chamber above. He missed his footing, stumbled, and fell, wrenching his knee again—he hadn't been able to see exactly where he was going to appear from the chamber below, and he'd picked a spot where the wreckage of old furniture littered the ground. Rain drummed down in the street outside, and scores of leaks in the roof of the old palace or temple allowed steady streams of rainwater to pour inside. That must have been the source of the water standing in the cellar below, he realized. Quickly he covered up his light again, leaving just a tiny glimmer peeking between his fingers as he stood and hobbled to the archway to peer up and down the street.

It seemed abandoned, but it was hard to be certain; the night was black, cold rain fell in sheets on the old cobblestones and broken tiles, and the wind blew in short, stiff gusts that rustled the trees and rushed through the wiry grass growing up between the ancient walls. A whole flock of gargoyles could have been standing in the street thirty yards away, and Geran wouldn't have known it. He decided to risk a little more light, and let more of the illumination show from the stone he held. Sulasspryn in its day had been much like old Hulburg, a small city huddled around a good harbor on the north shore of the Moonsea. Most of the old buildings were made of well-dressed stone, with slate tiles for roofing and broad avenues of mortared flagstones. Unlike Hulburg, it had never been rebuilt after its collapse; no one had ever come to clear the streets of rubble, cannibalize stone from old buildings, or build atop the ruins. If the Hulmasters had never resettled in Hulburg, this is what Hulburg would have looked like, Geran thought.

He limped across the street to the place where the gargoyle had dropped him, and found the cedar tree he'd fallen through. He searched beneath its boughs for a long time, shivering in the cold and the wet, and found nothing. He allowed the light to shine brighter still and peered into the branches, wondering if the satchel had been caught somewhere higher up, but it was not there either. "Think, Geran," he growled. "Where did you drop it?"

He tried to recall those last dizzy moments of the fight by the beach. The gargoyle had seized him in its talons, struggling to carry him aloft. He remembered the bluffs overlooking the harbor passing under his feet in a wild whirl, then the first few buildings by the edge, looking down and seeing the satchel fall toward the ruins below. The gargoyle had kept flying inland, toward the ruined citadel in the heart of the city, carrying him along. If he had to guess, the satchel was somewhere between the edge of the bluff and the place where he'd fallen, probably not more than a hundred yards from where he stood.

Closing his eyes, he whispered the words of a minor charm intended to reveal the presence of magic nearby. He felt nothing, but that didn't surprise him. He would have to be close to the starry compass in order to detect its enchantment in that way. Unfortunately, he had no other method for locating the compass besides groping through the rain and darkness in the hopes that he might physically stumble over it. The best thing to do would be to retrace the gargoyle's dizzying flight over the ruins as best he could, stopping frequently to repeat the minor divination. But even that would be nearly impossible, because he wasn't sure exactly which way he'd come before, and even if he were, he couldn't cut directly over the intervening ground. He'd have to find avenues that led back in the way he wanted to go without diverting him too far from the gargoyle's path.

"Or would it be wiser to remain here and wait for a rescue party?" he muttered to himself. He had no idea if *Seadrake* was still in Sulasspryn's harbor or not. He didn't think they would have left without him, but if the monsters had driven them off, Hamil and Sarth might have had no choice but to flee. They'd seen him carried off by the gargoyle, after all; they might very well assume that he was dead. Geran sighed. It was all too likely that he was stranded in Sulasspryn, alone and injured. In which case, the sooner he recovered the compass and made his way out of the ruins, the better off he'd be. He set out cautiously in the direction he guessed was most likely to lead him toward the place where he thought he'd dropped the compass.

He spent an agonizing hour groping his way through the streets, slowly working his way back toward the harbor. He blundered into blind alleys, climbed painfully over the rubble of ruined buildings, and backtracked dozens of times to try to stay as close as he could to his guess at the straight-line path back toward the harbor. Every fifty steps or so he paused to repeat the charm, hoping for some faint glimmer in the darkness. Several times he heard things moving in the ruins around him—the grating sound of rubble shifting, distant croaking cries that echoed from the stones, and one time the sudden flurry of heavy wingbeats somewhere overhead. For that one, Geran froze where he stood, not daring to move or make a sound until he was certain the creature was gone. But even after the wingbeats faded, he couldn't shake the feeling that something was lingering nearby, something that had his spoor and was patiently stalking him through the rain and the gloom. Icy tendrils of dread began to creep down his spine, and he hurried along as quickly as he could.

He turned a corner into a small, cluttered alleyway—likely a workshop district in Sulasspryn's better days—and pressed himself into a doorway, straining eyes and ears to detect any motion in the night around him. Something was abroad in the darkness, of that he was sure, and he did not care to meet it. He waited for a short time, watching back the way he'd come, but he could see nothing but the faint glimmer of puddles in the street and the dim, jagged shadows that marked the rooftops of the ruined city. He murmured the words of his detection charm again, stretching out his senses for the peculiar psychic impressions of magic nearby . . . and this time he felt a distinct answer, a faint vibration like a harpstring plucked in a nearby room. He turned and stared, trying to discern exactly which direction he'd felt the enchantment from, and decided that it was down the alleyway and a little to one side, perhaps in one of the old houses along the lane or just behind them.

He turned to leave, and in the corner of his eye he glimpsed a dark shape slipping across the street behind him. The air grew colder, and Geran jerked his head back, afraid he might have been seen. *Best to move on while it's not in sight,* he told himself. Quickly he hurried down the alleyway, moving toward the place where he'd felt the glimmer of enchantment. It still hovered at the edge of his awareness, and he fumbled toward it as he slipped and stumbled through the rubble. A doorway loomed up to his left; he cautiously stepped through, one hand on the hilt of his sword, the other cupped around his light-pebble.

The roof of this small home had fallen in long ago and was now an overgrown mound of rubble in the center of the floor. Rain spattered down from the open sky—and there, half hidden in the underbrush by one wall, the leather satchel gleamed wetly. Geran crossed the room and picked it up. It felt full, but to be certain he undid the latch and reached in. The fall might have damaged the orb, after all . . . but smooth, unbroken crystal met his fingers. He pulled out the starry compass and quickly examined it. In the darkness the tiny pinpricks of white light embedded in its substance seemed to glow faintly. He sighed in relief and put the magical device back into the satchel.

With the compass in hand, now he was free to find his way out of the city by the most direct route available. He hurried back to the alleyway outside and turned left, hoping that the next big street might lead him toward the bluffs overlooking the harbor. If he remembered rightly, there were old stairways zigzagging down from the street-ends to the strand below.

Something was waiting for him in the street.

He froze in midstep as he emerged from the alleyway, aware of a presence—several presences—gathered in the shadows outside. Again, cold dread welled up in his heart, stealing his voice. He heard the creature this time, a thick wet gurgling sound that wheezed in the darkness. And then that sound shaped itself into words and spoke. "Geran Hulmaster," it bubbled. "Geran Hulmaster."

Geran recoiled several steps, until he sensed another one close behind him. He swept out his sword and turned in a circle, trying to menace all the things around him with its deadly point. The last thing in the world he wanted to do was look upon the creatures closing in on him . . . but he needed some light to fight by. He opened his hand and held high the stone with the light spell. Blue-white radiance flared brightly in the shadowed street, revealing the leaning cornices and cracked facades of the ruins around him.

The dwarf Murkelmor crouched before him. At first Geran thought he was wearing some kind of strange, tattered cape, but then he realized that the flesh of Murkelmor's chest and shoulders had been ripped to ribbons. Murkelmor raised his eyes to meet his horrified gaze, and Geran saw that half his face had been clawed off as well. His eyes were a dead, pupil-less white, and his teeth had grown long and sharp. Black gore crowned him like careless splatters of paint. More of *Moonshark*'s crew stood in the street behind Murkelmor or stared at Geran through crumbling doorways. They were all dead, with torn, pallid flesh and lifeless eyes.

"Get away from me!" Geran cried. He'd faced ghouls and other such undead before, but never had he seen one he'd known as a living man. It was a peculiarly horrifying experience. Murkelmor bared his fangs and shambled forward a few steps; others of the crew closed in from behind Geran, reaching out with hands whose blood-caked nails had grown into filthy claws.

"Geran Hulmaster, you slew us," Murkelmor rasped. "You betrayed us, you drove us here, and here we died. A heavy debt you owe us."

Geran shivered at the idea of what he might owe to *Moonshark*'s crew. Still, he tried to answer. "You meant to pillage Hulburg, murder its defenders, enslave its women and children," he said to the gruesome thing that had been Murkelmor. "It was my duty to fight you. I didn't mean for you to come to Sulasspryn, Murkelmor, and I'm sorry that *Moonshark* came to a bad end here. But it was not my fault that you chose the course you did."

Behind him, a tall shape stumbled out of the shadows. Geran swung his sword point to menace the new threat and found himself facing Skamang. The big Northman had been eviscerated, and his ruined face was a mask of gore. Skamang bared his fangs and hissed at him. "Look what you've done to us! You must die to set matters right. A heavy debt you owe, Geran Hulmaster!"

The crewmen behind him edged closer. Geran tried to keep them at sword point, hoping to keep the dead pirates from attacking. He was in no condition to fight, and he doubted very much whether he could outrun them. Besides, something did not make sense to him. Murkelmor and Skamang had known him as Aram, a rootless brigand. As far as Geran knew, there was no way either of them—or their undead corpses—should know his true identity. Perhaps the dead saw through such things more easily than the living, or perhaps there was more to this meeting in the shadows of Sulasspryn.

"How do you know my name?" he demanded.

The dwarf snarled in anger and gnashed his long, pointed teeth. For a moment he rocked back and forth, moaning, as if he did not want to answer. But then he let out a thick, bubbling breath from his ruined chest and said, "We've been given a message for you."

"A message? What message? From whom?"

"King Aesperus sends his greetings, Geran Hulmaster," Skamang said, speaking from behind him. "He bade us tell you that the fates of Hulburg and the family Hulmaster now hang upon your choice. Follow your intended course, and the harmach's enemies will triumph over Hulburg. Return home, and you can prevent the harmach's defeat for now—but Grigor will be the last of the Hulmasters to rule, and his enemies will lay the city in ruins before he dies."

Geran shivered. He'd met Aesperus once, on the slopes of a barrow in the Highfells a few miles outside of Hulburg. The mighty lich-king was master of the undead in these lands, and he'd known Geran for a Hulmaster. He didn't know why the King in Copper had decided to speak to him through the dead of *Moonshark* . . . and he didn't like the message, either. "Which enemies?" he asked Skamang. "What danger in Hulburg can I avert?"

"An adversary you've forgotten threatens the harmach's seat," Murkelmor said. "But if you defend Hulburg, the Black Moon escapes. The two you seek'll be lost t' you forever, and in time the Black Moon'll work your ruin. If you pursue the High Captain, you may save the two you seek, but Hulburg is doomed t' fall under the power of your foe. Others dear t'you will suffer in their stead."

Geran frowned, puzzling over the lich's rede. How could defeating his enemies lead to Hulburg's fall? And who was the forgotten enemy—the Vaasans who had aided the Blood Skulls in their war? Some other tribe of Thar? It would seem that defeating his enemies and protecting the city went hand in hand, yet Aesperus said otherwise. And even if Aesperus was being truthful, which choice was the lich trying to lure him into making? To give himself a moment to think, he looked at Murkelmor and asked, "Did Aesperus make you into what you are?"

"There be other powers beside King Aesperus in dead Sulasspryn," the dwarf answered. "But none return from th' grave within the bounds o' his old kingdom without his knowledge."

"Why does Aesperus want me to know this fate?"

Skamang laughed softly behind him, a horrible sound. "King Aesperus has no more words for you, Geran Hulmaster. And now that we've delivered his message, he no longer has any hold on us. We can do with you as we like." He lurched forward, reaching out with his clawed hands.

"Reith arroch!" Geran shouted, summoning a sword spell. Instantly his elven blade flashed with a brilliant white light, throwing shadows back against the night. The ghouls that had been the crew of *Moonshark* shrank from the light, which seared their undead flesh. Geran took a half step toward Skamang and slashed the dead Northman across the face before he could recover. Skamang shrieked and collapsed to the ground, blinded by the searing light.

Geran swung wildly, keeping the dead crewmen at bay. Then he used his teleport spell, choosing a spot on the other side of a large building's crumbling wall. He appeared in a tangle of underbrush, slipped, and then climbed to his feet. Sheathing his sword and cupping his light closely, he scrambled through the ruins at the best speed he could manage, hoping that he'd given himself the head start he needed to escape from the vengeful crew. He could hear them scrabbling over the rubble and moaning in frustration behind him.

Geran pressed on, ducking through ruined doorways and climbing over decaying walls until he could no longer hear *Moonshark*'s undead crew behind him. He slowed down, moving more cautiously, and found a street leading downhill—toward the harbor, he guessed. He made his way down through an area of dense overgrowth, fighting his way through thorny thickets, and then emerged on the shore. He couldn't see if *Seadrake* was still out in the harbor, but *Moonshark*'s battered hulk creaked in the gusts somewhere not too far away.

"I hope Hamil and the rest are out there somewhere," he muttered. He shrugged the satchel off his shoulder, took out the starry compass and tucked it inside his shirt, and put the small stone with its light spell in the satchel. Then he went down to the water's edge and held the satchel open, facing out toward the harbor. The satchel shielded the stone's bright glow from anyone in the ruins above and behind him, but allowed the bright blue-white illumination to show toward anyone out at sea.

They might have had to pull off, he told himself. He'd seen a number of gargoyles flying out to attack the ship while the landing party battled the monsters on the shore. For that matter, it was possible that *Seadrake*'s crew had met the same end as *Moonshark*'s, torn to pieces to a man. But then, faintly, he saw a yellow light far out on the water shining back at him. It gave two short blinks.

Geran lowered himself to the rocky beach and hunkered under his sodden cloak. He kept a wary eye on the dark bluffs behind him, half expecting the beat of gargoyle wings or a sudden rush from the shadows by his former shipmates. Half an hour later, he heard the muffled clinking of oarlocks and the soft splash of oars in the water.

Geran, is that you? Hamil asked silently.

"I'm here, Hamil!" Geran called. He pushed himself to his feet and limped out to meet *Seadrake*'s boat. Ten Shieldsworn pulled the oars; Hamil stood in the bow with an arrow on his bowstring, and Sarth scanned the skies nervously from the stern.

The halfling vaulted over the bow and splashed ashore. "Where have you been? What happened? Are you hurt?"

"The curse on these ruins interfered with my divinations," Sarth added. "In truth, we feared you were dead."

"Am I hurt? Yes, but nothing fatal. As for the rest, I'll tell you the tale on the way back to the ship." Geran could not suppress a shiver. "I found the rest of *Moonshark*'s crew. They're all dead . . . but they don't rest yet. The King in Copper's got them."

"Aesperus?" Hamil frowned and shook his head. "I wouldn't wish that fate on anyone, not even Skamang. You're lucky we didn't leave you here with them; we intended to sail at first light."

Geran glanced once more at the ruins of Sulasspryn and shuddered. "The sooner we're away from this accursed spot, the better." He and Hamil climbed into the longboat, and they shoved off the shore and rowed through the rain back out to the waiting ship.

TWENTY-THREE

16 Marpenoth, the Year of the Ageless One (1479 DR)

When they returned to *Seadrake,* Geran learned that they'd lost nine men from the landing party and two more aboard *Seadrake*—a heavy toll, but not as bad as he'd feared in the first chaotic moments of the gargoyle attack. Many more were injured to a greater or lesser extent, but Brother Larken, the young friar who sailed as the ship's prelate, proved to be an able healer. After the first skirmish with the gargoyles, Larken saved the lives of several severely injured men and repaired injuries that might have crippled others. He looked after Geran as soon as Hamil and his rescue party brought the swordmage back on board, speaking healing prayers over the worst of his injuries. Geran met the morning stiff and sore, but his left wrist was knitting, and he was able to stand up straight on the quarterdeck with only a few aches and pains to remind him of his hours among the ruins.

Behind them, Sulasspryn receded into the morning mists. The rain had finally slowed in the hour before dawn, becoming a steady drizzle instead of a downpour. The first thing Geran did as they sailed away from the ruins was to summon *Seadrake's* carpenter—one of the sons of old Master Therndon, Hulburg's master shipwright—to the quarterdeck and start him working on a frame for the starry compass similar to the one that was on *Moonshark*.

Andurth Galehand watched the carpenter with a disapproving

frown. Many dwarves didn't think much of arcane magic, and seafarers were a superstitious lot in the best of circumstances. After a moment he shook his head and turned to speak to Geran. "We're standing sou'west because that was the best course to take us away from Sulasspryn," he said. "But I reckon we're clear now. What course, m'lord?"

Geran glanced up at the sky. The overcast seemed like it would be with them for a while yet, and the gusty winds of the previous night had settled into another steady blow from the northwest. He didn't think it would matter much where they were when they used the starry compass, but it couldn't hurt to steer toward Umberlee's Talons. That was where *Kraken Queen* had left the Moonsea, after all. On the other hand, if Aesperus had been speaking truthfully through Murkelmor and Skamang, then he ought to consider turning toward Hulburg instead. "Keep her on this heading for a while," he finally told the sailing master. "I'm not sure where we're bound, but we might as well work westward while I'm thinking about it. We might return to Hulburg before we do anything else."

"Aye, m'lord," Galehand answered. "Steady as she goes."

Geran decided that it wouldn't help the carpenter finish any faster if he stood and watched the fellow work, and went below to his cabin. He sent his steward to ask Hamil and Sarth to join him then sent the young fellow off to fetch a hearty breakfast from the galley. When his friends arrived, he motioned for them to join him at the table.

"I told you that I met Murkelmor and some of *Moonshark*'s crew during the night," he began. "I didn't want to say more around the crew or the armsmen, but here's the rest of the tale: They carried a message from the King in Copper. Aesperus said that if I continued after Mirya, Hulburg would fall into the power of a forgotten enemy . . . whatever that means. But if I abandon Mirya to protect the harmach, both she and Selsha would be lost. The Black Moon would escape us, and a different disaster would befall Hulburg in years to come."

"A grim prophecy," Sarth observed. "Doom awaits on either hand."

"So it would seem," Geran said. He leaned back in his chair, gazing out the stern windows at the shore behind them, now a dim gray line along the horizon. He could see nothing more of Sulasspryn.

"Do you have any reason to believe that the King in Copper is telling the truth?" Hamil asked.

"I have no reason to think that he isn't. I only met the King in Copper once, but I came away with the impression that he's not the sort to waste words. In his eyes, the living aren't worth lying to."

Hamil nodded slowly. "I had a similar impression," he admitted.

"Aesperus is certainly capable of lying," Sarth said. "While I have not met him as you have, I studied him through historical accounts and his own correspondence for many months. He probably would not break his word once he gives it, but he has a way of honoring his bargains with unfortunate consequences." The tiefling stood and paced, his slender tail swishing behind him. "The question that interests me is *why* Aesperus would choose to give you this warning. He would not do it for your benefit. He hopes to influence your decision to his own advantage."

"Assume that Aesperus is right, then," Hamil said. "Something bad will befall Hulburg if Geran keeps after the Black Moon now. But he also said that abandoning the effort to chase down the Black Moon would bring ruin too. Both options would seem to be disastrous. How is that supposed to influence Geran's decision?"

"Aesperus wants me to seek some third option?" Geran mused aloud. "I suppose it's possible to abandon both causes, although I hardly see how that could help."

"Or perhaps he suggests that you should return to Hulburg, leaving *Seadrake* to pursue the Black Moon pirates," said Sarth.

"Which might in fact bring down *both* dooms that Aesperus warned you against," Hamil answered. "That might be the point of his warning, in fact—choose one or the other so you don't stumble into both."

"This is maddening," Geran muttered. "It might be that his only purpose was to see if he could get me to second-guess everything I do and jump at my own shadow, in which case, he's well on his way to succeeding. It would have been better if he hadn't said anything at all." He shook his head. "In every tale I've ever heard told about an omen, prophecy, or prediction, efforts to cheat fate invariably fail. Why try to avoid it?"

"You do not strike me as a fatalist," Sarth said.

"I don't intend to surrender meekly to whatever doom is approaching." Geran sighed and looked away from the window. He couldn't imagine why Aesperus had deigned to warn him about the dangers ahead. In truth, he wished the King in Copper had no idea who he was. But the lich had taken an interest in him, whatever the reasons, and somehow Geran doubted that Aesperus would bother with any petty falsehoods or misdirections. That meant he had to choose. On the one hand, his family and his home stood in jeopardy. On the other, a woman he cared for deeply, even loved, and her innocent daughter faced a terrible fate . . . and his traitorous cousin seemed all too likely to escape him again.

Hamil watched him struggle with his thoughts. "So what will you do, then?" he asked.

Geran weighed his words before he answered. "I'll do my best to forget what Aesperus had to say, and carry on as I intended," he finally said. "I don't know what threatens Hulburg, but I certainly know the peril Mirya and Selsha are in. I simply can't leave them to their fate. And if Hulburg is doomed no matter what I do, then I might as well see to it that Kamoth and Sergen aren't the ones who bring it about. What happens after that, happens. I have to believe that even Aesperus can't foresee every outcome."

The steward returned with their breakfast then, and Geran was surprised to discover how famished he was. Of course, he'd been outdoors in cold, damp weather for most of the last day, and that always left him starving afterward. When they finished, the three comrades went back up on deck and found that young Therndon's frame was ready for the starry compass. With care

Geran, Sarth, and the carpenter installed the dark orb in its new place just ahead of the helm.

When they finished, Geran waited for the pinpricks of starlight he'd noticed the previous evening to appear, but nothing more happened. He looked to Sarth. "I think that's exactly the way it was fixed to *Moonshark.* Have we missed something?"

Sarth shook his head. "No, I do not think so," he said slowly. "The device is enchanted to carry the ship to the Sea of Night, but it's the middle of the day now. I think we'll need to wait for the sun to set."

"Just as Kamoth did the other day with *Kraken Queen,"* Geran said. He looked up at the sky and frowned. That would explain why the corsair ship hadn't fled into the skies at the first sight of the Hulburgan warship. "All right, we'll try again at dusk." He mastered his disappointment and went back down to his cabin to get a few hours' rest. He'd been awake for the better part of three nights running, and the time he'd spent unconscious in the cellar in Sulasspryn hardly counted as sleep.

A little before sunset, he roused himself and went back up on deck. Gray ramparts of cloud scudded along the horizon to the north, and the wind was growing stronger again. Geran had Galehand order all hands on deck, since he didn't know what would happen if the compass worked, and he waited for the last orange gleam of daylight to fade in the south. Then he turned to Sarth. "Let's try it now," he said.

"You should remember, this is not my field of expertise," the sorcerer replied. Sarth murmured arcane words and laid his hand on the surface of the compass. The pinpricks of starlight embedded in the crystal orb began to glow brighter and swirl slowly under his touch. Geran held his breath, watching intensely. Nothing else happened. Sarth frowned and tried a different incantation. That failed as well. Then he attempted a third, with a similar lack of effect. "I am sorry," Sarth said. "There must be a specific incantation to address the device."

Geran turned away and slammed one fist against the ship's rail. "Damnation!" he snarled. Now what were they supposed to do? He'd assumed that the operation of the starry compass would be no obstacle, but it seemed that wasn't the case.

"Wait!" said Hamil. "I forgot that I had this. Try the incantation from Narsk's letter!" He reached into his pocket and pulled out a scrap of paper. "It's a little sodden from that swim in the harbor the other night, but you can still make out the words."

Sarth took the paper and looked at the words. "Very well," he said. "Perhaps the Red Wizards who gave Narsk the compass gave him this incantation to awaken it." He laid his hand atop the compass again and read aloud from the damp paper. *"Jhel ssar khimungon, jhel nurkhme thuul yasst ne mnor!"*

Around the circumference of the device, ghostly white runes became visible. A tiny dot of white light appeared near the top of the compass. Geran could sense the arcane power of the device at work. A faint silvery sheen appeared around *Seadrake*'s deck and masts, like moonlight caught in mist, and the ship leaped swiftly over the wavetops. "I think it's working this time!" he called to Sarth.

"You have the helm, Geran," Sarth answered. "The compass should be answering to you."

Geran nodded. He wondered how he was supposed to steer *up*. After all, there was no set of sail or rudder he knew of that would carry a ship aloft. But he hadn't seen any special gear on *Kraken Queen* in the brief time he'd been alongside the Black Moon flagship, so he didn't think he needed any. The device was magical; perhaps it answered to the helmsman's voice or will.

Feeling a little foolish, he fixed his eyes on the compass and said aloud, "Ascend slowly."

Whether it was the sound of his voice or his simple intent, the starry compass heard him and answered. Its pinprick lights glowed brighter, and Geran let out a startled exclamation as some unseen force began to push the deck up under his feet. From either side of the hull the silvery sheen playing over the deck extended into two ethereal wings, seemingly made of nothing more than stardust and moonlight. He heard the sudden rush of water under the hull, the ruffle of the confused wind in the sails, and the mix of curses, gasps, moans, and whoops from the crew. The bowsprit rose high into the sky, and the ship leaped clear of the Moonsea in a burst of white spray. Almost immediately she heeled over in the breeze, carrying far too much canvas aloft now that there was no longer the weight of her hull in her water to hold her upright. Geran automatically spun the wheel to turn straight downwind and correct the dangerous heel, and the ship answered to his direction easily even though the rudder had no water to bite into.

"We're flying!" Hamil said with a laugh of delight. He leaned by the rail, one hand knotted in the shrouds as he looked over the side.

"Lord Geran, I'll give ye every gold coin I own if ye'll only set us down again," Andurth Galehand answered. "It's no' right for a ship to behave in such a way!"

"We've more flying ahead of us, so you might as well learn to like it," Geran told the sailing master. "I'll hold her steady for a bit. Have the crew take us down to half-sail or less. I don't think we need much canvas at all right now."

The dwarf looked pale, but he nodded. "Aye, m'lord." He turned and started shouting orders at the crew.

Geran looked at the compass and said, "Level now, and steady as she goes," he said. The bowsprit dropped a bit, and the deck slowly leveled in front of him. Now they might be sailing along on a smooth, calm day—but the Moonsea was hundreds of feet below their keel. He realized that he could see quite a distance from their height. Off his port bow he could make out the distant peaks of the Galena Mountains, glimmering orange with the sunset above a mantle of clouds that blanketed their lower slopes. And on his starboard beam he could faintly make out the snowy slopes of the high Earthspurs, rising in the wild lands south of Mulmaster—the better part of a hundred and fifty miles off, if he was right in his reckoning.

"Amazing," he murmured. He watched the crewhands taking in sail. When he was satisfied, he turned gently to run across the wind again. The ship heeled over, but much less than before; it was about the same as running across a stiff breeze in a waterborne vessel. "Ascend normally," he said aloud. This time the bowsprit came up even higher, and the ship seemed to soar upward as she climbed. A glance over his shoulder at the Moonsea dropping away below convinced Geran that he wouldn't ever need to order the ship to ascend at its best rate; he already felt as if he'd better hang on to the helm to make sure he didn't fall over the sternrail. He was surprised to see a small wisp of cloud pass by beneath them.

"How high can we go?" he wondered. "The air grows thin and cold atop the highest mountains. If we sail into the high reaches of the sky, wouldn't we encounter the same conditions?"

"What little I have read of voyaging in the Sea of Night suggests that we will," Sarth said. "The aether above the world is too rare to breathe, but artifacts such as the compass or magical helms gather it closely about the vessel—or so I have read. I recommend a cautious ascent, so that we can turn back if I am mistaken."

"A wise suggestion," Geran agreed. He glanced again at the compass and saw that the symbols along its equator were glowing brightly. The skies were darkening overhead, and he could make out the first dim stars glittering in the sky. Symbols and stars . . . he smiled at his own thickheadedness. "The compass symbols are constellations!" he said to Sarth and Hamil. "Look, that one right in front of us, that's the Swordsman," he said, pointing at the compass. "And look where our bow is pointed—the Swordsman is rising right in front of us. And that one to the left of it, that must be the Phoenix."

Sarth leaned close to inspect the compass. "I think you are right, Geran," he said. "Terrestrial directions must become meaningless in the Sea of Night. With no north, no south, a voyager must find some other way to mark his course. The constellations keep their places in the sky as Toril turns beneath them."

Seadrake continued to climb up through the twilight. Galehand peeked over the rail and quickly retreated with a sick look on his face. "Where are we bound?" he asked Geran. "Just how high d'you mean to sail?"

"That's a good question," Hamil said. "Where *are* we bound? I'd sort of hoped it might be obvious once we got aloft, but now I'm not so sure. *Kraken Queen* could be anywhere!"

Geran pondered the question for a moment. Narsk might have had some instruction from the Red Wizards in Mulmaster, but he doubted that Kamoth would have entrusted them with the location of his hidden isle. It was more likely that he'd told Narsk how to find his retreat beforehand. "Kamoth's letters," he murmured. He frowned and brought them to mind again. In the second letter there'd been a strange phrase, something he hadn't understood at the time: Neshuldaar, the eleventh tear.

He focused on the starry compass, with its slowly turning constellations and bright pinpricks of light. "Show me the course to Neshuldaar," he said to the device.

The small pinpoint of white light at the top of the compass abruptly moved and disappeared. It returned a moment later at the side of the compass, but this time it was a bright, six-pointed star, the brightest symbol visible in the device. Geran grinned and slowly turned the helm in that direction; the six-pointed star swung around like the needle of a lodestone until it rested in the center of the device, and there Geran steadied the helm. Their course seemed to lead a little to the right of the Swordsman.

"Look there," Geran said to Hamil. He pointed at the flickering star. "That's where we're bound. Neshuldaar, whatever or wherever it might be."

They were higher than the tallest mountain peaks now, and the world was passing into night below them. Geran thought he could make out the lights of Mulmaster far below their keel, but it was possible that it was some other city altogether; their speed was increasing as they rose, and they were sailing far faster than the wind could ever have carried them. The air grew thin, and frost glittered on the decks and rails, but Sarth's prediction seemed accurate—conditions remained tolerable, if not particularly pleasant, even as the blue haze of the world began to give way to the pure dark of the Sea of Night. The ship's crew began to break out heavy cloaks for all hands on deck.

Geran relinquished the ship's wheel to the helmsman of the evening watch after careful instructions about the ship's handling. He stepped over to the rail to join Hamil and Sarth in admiring the night sky, now brighter and clearer than anything he'd ever imagined possible. Selûne and her Tears seemed as bright as silver suns as they rose over the port bow, and Geran noted that their course seemed to be taking them swiftly in the moon's direction. Was that the meaning of the Black Moon's name? A reference not to the Moonsea, but to Selûne itself?

They kept to the destination indicated in Narsk's letter, and the world fell farther away under the keel. After several hours, Geran came to realize that they might be at sea—so to speak—for what might amount to a day or two of voyaging, perhaps more. He told Andurth to set the normal sailing watch and arranged a rotation of trusted helmsmen. He wanted Sarth, Hamil, or himself on deck at all times, just in case the journey took some unexpected turn. Then he went below to rest for a while.

When Geran came back up on deck after sleeping a few hours, Selûne filled half the sky. A quarter crescent of the moon's silver-white surface glowed with such brilliance that *Seadrake*'s deck was almost as bright as it would have been at twilight on a clear day, despite the black skies around them. Most of the moon's surface was in shadow, but Geran could still make out its warm gray outline against the blackness of the sky. Behind the moon a long, disorderly line of lesser bodies trailed behind the great orb, slowly tumbling and drifting against the starry dark—the Tears of Selûne. From the world below they were a crown of gems sparkling to the west of the moon, but from his new vantage Geran could see that they were tiny island-worlds that formed a great archipelago across the dark sky.

"The eleventh Tear," he murmured. Not even the wonders of Myth Drannor's glass towers compared to the marvels they sailed toward. He looked back toward the great curve of Toril below and caught his breath. The world of his birth was now much farther away than it had been when he went below. It was a blue-green orb hanging in the sky opposite Selûne's gleaming white. He realized after a moment's thought that Toril was much larger than Selûne; when he was on Toril gazing up at the moon, it was not much wider than three fingers held at arm's length, but now that he was near Selûne looking back at Toril, both his hands together could not completely occlude it.

The air was bitterly cold, and he quickly returned to his cabin for a heavy cloak before mounting the steps to the quarterdeck. There he found Hamil at the helm, standing on a footstool to see better over the wheel. "What are you doing at the wheel?" he asked. "Your turn isn't for hours yet."

Hamil shrugged. "I asked Sarth if I could have his turn, and he agreed. I was up on deck anyway, taking in the sights."

"I've seen some strange and wondrous things in my travels, Hamil, but I have to admit this is about the strangest and most wondrous yet." Geran shook his head. "No one will believe a word we say about this when we return."

Hamil smiled. "I've been looking at the moon. You can see mountains now, and seas. And if you look closely, I think you can make out plains and forests."

Geran turned his attention to Selûne's surface. It was marked by great round craters, just as he would have expected. But he could make out the distant glitter of pale blue waters shining in the sunlight in the largest craters, and the knife-edged shadows of mighty mountains. He wasn't sure he could make out anything he could definitely call a forest, but there were dark gray-green smudges around the knees of the mountains or the crater walls, and some stretched far out over the plains. "It's a world of its own," he said. "Why shouldn't it have its seas and mountains?"

"I suppose, but why is it so white? I don't think it's snow or ice. Maybe its grasses and trees are silver-white in color? Or maybe much of it's covered in white sand?" Hamil looked up at Geran and grinned. "You know, we could go have a look when we're finished with your cousin."

"Why not?" Geran answered. He looked at the starry compass; the six-pointed star that served as the indicator of their course was quite bright now. He pointed it out to Hamil. "I think we're getting close to our destination."

"Well, if you're right about the symbol the compass is showing, then the Black Moon's hiding-hole should lie straight ahead of us. What's out that way?" Hamil peered over the wheel, trying to see past the ship's bow. Geran moved over to the rail and leaned out to gain a better view of what was directly ahead.

Their course now seemed to lead them across the moon, since the bowsprit was fixed in the center of the Tears. They might be heading for any of three or four of the dark islets, but they were still a long way off. "We'll keep on like this, but keep a close eye on the compass," Geran said. "The closer we come, the more quickly our bearing to Neshuldaar might change. If we start to sail by it, the indicator might fall off abruptly."

They sailed on for another hour or more, now seeming to glide past the surface of the moon. They were so far above it that its mountains were merely wrinkles in its gray-white surface. Geran wondered if anyone—or anything—lived in the shadow of those mountains, and what they saw when they looked up into their own sky. Stories about the moon and its people belonged in children's rhymes, but here he was, sailing past it at a speed that must be unimaginable. If this was possible, then anything was. Eventually Selûne began to fall astern, and *Seadrake* glided silently toward the Tears.

After a time, he stepped in to take the wheel and relieve Hamil. Geran kept his eye on the starry compass and the six-pointed mark glowing brightly in the center of the dark glass. As it drifted out of the center, he steered to correct it, following the course as closely as he could. Soon the Tears shone all around *Seadrake*—each a great drifting mountain, slowly tumbling through shadow and silver light. It was impossible to be sure of their size, since there was nothing to compare them to, but Geran guessed that the smaller ones were perhaps a couple of miles across, while the largest might have been as much as fifty or more. The Tear in front *Seadrake*'s bow showed itself to be one of the larger ones, an asymmetrical body whose shape reminded him of a giant's foot. He could make out a dense, world-girdling jungle of purplish vegetation, dotted with small sapphire lakes and wreathed in silver mists.

"The hidden isle of the Black Moon," Hamil murmured. "Is that it?"

"An island of sorts, I suppose," Geran said with a frown. It didn't seem like much from their vantage, but as he studied it he came to realize that the whole thing was rather like three or four decent-sized mountain ranges mashed together and joined at their bases. It might be fifty miles or more from one end to the other—quite a large island indeed. Finding *Kraken Queen* in that maze of cliffs and misty forest might be much harder than he thought, even assuming that no dangerous creatures lurked in the area. He glanced again at the compass and adjusted his course. "Descend slowly," he said aloud, allowing the bow to begin dropping toward the worldlet below.

"Look, there!" Hamil said. He pointed over the rail. Geran summoned a crewman to mind the helm and rushed to join Hamil at the rail. Far below them a tiny flicker of firelight glimmered by the shore of one of the lakes. Geran drew out his spyglass and peered at it; a strange, square keep of black stone stood clinging to a sheer cliffside overlooking the lake. The flicker of firelight seemed to be a beacon fire in one tower of the keep. Smaller lights illuminated a wharf by the lake, the battlements of the keep, and a black-hulled galley lying alongside the dock.

"It's *Kraken Queen,*" Geran said. He passed the spyglass to Hamil and straightened up. "Master Andurth! Douse the ship's lanterns, and bring us down low to the hillside there. Tell the ship's company to don armor and make ready for battle."

"What is your plan?" Sarth asked him.

"First I'll take the ship to cut off their retreat," Geran answered. He gripped the rail and fixed his eyes on the tiny castle below. "Then . . . then I mean to storm the keep. One way or another, the Black Moon dies tonight."

TWENTY-FOUR

17 Marpenoth, the Year of the Ageless One (1479 DR)

The second time Kamoth Kastelmar came to visit Mirya in her cell, she knew she had to escape or die trying.

The pirate lord had stopped by once on the second day of their imprisonment to check on their accommodations—or so he said. But the whole time he'd been discussing routine matters such as bedding, fresh water, and the quality of their meals, he'd stared at Mirya through the bars with a cold smile beneath his beard. A few hours later, a dour-faced slave woman had come by with an armful of new clothes for her and, asked for her to remove what she'd been wearing for days now so that it could be washed. Mirya was none too happy to strip in her cell, but no men were in sight, and her dress sorely needed a washing. She'd complied, only to find that her new clothing was more than a little scandalous by Hulburg's standards. Instead of her sensible, neck-to-ankle, long-sleeved dress of blue wool, she was given a thin gown of crimson silk with a plunging neckline and diaphanous sleeves. At least Selsha was decently covered; the slave had brought her a small servant's tunic and smock that Mirya was able to fit to her with a couple of strategic tucks and knots.

Late the following day, Kamoth stopped by for the second time. He leaned against the bars of her cell and grinned broadly. "Well now, Mistress Erstenwold, perhaps I did you a discourtesy when I said you'd fetch a better price in the markets of Chessenta if you hadn't seen your twentieth year yet," he said. "That's a far more fetching outfit you have on today. You're a fine sight, you surely are. Why, it seems a shame to leave you locked up in my cellar. There's a much better room for you in the keep."

Mirya shivered, but she stood her ground with her arms folded over her chest. It was about the only way she felt decently covered. "I don't want to be any trouble," she said. "We're comfortable enough, unless you're willing to bargain our release."

"As I told you before, Mistress Erstenwold, your money and property are of no great value to me here." He studied her closely, and his dark eyes glittered in the torchlight. "But perhaps other arrangements might be made."

Mirya flushed. She took a deep breath to calm herself. "I'm sure you've no lack of women at your call, Lord Kamoth. You can hardly need me for . . . company."

Kamoth shrugged. "Perhaps, my dear, but I simply don't see what else you have to bargain with. Besides, you're being modest. I like my women tall and slender, and I admire your courage. I surely do."

Mirya started to answer with the idea of begging the pirate lord to be kind for Selsha's sake if not her own, but stopped herself short. The last thing in the world she wanted to do was to remind Kamoth that her daughter was in his power, as well. There was nothing she wouldn't do to protect Selsha, and that was all there was to it. Instead she said, "Geran Hulmaster will be looking for me. Let me go, and he'll have no quarrel with you."

The pirate lord enjoyed a long laugh at that. Mirya frowned, wondering what it was that he knew that she didn't. When he finished, he passed a hand over his face and shook his head. "Geran Hulmaster is very unlikely to forget his quarrel with me at this point, my dear. He's welcome to look for you all he wants, though. It'll be a long time before he comes to storm our battlements. A long time indeed!"

"Why?" Mirya demanded. "Where are we?"

Kamoth chuckled again and turned to the guards who flanked him. "Have Mistress Erstenwold bathed and brought to my chambers this evening," he said. "Take the girl and put her in the common pens. No need to be unkind to her—as long as Mistress Erstenwold remains pleasant company, well, little Selsha here will be quite taken care of with the keep's servants. Am I clear?"

"Don't take me away from her!" Mirya objected. She flung herself to the bars of her cage, but Kamoth was already leaving. "Please! Let Selsha stay with me!"

The pirate lord paused to glance over his shoulder. "Now, now, don't make a scene. I hate scenes, Mistress Erstenwold." Then he strode out of sight down the corridor. The guards leered at Mirya then followed their lord.

Selsha threw her arms around Mirya's waist. "I want to stay with you, Mama!" she said. "I don't want to be by myself here!"

Mirya hugged her daughter to her. "I know, darling. I'm afraid too." If she had to, she'd do her best to be pleasant company to Kamoth . . . but she suspected that Kamoth was the sort of man who quickly tired of his toys. She interested him now because she looked him in the eye and refused to let him see how terrified she was. That would not last long once she surrendered to him. He'd discard her soon enough, and then where would Selsha be? She couldn't leave her daughter alone in a place like this. She simply couldn't.

"Better to be hung for a goat than a sheep," she muttered to herself.

Selsha looked up at her. "What did you say?"

"We can't wait for Geran any longer. If we can get away from here on our own, now's the time to try. Otherwise the pirates will split us up, and I'll never have the courage to try it."

Selsha nodded. "How can we get out?"

Mirya smiled. "Well, I've given it some thought, and I've an idea how it might be done. I think you might be able to squeeze between the bars if I help you a little."

"But what about you, Mama?"

"I'll need a little more help." Mirya kneeled to bring her face closer to Selsha's. "When you get out of this cell, you'll have to go down the hallway here to one of the storerooms we passed, find me a good sturdy bit of rope or a chain, and bring it back here."

"I . . . I don't think I can," Selsha said in a small voice.

"My darling, you must, or we'll be in the power of these wicked men for the rest of our days." Mirya cupped Selsha's face with her hand. "I know you can do it. You're the bravest, most clever girl I've ever known. Now, let's see if we can get you through the bars."

Mirya stood up and took a closer look at the bars of the cell. She'd studied them thoroughly during the last day or two—after all, what else did she have to occupy herself, other than entertaining Selsha and keeping her calm? The cell's bars were inch-thick iron, anchored firmly at floor and ceiling, with two horizontal braces to secure them: one at her midthigh, the other a little above her shoulders. "Come over here and try to fit your head between the bars," she told Selsha. "Carefully, now!"

Selsha kneeled and leaned her head against the bars. It would be very close. Mirya looked carefully to see how much more she'd need. "All right," she breathed. "Selsha, I want you to strip down to your underthings and use our washbucket and soap to get yourself slippery all over. Make sure you soap up head and hair best of all. I'll see if I can bend this just a little bit."

She braced one foot against a bar, gripped the opposite bar, took several deep breaths, and threw all her strength into bowing the bar, even if it was just a little bit. She strained until a gasp of effort burst from her lips. Then she reversed her position and started on the opposite bar, pushing it in the other direction.

"I'm ready, Mama," Selsha said. She grinned at Mirya from underneath a head full of suds; the prospect of adventure had lifted her spirits.

Mirya slowly pushed herself upright and looked at the bars. She hadn't moved them much at all, but perhaps it was far enough. "Covered in soap, are you? Good. Now come here, and let's see if you can get out. Try your head first—if your head goes through, the rest of you must follow."

She moved out of the way to make room for Selsha. The girl pressed herself against the bars at the place where Mirya had tried to widen the gap. For a long moment, she struggled in vain, and Mirya despaired. This was the only plan she'd been able to come up with, and the bars were just too strong for her. But then, with a sharp cry, Selsha forced her head through. "I'm stuck!" she wailed.

"No, you're not!" Mirya answered. "We'll get you through!" She helped Selsha to turn her shoulders and pushed as hard as she dared. Selsha caught again at the chest, but Mirya had her exhale as far as she could, and in one more push she spilled out onto the floor of the hallway.

"I did it!" Selsha exclaimed. She did a little dance in the hall, and despite the desperation of the moment Mirya smiled at the sight of her daughter shaking suds all over the floor. "But now I've got soap in my eyes!"

"And I'm sorry for that, Selsha, but look—now you're out!" Mirya answered. She handed Selsha her tunic through the bars. "Here you go. Dress quick, and then off with you! The longer we take, the more likely it is that we're caught. There's a storeroom just a few feet down the hallway there. I need a rope, a chain, something like that." She smiled. "Or the key to the cell, if you see it hanging near."

Selsha pulled the simple servant tunic over her head and ran off down the hall. Mirya pressed her face to the bars, trying to see where she'd gone. Fear for her daughter left her heart hammering in her chest, but this was the best chance that she could see. She consciously resigned herself to endure the wait as calmly as she could—but Selsha hurried back into sight only moments later with the clinking of chain links.

"What about these, Mama?" She showed Mirya a pair of thick manacles. "Would they work?"

Mirya nodded at her daughter. "They ought to. Let's see." She took the first pair of manacles, closed the cuffs around one of the cell's horizontal slats, and then looped the chain over the next slat higher. She hurried over to one of the bunks, turned it on its side, and worked its leg free. Then she inserted the sturdy length of wood in the loop of the chain and began to twist. Slowly she pulled the horizontal brace upwards. When she'd moved it as far as it could go, she moved the manacle to one of the bars she'd already bent and looped the chain around another bar. Repeating the effort, she twisted the chain, this time widening the imperceptible gap she'd started before. It took all of her strength, and she had several painful slips and bashed her knuckles against the bars more than once. But now one of the bars was bowed several inches out of place.

"You're doing it, Mama!" Selsha exclaimed.

Quickly Mirya shifted her chain to the opposite bar and once again twisted the thick wood of the bunk's leg through the loop. She pulled it as far as she could and decided that it was enough. She slipped her head and leading shoulder through the gap and then slowly worked the rest of her body out of the cell—not without more bruises and scrapes. Finally she stood in the hallway, her arms and legs trembling with fatigue.

"Now what do we do?" Selsha asked her.

"Leave this awful place behind us, and soon," Mirya replied. If she was lucky, they might have an hour or two before someone noticed their escape. The best option would be to steal a small boat from the wharves, but it seemed unlikely that they could make off with a boat right under the pirates' eyes. It might be better to leave the vicinity of the keep as quickly as possible, staying near the coast in the hope that they might come across friendly traders or a port where she might arrange passage. In any event, the longer she hesitated, the less likely it was that their escape would succeed. The first order of business was to get out of the keep's dungeons.

"Come, let's try this way," she said. She took Selsha's hand and led her down the hallway to the left. It wasn't the way they'd come, but Mirya didn't like the idea of retracing her path back to the dock where *Kraken Queen* was tied up. At least one of the gates was guarded, the docks by the pirate ship would be busy, and there were monsters down some of those passageways. It seemed better to find some other way out of the keep.

They crept carefully down the hallway, passing more cells—most unoccupied, some not—and more storerooms. Several times Mirya pulled Selsha swiftly into the shadows, hiding as

Black Moon corsairs or their servants passed through intersecting corridors. Once they had to duck into a storeroom and hide behind several large casks of salted meat when a pair of pirates came straight down the hallway toward them. Fortune was with them for the moment; the pirates passed by without seeing them.

Two or three halls from the cell, Mirya stumbled across a small servants' stair leading up. She listened carefully for any sign that someone might be waiting above, and then nodded to Selsha. "Up the stairs, soft as a cat's step," she whispered. Selsha nodded, and together they climbed the stair.

They passed by one floor that looked far too busy for Mirya's taste—she could hear the bustle of kitchen work and a number of voices murmuring from that direction—and kept going to the next floor up. Hoping that she was not about to blunder into the part of the keep where Kamoth expected her to arrive in a few hours anyway, Mirya led Selsha down a hallway with doors on either side leading to what were likely barracks rooms or private suites. At the end of the hall stood a sturdy door reinforced with iron bands; she guessed that it might lead outside and decided to risk a quick look to gain her bearings. Mirya opened the door as quietly as she could and stepped out onto a dark rampart in the open air.

She took three steps toward the battlements, and then Mirya stopped where she stood and stared up at the sky. It was night, but the night was ablaze with stars. Climbing into the dark sky, a dozen or more small moonlets formed a heavenly stairway of silver and shadow, leading to Selûne—but here the moon filled almost half the sky, a titanic presence that left her unable to move or speak for ten full heartbeats. The keep on whose battlements she stood was raised on a steep-sided hill beside a lake of dazzling sapphire waters, overlooking a great dark forest or jungle of fantastic plants colored in hues of scarlet and purple. A soft silvery mist hung in the air, clinging to the hillsides almost like intangible waves that slowly undulated with no breeze to stir them.

"By the Dark Mother," she whispered. "Where *are* we?"

Selsha gripped her hand. "Ooooh," she said in a small voice. "Look at the moon, Mama! And the stars! We're in the Sea of Night, aren't we? I didn't think anyone really lived there!"

"I . . . I couldn't say." Mirya shook herself and tried to master the dizzying terror of her circumstances. They certainly weren't in Faerûn any longer. In fact, she doubted that they were anywhere in the world. No sky such as this could exist in Toril. Either they were in some other plane altogether, or—as the fantastically close face of white Selûne suggested—they were on some islet, some black moon, in the midst of the Sea of Night. Mirya had heard tales of magic doorways and ships that sailed the skies, but she'd never paid them any mind. She had learned long ago not to waste her time on foolishness and dreams. Yet here she and Selsha were, seemingly in the middle of some mad dream, and she could not even imagine how the two of them would ever see their little house in Hulburg again.

She wondered if they still had time to return to the cell before their absence was noticed. Where else could they go? Even if they found some place out in the jungle where they could hide from the pirates and their monsters, they couldn't go home. And Mirya didn't like the look of the scarlet forest in the least. The Dark Lady alone knew what sort of fierce moon-beasts might lurk in its shadows. Perhaps they could find some place to hide within the keep itself, some forgotten cellar or unused tower where they could avoid Kamoth until she could learn more about the black moon and its secrets.

Selsha suddenly grabbed her hand. "Mama!" she whispered.

Mirya heard it then too—the high-pitched, hissing voice of one of the spider-monsters, and a moment later the voice of another one. The creatures were coming toward them. Without a moment's hesitation, she turned and dashed for the other door leading up onto the battlement, Selsha's hand in hers. She fumbled at the door, and at the other doorway two of the neogi scuttled into view, with one of their hulking servant-monsters shambling along behind them.

The little monsters shrieked like angry teakettles. "You humans!" one snarled. "Stop there!"

Mirya managed to get the door open and pushed Selsha inside. The passage beyond descended a flight of stairs, leading down again. She felt something then, a baleful will that started to encircle her mind with unseen talons, but before it could seize her in its sinister grasp, she staggered through the door and slammed it shut behind her. It was fitted with a heavy bolt, and she shot it home just as the neogi's claws scrabbled at the door. Selsha whimpered, but Mirya grabbed her hand and fled down the stairs.

This part of the keep was lit only by the dimmest of lights, small glass orbs filled with a strange milky fluid that glowed greenish white. She had to grope her way down the stairs, feeling her way along the walls. Mirya guessed that the neogi liked it that way, and shuddered. The last thing she wanted to do was blunder into more of the spidery little horrors in the darkness. She pried one of the small glass orbs free of the wall, and found that it was cool to the touch. "Take hold of my gown," she whispered to Selsha, and they continued down the hall.

"Yes, Mama," Selsha whispered. She seized the hem of Mirya's thin robe.

Mirya led the way through the darkness until they emerged in a large hall or guardroom. There was a door nearby, with a pair of narrow stone embrasures beside it. She glanced out from one and realized that she was looking out of an arrow slit that protected a postern gate leading outside. The sinister jungle crowded close to the base of the keep here. Then she chose one of the other passageways and advanced cautiously into the bowels of the keep, hoping that she'd come across *something* that she could turn to her advantage—a good hiding place, a slave who might be willing to help her, or perhaps supplies and a weapon so that she might at least face the jungle outside with some amount of preparation. She came to a place where several passages met, and paused to consider her next turn. The last thing she wanted to do was to become completely lost in this place.

The click of talons on stone and the evil chittering of the neogi speaking in their own tongue came from the passage directly in front of her. She stood paralyzed for an instant.

"Hide!" she whispered to Selsha, pushing her into one of the passageways. She started after her daughter, but realized that the glowing orb she carried gave them away. Quickly she stepped back out into the intersection and rolled the light down one of the other passages—and then the neogi appeared. Mirya pressed herself into the shadow of one of the other doorways and prayed that the creatures hadn't seen her.

Several of the monsters chattered to each other, pausing for a moment in the intersection. Then they continued on their way—turning down the hall where Selsha was hiding. Another of the huge, apelike monsters followed after the little spider-creatures, and Mirya almost gave herself away by stepping out of the shadows too soon. She waited a moment for the creatures to pass and then crept out of her hiding place. Heart hammering in her chest, Mirya hurried after the neogi and their hulk, following as closely as she dared. Selsha must have fled down the passage in front of the monsters. Mirya prayed that her daughter was calm enough to seek out a side passage to duck into, or a small room where she might find a place to hide and let the monsters behind her pass. Selsha was a small girl, and she was good at hiding . . . but the moon-keep's monsters terrified the child. It was more likely that she was fleeing in blind panic, in which case there was no telling where she might turn.

Mirya came to a large open room and realized that they'd returned to the room by the postern gate again. The party of monsters she followed turned and disappeared up one of the other hallways that met here, and Mirya advanced cautiously into the room behind them. Selsha might have fled down any of the passages leading away from the room. She wheeled in a circle, hoping for some hint of which way her daughter might have gone. She listened for a moment, but all she could hear were loathsome scuttling footsteps of the neogi drawing away. Then she realized that the postern gate was standing open by a double handspan. "Oh, no," she breathed. She hurried to the gate and peered outside.

One of Selsha's shoes lay on the stone landing, atop a short flight of stone stairs that led down into a tiny clearing at the keep's foot.

She closed her eyes, sickened with fear. Selsha was out in that jungle somewhere, with its monstrous plants and its unknown perils.

There was no choice for it, then. Mirya quickly pulled the keep's gate closed behind her, hoping that their pursuers inside would assume they'd fled down one of the other passageways inside. Then she picked up Selsha's shoe and hurried down the overgrown path leading into the black moon's mist-wreathed jungle.

TWENTY-FIVE

17 Marpenoth, the Year of the Ageless One (1479 DR)

Seadrake dropped down out of the moonlet's black sky like a hawk stooping on its prey. The starry compass glowed with silver light in front of the ship's wheel, its strange symbols spinning swiftly with the precipitous descent. Geran stood at the helm and grinned fiercely, feeling the sails fill with the strange winds of the dark moonlet and the deck trembling to the rush of iron-shod feet. He had no idea what waited for him below the battlements of the ebon keep, but he meant to meet it with fine elven steel in his hand and spells of ruin on his blade. Whatever else happened, he'd teach the Black Moon a lesson or two about preying on Hulburg . . . and if Sergen was somewhere in that dark fortress, he wouldn't escape Geran's wrath a second time.

"Lord Geran! We're fallin' too fast!" Andurth Galehand shouted in his ear. The bowsprit pointed directly at the midships deck of *Kraken Queen,* tied up alongside its wharf under the black battlements, and *Seadrake* raced down on the pirate ship with such speed that Geran's stomach was left behind. "Slow th' approach, I beg ye!"

"Speed and surprise are our best weapons!" Geran answered. He could see the pirate ship's crew desperately running for their stations, even as others poured out of the keep's gates or hurried to man the battlements. *Seadrake* was low enough now that she seemed to sail through the skies of this strange, small world instead of skimming across the empty blackness of the Sea of

Night. The pirate keep stood atop a steep-sided hill overlooking the lake; strange-looking trees and thick, coiling vines in a dozen hues of red, purple, and blue crowded in close around the keep and the shore. A weird silver mist seemed to hang in the air, cool and humid, and tendrils of cloud seethed slowly through the low spots in the hills ringing the lake.

"There are ruins in the jungle," Hamil said. He pointed at the closer shore of the glittering blue lake. Geran glimpsed crumbling towers of black stone half hidden in the vales near the lakeshore. "Do you think the Black Moon's got allies nearby?"

"I don't know, but the sooner we take the ship and get into the keep, the less likely it is that anyone else can interfere." Geran spared a glance for Hamil. "As I said—speed and surprise."

He looked back to *Kraken Queen,* and judged that they were indeed closing too fast. "Slow the descent!" he said aloud. The ship replied, lifting her bow a bit and leveling out. *Seadrake*'s company—almost seventy Shieldsworn and veteran mercenaries from the merchant companies plus almost forty more sailors eager for a fight—lined the rails, armed and ready to give battle to the Black Moon corsairs. "Grapples, stand ready!" he called to his crew. "Archers, fire as you will!"

The crew raised a ragged chorus of war cries and defiant shouts. Bowstrings sang and crossbows snapped sharply, sweeping the deck of the pirate vessel below. Sarth blasted a knot of pirates trying to ready one of *Kraken Queen*'s catapults with a crackling ball of green lightning. Geran held his course until the last possible moment before turning the wheel sharply and willing the bow up and the stern down. "Make ready to drop sail!" he shouted. "Brace for impact!" The ship veered wildly before alighting in the sapphire waters of the moon-lake with an immense splash. Despite Geran's warning, fully half the hands on deck were knocked off their feet . . . but now *Seadrake* surged forward in the water, coming up alongside her quarry from astern. The Hulburgans leaped back to their feet, and deckhands swarmed aloft to lower the warship's sails as Geran turned the wheel the other way to drive his bow alongside *Kraken Queen.* Grapple-throwers heaved their hooks across the gap. The Hulburgan ship came to a jarring stop, tangled up with the Black Moon flagship.

"Over th' side!" Andurth Galehand yelled. It was unnecessary, since *Seadrake*'s company was already swarming across to *Kraken Queen.* Hamil vaulted up to the rail, seized a hanging shroud, and swung over to the pirate ship's quarterdeck. Geran followed an instant later with his teleport spell, spanning the gap with a single, bold stride. He immediately found himself in the middle of a furious fray by *Kraken Queen*'s mizzenmast. Dozens of pirates swarmed up on deck from every hatch and companionway imaginable, desperate to repel the attack.

"Arvan sannoghan!" Geran shouted. The mystic words evoked a sheath of brilliant flame along his blade. He hurled himself against the pirates, great arcs of razor-sharp fire trailing from his sword strokes. He slashed down one man with a searing cut from shoulder to hip, took the head off a goblin creeping up on his right flank, and drove another pirate to the deck with his assault before finishing the man with a thrust to the midsection. Hamil fought beside him, a dagger in each hand, guarding Geran's back or darting out to hamstring an unwary foe. By *Kraken Queen*'s mainmast, Sarth burned pirates down with fiery blasts from his rune-carved scepter or blasted them overboard with words of arcane power.

"We've got them!" Hamil cried.

"I think you're right!" Geran shouted in reply. *Seadrake*'s sudden appearance had indeed caught the pirates off-guard; many of the corsairs were off inside the keep, leaving only half a crew on the pirate flagship. Those pirates who were on hand to defend their ship were disorganized and poorly armed. They wore leather jerkins or no armor at all, and many fought with boarding axes, belaying pins, or daggers. Against them the Shieldsworn and the merchant armsmen were fitted out in mail, with swords and shields. More to the point, the Hulburgans were spoiling for a fight. With Sarth's destructive spells and Geran's swordmagic to lead them, their disciplined ranks swept across *Kraken Queen,* cutting the pirates on board to pieces.

Geran found that no enemies were within sword's reach and paused to take stock of the battle. *Seadrake* warriors held *Kraken Queen* . . . for the moment. But more pirates streamed out of the keep's gate, hurrying to join the fight. And others took up positions on the battlements overlooking the docks, sniping at the invaders with crossbow fire. A Jannarsk armsman near him shrieked in pain and fell to the deck, hands cupped around a bolt quivering in his face, and a Shieldsworn grunted and staggered back when a quarrel punched through his shield and transfixed his arm underneath. Then the pirates from the keep stormed aboard *Kraken Queen* from the wharf.

"I spoke too soon—here they come!" Hamil said. He crouched down behind the gunwale, sheathed his daggers, and shrugged his shortbow from his shoulder. Then he popped up to send an arrow winging up to the battlement overlooking the wharf. A Black Moon archer cried out and tumbled from the rampart.

"They would've been wiser to turtle up inside their keep," Geran said. He ducked down by the gunwale, trying to gauge how much the pirate reinforcements had changed the course of the battle. So far, the Hulburgans were standing their ground. "We don't have any siege gear!"

"They can't afford to let us take this ship. It's their only way back to Faerûn."

Geran realized that Hamil was right; the pirates had to retake their ship, or else the Hulburgans could simply sail it off and strand them in their moon-keep. A sudden inspiration struck him, and he looked around the pirate vessel's quarterdeck. *Kraken Queen*'s starry compass sat in a hooded binnacle just in front of the helm. It looked much like the one from *Moonshark,* although its color was more of a rich violet hue. He picked up a boarding axe from a dead pirate's hand and wrecked the device's frame with several hard strokes. Then he picked the orb out of the ruined frame. "There, that should do it. *Kraken Queen*'s going nowhere for now."

Hamil raised an eyebrow. "Stealing Kamoth's magic compass?"

"I don't see why he should have one. If the fight turns against us, we can retreat, and he'll be stranded here forever." The starry compass would also make for a very valuable bargaining chip if Kamoth put a knife to Mirya's throat. He couldn't be sure, but he had to believe that the pirate lord would part with his hostages in order to get the device back. Geran handed the orb to Hamil. "Here, take this back to *Seadrake,* and put it someplace safe. It might prove very useful. I'm going to see what I can do about breaking this stalemate."

"Done," Hamil said. He tucked it under his arm and hurried forward, looking for a good place to cross back to the Hulburgan warship.

Geran turned his attention back to the fight. A crossbow quarrel ricocheted from the unseen wardings that protected him, spinning away through the air. The fight had grown more heated while he sabotaged the ship's magical compass; scores of pirates in a howling, reckless mob fought to win back their ship. *Kraken Queen* was in Hulburgan hands, but the fighting had moved down to the wharf between the keep and the moored ship. Here *Seadrake*'s assault had momentarily stalled. For the moment, the numbers on each side seemed close, and if the Hulburgans had the advantages of armor and discipline, the pirates had the raking fire from the keep and fierce desperation on their side. Then he spotted a figure at the head of the pirate counterattack, a bearded man who wore scarlet armor worked in the shape of fishlike scales. Behind him, the Black Moon pirates hurled themselves into the battle with fresh zeal.

"Kamoth," Geran breathed. He vaulted down from the quarterdeck to the wharf and threaded his way through knots of battling soldiers and corsairs. He parried or dodged several blows aimed at him as he darted forward to confront the pirate lord.

Kamoth led the way with a cutlass in one hand and a hatchet in the other as the pirates fought their way back toward their flagship. He cut down a pair of Hulburgan sailors who stood against him then whirled to face Geran's attack. Their swords flashed and rang together in the furious melee at the foot of the gangplank. Geran attacked with a high slash at Kamoth's face, but the pirate lord blocked it and countered with a vicious cut of his left-hand axe. He pushed forward, pressing Geran closely, keeping their blades locked as he tried to get Geran in reach of the hatchet. Geran gave almost ten feet of ground across the blood-slicked wharf before he freed his blade and opened the distance again. The two men circled each other warily while the battle raged all around them.

"I know you, Geran!" the pirate lord said with a fierce laugh. "But I remember you as a lad of fifteen or so. You've learned to be handy with a blade, I see."

"I studied four years in Myth Drannor." Geran was careful to keep up his guard. "This blade I won in the Coronal's Guard."

"Well done, my boy!" Kamoth said. He wore the same fierce grin Geran remembered from years ago, as if all that stood between them even now were a few boyish pranks he'd been caught at and hoped to laugh away. "I never had the benefit of much formal study in sword play. I had to pick it up as I went along." He attacked suddenly with a furious onslaught. He was quick, and Geran saw where Sergen had gotten his speed from. His style was just as unschooled and unorthodox as he claimed. When Geran parried Kamoth's thrust, the pirate lord hooked the curving blade of his hatchet over Geran's sword, trapping their blades together, and nearly wrenched Geran's sword from his hand. Geran twisted his blade sideways and pulled it free and then ducked under a wild swing at his head as they spun past each other and separated again.

"That's *Seadrake* there, isn't it?" Kamoth asked, breathing hard. "How'd you manage to follow me here, my boy?"

"I've got *Moonshark*'s starry compass," Geran answered. He circled warily, looking for an opening. "And Narsk's letters led me here."

"Damn it all!" the pirate lord snarled. "It was you at *Moonshark*'s helm in Hulburg harbor, wasn't it? You cost me three ships in a single night!"

Geran replied with a lunge at Kamoth. The pirate lord parried several quick thrusts, and when Geran repeated the same attack, he tried again to catch Geran's blade with his own weapons. But Geran was waiting for him. The instant the blades caught, Geran snarled the words of a sword spell: *"Ilyeith sannoghan!"* Lightning flew from the elven steel, leaped to Kamoth's cutlass and hatchet, and raced up the pirate lord's hands. Kamoth howled and dropped his weapons, jolted by the sudden shock. Before he could recover, Geran lashed him across the face with the crackling blade. The pirate lord's helmet took much of the impact, but the ringing blow sent Kamoth spinning to the wooden boards, streaming blood and wisps of smoke from the rent in the side of his helmet. He stirred feebly and fell still—dead or unconscious, Geran didn't know.

"The High Captain's fallen!" one of the pirates nearby cried out. Others took up the cry. Some of the pirates began to retreat; others hurried toward the scene to protect their fallen leader. Several rushed Geran all at once, and for a moment the swordmage was caught up in the middle of the melee again, fighting furiously. The press of the attack carried him back across the wharf again, until Sarth's sizzling bolts of fire broke the last desperate Black Moon effort to retake their ship. Geran tried to battle his way back to Kamoth again as the Hulburgans rallied and drove the remaining pirates back to the castle gate. He caught a glimpse of several of the corsairs dragging Kamoth back toward the keep as the Black Moon gave up the battle for the dock. The wharf was littered with the dead and dying, most of them Black Moon men; he lowered his sword, panting for breath, and discovered that during the fighting he'd caught a shallow but bloody cut high on his left arm.

Hamil appeared at his side, his daggers bloody and a thin cut across his scalp. Geran hadn't even realized that his small comrade had returned to the fray. "Mind the sharpshooters!" he said to Geran, pulling him down by a high stack of crates that offered some cover against the fire coming from the ramparts. "*Kraken Queen*'s compass is locked up in your cabin. Do we try to take the keep, or do we offer terms? The Black Moon men might not have much more fight left in them."

Geran thought quickly. Mirya and Selsha were somewhere inside; if he didn't get into the castle quickly, he'd find it barricaded against him. The Hulburgans had *Kraken Queen* well in hand, and they had control of the docks as well. The Black Moon leaders inside realized that too, and the gates of the keep were beginning to close against the attackers. He stood again and raised his sword over his head. "To the keep!" he shouted. He spotted Sarth near the pirate ship's forecastle, and waved his arm at the sorcerer. "Sarth! Secure the gates!"

The tiefling glanced back and gave him a quick nod of understanding. He leaped from *Kraken Queen*'s deck, taking to the air as he did so. With blasts of fire and snapping arcs of lightning, he scoured the battlements overlooking the keep's gate clear of foes then hurled a glowing orange bead through one of the arrow slits into the gatehouse. An instant later a tremendous burst of flame shot out from each of the gatehouse's windows, and the tower shook with the force of the explosion. The gates below stopped moving. The sorcerer's fireball had wrecked the hidden windlasses, and likely had killed the pirates furiously working them. The gates remained half open, and Shieldsworn began pouring through into the keep.

Geran looked around for any of *Seadrake*'s officers, and found Andurth Galehand manning one of the arbalests on the warship's quarter rail. "Master Galehand! Keep half your sailors here and guard the ships!"

Seadrake's sailing master scowled in disappointment. "I'll do as ye say, Lord Geran, but only if ye promise me ye'll save a few for me later!"

"You're now standing on the Black Moon's only escape from this place," Geran called back. "Unless I miss my guess, you'll see a fight before we're done inside."

"Aye, m'lord!" Galehand left his arbalest in the hands of one of the crew and began shouting orders to get his sailors in order.

Geran left the sailing master to take charge, and rushed toward the keep. Hamil followed a step behind him, while Sarth hovered in the air, systematically blasting any arrow slit from which a bolt or quarrel flew. Geran could hear the ringing of steel echoing under the walls of the pirate keep, the furious shouts and roars of men in battle, the screams of the wounded. In midstride he invoked his silversteel veil, the swirling silver aura that might save him from an unexpected thrust or a shot fired at his back. The air was thick with the reek of smoke and the strange sweet scent of the moonlet's dark jungle. Overhead the Tears of Selûne mounted to the sky like islands of shadow and silver light, drifting across a black sky ablaze with more stars than he'd ever imagined might exist. What a strange place to fight a battle! he thought. He'd fought in skirmishes on the Sea of Fallen Stars, ambushes in the shadows of Cormanthyr, and desperate frays in deep, foul dungeons where monsters lurked, but never had he fought in a battle like this.

"Follow me, warriors of Hulburg!" Geran shouted. He ran through the gates and into the moon-keep's lower hall. At his back, armsmen and sailors charged in after him. A dozen or so of the Black Moon men tried to hold the hall against the attackers. Several crossbow bolts hissed past Geran, and one grazed his hip, catching in his leather jerkin despite his wardings. A Shieldsworn at his side stumbled and went to the ground, clutching at a quarrel in his belly—but then Geran was in among the keep's defenders, with the rest of the attackers a step behind him. He cut down one of the crossbowmen and darted past the fellow to engage a burly half-orc mate who seemed to be leading the pirates in the hall. He traded only two passes of steel with the half-orc before a *Seadrake* sailor buried a boarding axe between the mate's shoulder blades. The swordmage searched for another foe, but the keep's lower hall belonged to the Shieldsworn—the only pirates remaining here were dead on the floor. The Hulburgans raised a ragged cheer.

"Where to now?" Hamil asked. "There must be more of these fellows skulking about in here."

Geran studied the room for a moment. Several large passageways led away from the room, including a stair that climbed up from the gate. Like the castle of Griffonwatch that Geran had grown up in, the moon-keep was at least in part delved from the rock of its steep hill. Here at its foot, hallways led to subterranean vaults, while the stairs led up to levels and ramparts higher in the hillside. "We'll split up and search the place," he decided. "Master Worthel, take your warriors and ransack the lower levels. I'll take a squad of soldiers upstairs. Look for captives, and take or kill every pirate you catch. Keep your lads together in case you run into opposition. Sergeant Xela, take your Sokols and the Marstels, and go with Sarth. I can still hear him outside. Brother Larken, keep the rest of the soldiers here and hold this gatehouse. You're our reserve. Guard our retreat, and stand ready to help in case one of the search parties runs into strong resistance somewhere. Now go!"

The Hulburgans split up as Geran had ordered, some rushing down the passages below, others returning to the fray outside, while still others spread out to take control of the gatehouse and hold their conquest. Geran waved to the armsmen at his back and led them off into the keep. The main passage climbed a broad set of steps to a great hall, festooned with dozens of captured banners and standards. He could hear the distant ring of steel on steel from the other search parties, and shouts echoing through the stone corridors. The armsmen with him spread out to search the room; Geran headed for the first large passage leading out of the hall and peered down it, wondering just how big the keep really was. The portion built atop the hill was not very large, not much bigger than the upper bailey in Griffonwatch, but there was no telling how far the subterranean halls and vaults extended. Depending on just how long the Black Moon Brotherhood had held the keep and how industriously they'd worked, there might even be several escape tunnels hidden below, leading to secret exits in the jungles outside . . . possibly with smaller skyfaring vessels close by. Even now Kamoth and Sergen might be making their escape.

A call from one of the Shieldsworn interrupted his brooding. "Lord Geran?" he called. "We've found several people held captive here."

"Mirya and her daughter?"

The soldier shook his head. "No, but a woman here says there are other captives in the dungeons."

Geran hurried over to the fellow and found him standing by the entrance to the kitchens that served the great hall. Seven or eight people in threadbare servants' garb stood in a confused knot inside, staring at their unexpected rescuers.

The soldier motioned to one of the freed captives. "Here she is," he said. "This is Olana. She was taken captive four years ago near Phlan."

A dour-faced woman of middle years stepped forward. "Long I've dreamed of this day, m'lords, but never I thought to see it with mine own eyes. You're a welcome sight, you are."

"We'll take you home as soon as we've finished here, Olana," Geran told her. "But first, is there a woman named Mirya Erstenwold here? She's tall and slender, with black hair and blue eyes. She might have had her daughter with her, a dark-haired lass of about nine years. Have you seen her?"

"I did see those two, m'lord. I've brought them their food and water for a couple of days now, and Lord Kamoth had me bring them new clothes as well. They were held down in the lower dungeon. But—they're gone now." Olana fell silent.

"Well, where are they then?" Geran demanded.

"They've escaped, m'lord. I went by their cell to bring them their breakfast and discovered the bars bent wide enough for them to slip out."

"When was this?"

"It was only an hour or two ago, m'lord. I don't think the Black Moon men know she's gone yet. I wasn't about to tell, not until they'd had a good chance to slip away."

"Good woman," Hamil said in approval. "But where could they slip away to?"

The woman frowned. "I expect your Mirya and her daughter ran off into the jungle."

Another of the servants, a stooped old man with a bushy, white beard, spoke up. "Beggin' your pardon, m'lords, but I think they must have done just that. I was with a party sent to cut firewood this morning. We found the postern gate standing ajar when we came back in. I'd wager that's the way your friends went."

"Did the Black Moon pirates go after them?" Hamil asked.

"No, m'lord. They figured one of us had left it open when we went out in the morning. Besides, they only venture into the jungle in large parties, and well-armed at that."

Geran gripped the hilt of his sword and turned away, teeth bared in pure frustration. If they'd only been an hour or two swifter, they might have found Mirya and Selsha before they slipped out of their cell. Now they might have the whole black isle to search! He took a deep breath to master himself and then looked back to Olana and the older servant. "I'll need you to show me to the postern, and quickly," he said.

Olana bowed. "Of course, m'lord."

"Hamil, you take over here. Make sure we cover every inch of this keep, and keep an eye open for Sergen. He's still around somewhere, and you know the sort of trouble he can cause."

"My apologies, Geran, but I can't do that," Hamil said. "I'm coming with you. Mirya's my friend too, and I'd fight a whole moon full of monsters to keep Selsha from harm."

Geran started to argue, but thought better of it. He could use Hamil at his back, and things seemed well in hand with the pirate keep. "All right, then. Sergeant Xela, send messengers to find Sarth and Larken. Tell Sarth he's in charge until we return. I trust you to do what needs to be done here."

The Shieldsworn soldier nodded. "Aye, we'll look after things, Lord Geran. As soon as we can, we'll send some soldiers out after you and Master Alderheart."

"Good." Geran clapped a hand to the armsman's shoulder and then looked back to Olana. "Show us the quickest way to the postern, Olana."

The woman curtsied. "Of course, m'lord. I hope you find her—the jungle of the black moon's no place to wander. It's this way." She hurried off for one of the servants' stairs leading off the great hall. Geran and Hamil followed her into the mazelike passageways of the keep.

TWENTY-SIX

17 Marpenoth, the Year of the Ageless One (1479 DR)

The alien jungle of the black moonlet crowded menacingly against the walls of the pirate keep. Its fronds and grasses, its brush and its trees grew in a riot of fantastic colors unlike anything Geran had ever seen before. A dozen strange, sweet scents hung heavily in the air, and he could hear the chirps and croaks of small creatures—birds, frogs, or something like them—echoing in the dim light. The air was damp and cool, with a faint white mist clinging to the ground. More than a few of the plants had a distinctly unwholesome look to them, and he wondered if any of them were carnivorous.

"Out of the frying pan and into the fire," Hamil said softly. "I don't like the looks of this place. I hope Mirya stayed on the trail."

"So do I. Even Kara couldn't track her through this." Geran looked around the stone steps leading down from the keep's postern gate. There was a small clearing right by the gate, with overgrown paths leading in either direction immediately below the walls. In theory, the postern allowed the keep's defenders to send out parties of raiders to counterattack an enemy concentrating on the front gate. He saw no sign that Mirya or Selsha had circled the keep at the foot of the wall, though. If they'd fled the keep, they wouldn't want to skulk around by the base of the wall; they'd want to get as far from the place as they could, and would hope to outrun or evade any pursuers out in the jungle.

Across the clearing, a single footpath led off into the jungle. Geran headed for it while still watching for any tracks along the trail. If he had to guess, he'd say that the path saw infrequent use at best; it was mostly overgrown, but a strip of bare dirt in its center suggested that people came this way from time to time. Fifty yards from the gate, the trail met the edge of the moonlet's dark forest . . . and here Geran found something more familiar. He stopped and kneeled in the violet grass by the trailside. The impression of a small, bare foot lay in the center of the path. "Look here," he said to Hamil.

The halfling kneeled beside him. "Selsha?"

"I think the size is about right. And I don't think it's more than a few hours old. It's hard to tell, since I have no idea what sort of weather this place gets, but look—the grass that's bent under the heel, there, it's still damp and the same color as the rest."

Hamil stood up and circled around the area, looking down. "Over here," he said. "I think this may be Mirya."

Geran moved over to look at Hamil's find. This print was a smooth slipper of some kind, with a pointed toe, but the size was about right. It could have been any of the women enslaved by the pirates, of course, but he didn't see any reason why serving women would leave the keep by this door, at least not in shoes such as those. "I don't think those are Mirya's shoes," he said. "But then Olana said she brought Mirya a change of clothes. Maybe she brought slippers too."

They set off again, following the footpath as it wound through the forest. After a few hundred yards, it emerged briefly along the lakeshore; they could look back and see the keep atop its hill, and the two ships grappled alongside the dock. A few thin streamers of smoke rose up into the dark sky, but no other signs of strife were evident from their distance. Several other footpaths—or gametrails, possibly—met by the shore. They searched the ground for any signs of which way the Erstenwolds might have gone, and Geran spotted something on the bole of a tree near the path they'd just emerged from. He took a closer look and found the tree's fleshy bark scored in two rough horizontal lines. Beads of dark sap welled up from the marks.

"I think Mirya might have marked this tree," he told Hamil.

"But that's the way we just came. Why would she mark the trail leading back to the place she was escaping from?"

Geran frowned, thinking for a moment. It could have been simple caution; Mirya might have decided that she wanted to know how to get back to her captors if the wilderness outside the keep proved too dangerous. None of the other pathways had such a mark, so she clearly wasn't trying to leave signs showing which way she'd gone. But studying the ground, he saw that Mirya—if the slippered footprints were in fact hers—had looked at each of the trails branching away from the lakeshore before finally choosing one. "We'll ask her when we find her," he told Hamil. "Come on, let's keep going."

They jogged along the new path. This time they went a mile or more before coming to an intersecting trail. Once again they found the trail leading back the way they'd come marked with a fresh blaze. "Mirya!" Geran called. "Mirya!"

There was no answer. With a grimace of frustration, he searched until he found the path whose prints seemed most like the ones he'd been following, and started off again. But something else on the ground caught his eye. Quite near to Mirya's step—overlapping it, in fact—was the mark of a taloned foot as big as Geran's own. It had two large toes and a third, smaller one back toward the instep. As he moved along the trail, he found more of the creature's marks, paralleling Mirya's. He was fairly certain that he hadn't seen those prints back by the lakeshore; something had dropped out of the jungle and taken up the Erstenwolds' trail, or so he guessed. He picked up his speed, now loping along at an easy run. Hamil kept up without complaint, sensing his increasing urgency.

They splashed across a rock-strewn stream and found on the farther shore that the old footpath led into the ruins of an ancient road of glossy black stone. Hexagonal blocks fitted together untold years ago marked the old highway, although scarlet grass pushed up in the gaps between the pavers, and vines hung down over the path. Geran halted in confusion, staring at the ground. The hard stone held no impression that he could make out. "Damn the luck," he muttered. Somewhere in the forest nearby, an animal gave voice to a strange hooting cry. "Hamil, I've lost the trail."

The halfling looked up and down the path and frowned. "Left or right?"

"Kara could tell us, if she were here." Geran kicked at the ground in frustration. He'd exhausted what small store of woodcraft he possessed, but he kneeled and began to examine the stones more closely, hoping for a sign he'd missed. Hamil did the same.

"This stonework's much older than the Black Moon keep," the halfling said. "I wonder who put a road here?"

"It might lead to those ruins you saw as we descended. They'd be uphill from here, I think." Geran peered up the overgrown road, searching for a glimpse of old towers and walls in that direction, or at least some sign that Mirya and her daughter might have gone that way. Then he looked down the road, which followed the stream back toward the lake. Another unseen animal on the other side of the stream hooted back at the first one. "Which way would Mirya and Selsha turn?"

Hamil shook his head. "Mirya would be looking for a place to hide, wouldn't she? If she saw those ruins from the air, she might have decided to head for them. They'd be clear of the forest, anyway." He waved his arm at the downstream direction. "That probably takes you back toward the lake, and then who knows where?"

"We could split up and cover both possibilities," Geran said slowly.

"Not a chance. The last thing I want to have to do is go looking for you after I find Mirya and Selsha. In fact—" Hamil started to say something more, but he was interrupted by another of the hooting cries. His eyes narrowed, and he turned slowly, his head cocked to one side as he laid an arrow across his bowstring. *In fact, we're about to be attacked,* he finished silently. *Whatever they are, there are three or four of them closing in on us from the forest.*

Hamil had an uncanny sense for trouble, and Geran trusted it. He eased his sword from the sheath and moved to put his back to Hamil's. "Never mind about the splitting up idea," he said softly. More of the cries sounded in the forest, now closer and around them on all sides. The swordmage stared into the gloom of the forest floor, straining for some glimpse of the creatures stalking them—and then the monsters attacked.

They hurled down from the treetops, leaping in great frog-like bounds. Geran glimpsed mottled greenish white bodies and great yellow-orange eyes, a single orb that formed almost the entire head of each of the creatures. Behind him Hamil's bowstring thrummed, and an uncanny screech split the air. Then the first of the things was on the swordmage. Its talons raked at him, scoring the flesh of his shoulders. He slashed furiously at it and felt his steel bite into its warty hide; dark ichor splattered the ground, and the thing bounded away again.

He wheeled to face the next of the monsters and saw it crouching in the fork of a moss-covered tree, staring at him. The creature was the size of a grown man, but it had a hunched, stooped posture, with long arms and knees bent into an awkward crouch. Its single great eye was almost the size of a human head and glittered with a bright golden malice. Beneath it a tiny mouth filled with needle-sharp teeth opened to hiss at him. The eye focused on him, and a sudden wave of lightheadedness and nausea swept over him. His face felt hot and flushed and began to itch furiously. He tore his eyes away from the monster's gaze and raised his left arm to guard his face; to his horror he saw the skin growing dark, dry, and hot in front of him, until small cracks appeared and fluid began to seep out.

"Ilmater's holy wounds!" he cried out in horror. "Hamil, don't let them look at you! Their gaze sears flesh!"

A strangled cry behind him warned that Hamil had discovered that for himself. In pure desperation, Geran turned away from the monster staring at him and did his best to hide inside his own cloak, averting his gaze. The suppuration of his left arm ended abruptly; he bounded past Hamil, charging at a monster that squatted on a boulder by the stream, transfixing the halfling with its horrid gaze. The creature hissed in anger as Geran broke its hold on Hamil, and shifted its gaze to the swordmage—but now Geran was within sword's reach. He lashed out with a wild slash at the thing's face and caught it across its great foul eye. The orb burst open in a gush of dark liquid, and the creature screeched horribly. It fell to the ground, its limbs jerking and flailing, and he finished it with a thrust through the center of its narrow chest.

Geran turned back to the one he'd left behind him. The creature was bounding closer, charging at the two companions while neither was looking at it. This time he shielded his eyes with his hand, keeping his gaze at the middle of its chest and guarding himself with his cloak as he moved forward to meet it. Swinging his sword wildly, he forced the monster to break off its rush. Talons raked at him, but Geran leveled his sword and thrust straight ahead, where he guessed the middle of its body to be. Steel bit into flesh, and his adversary hissed and jumped away; when he cautiously raised his eyes to find where it had gone, he glimpsed only a flash of pale hide disappearing back into the jungle.

"I *definitely* don't like the jungle," Hamil muttered. He held his bow with blistered hands, peering into the trees. "Did that last one get away?"

"I wounded it, possibly mortally. But it's gone now. So is the first one I cut."

"Well, these two here are certainly dead." Hamil moved over to kick at the body of the one he'd shot through with his arrow. "What in the world are these things?"

"Nothing in the world, and that's the problem. We're a long way from Faerûn." Geran glanced at the ancient roadway winding through the forest and grimaced. If more creatures like the eye-monsters haunted the black moon's jungle, Mirya and her daughter were in terrible danger. He could only pray that the Erstenwolds hadn't run across any of these creatures, or worse.

Somewhere close at hand in the forest shadows, the hooting cry went up again. It was answered by another off in the distance. Hamil swore and looked up at Geran. "They're talking to each other, damn it! I don't think they're done with us yet."

"Then we'd better move on, and quickly. No sense waiting for more of them to get here." The swordmage chose to head uphill, following the road as it climbed toward the hilltops ringing the lake, and set off at a trot. He wanted to cover ground, but he had to make sure he didn't miss any trail signs or run headlong into some other jungle monster. The thought of Mirya and Selsha wandering in this dreadful place chilled him to the marrow.

He knew he should be careful of getting too far away from *Seadrake* and the pirate keep—after all, there was always the possibility that the battle had turned against the Hulburgans again, and he and Hamil might be desperately needed to finish the Black Moon Brotherhood. But he couldn't bring himself to even consider turning back. In the two years since he'd last walked under Myth Drannor's golden leaves, the days he'd spent with Mirya and her daughter had been the only ones when he'd been able to truly forget the loss and loneliness of his exile. He couldn't leave this place until he knew that she was safe. If he had to, he'd send *Seadrake* back home and stay to search the worldlet from one end to the other himself.

The road climbed steeply upward through the shadows of the forest in a set of moss-covered steps and then broke out of the foliage high on a hillside. The sapphire lake glittered below, stretching for several miles through the jungle-covered hills. Ruined walls of glossy black stone tumbled around them, marking out the overgrown outline of some ancient temple or palace. Geran looked back the way they'd come; he guessed they stood nearly two miles from the keep now. *Kraken Queen* and *Seadrake* still lay side by side at the wharf, so he supposed that the fighting hadn't yet taken any truly disastrous turn. It was cool and still in the open air atop the hill.

"Mirya!" Geran called. "Selsha! Are you here?" No one answered. He jogged across the old plaza to the far corner and shouted again. "Mirya! Selsha!"

The ruins remained silent. Dark archways and scarlet creepers brooded under the heavy black stones of the walls. In growing desperation, Geran ran from side to side, looking frantically into old doorways and around corners. Hamil followed, keeping an arrow on his string, watching Geran's back. With a cry of pure frustration, Geran turned back toward the lake view. "They're not here!" he said. "We should have followed the road down instead of up—assuming we didn't lose the trail somewhere before that. Come on, Hamil."

"Wait a moment. Let's be sure before we give up on this choice." Hamil scrambled to the top of a low wall, followed it to the place where it met a building facade, and then scaled the crumbling roofline. From his vantage he took a long moment to study their surroundings. Geran glanced up at the sky and saw that bright glimmers of pale violet were beginning to streak the absolute blackness overhead. There was a bright gleam on the trailing limb of the moon; dawn, such as it was in this place, was not far off. Then from somewhere close by in the ruins, a chorus of hooting calls and brash yips erupted, echoing loudly in the ancient stone walls.

Hamil winced and crouched low to the roofline. *More of the eye-creatures,* he observed. *They're almost on top of us!*

"Of course they are," Geran growled. He glanced around and spied a narrow street of sorts that led down off the hilltop. High stone walls offered some hope of concealment, and would keep monsters from surrounding them. "Quickly, this way!"

He darted for the alleyway, listening to the creatures calling to each other in the ruins. Hamil slid down from his perch, alighted on his feet, and raced after him. The alleyway wound past the shells of several old buildings on the hilltop before descending sharply on the other side. The old walls pressed in closely around them, and thick clumps of blue-glowing fungi gathered along the worn stone steps. Geran found a low doorway to one side and ducked inside. The building was open to the sky, its roof long since vanished, but the high walls and narrow doorway offered a defensible retreat. He drew his sword and waited by the opening; Hamil readied his bow and stepped back to watch the walltop in case the moon-monsters scrambled over.

"I think I'd like to go back to the keep and fight pirates now," Hamil said in a low voice. He laid an arrow across his short bow.

Geran allowed himself a grim smile and tightened his grip on his blade. He heard the monsters moving through the ruins close by—the soft padding of pale, taloned feet on old stone, the maddening notes as the creatures called to each other. He drew his sword back, ready for a lethal thrust through the center of the archway at the first creature to appear . . . but none of the monsters appeared. The calls continued, but started to move off again. He risked a peek out the doorway and glimpsed one of the monsters bounding past, already by them. It vanished into the ruins.

Did they miss us? Hamil asked.

"I don't see how they could have." Geran peered down the alleyway. The moon-creatures hadn't had any trouble finding them before. Maybe they were on the scent of some other prey . . . "Bloody hell. They're after Mirya and Selsha!"

Before he could second-guess himself, he hurried back out into the narrow street and ran after the moon-creatures, following their calls as best he could. Hamil shot him a stern look, but raced after him. They fumbled their way through the maze, now dropping steeply down the shadowed hillside. He bounded around a corner and found himself in a smaller plaza, this one surrounded by leaning five-sided towers whose tops were broken rubble. Trapped in a shallow alleyway between two of the towers, a woman in a thin gown of red silk stood with her back to the wall, fending off several of the eye-creatures with thrown rocks. "Mirya!" Geran shouted.

She glanced up, looking over the pale monsters closing in, and their eyes met across the small courtyard. "Geran?" she said in amazement. She brushed her hair from her eyes.

The moon-creatures wheeled to confront Geran and Hamil. The halfling raised his bow, took aim, and loosed his arrow in the space of a heartbeat. The nearest of the eye-monsters shrieked and leaped into air before flopping to the ground, an arrow buried in its ribs. The others glared at the alleyway and charged across the small plaza; Hamil ducked back out of sight, but Geran fixed his eyes on a spot of ground by another of the creatures and summoned the words for his teleport spell. In an instant he stood beside the thing, sword at the ready. The monster leaped for him, talons outstretched; Geran crouched and drove his elven blade straight into its foul heart, shouldering the stumbling corpse aside as it staggered past him and fell. He rose and shook the ichor from his sword.

Two of the monsters hissed and fixed their terrible gazes on him. He felt his flesh searing under their eyes and stumbled blindly toward the next of the monsters—but Hamil shot again and blinded one of the creatures, and a fist-sized rock sailed out of the alleyway to knock the other one to all fours. With a yip of pain, it scrambled up and bounded off into the ruins; the rest of the pack scattered just behind it. Geran slowly straightened up, searching for any more of the monsters, but they vanished as quickly as they had appeared.

Mirya Erstenwold picked her way out of the blind alley, holding another rock in one hand. Geran blinked in surprise; the red silken robe she wore was hardly decent at all, leaving her long legs and slender arms bare and showing an impressive décolletage. "Geran Hulmaster," she said, lowering her rock. "You're a sight for sore eyes! What in the world are you doing in this strange place?"

"I'm looking for you, of course." Geran sheathed his sword and hurried up to catch her in a quick, fierce embrace. For a moment he allowed himself to forget everything that stood between them, and drank in the sweet relief of finding her alive and unharmed. Whatever else might happen on Neshuldaar this day, at least he'd accomplished that much. "Thank the gods you're safe!"

"Aye, for the moment." She closed her eyes and sighed in relief. He couldn't imagine what she'd been through in the last few days, but Mirya was made of stern stuff; she allowed herself only a moment before she disentangled herself from his arms. A worried frown creased her brow. "Have you seen Selsha anywhere?" she asked.

Hamil looked around the ruins looming over them. "She isn't with you?"

"No. She's still lost out here somewhere." Mirya wrapped her arms around her shoulders and shuddered. "We escaped from our cell in the pirate keep, but we were parted. She fled out the side gate. I heard her shouting and followed her all the way up to this awful place, but then those . . . *things* . . . found me." She nodded at the dead monsters by Geran's feet. "They chased me all through these terrible old ruins. Where Selsha is now, I've no idea."

Geran winced at the bitter irony. Mirya had managed to escape from her captors only an hour or two before her rescuers arrived . . . and now Selsha was lost and alone in this terrible dark forest. If only they'd stayed where they were, they might both be safe now—or at least as safe as Geran and Hamil could keep them. But then again, if they'd stayed where Kamoth and Sergen had left them, the lords of the Black Moon might have done something horrible with their captives once they realized the keep was lost. Either way, it was done now; there was no point in fretting over might-have-beens.

"We'll find her, Mirya," he said gently. He took his cloak from around his shoulders and offered it to her; her robe was hardly decent at all, not by Hulburg's standards. "If she found her way from the moon-keep up to these ruins, there's no reason she wouldn't be hiding close by."

"I know it, Geran." Mirya drew his cloak around her shoulders with a grateful smile, and composed herself.

"Where was the last place you saw her?" Hamil asked.

"I didn't see her, but I heard her calling for me from the top of the hill, there," Mirya said, pointing. "I came down this way after her, and then I met the eye-monsters."

"So she's likely somewhere in these ruins," Geran said. "We won't leave without her, that I promise you." He turned to study the ruins nearby and drew in a deep breath. "Selsha!" he called, as loudly as he could, monsters or no monsters. It might take hours to find one small girl hiding in the maze of old buildings and shadowed trees. With luck, they'd find her before the eye-creatures regrouped for another attack . . . or so he hoped.

I don't care for the idea of shouting out our location for every hungry moon-monster within earshot, Hamil told him silently. But he shouted, "Selsha! We're here!" a moment after Geran. Mirya joined them, calling for her daughter with her clear, high voice.

Together, they followed the narrow alleyway deeper into the ruins.

TWENTY-SEVEN

17 Marpenoth, the Year of the Ageless One (1479 DR)

The sounds of combat grew steadily louder as Sergen peered from the window of his suite high in the keep's central tower. From his vantage he could see that the surviving Black Moon pirates had abandoned the gatehouse battlements. The fighting on the quay and the decks of *Kraken Queen* was over; the dead and dying littered the decks and sprawled across the wharf. He glowered at the Hulburgan caravel lying alongside the Black Moon flagship, fuming at the turn events had taken in the last hour. Only this morning he'd had his breakfast on the balcony of his room, sipping from a goblet of chilled white wine as he contemplated his return to Melvaunt and the best use he could make of Mirya and her daughter against his accursed cousin, Geran, and the rest of his accursed stepfamily. Well, it seemed that Geran—it had to be Geran, who else?—had followed him all the way to the hitherto hidden refuge in the Sea of Night, determined to once more foil his carefully laid plans. It was beyond infuriating.

"My lord, we are ready," his armsman Kerth said. Kerth and the five magically tattooed warriors in his detail had spent the last quarter hour stripping the suite of everything that might be of use, including a small fortune in gemstones and gold. If Sergen had had all of his armsmen present, he might have tried to influence the course of the battle by throwing his soldiers alongside his father's pirates . . . but most of his personal guards were still in Melvaunt, watching over his interests there. The armsman glanced out the window and asked, "What are your orders?"

"The keep is lost," Sergen replied. "But it seems to me that the Hulburgan ship is lightly guarded. With a little luck, I think we may be able to make our escape on *Seadrake.* But I'd like some insurance in the event that proves impractical."

"We could slip into the forest and hide, my lord. The Hulburgans would never find us." That was his magical conditioning speaking, of course; Kerth had to think first and foremost of Sergen's personal safety.

"I don't care to be marooned here, Kerth. Now come with me, and stay close." Sergen glanced around the chamber one more time and then strode out into the corridor beyond. Kerth and three of his soldiers followed closely after him, swords bared in their hands; the remaining two struggled to keep up, carrying a heavy chest full of Sergen's treasure between them. He wondered briefly where his father was, and whether he still defended any part of the keep, but then he put Kamoth out of his mind. If the pirates were still fighting somewhere in the fortress, it would serve as an excellent distraction for what Sergen intended to do. His father would understand.

He led his guards to one of the servants' stairs in the center of the tower and quickly clattered down the steps. At each floor he paused and listened carefully, but fortune favored him; the squads of Hulburgan soldiers and mercenaries roving the keep's lower floors didn't chance to cross his path. He detoured carefully around the great hall on the keep's main floor, slipping through the kitchens—as he'd guessed, the servants who worked there were no longer at their places—and then used a freight ramp that led from the back of the kitchen to descend to the granaries and cellars below. Two more turns and a narrow stairway later, and he emerged in one of the gated corridors on the second level of the dungeons.

There he found seven of *Kraken Queen*'s crewmen gathered around the gate of one of the treasure vaults. "Here, now," Sergen said. "What's this about?"

The pirates exchanged looks, but none of them spoke. Sergen smiled to himself. "Allow me to make a guess, then. You all thought you'd fill your pockets with Black Moon loot before taking your chances in the jungle. Am I right?"

A bald Turmishan with a square beard of tight black coils straightened up and looked Sergen in the eye. "What other chance have we got? The harmach's soldiers hold the keep. When the ship founders, it's every man for himself."

"Can you eat your gold?" Sergen asked. "Do you think you can bribe the nothics and chuuls and tall mouthers out in the forest with a few pretty coins? No, you'll be dead within a day if you run off into the jungle. It seems to me that's not much of a chance at all."

"Then we'll die with our pockets full of gold," the man snarled. "What else can we do?"

Sergen's lips twitched toward a smile at the irony. He was not far off from that very situation, but at least he had his armsmen to carry his gold for him. With more boldness than circumstances warranted, he met the Turmishan's eyes and answered. "Follow me," he said. "I'm going to make a try for *Seadrake*. Most of the harmach's soldiers are searching the keep. With you seven and my armsmen, we'd have about as many crew as they've got guarding the ship. I tell you frankly that it'll be a hard fight at best—but at least it's a chance. Are you willing to try it?"

The bald Turmishan thought about it for a moment, and then he nodded. "Aye, I'm with you. It's better than anything we had in mind." The other men looked at each other and then nodded at Sergen or spoke up with an "I, too!" for him.

"Good," Sergen said. "Leave off there, and come with us, then." The pirates joined his band, and he set off again, striding along at a quick pace but careful not to run. If he wanted to keep the Black Moon pirates with him, it would be best to affect a calm, deliberate confidence. The last thing he wanted to do was appear desperate, and he did in fact desperately need those pirates. Assuming that he succeeded in taking one of the two ships lying alongside the keep, he'd need at least a few experienced deckhands to help him get home. He knew very little about sailing himself, and his personal armsmen were likely not much better.

They passed through one of the gates—standing open, its guards nowhere in sight—and turned down another passageway. Sergen allowed himself a smile of relief. They'd reached the Erstenwolds without a fight, and that meant he now had hostages he could use if he couldn't seize the ship he needed by force. He approached the cell where Mirya Erstenwold and her daughter were being held, and his confident footsteps faltered.

The cell was empty. A set of manacles hung around the bars, showing where they'd been pulled apart with a thick wooden lever thrust through the chains.

"The Erstenwolds escaped," Kerth said—a statement of the obvious if ever Sergen had heard one.

"Clearly," Sergen snapped. He stared at the empty cell for a long moment, thinking hard. Obviously none of the Black Moon corsairs were responsible. They would have fetched the keys from the master-at-arms in charge of this level instead of bending bars to get her out. Either the Hulburgans had already found her and set the Erstenwolds free, or Mirya had managed her own escape. Either way, he was sorely displeased to discover that he did *not* have the hostages he feared he might need.

He took a breath and then set aside his frustration. The mark of a man's ability to deal with a crisis was his willingness to make use of the facts as they were, not as he wished for them to be. "Clearly," he repeated. "Very well, then. If we run into Mistress Erstenwold and her daughter again, we'll take them with us, but we don't have the time to search for them now. To the postern, then."

Sergen led his band of bodyguards and corsairs down through the deserted hallways toward the keep's side gate. He managed to pick up two more Black Moons along the way, although both were so badly wounded that he doubted they'd be any use to him. Then they reached the dimly lit halls where the keep's neogi lurked, and turned toward the gate leading toward the dark forest outside. In the mustering hall just inside the gate, they found five of the spiderlike neogi arguing with each other, accompanied by their umber hulk slaves. Four of the hulks were laden with even more treasure than Sergen had seen fit to carry away, and several others watched over a chain coffle with a dozen vacant-eyed captives waiting to be marched away.

The neogi ended their argument as soon as Sergen and his soldiers appeared. "Lord Sergen, this is a disaster!" one of the creatures hissed at him. "You let your enemies follow you here, and they have ruined us! Your carelessness has cost us a very valuable station!"

"I regret the inconvenience," Sergen retorted. "If you help me throw back the Hulburgan attack, we won't have to give the place up."

"Unthinkable!" The spider-monster recoiled in horror, and Sergen snorted to himself. Neogi were cowardly creatures, unless the hope of a rich prize inflamed their avarice and drew them out of their habitual caution. "That would entail exposing ourselves to physical danger! There is no profit in that!"

"Then what use are you?" Sergen retorted. He didn't care much for the neogi. They were valuable trading partners, of course, since they eagerly bought up any goods the Black Moon carried off from the seas of Faerûn. Years ago they'd sold Kamoth the starry compass that made him the master of Neshuldaar, and they'd reaped the benefits of the Black Moon's depredations. Their spiderlike ships called at the keep from time to time to deal with the human corsairs, and Kamoth was only too happy to let them use the place as a storehouse and port of call. But they were detestable, untrustworthy creatures, and they had no love or loyalty for anyone but themselves.

"Fighting is for slaves," another of the neogi answered him. "We will take shelter in the moon's forest and await our clan's next tradeship. Deal with your foes yourself."

Sergen started to retort in anger, but he bit back his words. There was no point in antagonizing the creatures . . . and it might be that he hadn't found the right way to ask for their help yet. "Fine," he said. "You need not fight. However, I would like to hire the services of your umber hulks for the day, and I will pay handsomely for them."

The neogi looked at each other and then back to Sergen. "They are very valuable servants, and there is an excellent chance they might be damaged or killed in battle," the first one answered him. "Moreover, we cannot be certain of your success. We must reserve several for our own protection in case you fail."

"Then it is simply a matter of determining how many of your hulks I can use, and fixing a fair price for them."

The neogi grinned at him, showing a mouthful of needle-sharp fangs. Sergen sighed. The one thing for which neogi could be counted on was to try to exact every loose copper piece in your pocket if they thought they could sell something to you. It took several minutes of hard bargaining, but they soon struck a deal that gave Sergen the use of four of the monsters at an exorbitant rate, which Sergen directed his guards to pay from the chest they carried. He would have struck a better deal with more time to negotiate, but he tried not to concern himself with the details; he was quite possibly buying his freedom, after all, and he might even be able to recoup his expenses by selling the neogi passage on whatever ship he managed to capture. The neogi pulled aside the umber hulks in question and spoke to them in their own language for a moment; the monsters looked at Sergen and bowed their huge heads.

"We have instructed these four to obey your orders," the neogi said. "They will serve you to the best of their ability until sunset, or until we instruct them otherwise."

"Very good," Sergen said. He'd delayed here as long as he dared, but consoled himself with the thought that adding the umber hulks to his improvised little army drastically improved his chances of success. He inclined his head to the small creature. "I think I hear the fighting drawing closer. If you mean to depart the keep, now would seem to be a good time."

"We will wait and watch from the temple ruins," the neogi said. "Remember, we expect our property to be returned before we part ways."

"I understand," Sergen said. The last thing he intended to concern himself with was returning any remaining umber hulks to their neogi masters, but he didn't see any reason to tell the horrible little creature that. Then a sudden thought struck him. "One more thing before we go. Do you know the two captives I brought back from Hulburg? A tall, black-haired female and a young, dark-haired girl?"

The neogi peered at him. "I know those two. The small one was badly frightened when she saw us. I told her guards that they should cut out her tongue if she kept making sounds like that. What of them?"

"They escaped from their cell. Have you seen them?"

"Yes," the monster admitted. "We saw them here at the gate an hour ago. They managed to elude us and flee into the jungle."

Sergen suppressed his irritation. No doubt the neogi hadn't bothered to tell the Black Moon about their escaped prisoners because they intended to catch the Erstenwolds and sell them back. Still, he might as well see if he could encourage the neogi mercenary instincts. "They are of some value to me. If you recapture them, I will pay you handsomely for them. Two hundred pieces of gold each." That was several times the value the neogi would expect for routine slaves; perhaps they'd actually make an effort to track Mirya and her daughter.

"Done," the neogi answered. It hissed to the others, and the five small creatures scuttled out the door, heading for the jungle. Behind them, their umber hulks and slaves followed, leaving behind the four who now served Sergen.

Sergen looked at the monsters. "Stay close to me," he told them. Then he gathered his bodyguards and the pirates who had joined him, and followed the neogi party out of the keep's rear gate. He saw the neogi and their slaves disappearing into the jungle ahead, but he turned toward the left and took the path that circled the keep just under its black walls. The situation was not irretrievable. He thought he had enough men—and monsters—to seize one of the ships, if they moved quickly and the Hulburgans were slow to realize their danger. He'd burn whichever ship he didn't take, which should strand any possible pursuit on Neshuldaar. Within a day and a half he'd be back in Melvaunt, safe in his palace and ready to continue his efforts against the Hulmasters with whatever tools he found ready to his hand. But there was no doubt that the breaking of the Black Moon Brotherhood was a sore setback. It *had* to be Geran Hulmaster behind it. Who else but his hateful stepcousin could have found a way to overthrow his pirate allies in such a remote and presumably secure anchorage?

Sergen scowled darkly. He would dearly like to make certain that Geran met a lonely death under the walls of the Black Moon keep before he abandoned this place . . . but stranding Geran and his handpicked crew thousands of miles from home was some consolation. Maybe he'd be stranded in the Tears of Selûne for years, hunted by moon-monsters and helpless to thwart Sergen's plans. It was a pleasing thought.

They came to the corner where the keep's wall met the dock, and Sergen motioned for his men to halt. He crept forward and risked a quick look. The front gate to the keep stood open, but there were few soldiers on the wharf. A score of sailors busied themselves in and around *Kraken Queen* and *Seadrake.* They did not concern him; he was much more worried about the possibility of Shieldsworn and armsmen from the keep hurrying out to join the fighting once they realized the ships were under attack. He'd need to do something to block any reinforcements from coming to the sailors' aid.

"You two," he said to the closest umber hulks. "When the rest of us charge, I want you to go to the front gate of the keep, there. Go inside to the lower hall, and slay any Hulburgans you find there. Hold the lower hall and keep any soldiers inside the keep from using that gate until I tell you otherwise. Do you understand?" The monsters stared down at him with their bizarre insectile eyes, but they nodded. Sergen guessed that each was worth at least five soldiers in a fight; with some luck, they might pin the Shieldsworn inside the keep for quite a while before they were overcome.

He studied the two ships locked together at the wharf, and made his decision. "We'll try for *Seadrake,*" he told the rest of his band. "Deal with the sailors first, then we'll cut her free and fire *Kraken Queen.* Hold nothing back—this is our only chance. Now follow me!"

Drawing his rapier and poniard, he broke cover and ran for the ships. His bodyguards followed after him, striving to get in front and screen him from attack; the umber hulks lumbered out after him, two turning toward the keep's gate as he'd instructed. So sudden was his appearance that Sergen actually reached the deck of *Kraken Queen* before the Hulburgan sailors began to shout the alarm. He met a cutlass-armed sailor at the top of the gangplank, parried the fellow's clumsy attack, and ran him through. The man groaned and started to sag; Sergen unceremoniously kicked him off the point of his blade and stood aside to let his followers swarm up from the dock.

"To *Seadrake!*" he shouted. "That's the one we want!"

He crossed *Kraken Queen*'s deck and leaped over to the warship lying alongside. Here, despite their surprise, the Hulburgans stood their ground and put up a stout defense, fighting furiously to protect their ship. Sailors, pirates, and mailed guards shouted and cursed, tangled together in a furious melee of knife, axe, cutlass, and sword that sprawled over the ships' decks. For a moment Sergen doubted the outcome, as soldiers fell on both sides of the fight, and the attack seemed to stall, but then the two umber hulks he'd kept with him clambered across the deck and joined the fight. The creatures were horrifically strong and protected by chitinous carapaces thicker than plate armor. Worse yet, anyone who chanced to look one in the eye stood mesmerized by the monster's maddening gaze. Rooted to the spot, unable to raise a blade in self-defense, they were torn limb from limb by the monsters' stone-crushing claws or cut down from behind by opportunistic pirates while they stood helpless.

Well worth the money, Sergen decided, watching the monsters rip his foes to pieces. Then a deep-voiced *thrum* rolled across the deck, and a thick black quarrel as long as his forearm took one of the hulks right between its eyes. The powerful missile split the monster's chitin with an audible crack. It squealed once and staggered back, before it crashed through the rail and disappeared over the side. The creature sank like a stone in the sapphire waters and did not come up again.

"By all the gods!" Sergen snarled in frustration. He whipped around, searching for the source of the quarrel, and spied an old, weatherbeaten dwarf standing by an arbalest mounted on the quarterdeck rail.

"How'd ye like that, ye great overgrown bug?" the dwarf shouted. He grinned fiercely and began cranking his engine furiously, drawing back the oversized crossbow for another shot as he eyed the second of the hulks.

Sergen dashed up the steps leading to the quarterdeck and charged at the dwarf. The dwarf saw him coming and backed away from the arbalest to meet him with a boarding axe in hand. He managed to bat Sergen's point aside with the axe haft and lunged out with a vicious counter—but left himself open. Sergen slid back a half step and ran a foot of his steel between the dwarf's ribs. The dwarf staggered on three more steps, swinging weakly, and then sank to the deck.

"Ye'll no' get far, Sergen," he gasped through blood-flecked lips. "Geran Hulmaster will see t' ye soon enough."

Sergen raised an eyebrow. "Perhaps, but I'll get farther than you, my friend," he said. He moved back to the rail and took stock of the fighting. Few of the Hulburgans were still on their feet, and several of his personal guards were already setting fire to *Kraken Queen*. It was a shame to destroy such a fine ship, but Kamoth—if he still lived—would have fired her with his own hand rather than allow her to be captured.

"Cut the grapples! Make ready to sail!" he shouted to the soldiers below. He turned his attention to the lines nearby, yanking the hooks free and throwing them over the side one by one. He paused to peer toward the main gate of the keep, looking for any sign of Hulburgan soldiers. He thought he heard the sounds of fighting from that direction, but it was difficult to be certain. All the umber hulks there had to do was keep the Hulburgans busy for a few minutes more, and that would be enough to satisfy him.

"We're free, Lord Sergen!" his armsman Kerth called. The big swordsman slashed the last of the lines holding *Seadrake* to *Kraken Queen*.

"Very good. Now get us aloft!" he shouted at the Black Moon corsairs still on their feet. "Hurry, now!"

"Aye, Lord Sergen!" the bald Turmishan pirate answered. "But we're sorely shorthanded for this ship."

Sergen looked at the main deck and realized that he'd lost several pirates in the desperate fight on the deck, along with one of his bodyguards. He bared his teeth in frustration. The Hulburgans had put up a better showing in the brief, violent fray than he'd hoped. "We don't have a choice," he snapped. "Just get us into the air and do your best! They can't follow us!"

The Turmishan pirate grimaced, but he climbed the steps leading to the quarterdeck and took the helm. "Raise the foresail!" he called to his fellows. "It'll give us a little steerageway! Lord Sergen, tell your lads to lend a hand!"

Kerth looked questioningly at Sergen. "Do as he says!" Sergen told him. The bodyguards knew little more about sailing than he did, but they ran forward to help the Black Moon sailors as best they could. *Seadrake* drifted slowly away from *Kraken Queen;* Sergen could feel the heat of the flames that were beginning to consume the pirate flagship beating against his face and hands. For a moment he feared that they wouldn't get clear of the burning ship before catching fire themselves, but then he heard the ruffle of canvas flapping in the wind. Inch by inch, the foresail was rising into place . . . and as the wind began to catch the sail, the warship's hull slowly began to lift clear of the water.

"The mainsail now!" the Turmishan mate at the helm shouted. Side by side the Black Moon sailors and Sergen's guards lashed down their lines for the foresail and then hurried to the mainmast to begin the work of raising the mainsail.

Sergen looked back toward the wharf, slowly drawing away from them. Shieldsworn soldiers spilled out of the front gate and ran along the dock, with shouts of alarm. Some leveled crossbows or longbows at *Seadrake,* firing in futility at the warship as it began to climb away from the keep. Others raced to battle the flames spreading across *Kraken Queen* in a desperate effort to save her. He smiled in cold satisfaction. "I have your ship, Geran!" he shouted toward the wharf. "Enjoy your stay here, Cousin!"

A small figure in scarlet robes appeared on the battlements above the gatehouse. Sergen frowned as he recognized the sorcerer Sarth. The tiefling gestured, his mouth moving as he snarled the words of a spell Sergen could not hear. Golden fire gathered around his rune-carved scepter, taking on an arrow-like shape—and then with a flick of his hand, Sarth sent the quarrel hurling up at him. Sergen swore and threw himself flat as the fiery bolt blasted through the spot at the rail where he'd been standing.

The Turmishan pirate at the helm gave a strangled cry, and suddenly the bow of the ship began to droop. Sergen glanced back to the wheel and saw the man standing there with a charred, smoking hole burned through the base of his throat. He looked at Sergen, his eyes startlingly wide and white in his dark face, and tried to say something, but blood pooled from his mouth and dribbled down his chin. He leaned on the wheel, his hands knotted on the spokes, and as he slumped to the deck, the helm spun wildly in his dying grip. *Seadrake* lurched to the side, and one of Sergen's bodyguards scrambling aloft in the mainmast lost his grip. The man tumbled from his precarious perch and fell past the rolling deck, splashing into the lake below.

Sergen realized he was the only person anywhere near the wheel. He threw himself forward and seized the helm, trying to right the ship's careening course. The ship was heavy beneath the wheel, and he struggled to steady her. The vessel picked up speed on the fresh breeze as Sergen fought with the helm. He finally managed to level the deck again, just in time to see the scarlet foliage of a forested hillside looming just ahead. "Up! Up!" he screamed at the helm . . . but it was too late. Even as the bow began to rise sharply, the wind carried *Seadrake* into the great trees mantling the hillside. Branches cracked or whipped across the deck like scythes, hurling loose gear into the jungle below, and the ship came to a halt canted steeply to one side, snagged among the branches.

"Damn it all!" Sergen snarled. He clawed his way to the rail and looked back at the keep. They'd come a mile or more in their brief flight, and it was clear that *Kraken Queen* wouldn't be coming after them any time soon . . . but *Seadrake* was snagged in plain sight on the hillside. The Hulburgans could give chase on foot. Maybe it would take them half an hour to get to *Seadrake* in its precarious perch, or maybe it would take them less than that.

He hurried down from the quarterdeck to his sadly diminished crew, most of whom were picking themselves up off the deck or looking around with stunned expressions on their faces. "Don't just stand there!" he shouted. "Cut us free! Cut us free!"

I can still escape, Sergen told himself. A few minutes' hard work with axe and knife, and *Seadrake* would be free to carry him to safety. He hurried to the rail and looked back toward the keep, where smoke billowed from the burning ship, and watched anxiously for any signs of pursuit.

TWENTY-EIGHT

17 Marpenoth, the Year of the Ageless One (1479 DR)

The strange old ruins proved more extensive than Geran would have guessed from the vantage of the hilltop. Walls and plazas, tumbled towers and rambling palaces ran for hundreds of yards beneath the dense canopy of Neshuldaar's strange, mist-wreathed jungle. Below the crown of the hill, the ruins took on the character of a strange, walled maze—an old stronghold, monastery, or fortified town of some sort, but not one raised by human hands. The doorways stood only four feet tall, there were no windows to speak of, and the cell-like buildings were piled up on top of each other, linked by what Geran guessed had once been trap doors in ceilings and floors. Large standing stelae marked the small plazas, each covered in carvings of grotesque, monstrous creatures. There were very few streets, and the whole place had an almost warrenlike feel to it even without the overgrowth of trees and vines.

Geran, Mirya, and Hamil picked their way carefully through the ruins, descending deeper into the forest. From time to time they called out for Selsha, but the moon's strange mists grew thicker as the trees closed in around them. Their shouts didn't seem to carry very far, and Geran began to wonder if Selsha would hear them even if they happened to come close to wherever she was hiding. The idea of combing the ruins for hours was not particularly appealing.

Hamil led the way, with Mirya close behind him. She carried Hamil's bow and quiver. Geran knew her for a fair shot with the bow; at least, she'd been pretty good in the days when she'd tagged after her brother Jarad and him on their forays into the Highfells. She might not shoot with Hamil's speed or accuracy, but he felt better having her armed. Geran brought up the rear, keeping a wary eye over his shoulder for any more jungle monsters. He tried to ignore the graceful curve of Mirya's hip beneath the borrowed cloak and the thin silk robe and was not entirely successful. It wasn't that hard to see the girl he'd loved ten years past in the strong stride and carriage of the woman walking before him. Somehow he doubted that his lost love, Alliere, would have shown Mirya's strength and resourcefulness in similar circumstances. Strange to compare a common woman from rustic Hulburg to a highborn lady of an elf noble family and find the princess of the *Tel'Quessir* wanting, he reflected.

After they'd wandered through the ruins for a half hour or so, Mirya glanced over her shoulder and caught him as he happened to be admiring her. Geran quickly raised his eyes to meet hers; she gave him a stern look, but the ghost of a smile crossed her lips before she spoke. "I'd like to know how you found this place," she said. "We're a far way from Hulburg, and there's no doubt of it."

"We followed you, of course," he answered. "We found that you'd been carried off only an hour or two after the Black Moon raid on Hulburg. I set out after you as quickly as I could. We chased Kamoth and *Kraken Queen* halfway across the Moonsea—"

"And then Kamoth took to the skies," Hamil interjected. "We had no idea that he was using magic like that to come and go from the Moonsea."

"We had to locate an enchanted compass of our own to sail the Sea of Night. As soon as we did, we fitted it to *Seadrake* and followed Kamoth here," Geran continued. He smiled grimly. "We've been searching for the Black Moon's hidden lair for tendays now, but we never imagined that it wasn't anywhere in the Moonsea—or Toril, even. In any event, we've taken *Kraken*

Queen and the pirate keep. The Black Moon Brotherhood is finished. As soon as we find Selsha, we can all be quit of this place forever."

"How bad was the Black Moon raid?"

"Not as bad as it might have been," he told her. "Sarth, Hamil, and I were disguised aboard *Moonshark,* one of the pirate ships. Sarth managed to carry a warning to the harmach just before the Black Moon ships sailed into the harbor. We took our ship in after them—we had command of *Moonshark* by then—and helped to sink two other ships before our crew chased us over the side." He paused, thinking about the events of the night. "We only stayed in Hulburg a few hours before we set out again in *Seadrake,* so I know only what I saw with my own eyes. Parts of the harbor district were burned, and many people were killed. But the Shieldsworn, the Spearmeet, and the merchant company armsmen threw back the attack after an hour or two of hard fighting. I did see that Erstenwold's seemed mostly undamaged."

"I'm glad of that, but Hulburg should have been ready. With more warning—"

"I did the best I could, Mirya," Geran said. "The weather that night was terrible, and we made the best speed we could for Hulburg. It was all we could do to give the harmach any warning at all."

"No, it's not that, Geran," Mirya said. She halted and turned to look at him. "I knew the raid was coming. I spied on the leader of the Cinderfists and overheard him conspiring with the Master Mage, days before the Black Moon attacked. I thought I'd gotten away with it, and I meant to tell the harmach first thing the next morning. But they came to my house and caught Selsha and me both." She looked down at the ground. "The gods alone know how many folk died because I didn't go up to Griffonwatch straightaway."

"The Master Mage?" Hamil asked. "Marstel's House wizard?"

"Lastannor, aye. He brought word of the attack to the Cinderfist leader. That one's a priest of Cyric named Valdarsel.

I eavesdropped on them in the Three Crowns." Mirya shivered. "The wizard came for me later with his horrible servant at his side—a huge, pallid, man-shaped *thing* with dead eyes and cold flesh. The servant broke down my door, and Lastannor struck me senseless with his spells. He kept me that way until I woke up on Kamoth's ship."

"What in the world led you to play at spying on wizards and Cinderfists?" Geran asked. "You were gambling with your life!"

"Selsha stumbled across Valdarsel's shrine. He found her out. I feared that he might do something to make sure she didn't tell anyone else what she'd found. The Shieldworn couldn't help me because they had no idea who he was or where he was hiding. I . . . I heard something of his whereabouts, but I had to go have a look to make sure of it before I could turn the matter over to the Shieldsworn."

Geran frowned. He was about to say, "you should have told me," but of course he'd been away from Hulburg for tendays now, boring his way into the Black Moon by playing pirate. Still, Mirya had just given him a great deal to think about. If she was right, then House Marstel—or its chief mage, anyway—was in league with both the Black Moon Brotherhood and the Cinderfist gangs. And he'd sailed off after *Kraken Queen,* completely ignoring the enemies he'd left at his back. Was that what Aesperus had been hinting at with the cryptic warning dead Murkelmor, delivered in the ruins of Sulasspryn? He still had no idea what the lich-king's interest in the whole business was, but suddenly he was much less sure that venturing into the Sea of Night to chase after Kamoth was as right as it had seemed at the time.

It's done, he told himself. And if I hadn't come, what would have become of Mirya and Selsha? Whatever happens at home while I'm away, at least I've spared Mirya the fate Kamoth and Sergen had in mind for her. "As soon as we get back to Hulburg, we'll deal with Lastannor and this Valdarsel," he told her. "They conspired with the Black Moon and kidnapped you and Selsha. That's enough for the harmach to exile both of them, at the very least. You shouldn't have to worry—"

A distant scream interrupted him—the scream of a child in terror, echoing from somewhere ahead of them in the ruins.

"Oh, dear Lady," Mirya breathed. "Selsha!" She dashed off down the street, leaping down the steps.

Geran and Hamil exchanged a worried glance. Mirya was off without a moment's hesitation, reacting with a mother's instincts regardless of what else might be waiting in the shadows of Neshuldaar's forests and ruins. "After her, quick!" Geran snapped. He sprinted after Mirya, determined not to lose her again. Hamil followed a step after him as they rushed headlong into the sinister black ruins at Mirya's heels.

Selsha's scream echoed in the air as Geran and Hamil ran down the steep steps in the mazelike alleyways. Mirya appeared and disappeared in the gloom ahead of them, a glimpse of white limbs and sheer red silk fluttering amid the black stone. She took several quick twists and turns, and Geran almost lost sight of her completely. Hoping that she was navigating her way toward Selsha with more confidence than he was, he simply followed her as she went. A few steps behind him Hamil pelted along, doing his best to keep up. Halflings were quick despite their short strides, but few could keep up with long-legged humans for long.

Keep Mirya in sight! Hamil told him. *I'll catch up soon enough.*

Geran redoubled his pace. He saw Mirya turn a corner just ahead, and he sprinted around the turn behind her—only to skid to a stop just on the other side, nearly knocking her down. They were looking out into another plaza, but this one was larger and had no towers. Instead, it seemed to be a square just inside the ruin's encircling wall, with a crumbling gatehouse of several stories guarding an ancient archway leading to the jungle beyond.

Selsha Erstenwold clung precariously to the topmost part of the old gatehouse, which was little more than a leaning heap of stone about fifteen feet tall. On the plaza below her feet, several small arachnid monsters, with long eel-like necks and furred carapaces dyed in strange whorls and marks, hissed and chittered to each other, eyeing the girl hungrily. A spearcast behind the spider-monsters plodded enormous, insectile apelike creatures that Geran recognized as umber hulks. He'd encountered them before in a long-ago venture into the Underdark as a member of the Company of the Dragon Shield. The hulks were burdened with heavy chests.

Mirya swore a startled oath. "The monsters from the keep!" she cried. The spider-monsters at the foot of the ruined gatehouse hissed in surprise at the three adults' sudden appearance, and then began shouting orders in their own strange tongue. The hulks coming up behind them set down their chests and began to lumber forward.

Geran glanced at the umber hulks and back to the small arachnids. If he was swift, he could reach Selsha before the hulks . . . but he'd have to chase off the arachnid monsters quickly. Best not to think this through, he decided. "Get away from her!" he shouted at the spider-things and charged recklessly straight at them. Hamil shouted and followed on his heels.

"Geran! Hamil!" Selsha shouted. She scrambled back another foot from the spider-creatures, rubble sliding out from under her feet. "Watch out for the monsters!"

The arachnids recoiled with hisses of agitation, apparently none too eager to let Geran come within sword's reach, but the umber hulks were hurrying to the aid of their small masters. Geran's feet flew over the mossy old stones of the plaza, and he raised his sword for the first strike—but suddenly a black, hopeless malaise descended over him, a hopelessness so powerful and complete that he stumbled to a halt, his knees buckling and his sword point drooping to the ground. He *knew* that he had to drive off the spider-monsters before their towering servants caught up, but the effort simply seemed impossible. Try as he might, he couldn't muster the volition to even take another step toward the little eel-spiders. Three of the creatures stood before the gatehouse, weaving their forelimbs in strange passes as their small black eyes, fixed on him, glittered with malice. They're spellcasters of some sort, he realized. Yet the knowledge that they had somehow conjured the torpor that held him motionless while their monstrous servants rushed to their aid still was not enough to break their grip on him.

"Geran, what's wrong?" Selsha called. She slipped a few feet down, dislodging more rubble, but she caught herself and looked at her mother. "Mama! There's something wrong with Geran!"

Hamil did not hesitate. He darted past Geran, daggers in hand, and struck with serpentlike swiftness against the nearest of the spider-monsters. The creature shrieked in anger and fear and scuttled back from the halfling's attack. *Geran!* he shouted mind-to-mind. *They're using magic against you. Fight back!*

The swordmage tried to muster his willpower against the insidious assault, to summon up anger or denial, any emotion that might give him the beginnings of resistance. He struggled, searching for something as the spider-things circled closer and their umber hulks rushed into the old plaza. He wondered if they'd have the hulks tear him to pieces, kill him with their own sharp teeth, or simply disarm him and leave him helpless where he stood, unable to move or act to protect himself against the first jungle monster that came along.

"Take them alive!" one of the small creatures hissed. "They may be valuable slaves!"

A bowstring sang behind Geran. He felt the arrow speed past him, its passage a faint breath of wind on his cheek, before it sank deep into the body of one of the three spider-creatures holding him with their enchantment. The creature leaped into the air with an agonized hiss and fell on its back with its legs kicking . . . and the malaise holding him in its grip vanished, as if it had never existed.

With a sudden shout Geran lunged at the nearest of the spider-monsters drawing close and half-severed its neck with his thrust. "Don't look the hulks in the eyes!" Geran cried. That much he remembered about the creatures; umber hulks could drive a human mad with their magical gaze. The rest of the spider-monsters retreated at once, spitting and snarling in anger. An umber hulk reached for the swordmage with one enormous claw, its sharp mandibles clacking together, but now Geran was free to move. He turned his back on the monster, refusing to look at its face, and rushed over to the spot where Selsha clung to the wreckage of the gatehouse's upper walls.

"Jump, Selsha!" he cried. "I've got you!"

Selsha took one glance at the monsters surging close and leaped down into Geran's arms. He staggered under her—it was a good drop, and he only had one hand free—but he caught her and lowered the girl to the ground. Hamil chased off another of the spider-monsters, but then he gave ground himself as he saw Geran falling back from the terrible umber hulks. Mirya loosed one more arrow that bounced from the thick chitin protecting an umber hulk's torso; the creature bellowed and turned toward her.

As matters stood, discretion was clearly the better part of valor. "Through the gate, quickly!" Geran shouted. "We'll outrun them!"

Mirya drew another arrow and took aim, but Hamil seized her by the arm. "No more of that!" the halfling said. He pushed her ahead on the path. "Run!"

Geran took Selsha by the arm and led her out of the gate and down the road outside the old city walls. The hulks' mandibles clacked eagerly as they lunged after their quarry. It was a very near thing for the first thirty yards or so, but then Hamil, Mirya, Geran, and Selsha began to pull away; the umber hulks had the size and power to flatten most of the undergrowth in their way or tear their way through hanging vines and creepers, but each time they did so, they lost a step or two on their smaller quarry. Geran was momentarily tempted to try to lead their pursuers off into the forest, but he discarded the idea at once. The last thing he wanted to do was split up now that they'd finally found everyone, and there was always the chance that the umber hulks and their small masters wouldn't fall for the ruse. He plunged into the new trail behind Mirya and concentrated on speed. If they could outdistance the umber hulks, he doubted that the smaller creatures would be very eager to follow too closely.

After a couple of hundred yards, they struck an intersecting path. "Turn right!" Geran called to Hamil; if his reckoning was true, that should lead them back to the lakeshore and the Black Moon keep. They hurried in the new direction for a long time, until the path began to climb slowly upward again, ascending another hill. There they paused. Their pursuers were nowhere in sight, at least for the moment.

Hamil looked at Geran with a wry smile. "I suppose the little ones don't fancy the idea of catching up to us without the big monsters to lend a hand," he said.

"Mama!" Selsha threw herself into her mother's arms. Mirya met her halfway, dropping to her knees to wrap her arms around her daughter and weeping with her face buried in Selsha's hair. "I was so scared! The monsters chased me!"

"I know, my darling, I know," Mirya said softly. "But you're with me now, and I'll keep you safe from them."

The two Erstenwolds stayed that way for a long moment. Geran could hear the distant thrashing of the umber hulks in the forest behind them, but he smiled to see Mirya and her daughter together nonetheless. To the darkest Hell with Aesperus and his words of warning, he decided. He knew it couldn't have been the wrong choice to rescue Mirya and Selsha from this terrible place. He'd gladly bear the cost of his decision later, whatever it proved to be.

Hamil glanced at the Erstenwolds, and he smiled too. But he looked back to Geran with a troubled expression. *We should get moving, Geran,* he said silently. *We don't know if there are more creatures around like the eye-monsters. The sooner we're all out of this accursed forest, the happier I'll be.*

Agreed, Geran answered. *And we need to get back to the keep. The fighting seemed well in hand when we left, but I'd like to be sure of it.* He moved over to the Erstenwolds and cleared his throat. "We probably shouldn't linger here," he told them. "We can celebrate your rescue aboard *Seadrake* when we're on our way back home."

Selsha looked up at him and beamed. She let go of Mirya and threw herself into Geran's arms, hugging him tightly. "Thank you for coming to save us, Geran," she said. "Mama said you would, and you did! But I want to go home now."

He looked over to Mirya. Her face colored a little, but she gave him a warm smile. He kneeled down to return Selsha's hug and patted her back. "I'm glad I was able to help," he told her. "But I'm ready to go home too. We'd better get started."

They hurried along the path at the best speed Selsha could manage. The twists and turns soon left Geran with no very good sense of which way the path was taking them, but he thought the trail was meandering back toward the keep. Whenever he paused, he could hear the thrashing of the umber hulks as they battered their way through the moonlet's forest along the trail behind them—but Geran and his companions were steadily gaining ground now. As long as they could keep moving, they'd be able to stay ahead of the monsters. The only question was whether this trail they were now on would eventually lead them back to the keep.

The path started to climb steeply, and Geran realized it was leading them to the hill top. Old black stone steps began to appear underfoot, marking out another ancient roadway—this one a staircase ascending the hill.

Hamil paused at the foot of the steps. "Keep going, or turn off the path and strike out for the keep?" he asked. "I don't think this trail leads where we'd like to go."

"I've no liking for the looks of the forest," Mirya said. "I don't want to leave the path until we're certain that we have to."

"Well, it would be inadvisable to go back." Geran nodded in the direction they'd come. He could still hear the umber hulks behind them. "I think we should keep going for now. Maybe we'll find another way down from the next hilltop."

Maybe we'll find more monster-haunted ruins, Hamil observed sourly. But he pressed on, leading the way as they scrambled up the old stone stairs and emerged in another clearing at the hilltop. This one was occupied with a large, round building whose dome had long since fallen in. To Geran's eyes it had the look of an observatory, the sort of place where priests and sages might study the stars and cast horoscopes. He started to look for another way down from the hilltop, as did Hamil and Mirya.

"Geran?" Hamil called. He'd scrambled to a better vantage on the terrace surrounding the old observatory. "You'd better come here."

The swordmage jumped up to where Hamil stood, and followed his gaze. He saw that they were closer to the keep than they'd been before; it wasn't much more than a mile away. A great plume of smoke billowed up from the docks, where *Kraken Queen* was engulfed in leaping flames, but *Seadrake* was missing. "What in the world is going on down there?" he asked aloud. "They haven't left us, have they?"

"Well, if they did, they didn't get far," Hamil replied. He pointed in the other direction. On the lower shoulder of the hill they stood on, perhaps five hundred yards away, *Seadrake* lay tangled in the treetops. Her deck was canted to one side, and a handful of men worked busily to free her from the branches. When Geran listened closely, he could hear the distant sound of axe blows and the ruffling of the wind in the ship's sail.

"Can you make out who's on deck?"

Hamil shook his head. "Not from this distance. My eyes are good, but not that good."

"If *Kraken Queen* caught fire, Galehand might have cast off shorthanded to avoid burning too. He would've taken the ship aloft to open the distance."

"Or Black Moon corsairs took the ship and wrecked her." Hamil shook his head. "There's no way to know from here."

"The monsters from the keep aren't far behind us," Mirya said in a low voice. "We can't stay here much longer."

Geran looked at the caravel, caught in the treetop like an oversized kite. Either she was in friendly hands, in which case they'd have allies there and might be able to lend a hand with extricating *Seadrake* from her situation . . . or she was in unfriendly hands, in which case their only escape from Neshuldaar was about to sail off into the Sea of Night, leaving them here with no way home. They had to get down to the ship, and the sooner the better.

"We'll make for *Seadrake,*" he said. Marking the ship's position carefully in his mind's eye, he chose a path that looked like it might lead them in the ship's direction and set off once more into the moon's sinister forest.

TWENTY-NINE

17 Marpenoth, the Year of the Ageless One (1479 DR)

Geran followed the sound of the axe strokes as he slipped and scrambled over the jungle floor. The path down from the ancient observatory had brought them several hundred yards closer to where he guessed *Seadrake* was snagged, but it soon became clear that they would have to leave the trail to reach the ship. He chose a place where a small streambed crossed the trail, and he scrambled up the rocky creek, splashing through the cold, clear water. Overhead he could glimpse white canvas through the crimson leaves and make out the voices of sailors shouting and cursing as they hurried to free the vessel from the treetops. Great branches creaked and groaned as the ship's weight shifted. He climbed up the streambank and found himself standing at the base of a mighty tree whose trunk was easily twenty feet thick. Several other giants stood nearby; *Seadrake* was caught in their upper branches. He could see the damp curve of the ship's hull suspended overhead.

"Now that's something you don't see everyday," Hamil said in a low voice. "It takes some seamanship to run your ship aground sixty feet up a tree."

"They're freeing her fast enough," Geran observed. It was hard to tell from the ground exactly what else was holding the ship in place, but based on the number of axe-cut branches and limbs lying near the base of the tree, the crew had already made good progress on their work. He could hear cries of "Hurry,

hurry!" and "This one now—all together!" echoing down from above. Then he heard a voice he knew. Somewhere out of sight on the decks above, Sergen Hulmaster called out, "Quickly, now! The harmach's soldiers could be on us at any moment!"

Hamil glanced at Geran. "I think that was your cousin Sergen."

"It was," Geran answered. He stared up at the ship and scowled in anger. He should have known that his venomous serpent of a stepcousin would have found a way to slip away from the destruction of the Black Moon Brotherhood. "I'll be damned if I'll let him leave us all stranded here!"

"How many men does he have with him?" Mirya asked.

Geran shrugged. They'd certainly be outnumbered, but with a little luck they'd have the advantage of surprise; the corsairs were busy with their work of cutting *Seadrake* out of the treetops and likely didn't expect him and Hamil to be anywhere nearby. He turned his attention to the tree trunk and decided that it was not a difficult climb. The tree forked into thick limbs fairly close to the ground, and thick vines clung to its surface. He could pick out a path that would get them to the windows of the stern cabin or the rail of the quarterdeck with a little effort.

"You're going up there, aren't you?" Hamil said.

"We can't let them have the ship," Geran replied. "Mirya, it might be best if you and Selsha waited here."

"I'll thank you for your concern, but I've seen all of this forest I care to," Mirya said. She held up her bow. "And I may be able to help you."

"Out of the question. You could be hurt or killed. Sergen and his corsairs won't be in any mood to take captives if we fail."

"Better that than the monsters roaming this black forest."

Geran started to argue the point, but then he thought of the umber hulks and spider-creatures following behind them. The creatures might miss the place where they turned off the trail . . . or they might not. He wouldn't want them to come upon Mirya and Selsha here on the forest floor while he and Hamil were on the decks of the ship above. "All right," he said. "You can come up with us. But you'll find a safe place to keep out of the way until I call for you."

"Well enough," Mirya said. "We'll follow you."

Hamil led the way as they scaled the tree. It proved to be an easy climb; the heavy vines helped in the few difficult parts. Geran feared at first that it might be too hard for Selsha, but she scampered up the trunk like a nimble little monkey. Of course, she likely spent more time climbing trees than he did. A few feet below the level of the stern windows, another large fork provided a reasonably comfortable perch that was safely out of sight from the deck above. Geran silently motioned for Mirya and Selsha to wait there, and the two Erstenwolds nodded in acknowledgment. Then he continued up after Hamil.

Better let me have a look first, Hamil said silently. He crept up the last few feet and peeked over the rail, studying the decks above. *Seven sailors, three armsmen in mail, your cousin Sergen—and another umber hulk. They're working up at the bow. It's driven deep into the trees. No one's on the quarterdeck.*

"An umber hulk too?" The odds were long for Geran's taste, just with Sergen and his Black Moon allies. He was fairly confident that he could best Sergen—they'd crossed swords before, and he'd had the better of the match—but the presence of ten more enemies and a powerful monster made it simply impossible. Frustration and despair settled over him. Perhaps he could kill Sergen and a pirate or two before he was cut down, but what was the point of that? It wouldn't keep the rest of the corsairs from sailing off with *Seadrake* and stranding the Hulburgans in Neshuldaar. He thought hard for a moment, and then he heard another large branch crashing to the forest floor from the ship's forecastle. If he waited too long, he'd lose his chance altogether. But what chance was there?

Hamil read the despair in his face and grimaced sympathetically. *We might be able to stow away,* the halfling suggested. *Hide somewhere belowdecks until we can thin out their numbers one or two at a time.*

A desperate strategy, Geran answered him. *And we couldn't put Mirya and Selsha at such risk.* Still, he didn't see any other possibilities.

A sudden chorus of shouts from the deck above interrupted

him. "Stand to your arms! The sorcerer approaches!" the armsmen cried. Footsteps hurried across the deck, and the axe strokes ceased.

"Break out crossbows!" Sergen shouted. "Man the arbalests! He'll stand off and slay us all with his magic if we can't drive him off!"

"Sarth?" Geran whispered. He risked a quick scramble up to the rail and peeked over. Sergen and his men scurried all over the deck, seizing weapons and taking cover. A pirate on the quarterdeck hurriedly cranked one of the heavy arbalests mounted at the forward rail. Others crouched by the gunwales, their attention fixed on a distant figure. Streaking over the treetops with his flying magic, Sarth arrowed through the air toward the entangled ship, resplendent in his robes of scarlet and gold. The tiefling aimed his scepter and let loose a searing barrage of bright blue-white sparks. Spitting and crackling, the sparks seared great black marks in the deck; one caught a half-orc pirate who ducked a little too late. The half-orc shrieked and fell smoking to the deck, limbs flailing uncontrollably. Crossbows snapped and hissed in reply, but shields of unseen magic kept the quarrels from finding Sarth's flesh. Still the deadly bolts forced Sarth to dodge aside. Evidently he didn't trust his magic to halt a well-aimed quarrel fired at a stationary target.

Hamil grinned. "I think our odds just improved!"

Geran nodded. If the sorcerer's appearance wasn't the chance he was looking for, he didn't know what was. "Quick—tell him we're here, and get him to move toward the bow!" he said.

The halfling fixed his eyes on Sarth and frowned in concentration. He had to be fairly close to speak into someone's mind, and the tiefling was hovering a good distance from the side of the ship. But Sarth quickly glanced toward them with a surprised look. The tiefling's teeth flashed in a fearsome smile, and he swooped off to his left, moving toward the front of the ship. Sergen, his armsmen, and the Black Moon corsairs all turned to follow him.

"Get your bow back from Mirya," Geran told Hamil. The halfling nodded and slipped back down the trunk. Then

Geran cleared his mind to conjure up the best defensive spell he knew—the Scales of the Dragon. *"Theillalagh na drendir,"* he said. A rippling aura made of violet shards of magical force shimmered into existence around him, flowing over his body like a coat of scales. Hamil returned a moment later with the bow and quiver.

"The umber hulk first," Geran said softly. "If we can slay it quickly, we'll have a fighting chance against the rest."

I doubt I'll be able to drive an arrow through that monster's hide, Hamil told Geran.

"Give it a try. If nothing else, you might distract it for me." He surveyed the deck quickly. Sergen's small band had worked furiously to clear away the branches that snagged the forward shrouds and stays; the Black Moon deckhands and armsmen now crouched amid the cluttered branches and canvas, snapping off quarrels at Sarth whenever the sorcerer showed himself. Then, before Geran could think better of it, he swarmed up the last few feet of the branch and vaulted over the ship's rail.

No one noticed his appearance at first. He dashed forward and leaped down the steep steps leading to the main deck. Behind him, Hamil raced up to the forward edge of the quarterdeck and halted at the top of the steps, taking aim. His bow thrummed twice; the first arrow took the pirate by the arbalest in the middle of his back, and the second ruined one of the great insectile eyes of the hulk. The creature screeched in agony, its great claws flailing in the air. Geran immediately attacked the creature's flank. He stabbed it at the meeting of its leg and torso, and his point sank through the soft chitin of the joint. Dark ichor splattered the deck, and the monster's leg buckled underneath it, but it responded with a furious rake of one great claw that he barely ducked under.

"Geran!" Sergen snarled. He whipped his rapier from the sheath. "You two, keep working on getting us free," he snapped at his crew. "The rest of you, to arms! I want Geran Hulmaster dead!" Then Sergen threw himself to the deck as one of Hamil's arrows sped right through the place where he'd been standing.

Geran backpedaled from another of the enraged umber hulk's blows and saw a big, mailed armsman closing in behind him. The fellow's head was shaven, and his face was tattooed with arcane sigils. Leaving the umber hulk to flounder to its feet, Geran wheeled and leaped to meet his new foe. This fellow was a swordsman of some skill, and he parried Geran's high slash competently before returning a similar stroke. For several heartbeats they dueled fiercely, steel ringing shrilly as blade met blade. Geran gave back a step and suddenly turned his blade to throw his opponent's edge into the mainmast nearby. The weapon caught for an instant, and Geran leaned close to throw his right elbow into the man's face. It was nothing that his old teacher, Daried Selsherryn, would have approved of, but it worked; the big man reeled away, blinded by the pain of a flattened nose. Geran would have finished him then, but Sergen rushed him from his other side. The exiled lord attacked with a series of lightning-swift jabs and lunges, using his natural speed and light blade to good advantage.

Again Geran had to give ground, until he found an opportunity to snarl the words of a sword spell. With a cry of *"Reith arroch!"* he conjured a brilliant white gleam to his edge and launched a flurry of counterattacks. He gave Sergen a shallow slash to the left arm, and Sergen leaped back with a curse. But before Geran could press his stepcousin, the umber hulk hurled itself back into the fray with a roar of anger, splintering the deck with a single pulverizing blow of its massive claws. He managed to slash it once across the mandibles and then had to leap for his life.

"You seem a little overmatched, Geran," Sergen taunted him. "You would have been wiser to let me go, I think!"

There are too many of them, he realized. As soon as I corner one, the others will have me. He risked a quick glance toward Hamil and saw his small companion fighting against a pair of pirates with his daggers in hand. A brilliant flash of lightning, followed by a great thunderclap, echoed through the treetops as Sarth blasted a small knot of crossbow-armed Black Moons near the ship's foremast. The ship lurched to one side as one of the branches trapping the bowsprit shattered under the impact of the sorcerer's spell.

"I think the odds are improving," Geran replied. All he had to do was avoid getting killed by the umber hulk and keep Sergen and his bodyguard busy a little longer, and Sarth's magic would eventually sweep the deck clean of pirates.

"Geran!" Mirya scrambled over the rail back by the quarterdeck and then turned to help Selsha make the jump. "The spider-creatures found us! They're coming up after us!"

Sergen gave a single bark of laughter. "Ha! I see you've met the neogi, then. So much for improving the odds, Cousin!"

"By all the screaming Hells," Geran snarled. He scrambled back from another blow of the umber hulk's fist, trying to keep the mainmast between the monster and himself. The tattooed swordsman edged closer, and on the opposite side Sergen glided in with a grin of anticipation. He couldn't afford any more foes, not at the moment. He risked a quick glance forward and saw that the two pirates were still working on cutting the ship free. Another large limb cracked and dropped away, falling to the forest floor far below, and the ship's deck suddenly canted in the other direction. She's working loose! he realized.

He looked back to the quarterdeck. "Hamil! Take the wheel and get us away from here!" he shouted.

Hamil nodded. He drove back one of his pirates with a furious frenzy and then turned on the other one and rolled up under the man's guard to bury a knife in his belly. Before the fellow could even sink to the deck, the halfling dashed across the quarterdeck and seized the wheel. Hamil glanced once at the sails and then turned the wheel to the right and willed the ship's bow to rise. *Seadrake* twisted awkwardly where she was snagged, and the deck's list grew so precarious that Geran feared she might go over on her side and dump everyone on board to the ground. Then, with the splintering of wood and the snap of parting lines, the caravel heaved her bow free and pointed her nose to the sky.

Instantly the deck rolled hard in the opposite direction as the ship leaped skyward. Geran lost his footing and slid to the opposite gunwale, catching himself there. Mirya locked one arm around the sternrail and hugged Selsha tight with the other. The second of Hamil's pirates was not so lucky and was hurled off his feet when the ship rolled. He toppled over the side with a terrified wail. Sergen and his tattooed swordsman fetched up against the rail, but the two pirates who'd been at the bow working to cut the ship free now tumbled aft, rolling along the deck as the bow shot skyward. The umber hulk seized the mainmast in one claw, and reached out with its other arm to seize Geran. Its talons came up inches short of Geran's leg, raking the tough old oak of the deck like soft sand as Geran kicked himself out of the way.

"Kerth! Kill the halfling!" Sergen shouted. The tattooed armsman steadied himself against the rail and then climbed back toward the quarterdeck.

The halfling glanced back at Mirya. "Take the wheel! Hold her steady!" he cried. Mirya hurried over to seize the ship's helm, while Hamil retrieved his daggers and moved to meet the swordsman Kerth in the narrow space at the top of the quarterdeck ladder. But at that moment several arachnid legs appeared over the sternrail, and one of the neogi clambered over the side. It hissed at Mirya and her daughter, and Selsha screamed. The girl backed away from the spiderlike creature, which scuttled after her.

Geran struggled to get to his feet and go to her aid, but the umber hulk released its grip on the mainmast and lunged for him. This time its iron-hard talons ripped across his torso. Only his magical wardings saved his life, but even so the claws tore flesh and bruised bone. He was knocked spinning across the deck by the creature's incredible strength. It pounced on him with surprising speed for a monster so large. He threw his sword up to fend it off, and then he made the fatal mistake: he looked into its eyes.

Instantly, his thoughts seemed to splinter into vertigo and nonsense. He staggered back, unable to remember where he was or what he was doing. The roaring of wind, the crackle of the tattered sails, the dizzying rush of the forest-covered hillsides spinning away under the rail, and the brilliant stars reeling by in a sky of pure black—all these things crowded in on his senses in a fearsome jumble. Clumsily he threw his sword point out, hoping to fend off the monster looming over him, but the umber hulk batted aside the blade and pounded him into the deck. He groaned and tried to crawl away, but it seized him around the waist and dragged him to its huge mandibles. Its scythelike mouthparts clacked together and scissorred eagerly, anticipating the taste of his flesh.

"Geran!" Mirya shrieked.

He struggled to make sense of what he was seeing, and closed his eyes to shut out all of the things he didn't understand. His thoughts cleared a little, and he seized with all of his willpower at the fragile promise of calm, even as the hulk's talons ground into his waist, and the mandibles slipped against his magical scales. The pain jolted him into clarity. In pure desperation he stabbed blindly straight ahead with his sword and caught the monster in its mouth. It roared and let go of him; Geran hit the deck and fell, still helpless from its maddening gaze.

The creature raised both of its huge arms over its head, ready to crush Geran where he writhed. But then a searing jet of fire blasted the umber hulk. Sarth appeared thirty feet from the ship's rail, hovering in midair as he scoured the creature with his sorcerer's fire. "Desist, creature!" he shouted between the words of battle spells.

The umber hulk reeled away with a screech of pain, and abruptly Geran's mind cleared again. The huge monster floundered across the deck, retreating from Sarth's fire, and fetched up against the opposite rail. Geran picked himself up and charged the monster while it flailed under the sorcerer's flame. He reversed his grip on his backsword, capped his left hand over the pommel, and then drove the blade up under the hulk's jaws with all of his strength. The thing shuddered and then toppled over the rail, almost taking his sword with it. He wrenched it out of the carcass as it went over the side, and had to catch himself hastily on the rail. Then Sergen's sword point sank into the back of his left shoulder, missing his heart only because the umber hulk had dragged him around as it fell. Geran cried out as the sharp steel grated on bone before he twisted away.

"*Damn* you, Geran!" Sergen hissed. "You have meddled in my affairs for the last time!"

The swordmage clenched his teeth together and pushed the hot agony in his shoulder from his mind. He parried Sergen's next thrust and risked a quick glance around to make sure his cousin was not about to drive him into some new peril. Sarth burned down the last of the Black Moon men with a jagged lightning bolt that blasted splinters from the battered deck, and then wheeled in midair to trade spells with the spider-creature threatening Mirya and Selsha—the little horror was a sorcerer too, and their magic roared and thundered across the deck. Hamil fought grimly on against the tattooed swordsman, still trying to battle his way to the ship's helm. Beneath the rolling hull the serrated hills and crimson jungle of the dark moon drifted past, many hundreds of feet under the keel and falling away with every moment.

He returned his full attention to Sergen and adjusted his grip on his elven blade. The mithral rose of its pommel was splattered with blood, but the wire hilt was sure and certain in his hand. Anger, black and pure, swept over him—the same dark, cold loathing that had carried him away from himself in the golden woodlands of Myth Drannor on a fine fall morning two years past. He looked into Sergen's eyes and saw nothing but duplicity, murderous scheming, and sneering superiority. His blade flowed unconsciously into a high guard position as deadly intent welled up in his heart. "You're right about that, Sergen," he heard himself say in a cold voice, not even realizing that he'd intended to speak. "It's only the two of us. Time to settle scores, cousin."

Without waiting for a reply, Geran attacked. Sergen was a good fencer, and he had the lighter blade—so Geran started with his edge, an elegant pattern of figure-eight slashes and quick overhand cuts as he advanced boldly. Driving Sergen to the defensive, Geran forced him to parry his heavier backsword. Pass by pass he knocked Sergen's blade aside, until Sergen's face whitened and a feral snarl twisted his face. The exiled lord swore viciously and flung himself into a desperate counterattack, but Geran let the wild thrust pass by him and stepped in close to slam his sword's hilt into Sergen's face. Sergen staggered back and fell to the deck, spitting blood from his mashed lips.

Geran allowed himself a low laugh at the desperate fury growing in Sergen's face. "You're beaten, Sergen," he said. He held his blade at the ready and silently marked out the next wound he intended to deal his cousin in payment for all the misery and trouble Sergen had caused. His black wrath impelled him—but past the rogue lord's shoulder, Geran's eye fell on Mirya, who fearfully watched his duel with his cousin as she struggled to keep the helm steady. He hesitated, struggling to regain mastery over his anger. For a moment he feared that he would fail, but as quickly as the dark rage had come over him, it released him from its grip. For all the harm Sergen had done, for all the lies he'd authored against the Hulmasters, he was still a kinsman of sorts . . . and there was no doubt that he knew things that might be very useful in unraveling the plots against the harmach.

Geran grimaced, but he withheld his strike and forced himself to speak. "Surrender, Sergen," he rasped. "I'll spare your wretched life. You don't deserve it, but maybe you can put right some of what you've done to our family."

"Surrender? I hardly think so!" Sergen replied with a sneer. "It doesn't matter if you best me with your blade—I've already defeated you, dear cousin. What do you think's happened in Hulburg while you've been chasing after me?"

"What do you mean?" Geran demanded. "Answer me!"

"I think you'll find an old friend of yours is waiting for you when we get home." Sergen pushed himself to his feet, eyes narrowed, and settled back into his guard again. Then he attacked, making good use of his natural speed. His rapier point was a blur, darting quicker than a striking snake, but Geran stood his ground and weathered the onslaught. Sergen's attack slowed, and the momentum of the duel shifted back to Geran again. The swordmage counterattacked with a spinning combination of draw cuts and quick jabs, pressing the exiled lord back against the ship's rail.

Sergen parried the first two or three, and then he missed. Elven steel sliced through muscle and bone as Geran wheeled past him, laying open a long cut from right hip to left breast. Sergen made a single choking sound and reeled away, his rapier clattering from his fingers. "You . . . cannot . . . best me . . . so easily!" he hissed between his teeth. "I . . . will be . . . harmach . . ." Then he sagged over the rail and disappeared.

Geran rushed to where Sergen had fallen and peered over the side. The scarlet jungle wheeled slowly past far below the keel, and he spotted a tumbling figure in black and gold, cloak fluttering behind him. He watched in silence until Sergen's body vanished from sight against the moonscape below. "Farewell, Sergen," he murmured. He reminded himself that scores—perhaps hundreds—of Hulburgans had died in Sergen's petty schemes for power. But he did not look forward to telling the harmach that Sergen had died under his blade. Grigor Hulmaster had always hoped for the best from his sister's stepson; it would grieve him sorely that Sergen had died before finding some measure of redemption.

A sharp thunderclap sounded behind him. Geran whirled around just in time to see Sarth blast the last of the neogi from the ship with a crackling stroke of emerald lightning. The creature screeched piercingly as it fell, its legs jerking and kicking. Then a sudden lurch of the ship threw Geran off his feet and nearly pitched him over the side as well. He seized the rail with one hand and looked around for more foes—but there were none. Hamil had defeated his larger opponent, although he held his hat crushed against his left shoulder as an improvised bandage and didn't seem all too steady on his feet. Geran sheathed his sword and made his way back up to the quarterdeck.

Mirya looked at him, her eyes wide. "I saw Sergen fall," she said. "Are you all right, Geran?"

"Wounded but well enough," he answered. Part of him was glad to see Sergen dead, and he wasn't proud that he felt that way. But when he looked at it rationally, he knew that Sergen had forced his hand—not only in the duel he'd just won, but in all of the troubles over the last few months. He took a deep breath and set aside his tangled emotions. "Sergen chose his path a long time ago. I don't think there could ever have been peace between us."

"No, and I believe that's the truth of it," Mirya answered.

No one spoke for a moment, and then Hamil cleared his throat. "Well, the ship is ours again," he said. "Back to the keep?"

Geran nodded and then looked over to Sarth. The sorcerer watched over the ship's deck with his rune-carved scepter in hand, waiting for any more foes to appear. "I don't know where you came from, Sarth, but I was glad to see you at the rail."

"I am sorry I was so late," the tiefling said. A bloody hole in his sleeve showed where a crossbow's bolt had marked him, and blackened splatters across his fine robes spoke to the ferocity of the neogi's spells. "I was in the keep when Sergen made off with *Seadrake.* I hurried after the ship as quickly as I could, but I had to ready my spell of flying again before I could give chase."

"Better late than never," Hamil remarked. "I'm glad you dealt with the spider-creature, though. I certainly didn't want to get close to it. Never cared much for spiders, especially talking ones that are as big as I am."

"I am pleased to have been of service," Sarth said in a dry voice.

Geran smiled. Now that the fighting was done—at least for the moment—he became all too aware of his injuries. He ached in a dozen places from the clawing the umber hulk had given him, the back of his shoulder burned, and he seemed to have a few smaller cuts he hadn't even noticed during the fray. Well, with any luck, the voyage home would give him plenty of opportunity to rest. "Bring us about, Hamil," he said. "We'll pick up the rest of the ship's company, the captives they've freed, and any prisoners they've taken. Then we'll set course for home."

THIRTY

20 Marpenoth, the Year of the Ageless One (1479 DR)

It was a clear fall afternoon as *Seadrake* sailed proudly past Hulburg's towering Arches and began to take in her sails. The day was cool and bright, and the breeze carried just enough of the coming winter's chill to make Geran glad for his good wool cloak. He inhaled deeply, relishing the familiar taste of the air. For all the wonders of the Sea of Night, he was very glad to have the purple-hued waters of the Moonsea beneath the keel and the clean, rocky shores of his homeland before his eyes. The day might come when he'd set his course for the starry skies again, but for now he was content with the common sights and sounds of Hulburg. The Black Moon Brotherhood was broken, their ships destroyed and their members scattered. Sergen Hulmaster, traitor and would-be usurper, was dead by his hand and would never trouble the family Hulmaster again. And Mirya and Selsha Erstenwold stood by his side on the deck, even more glad for the sight of home than he was.

"For a time I never thought to look on Hulburg again," Mirya said quietly. "I knew we'd spend the rest of our days in chains in some far foreign land."

Geran shook his head. "I'd have found you."

"Why, Geran? That's the question that's been foxing me for days now." She looked into his face. "What am I to you that you'd sail to the moon to save me?"

"I don't know," he admitted before he even knew what he was

saying. "I mean, you and Selsha are dear to me. I *had* to come after the two of you, to make sure that you were safe and home." He searched for words for a moment before going on. "I've made mistakes in my time. Everyone has, I suppose. I can't go back and choose differently, but looking after you—and Selsha—makes me feel that there are things I can set right again. There's a darkness in my heart. Seeing the two of you safe and well lightens it."

Mirya didn't answer for a long time. Then she sighed. "I'm no penance of yours, Geran Hulmaster."

"No, it's not that. If you were—I mean, if that's the way I saw you—I'd resent the time I spend with you. But I don't, Mirya." He looked down at her and tried to find a smile. "Little by little, I think you're healing me of hurts I didn't know I had. That's why I had to come after you."

"In all the years I've known you, that's the first time I think you've ever allowed me a glimpse of what's truly in your heart." She frowned and pulled back, looking away from him. "There's nothing special about me, you know. I've darkness of my own, and some days it's near to drowning me. I don't know what power I have to heal anyone."

He didn't know what more to say, and so he returned his attention to the town. The familiar wharves of Hulburg drew closer, full of cart traffic and passersby on foot who were now stopping and looking seaward to see what ship was coming to call. The battered hulks of *Seawolf* and *Daring* rested on the bottom by the dockside in the center of the town, their masts and tangled rigging jutting crookedly up out of the water. "Take in all sails! Run out the oars!" called Worthel from the quarterdeck. Geran missed the gruff skill of Andurth Galehand, but Worthel was a competent shiphandler too, and he served as *Seadrake*'s sailing master as well as her first mate. Many of *Seadrake*'s sailors had more than one job to do on the voyage back from pirate's hidden keep. They were sorely shorthanded after the fierce fighting in the Tears of Selûne, having borne the brunt of the battle in Sergen's bold attempt to steal *Seadrake* out from under their noses, and so the Shieldsworn and sellswords went to the oars to lend a hand with the rowing.

"Look! The soldiers are lining up to welcome us!" Selsha Erstenwold, standing a short distance from Mirya and Geran, pointed over the rail and jumped in excitement. "And look at all the people!"

Geran followed her gaze. Several companies of armsmen in the colors of several different merchant companies had appeared by the wharves and were taking up station. "I suppose they caught wind of our victory in the Sea of Night," he said, thinking aloud. "But how they could have heard the news, I have no idea."

"A divination or sending, perhaps?" Sarth came to join Geran and Mirya by the rail, with Hamil close behind him. The tiefling frowned, puzzling at the question. "No, not a sending. Who was left behind in the keep to work such a spell, and why would they have done it? It must have been a divination of some sort. A merchant House wizard scried our return."

"Then where are the Shieldsworn?" Hamil asked in a low voice. "Where are Harmach Grigor and Kara?" He frowned. *No, I don't like the looks of this, Geran. Be careful!*

Seadrake shipped her oars and glided alongside the pier; sailors threw out the ship's mooring lines and brought the caravel to a halt, riding gently at the dock. As soon as the sailors laid the gangway in place, a detachment of armsmen wearing the red and yellow surcoats of House Marstel quickly boarded and made their way directly to Geran. Their captain was a short, broad-shouldered Damaran with a sandy goatee and eyes the color of steel. "Geran Hulmaster?" he asked. "You are summoned before the harmach. Come with us peaceably, or we will subdue you by whatever means are necessary."

"Who are you?" Mirya demanded. "And since when does the harmach send a Marstel man to carry his messages?"

"Since Maroth Marstel became harmach," the captain answered. "I am Edelmark, Captain of the Hulburg Guard. Now, if you please, Harmach Maroth is waiting."

Geran stared at the man, so stunned that he could not speak for a long moment. Harmach Maroth—Maroth *Marstel?* His uncle, Grigor, was no longer ruler of Hulburg? He'd only been gone from the city a little more than a tenday! Finally he found his voice again. "What happened? Where is Harmach Grigor? Where is Kara Hulmaster?"

"All the Hulmasters have fled," Captain Edelmark answered flatly. "Lord Marstel is now harmach of Hulburg, and he wants you brought to Griffonwatch without delay. I grow tired of repeating myself."

"Are you arresting Geran?" Hamil asked. His hands rested lightly on the hilts of the daggers at his belt.

"I will do whatever I have to in order to carry out my lord's instructions," the officer said. "I'd take my hands off those daggers, if I were you, little man. There are two hundred armsmen on the pier behind me."

"There are fifty here on this ship," said Worthel. The Red Sail first mate stood nearby with his arms folded across his chest. "Geran goes nowhere he doesn't care to, Captain."

Geran held up his hand. The last thing he wanted to see was a battle at *Seadrake*'s slip. Many good men would be killed, and Hulburg had already lost enough. "You may escort me to Marstel, Captain," he said. His voice seemed steadier than he felt. "But no one else aboard this ship is to be troubled. They've fought and bled for Hulburg in strange, far places, and they deserve a hero's welcome."

"My orders only concern you," Edelmark said. He motioned for Geran to precede him.

Sarth looked at the armsmen gathered on the pier and then back to Geran. The tiefling narrowed his eyes. "I will come too," he said. "Anyone who thinks to lay hands on Geran will have me to reckon with."

"And I," said Hamil. He shot the captain a hard look and very plainly left one hand resting on a dagger hilt. "You can bring ten men along, Captain. The rest of your little army can stay right here, or Geran won't go anywhere with you."

"Fine," the captain snapped. "Can we go now?"

"A moment," Geran said. He turned to Mirya and took her hand. "Go ahead and take Selsha home. It should be fine. I'll be by later, as soon as I straighten all this out."

She nodded, although she couldn't help but glance at the guardsmen waiting on the pier. "Mind your step, Geran Hulmaster. And, for all you've done for us—thank you." She leaned forward and kissed him on the cheek and then took Selsha by the hand and led her down to the pier.

With that, Geran looked to Sarth and Hamil and then followed Mirya to the wharf. Edelmark ordered ten of his men to come with him, dismissed the rest of his companies, and left a token force at the foot of the wharf. Then the Hulburg Guards—an army made up of the armsmen of the Merchant Council Houses, as far as Geran could tell—escorted the three companions through the streets of the town to the foot of Griffonwatch. It was a tense and silent walk, with little conversation. Edelmark refused to say more than he'd already said, and his men didn't dare say more with their captain on hand. But the signs of recent fighting in the streets spoke clearly enough for them. More burned buildings, familiar shops boarded up, small groups of Hulburg Guards stationed on the corners, and no sight of the Shieldsworn or the native-born militias who'd been keeping the peace in the streets for months now.

They marched beneath the castle gate, and Edelmark took them directly to the great hall. The Harmach's Council was gathered to await him, but as Geran approached, he realized that this was not the council he knew. In the places formerly reserved for Grigor Hulmaster's advisors and the officers of the realm, the heads of the large merchant companies sat—the masters of the Double Moon Coster, the Iron Ring Coster, House Jannarsk, and of course Nimessa Sokol, whose face was set in an unhappy frown. Marstel's former seat was vacant; instead the old lord now slumped in Harmach Grigor's great wooden seat. Wulreth Keltor still held his seat as Keeper of Keys, but no other councilor who'd served under Grigor was at the table. How many of the others had been forced to flee? Geran wondered. How many were dead? The murmur of voices in the hall fell still as he drew near, and the men and women gathered in Griffonwatch's hall silently watched him.

Captain Edelmark stepped forward and addressed Marstel. "Lord Harmach, I have brought Geran Hulmaster," he said.

Marstel stirred himself and peered at Geran. "So you have," he said. "Very good. We have some important matters to discuss, I believe. What of *Seadrake?*"

"She is moored to the old Veruna wharf. I left a company to guard the ship." Edelmark frowned tightly. "There is a detachment of almost fifty Shieldsworn aboard, my lord. They should be disarmed immediately, and the ship placed under guard."

"I would advise against it," Geran said. "Unless I order them to stand down, *Seadrake*'s company will resist any such attempt."

"They're outnumbered five to one," the captain said. "You'll have them stand down, or you'll be responsible for their deaths."

Geran turned his head slightly and spared Edelmark a single glance. "I do not answer to you," he said firmly. Then he looked back to Marstel. His surprise at the situation was rapidly giving way to a mounting anger. Marstel was seated in his uncle's throne, calling himself the harmach, and he was acting as if he'd always been there! He took two steps forward. "Lord Marstel, what is going on here?" he demanded. "Why are you in my uncle's seat? Where is Harmach Grigor?"

"The Hulmasters no longer rule in Hulburg," Marstel said. He sat up straight, and a spark came into his eye. "No longer! Your uncle's misrule nearly destroyed this realm. The Merchant Council intervened—we had no choice in the matter. Our armsmen moved to restore order, and Grigor Hulmaster opposed our actions. He has been removed from power. As the ranking peer remaining in Hulburg, I have duly assumed the title of harmach."

"Duly assumed?" Geran repeated. His anger was a hot, white blaze that threatened to sweep him away, and he clenched his fists as he spoke, but he held his temper for the moment. "By what authority do you claim power, Marstel? There is no peerage in Hulburg, no established precedence! You have no right to name yourself harmach. As far as I can tell you are a usurper, plain and simple. Now tell me: what have you done with my family?"

Easy, Geran! Hamil warned. *Keep your temper in check. There will be a time for anger and action later. Don't convince Marstel that he can't allow you to live.*

Marstel's face darkened, and he half rose from his seat. "I will not be spoken to in such a tone!" he roared.

"He deserves an answer!" Nimessa Sokol said loudly. Ignoring Marstel's apoplectic fit, she stood and met Geran's eyes. "Your family is alive, Geran. They've taken refuge in Thentia—or so we've heard."

Geran took a deep breath. Nimessa's loyalties lay with House Sokol, of course, but he couldn't imagine that she would have had any willing part in unseating his uncle, Grigor. In any other circumstances he would have greatly enjoyed the opportunity to tell her about the destruction of *Kraken Queen* and the small amount of justice he'd been able to extract against the Black Moon Brotherhood on behalf of her friends and servants killed aboard *Whitewing,* but that would have to wait. "Tell me, Nimessa. What happened?"

"As Lord Marstel said, the Merchant Council moved to restore order by disarming all militias," she said. "I argued against it, but the council was resolved; House Sokol had no choice. Harmach Grigor resisted, so the council resolved to recognize Lord Marstel as harmach. The council's armsmen and the council-sanctioned militias defeated the Shieldsworn and drove them back to Griffonwatch. It seems that Lady Kara found a way to spirit your uncle and the rest of your family out of the keep and get them away from Hulburg."

"A desperate act on the part of a weak man clinging to power, heedless of the welfare of his realm," Marstel rumbled. "Had he truly been concerned for Hulburg, Grigor would have abdicated honorably. I intended to see to it that he was comfortably established in any neighboring land. But, since he has not yet done the honorable thing by renouncing his claim, the Hulmasters are banned from all lands and possessions under the harmach's rule."

"Banned?" asked Geran. "Hulburg is *named* after the family Hulmaster, in case you've forgotten. Do you mean to tell me that my whole family has been exiled from the realm Hulmasters have ruled for two hundred years?"

Marstel sat back in his stolen throne and smiled to himself. "My edict stands. No Hulmaster is to set foot in Hulburg, on pain of death. Of course, you could not have known this while voyaging abroad, so—despite your rudeness and your hostile manner—I suspend my own edict until you are escorted to the border of the realm. I am not unreasonable, after all."

The warning of Aesperus becomes clear, Hamil observed. *You carried on with your intended course, and Hulburg fell into the hands of the harmach's enemies. But who is the forgotten foe?*

"My lord errs on the side of compassion," Captain Edelmark said. "Geran Hulmaster is well known as a scofflaw, rabble-rouser, murderer, and worse. Better to deal with him here and now than to let him go free."

Geran ignored the captain and looked at the other House leaders, their advisors and captains, and saw nothing but guarded expressions and stern frowns. Nimessa Sokol looked down at the ground, unable to meet his eyes. Then his eye fell on a figure he'd overlooked before, a slender man in a long, hooded cassock of dark gray who sat in the place that had once belonged to the Master Mage of the realm. The hood shadowed the man's face, but a dark suspicion fell over Geran's heart. He knew everyone else sitting at the council table, even if he did not know them well. But the hooded man he did not know, even though he felt that he should.

As if he sensed the weight of Geran's gaze, the hooded man reached up with his hands—one made from rune-carved silver instead of living flesh—and drew back his cowl. Geran stepped back with a gasp, sick astonishment momentarily overwhelming him. "Rhovann!" he breathed. "What are you doing here?"

"Me? I am Master Mage of Hulburg, as it so happens," the moon elf replied. He smiled coldly. "Lastannor the Turmishan decided his services were no longer needed. I have been retained in his place."

"Indeed." Sarth studied the sneering wizard, a stern frown on his ruddy face. "Who is this, Geran?"

"Oh, has he not told you of me?" The mage affected mild surprise. "Geran and I have been acquainted for years. We knew each other well in Myth Drannor. I am Rhovann Disarnnyl, of House Disarnnyl." The false humor in his eyes died, and he held up his silver hand. "Two years ago, your friend Geran gave me this to remember him by. I have given much thought to a suitable gift for him, let me assure you."

Geran stared at his old rival, barely able to form a thought in his head. Rhovann was here, in the house he'd grown up in, and in payment for the maiming he'd suffered under Geran's blade and his own exile from Myth Drannor he'd come to Hulburg to visit ruin in return. Rhovann simply smiled and contemptuously turned his back on Geran to address Marstel. "Lord Harmach, please forgive the interruption. As you see, Geran Hulmaster and I are acquainted with each other. You were about to banish him, I believe?"

"Yes, of course," Marstel rumbled. He rose to his feet and pointed to the door. "Geran Hulmaster, you are hereby banished from the realm of Hulburg. Do not return on pain of death! Captain Edelmark, you will take a detachment of guards and escort this man from the town immediately."

Edelmark set his hand on his sword hilt and bowed. "At once." He beckoned to the armsmen in the hall, summoning a dozen soldiers for the task.

Geran stood unmoving for a moment. For an instant he considered drawing his sword and rushing Rhovann, in the hope that by striking down the embittered mage he might put an end to the madness that had taken over Griffonwatch. But even if he succeeded, he'd have all of Marstel's guards to deal with, plus the mages and captains of the various merchant Houses. He'd die with his blade in hand, and most likely Hamil and Sarth would follow him to the grave. That was the thought that stayed his hand; destroying himself to throw down Hulburg's enemies was one thing, but his action would doom his friends as well. Rhovann evidently meant to savor the irony of arranging for Geran's banishment from his homeland, just as Geran had brought about Rhovann's banishment from Myth Drannor two years past. It was a sore blow indeed. But to rail against his fate, to fight off Edelmark or launch himself blindly against his foes—all he would do is give Rhovann the pleasure of seeing how badly he'd been hurt. Geran took a deep breath and resolved to deny his old enemy the satisfaction.

"I expect the crew and armsmen of *Seadrake* to be treated well," he told Marstel. "They have fought bravely for Hulburg. You need not worry about the Black Moon pirates again. I will order my crew to disperse peacefully and acknowledge Lord Marstel's authority, if you swear before Amaunator that they will be free to come or go as they like."

Marstel frowned, but nodded. "Agreed," the old lord said.

Geran looked over to Sarth and Hamil. "Watch over Mirya and Selsha for me," he said in a low voice. Then he squared his shoulders, turned his back on Marstel, Rhovann, and all the rest of the usurper's court, and strode off to meet his exile.

EPILOGUE

29 Marpenoth, the Year of the Ageless One (1479 DR)

Snow dusted the Galenas' foothills, a dozen miles northeast of Hulburg. In the lowlands sodden stands of alder and maple still wore their fall coats of yellow and orange, but the forest-covered hills and steep-sided vales were a couple of thousand feet higher than the Winterspear valley, and their rocky crowns had been streaked with white for tendays now. Kardhel Terov, Warlock Knight of Vaasa, stood by one of the windows of his iron tower and studied the snows of the slopes above him with a dour frown. He was a stern man of fifty years, with close-cropped hair of iron gray and a strong, clean-shaven jaw. His eyes were a startling crimson hue, the mark of a pact for power he'd made long ago. Here, in the sanctuary of his iron tower, he did not bother with his great armor of black plate; it rested on a stand against the opposite wall. Instead he wore long robes of scarlet and black, embroidered with draconic designs.

He glanced up at the leaden sky, and his frown deepened. He needed no magic to see that more snow was coming soon. There were no true passes between Vaasa on the east side of the Galena Mountains and Thar and the inhabited lands of the Moonsea North on the west side. The lowest saddles between the Galenas' mighty peaks remained choked with ice and snow year-round. But travelers of unusual determination could manage the journey in the summer and the early months of fall. Unfortunately, the weather seemed to suggest that unless

Terov returned to Vaasa soon, he would be forced to go home by another path—either the long and tedious voyage down to the Sea of Fallen Stars and back again through the realm of Impiltur, or the dark and dangerous route under the mountains, through the mines of forgotten dwarven strongholds and the warrens of fierce orc tribes. Not even a Warlock Knight and his entourage were guaranteed a safe passage by that road. No, it would be much more convenient to conclude his business in these lands and depart soon.

A soft knock at his chamber door interrupted his brooding. Terov turned his head. "Enter," he said.

Behind him, a pale, red-haired woman in a plain gray cassock and mantle of darker gray let herself into the room. She wore a thin black veil across her eyes. "Lord Terov, the priest from Hulburg has arrived."

"About time," the Vaasan lord muttered. "Very well. Show him to the great room. I will be down directly."

The veiled woman nodded and withdrew. Terov allowed himself one more look from the window—the snow on the mountains was strikingly pretty, even if it portended no small amount of inconvenience for him—waited a short time to show his guest that he was not in fact waiting on his arrival, and then left his chamber. A single, curving stairway of riveted iron led down to the tower's lower floors. The tower itself seemed not much larger than a farmer's grain silo from the outside, but its interior was much more spacious, and Terov kept it well appointed with comfortable furnishings and a small staff of guards and servants. It was his most prized possession, a small magical fortress that he could summon into existence wherever he traveled. The iron tower could easily accommodate half a dozen guests in great comfort, as well as twenty or more guards and servants in plainer lodgings, and it was virtually impervious to attack.

A large fireplace and a row of narrow, arched windows guarded by iron shutters dominated the tower's great room. It served as Terov's sitting room and dining room, and from time to time as his audience hall. Inside, the Warlock Knight found his guest waiting for him. "Welcome, Valdarsel," he said. "I trust your journey was not difficult?"

The priest of Cyric shook his head. "No, my lord. Not at all. The ride was only three hours or so."

"Good. I know I summoned you here on short notice, but I felt that it would be useful to speak face to face." For months now, Terov had relied on the occasional sending spell or carefully guarded letter to keep in touch with his servant in Hulburg. He trusted Valdarsel's ambition and competence, and he was so far highly pleased with the results of the Cyricist's assignment to organize a faction in Hulburg that could unwittingly serve Vaasa's purposes. Still, it was useful from time to time to make sure that Valdarsel remembered whom he worked for—hence Terov's visit to the borders of the harmach's domain. "So tell me, Valdarsel: how do matters go in Hulburg?"

"Well enough, my lord. As you instructed, I have secured a seat on the Harmach's Council. The gangs I control are restive, but so far I have held them in check with promises of property taken from native Hulburgans. Harmach Marstel cannot so much as scratch his nose unless the wizard Rhovann remembers to instruct him to do so. There may be some trouble on that front soon enough; despite his patents of nobility and Rhovann's guidance, Maroth Marstel is not much of a harmach, and I imagine that it will be hard to keep that fact hidden for much longer."

Terov shook his head. "The only opinions that matter are those of the merchant costers, and if Marstel continues to restore the leases and royalties they formerly enjoyed under Sergen Hulmaster, they won't trouble themselves with what sort of ruler he is. Continue."

"The Hulmasters have taken refuge in a modest estate—an old family holding from the time of Grigor's grandfather, it seems—in Thentia's lands. A small number of guards and servants accompanied them into exile. They aren't penniless, my lord, but I doubt that they'll have the means to mount a challenge to Marstel's rule any time soon."

Terov looked sharply at Valdarsel. "I fail to see why they are permitted to live at all."

"I am puzzled too. Certainly it would be wiser to eliminate any possibility that a deposed dynasty might someday reassert its claim. But the mage Rhovann has taken no steps to tidy up that little detail, at least no step that I've seen." Valdarsel shrugged. "In all honesty, my lord, I believe that Rhovann *prefers* the Hulmasters to live with their defeat, and does not especially care whether Marstel's rule is secure or not. He hates Geran Hulmaster far more than he enjoys wielding power through that hapless old oaf Maroth Marstel."

"Hmmm." The Vaasan lord considered the priest's words for a long moment. "If Rhovann is not inclined to act, then you must, Valdarsel. I require the Hulmasters to be eliminated—all of them. And if you can arrange to implicate Maroth Marstel, so much for the better."

"That shouldn't be too difficult, my lord." Valdarsel smiled coldly. "If anything unfortunate befalls the harmach in exile, suspicion will naturally fall on the man who seized his throne. But I will ensure that strong evidence of his involvement surfaces to confirm what everyone will suspect anyway."

"Good. With a little work, I imagine we might bring down Marstel and his Merchant Council as well—which will of course leave Hulburg with a crisis of leadership, to say the least. You should be well placed to exploit that. I mean for Hulburg to be under Vaasa's control by spring." Terov gave his guest a predatory smile. "You will be richly rewarded on that day, Valdarsel. I promise you that on my ring of iron."

The Cyricist inclined his head. "My lord honors me with his confidence."

"You have done well so far. Finish the Hulmasters, and the rest should fall into place." Terov reached out to set a hand on Valdarsel's shoulder. "Now, I am afraid I must turn you out into the weather again. I start back for Vaasa today, and I cannot delay any longer or leave the tower here."

Valdarsel bowed again. "Occasional discomfort is good for the character, my lord. Besides, you have the more difficult journey. May the Black Sun guard your steps as you make your way home."

"And you, my friend," Terov answered. He walked Valdarsel from the great room down to the foyer by the tower's door and waited as a servant gave Valdarsel a dry cloak to replace the sodden one he'd worn on his ride from Hulburg. Another servant waited in the drizzle outside, holding the reins of the priest's horse. Valdarsel mounted, touched his brow and bowed to Terov, and then rode off down the lonely trail leading back toward Hulburg.

Terov didn't waste time watching his underling ride off. He looked at the servants in the foyer and said, "Inform the staff and the guards to make ready for the march. We are returning to Vaasa, and I wish to depart within the hour."

The warlock lord spared one more glance for the leaden sky and the towering white peaks looming ahead, and then he went to prepare for his journey home. He'd tried once before to panic Hulburg into his arms with the threat of the Blood Skull orcs. Where violence and fear had failed to accomplish his aims, ambition and deceit were poised to succeed.

AVENGER

AN EXCERPT

Someone means to eradicate the Hulmasters this night, he realized—all of us.

"Damn it," he snarled into the darkened hallway. He whirled, trying to make sense of the chaos. To the right were the rooms of the young Hulmasters. In the opposite direction lay Harmach Grigor's chamber. The harmach was certainly the first target of the attackers, but Geran knew what his uncle would want him to do. Grigor would want him to make sure that Natali and Kirr were safe, regardless of the cost.

A child's scream rang out in the darkness. "Natali," Geran murmured. Without another thought he turned to his right and sprinted down the hallway, his sword bared. The harmach probably had Shieldsworn bodyguards close to hand already; if fortune smiled just a little, they might be able to hold off the attack for a while. He turned the corner at the manor's grand stair, and found several men and women in the harmach's colors lying dead or unconscious at the top of the steps. Two men Geran had never seen before were crumpled on the steps by the guards. They wore no colors at all other than their well-worn leather jerkins and dark, hooded cloaks, the sort of nondescript garb that scores of sellswords in Thentia's dockside taverns wore every day. Whoever was behind the attack had likely hired any killers he could find for the task—or wanted it to appear that way—and then reinforced the common sellswords with summoned devils.

Geran did not pause to study the scene more closely, leaping over one of the fallen guards and continuing down the hallway. He came to Natali's chamber, found the door standing open, and burst inside.

Two more Hulmaster servants were dead on the floor before him. Over them stood three more sellswords, already turning toward the corner of the nursery, where Erna huddled with her children. One of the sellswords, a bald man with Thayan tattoos on his scalp, raised a cleaverlike blade and seized Kirr's arm to haul him away from his mother. Natali and Kirr both wailed, but Erna glimpsed Geran past her assailants. "*Geran!*" she shrieked. "Help us!"

The two mercenaries between him and the Thayan holding Kirr wheeled around at her cry. "One more step and we'll slay the lot!" the first snarled. "Drop the sword, and we'll let the small ones go!"

He hesitated a moment before realizing that the man had to be lying. They had no intention of leaving any Hulmasters alive. Instead of releasing his blade, he fixed his eye on Kirr and the mercenary who gripped his arm, and formed a spell in his mind. *"Sierollanie dir mellar,"* he said in a clear voice.

An instant of utter darkness and icy cold flashed across his senses—then he was where Kirr had been standing, with the Thayan's hand locked on his left arm, while Kirr stood dumbfounded in the doorway where Geran had been a heartbeat before. The Thayan mercenary's eyes opened wide in astonishment, and he opened his mouth to say something before the heavy basket hilt of Geran's backsword slammed between his eyes with a sickening crunch. The fellow staggered back and collapsed to the floor; Geran turned to engage the remaining two swordsmen. "Kirr, get out of the hallway and find a place to hide!" he cried. "Erna, get Natali into the washroom and barricade the door!" Then his blade met the hard parry of the first of the two enemies he now faced, and the fight was on in earnest.

Unlike the Thayan sellsword lying motionless on the floor, these two were now fully cognizant of his skill and magic. He had no more surprises for them, and they were good enough blades that he couldn't simply overwhelm them with a quick assault. He tried anyway, and succeeded in driving them back two steps toward the doorway, steel crashing against steel as their swords danced with his. Behind the two mercenaries, Kirr glanced down the hallway. "More of them are coming, Geran!" he shouted. Then he darted out of sight to the left—Geran hoped Kirr was going to find some secure bolthole where the assassins couldn't find him. He risked a peek over his shoulder and saw Natali and her mother pushing the door of the garderobe closed behind them.

"A futile gesture," said one of the swordsmen dueling Geran. "We'll have all of them within a quarter-hour anyway!"

"Not while I still stand here, you won't," Geran retorted. He resumed his attack, trying to beat down the asassin's guard, but now his opponents were beginning to work together. Whichever he attacked gave ground and went on the defensive, while the other pressed hard and tried to catch him with his guard out of place. He grimaced, beginning to wonder if he'd been wise to transpose himself into the bedchamber after all. He'd caught the one holding Kirr off-guard, but in doing so he'd put two good swordsmen between him and the door. His quick stroke had left him pinned in the children's chamber, unable to fight clear quickly or affect events anywhere else in the manor. The youngest Hulmaster was out in the dark hallway somewhere, all too likely in need of Geran's help, and he could hear more fighting echoing throughout Lasparhall's fragrant chambers.

Steel flickered and shrilled in another exchange, and Geran ground his teeth together in growing frustration. He had to get by these two and find out what else was happening! Pressing forward recklessly, he sent lightning coursing down his blade and managed to shock the sword out of one man's hand. The man yelped and moved back, holding his sword hand, but Geran paid for it with a shallow cut to his left calf as the fellow's comrade struck back at him. Then the doorway filled again, this time with two more assassins and the hot, sulfurous stink of another bearded devil.

"I've got Geran Hulmaster here!" the swordsman fighting him cried. "Two more of them are in the garderobe! Cut him down!"

"Cuillen mhariel," Geran said. Thin streamers of silver mist appeared around him, the best defense he could summon at the moment. He might be able to escape with a spell or two, but he couldn't abandon Erna and Natali. He settled into a fighting crouch, standing his ground in the middle of the bedchamber, teeth bared in a grimace of determination. Here he would stand and, if fate ordained it, die, but he would not give ground.

The assassins and the grinning hell-spawn rushed him all at once. For a single, impossible moment Geran stood without yielding, his elven blade a silver blur as he parried and countered as fast and furiously as he'd ever fought in his life. The assassins closed in from all sides, sword points weaving and darting like steel serpents eager for a taste of his flesh, while the bearded devil hissed and bulled straight at him, slashing wildly with its iron talons. A point grazed his ribs, another pinked him in the thick of his left thigh, and raking talons furrowed his chest. Despite himself Geran faltered a step, trying to use his foes as shields against each other, but there were simply too many to deal with at once in the close quarters. So be it, he thought grimly. He'd try to take as many with him as he could, and hope that any assassins he delayed here missed their chance to kill more of the Hulmasters.

The rearmost assassin cried out, back arching as his arms flew up in the air. He took two staggering steps forward and then pitched forward on his face. Behind him stood Kara Hulmaster in her mailed coat, her saber dripping blood from its point. Her spellscarred eyes blazed with azure light, and a snarl of rage twisted her face. "Murderers!" she snarled. "You'll not see the sunrise, that I promise you!" She leaped into the fray, driving against the two remaining swordsmen, who turned to meet her. Kara was almost as skilled with a sword as Geran, and two more Shieldsworn followed close behind her.

Geran took advantage of the distraction Kara caused to duck beneath the slashing claws of the bearded devil and throw himself into the back of one of her opponents, driving the man into the wall. He seized the stunned assassin and threw him headlong into the face of the bearded devil rushing after him, briefly tangling the two together. While the assassin struggled to get free, the swordmage snarled a spell of strength and drove his point through the man's torso and into the body of the devil behind him. With the power of the strength spell, Geran shoved both his impaled foes to the nearest wall and drove his sword through until it grated on stone behind them. When he yanked the blade free, the assassin groaned and slid to the floor, while the bearded devil screamed in rage before vanishing in a foul cloud of smoke like the others had. He turned back around just in time to see Kara finish her last opponent with a graceful slash across the throat. A moment's calm settled over the room.

"Natali! Kirr! Are they safe?" Kara demanded.

"Natali's here. Kirr ran off to hide. I don't know where he is." Geran found that warm blood was dripping over his brow from a cut he didn't remember receiving. He wiped it away with the back of his left hand. "What of the harmach?"

Kara paled. "I'd hoped that you might know. I was making the rounds outside when I heard the fighting."

A terrible suspicion dawned in Geran's heart. He looked over to the Shieldsworn who followed Kara. "You two, stay here and guard Lady Erna and Natali," he ordered. "Watch out for Kirr, too, if you see him. Kara and I are going to the harmach."

MARK SEHESTEDT

Chosen of Nendawen

The consumer, the despoiler, has come to Narfell. His followers have taken Highwatch and slain all who held it–save one.

Book I
The Fall of Highwatch

Book II
The Hand of the Hunter
November 2010

Book III
Cry of the Ghost Wolf
November 2011

Vengeance will be yours, the Master of the Hunt promises.
If you survive.

Award-winning Game Designer

BRUCE R. CORDELL

Abolethic Sovereignty

There are things that we were not meant to know.

Book I
Plague of Spells

Book II
City of Torment

Book III
Key of Stars
September 2010

". . . he weaves a tale that adds depth and breadth to the FORGOTTEN REALMS history."
—Grasping for the Wind, on *Stardeep*